Alix Nathan's novel *The Warlow Experiment* was a Radio 4 Book at Bedtime and a *Sunday Times* Fiction Book of the Year. Her short stories have been published in *Ambit*, the *London Magazine* and *New Welsh Review*. She lives in Shropshire, where she owns some ancient woodland with her husband. Follow her @alixnathan

Praise for *The Warlow Experiment*

'An extraordinary, quite brilliant book' C. J. Sansom, author of *Tombland*

'A powerful and unsettling novel, both fascinating and infinitely strange' Andrew Taylor, author of *The Ashes of London*

'A meaty, gripping novel of obsession gone sour' Elizabeth Buchan, *Daily Mail*

'An original, compelling story of power and isolation' Elizabeth Macneal, author of *The Doll Factory*

'Original and gripping ... builds to a satisfying and fittingly macabre climax' Antonia Senior, *The Times*

'Smart and darkly entertaining' Jeffrey Burke, *Mail on Sunday*

'It is Nathan's scrupulous objectivity that enables the complexity of her characters to emerge ... For all the grim logic of its horrifying finale, what distinguishes *The Warlow Experiment* above all is how Nathan ... treats her subjects with unfailing dignity and compassion' *Literary Review*

'Warlow is a victim, outclassed in every respect by Powyss, and yet they mirror each other and partially become each other's double. Nathan's delicacy of touch makes this development ... both shocking and convincing ... It is a woman who shows sympathy for Warlow ... another woman derails Powyss ... The complications that ensue take us into the deep heart of blunted male emotion' *Times Literary Supplement*

'Skilful and assured ... a historical novel of note' *Daily Telegraph*

'Unusual, gripping and emotionally complex – I loved this book' Sally Magnusson, author of *The Sealwoman's Gift*

Sea Change

Alix Nathan

———

This paperback edition first published in 2022

First published in Great Britain in 2021 by
SERPENT'S TAIL
an imprint of Profile Books Ltd
29 Cloth Fair
London EC1A 7JQ
www.serpentstail.com

Lines from 'The Wild Iris' by Louise Glück reproduced
by kind permission of Carcanet Press

1 3 5 7 9 10 8 6 4 2

Typeset in Tramuntana Text by MacGuru Ltd
Designed by Nicky Barneby @ Barneby Ltd

Printed and bound in Great Britain by CPI Group (UK) Ltd, Croydon, CR0 4YY

The moral right of the author has been asserted.

A CIP catalogue record for this book is available from the British Library.

ISBN 978 1 78816 350 7
eISBN 978 1 78283 612 4

To the memory of MaryRose Romer

                    whatever
returns from oblivion returns
to find a voice

                    Louise Glück, 'The Wild Iris'

The celebrated Aëronaut M André-Jacques Garnerin
will Ascend in his gas Balloon
at Ranelagh
on 28 June 1802 at 5 o'clock
during an elegant Afternoon Breakfast
given by the Directors of the Pic Nic Society
in recognition of the new Peace of Amiens.
M Garnerin will be accompanied by
the renowned Artist and Engraver Mr Joseph Young
and, to prove the Safety of such Travel to
Members of the Fair Sex,
the well-known Proprietress of Battle's Coffee House
Miss Sarah Battle

They walk through the crowd towards the enormous balloon, thirty feet in diameter, forty-five feet high, as big as a four-storey house, shifting gently against its anchoring ropes despite a hot, almost breathless day. Its alternate dark-green and yellow segments are encased in a net, its oblong car draped in tricolours and Union Jacks. On the ground around it lies a cartwheel shape of barrels and pipes in which acid and iron filings have generated the hydrogen that fills the great globe.

The aëronaut waits for them in an elegant blue coat and French hat bearing the national cockade, chatting to bystanders and smiling, as if he were a showman at Bartholomew Fair encouraging people into his booth. Jacques Garnerin is sinewy and slight, his noble nose and thin, sharp features wind-burned, his skin toughened like a sailor's.

Sarah, in a large beribboned bonnet, her best dress with its low neckline and short sleeves fashionable enough to quell her anxiety about what to wear, steps forward slowly, weighed by regret. Her jibe, fired off in annoyance, that women are just as able to fly in balloons as men, has brought her here. She is red with heat and

1

self-consciousness. It's not unlike the first day she stood at the bar in her father's coffee house, replacing her newly dead mother, when men scanned her perpetually till she felt skinned.

Joseph strides ahead, can't stop himself, bags and satchels hung about his tall, ungainly person.

Sarah turns to hug her daughter Eve, to kiss the girl in her pretty blue gown, who looks with bright eyes from her to the balloon and back, understanding only that her mother has chosen to travel in it, aware of a vast murmuring, a heaving sea of smiles.

'I'll be back soon, my love. Tonight, I hope.' She moves over to the basket, wanting it all to be over.

Garnerin, the small, foreign entertainer, hands his two British aëronauts up steps into the car, springs into it like a boy. There's only just room, for in the centre is ballast, bags of sand marked in quantities from kilos down to grams, suspended by four cords from the hoop at the base of the balloon's netting. Attached to the car's ropes are a thermometer, impressive compass, telescope and a barometer for measuring altitude. Baskets of provisions are stowed in lockers under the seat where Joseph will sit together with all his boxes of pens, pencils, chalks, brushes, paint, sketchbooks and blocks, perspective glasses and his own telescope. Jacques calculates that large Joseph, his equipment and a basket of food and drink will balance the weight on the opposite side of the car to Sarah and himself.

A band strikes up 'God Save the King'. The Official Aëronaut of France, fidgeting throughout, stands to attention for the succeeding tune, which no one recognises.

'But that is not the "Marseillaise",' says Joseph, puzzled.

'It offend Bonaparte. I tell them they must play "Veillons au salut de l'Empire". Soon he become Emperor.'

After four verses, during which it is the crowd's turn to fidget and chatter, Garnerin unhooks bag after bag of ballast, hands them over the side of the car until the captive balloon pulls at its tethers.

At last he signals, assistants untie the ropes, restrain the great ball solely by muscle power. The crowds hush.

A dramatic sign, the ropes are loosed, a huge cheer breaks out, the ascent begins. Sarah feels the basket leave the ground, an upward pull through her body that makes her laugh aloud. Even as her child slips further from her, the little girl's face blearing in her sight, her legs weaken with pleasure and she grips the car to steady herself. Jacques, so many successful flights in hand, moves about with panache, making the balloon rise slowly, letting it hang over the gardens for maximum effect. He holds a flag of the République, gives Sarah a Union Jack and, with Joseph waving his sketchbook, they all three salute the crowds thronging the Gardens and all roads that lead to Ranelagh. The great vehicle moves massively, elegantly in a north-east direction, away from the packed banks of the river, from the waterworks, the creeks and sluice gates of Pimlico fenland. Still low enough for onlookers clustered in every window and housetop, perching in trees like cawing rooks.

Joseph, breathless with excitement, sketches rapidly as they sail over Green Park and St James's. Ducks rise up, quacking from the lakes as the huge shadow passes. Westminster to the right, Charing Cross beneath.

'Sarah, look! See the pillory in Charing Cross?'

'I hope there's no one in it.'

'Come now, it'll cheer a prisoner to see us fly over. At least it will distract the pelters. Here! Use my pocket telescope. I've not enough hands for it.' His steel spectacles have a second set of lenses, tinted, hinged up until needed, for all like mad eyebrows.

Everywhere upturned faces.

'Strand!' Jacques points out.

'The whores will lift their eyes instead of their skirts, Jacques,' Joseph smirks at him.

They gather speed, move between road and the river. Or rather, road and river seem to move past below, for they feel no motion, borne at the wind's pace.

'Over there in the distance, are those St George's Fields?' Sarah asks Jacques, whose thin brown finger traces a line on his map. She remembers a shining day.

'I think St George's Fields, yes. Now we release the bird.' He opens a small wicker cage and a pigeon with a tiny Union Jack round one leg, a tricolour round the other, flies out and away without hesitation.

Small boats jostle each other on the river. At this point there are no masted ships, held back by the multiple, stumpy legs of London Bridge. Anchored, the little vessels rock to the movement of their passengers, who follow the balloon, cheer the pigeon's flight, soon lost.

Fleet Street, Ludgate Hill and the glory of a dome from whose pinnacle stone seems to cascade like water. They're so near they almost touch it.

'Who wouldn't give their eye teeth to touch St Paul's?' Joseph's pencil runs over page after page. 'If only we could stop!'

'No balloon have ever flown this route before,' says Jacques. 'Look at the people. They leave their houses like in an earthquake!' He reads the altitude barometer. 'Three thousand feet. I keep it low for them.'

Cheapside. Sarah peers down. Somewhere near here is Winkworth Buildings, City Road, the place of her dismal marriage. Poultry, where her mother and adored childhood friend Ben Newton were killed. Can she see 'Change Alley with Battle's Coffee House in its dark corner? Her life passes beneath her.

The wind still carries them north-east. Such density of brick. Streets, insect tunnels bored through the heart of a great tree.

To their right, masts and sails appear beyond London Bridge.

'Look where they've pulled down the granaries in Tooley Street,' Joseph announces. Gulls screech. Foul grey smoke from a brick stack puffs up, floats away. The Tower, flag flying.

Goodman's Fields, market gardens, pastures where cattle stand. The wind is blowing them due north.

'Now we ascend,' says Jacques, the city finally behind them, the fields and hamlets of the East End shrinking to dabs of colour.

'Mme Battle, you will feel the coldness *un petit peu*.' He unhooks sacks of ballast and throws them out.

They rise through cloud mass. Sarah shivers, reaches for her bag of winter clothes, two shawls, a cloak, gloves. Someone had assured her she would freeze.

'Thermometer reads fifteen degrees,' says Joseph, ghostly in the mist, layer upon layer, three full shelves of cloud.

Then they are through: vast blue opens above and all around. The quicksilver shoots up five degrees more than summer heat. Whiteness lies thick beneath them.

'Have we stopped moving?'

'*Non*, Mme Battle, we merely *seem* stationary.'

'We can see nothing against which to locate our movement,' Joseph remarks, his sketchbook temporarily abandoned, his tinted lenses lowered against the glare.

'Yes! *C'est vrai*. And so we eat now. What have you brought for us, Mme Battle?'

They pull out the basket, balance plates on napkins on their laps, hold glasses cautiously, eat, drink, smile at each other. Sarah is famished, having eaten nothing since early morning, and then, too nervous for more than tea. There's ham and cold fowl, best plum cake and three bottles of orgeat, wine and spirits too dangerous to take because of the air pressure. Balloons and champagne: those were the early days, before war with France.

Eat, drink and smile again. M Garnerin leaps up constantly to check ropes, instruments, his markings on the map. His mood is imperturbable, his movements disturbing.

'Jacques,' says Joseph, 'stop for a minute and tell us about your imprisonment in Buda Castle.'

'No! It is without purpose. The past is finished, it is dead. I never think of it.'

'Oh, I can't agree with that,' Sarah says. 'You're quite wrong, M Garnerin.'

'The past, *c'est passé*! Only today is important. And tomorrow of course.' He checks the barometer.

'For me the past has the greatest importance.'

'All of it?' Joseph asks her.

'No. Not all of it. But some of it lives in my mind. My memories are alive.'

Joseph is searching through his baskets of materials. She wonders if he, too, thinks about his past, what she knows of it, so conveniently abandoned. Yet she is glad he's there with her now, excitable though he is. Over months, they have become used to each other, talk easily, even if his ideas are often wrong.

He shows her his sketchbook.

'Oh, Joseph, they're wonderful! Look at St Paul's, the ships on the river. Even people in the trees at Ranelagh. You seem to have drawn everything. Such skill.'

'You are not drawing me?' says Jacques, flicking through the pages.

'They'll make a most excellent book,' Sarah says, 'and increase your fame, too, M Garnerin.'

'Now that we are cut off from the earth by these clouds, Sarah,' Joseph says, 'are you afraid?'

'Mme Battle have no need to be afraid. I have much experience. I have ascended many times. You are safe, *Madame*.' Sinewy Jacques is practical, has never known doubt.

'I feel quite safe, M Garnerin, and not afraid at present, though a little apprehensive about the next stage, perhaps. It is not like anything I have ever known.'

They pack away the remains of the meal, plates, bottles, wrap glasses in the napkins, stow the basket. Joseph has removed his greatcoat, both men take off their jackets.

Suddenly the clouds below disperse and the world appears. The whole country spreads magnificently beneath and beyond them. Sarah gasps and Joseph, elated, grasps her hand.

'We are in heaven, are we not? To look down like this is perfection. I never felt so happy!'

She takes her hand from his, gently, holds on to the edge of the basket.

'Mme Battle, you feel dizzy?'

'Certainly not, M Garnerin.'

'You feel well?'

'I feel exhilarated.'

They are fifteen thousand feet above a boundless land, which at first appears as swathes and blocks of greens and browns like a canvas in preparation. The balloon's shadow moves across it, the only cloud. They lean over the side and are amazed to see objects picked out in extraordinary precision. Once again Joseph insists Sarah use his snakeskin-covered pocket telescope, but even without magnification, they point out to each other ruts in roads, furrows in fields, thatch in hamlets, chimneys in towns. Their hearing, too, has sharpened strangely, so that sounds reach them: the rattle of carriages, lowing of cattle, mewing of kites and buzzards, shouts of surprise and joy.

'This is remarkable,' Joseph says, 'quite remarkable.'

'When people ascend first time, sometimes they talk of God,' Jacques tells them.

'I can understand that,' Sarah says. Tom had spoken of the ordered beauty of the natural world. That day at the Schuylkill River. 'But then think of the thousands of lives below us. What tragedies, pleasure, what love, sadness, cruelty and kindness that we can neither see nor hear! Like the ship's captain who cares nothing for the mice on board.'

She thinks: My own life, too, is as nothing in the universe. Yet now for me each second is full, so full of everything that is happening, all that has happened.

They ascend higher and a west wind drives them over a forest. Jacques attends to his map.

'Here the forest of Epping.'

'The easist thing to sketch so far, let me tell you. Look, it's like a great gooseberry bush.'

He daubs and streaks, trying out greens merging into blue, black shadows, a distant sift of cloud while yet the sun still burns.

They move rapidly, high, to the east.

In the huge blueness Sarah's senses are keenly alert. She feels her body glow with the sun's heat, her mind open so that past and future spread like a magnified map. She sees like a blade.

And knows what she must do. Knows with complete clarity what she must do for Eve and for herself.

She must leave Battle's Coffee House. Sell it. Its darkness and smells, closed, inward-looking, a standing pool, black, stagnant. She will remove Eve from its influence. Sail once more to Philadelphia. Live there, work there. Publish and sell books herself. Take up where Tom and she left off.

I shall do what he would have done had he lived, what we would have done together. I learned something of the business there, enough to try. Sell reprints cheaply so as to publish more pamphlets and unknown writers. Universal suffrage. Education of women.

I can do it with the money from selling Battle's. Tom thought I was wasted in the coffee house. *She will find a new way in this new world*, he said. I shall!

I shall have his name once more as I did when we lived as man and wife. I can see it all set out: Sarah Cranch & Daughter, Books and Printseller, Market Street, Philadelphia.

Oh! It's like the moment when the clouds dissolved! I shall leave the darkness of England for the light of America again.

Joseph notices the change in Sarah's face, her features seeming both to sharpen and to shine. An inner exultation. Sketches her as well as he can without her knowledge. Catches illumination.

The balloon moves with speed towards lines of light and dark.

'*Joseph!*' Jacques shouts. 'For God's sake, we must descend. Look, la mer, *la mer!*'

The wind has driven them eastwards, over the marshes of Essex, extremely close to the sea. At the same time a summer storm cloud wells up immediately beneath them, black, heavy with disturbance.

Jacques shows no sign of panic – indeed he never feels it, he is coolness personified. But he must keep the worst from Mme Battle.

'*Il faut que nous passions à travers de ce drôle là,*' indicating the cloud. '*Accrochez-vous ferme car nous allons nous casser le col.*'

'He says to hold on tight,' Joseph tells Sarah as Jacques pulls on a rope to open the valve at the top of the balloon. 'We shall have to pass through this storm. Do you see it?'

Gas spurts, they plunge down into the cloud and the squall's centre, beaten by wind and rain as they descend with sickening velocity. They grip the sides of the basket and Sarah cries out as a particular buffet hurls her onto the floor.

Both men help her up. '*Vite, vite!* We strike the ground in a moment,' Jacques yells above the wind. 'Hold the hoop so. Do like this. Lift the feet!'

The basket is held by a hoop attached to the net around the balloon. Joseph lifts Sarah up, bids her hold on to the hoop for dear life, raise her legs, does the same himself. Jacques, monkey-like, jumps up, tucks his feet into the net, holds an arm out to Sarah and the three of them, newfangled acrobats, swing from the massive gas-emitting globe as the basket hits the ground.

Sarah, her bonnet long gone, her dress soaked against her body, her muscles jarred, is too cold to cry. Survival is all. Gusting wind pulls the balloon across fields, the car dragging behind it at speed, banging over the ground, knocking against trees while they hang on to ropes with both hands, glad to be down, though jolted mercilessly. At last the grappling iron fastens its claw-hooks onto a tree stump.

'Mme Battle, you are well?'

'I am alive.'

'We could have done with your parachute, Jacques,' says Joseph, half joking, watching Sarah.

'*Mais non.* Only madmen jump in this weather. *Regardez!*' People are running out of a nearby farmhouse and stand gawping and pointing. Not too close.

'Surely they will help, will take us in?' Sarah's hopes rise.

Jacques and Joseph throw ropes towards them.

'Anchor us! Tie the ropes to your trees!' Joseph yells. The people stare. Some of the men confer with each other, gesture violently to the women, who turn and run back to the house. A woman stumbles as she runs, shrieks with terror.

'They think we are Napoleon's invasion! With our tricolours,' says Sarah, for the Union Jacks blew off some time before. 'They have not heard of the Peace. *We are friends!*' she shouts. '*Please help us!*' But her voice is lost in the wind's roar.

'They think we're devils dropped from the sky,' Joseph says grimly. 'I'll jump out and secure a rope, Jacques.'

'You cannot, alone. You are not strong enough, even you. So much gas still in the balloon, *comprenez*? Many men are needed to secure it. *Ils sont idiots, ces gens!*'

And then a sudden blast of wind grabs them like a hand, breaks the anchoring cable and with extraordinary speed shoots them hundreds of feet into the air. Tosses them back in the direction from which they came. The flight resumes just when they want it to end.

Jacques stretches for the gas-release-valve rope, but it's blown out of his reach.

'It have slipped away,' he shouts. 'I cannot make us to descend. We shall continue.'

Sarah pulls her cloak about her tightly to calm her shivering body.

'Mme Battle, have courage.'

'There is no braver woman, Jacques,' shouts Joseph, shaking with despair. 'But look, we all need courage now. We're being blown back to the coast.'

He fastens the clasps of his sketchbook, wraps it in oilcloth, ties it firmly.

At least what I have drawn may survive even if I drown, he tells himself. Someone may find the sketch of her. It's the best thing I've ever done.

'Put on the cork jackets! There will be ships, boats,' Jacques proclaims, confident even though there's not a sail in sight.

Sarah longs for Eve. Rejoices in her plan of hope and reuniting as the damaged balloon scuds rapidly towards a lucent sea.

1

———

IN THE CARRIAGE NURSEY HOLDS Eve's hand between both of her own.

'You must not mind,' she says, sniffling.

Eve pulls away. The tears on Nursey's soft, wrinkled cheeks annoy her. Mama is dead and she *does* mind.

She heard them in the kitchen say, 'Dead fer sure. Er'll not come back from *vat*.'

'What'll appen to us now, I ask you? Sssh, the child!'

It's a knot in her mind. Mama's gone. Each day passes and she doesn't come back. Isn't there in the morning. Doesn't kiss her goodnight. A knot.

'I'll dry my eyes, my love. There now. We'll have a grand life, you and I.'

They draw up before a tall house and Joseph comes out. She's seen him often. He strides through the coffee house, nods to some of the men, calls for Mama, sits at a table drinking, eating, talks to Mama when she's not busy, interrupts her when she is. Sometimes they argue.

'That's ridiculous!' she's heard Mama tell him.

She's never been in Joseph's house with Mama. If only she were here to help her understand! She'd explain everything. One arm round her. Heads leaning together.

'Eve! Dearest child of dearest woman. Come! I'll show you my house. I'll show you your room. Nurse, bring the bags.'

He leans down as if he would lift her, but she dodges him and he pulls her by the hand upstairs. To an enormous room with windows to the ground. She runs over to them to look out, to look away from Joseph. A groom is taking the last bags and boxes from the carriage, the horses' heads half hidden in nosebags. Across the street a woman looks out from her house, stares straight at her, unmoving.

'Put the luggage on the landing and come in, Nurse. This is where I entertain my patrons when they come to discuss their portraits. Hence best furniture and frames! You may not use the room without my permission.

'Here, look now, through these doors is a smaller room in which you two may sit and read and play. You can see it's where I read, myself. And smoke. Do you object?'

'It's not my place to object, sir. Are there housemaids?'

'I've not troubled with servants except a cook and groom. I read your mind, Nurse. You think it dirty, a mess.'

'Sir. Eve is unused to such surroundings.'

'There's a great funk in the coffee house!'

'Not in the family's rooms, sir.'

'Well, I live a bachelor's life. But I dare say you have a point. For her sake I'll hire a housemaid. Now I'll show you where you'll sleep.'

This time he succeeds in hugging Eve. The thick smell of his hair and clothes is like that of the room: she half likes it, half wants to choke. She struggles and he lets her go.

In the bedroom she's to share with Nursey at the top and back of the house, the walls are painted with lines of green leaves. There are pictures of animals and houses, of children with dogs and birds in cages. Two beds stand together opposite the window under which there's a painted red box. The head of a toy horse sticks out, she sees a doll's skirt, skittles.

'Oh,' she thinks. 'Toys for little children. I shan't play with them.'

'That's grand, sir.'

'You will breakfast with each other, Nurse, but we shall all three dine together and I shall read to Eve each night before she goes to bed. Although I'm not her father I wish to guide her, to protect her, to ensure she grows like her mother.'

A while later this conversation takes place:

'*Must* we live here? When shall we go home?'

'This is our home now, Eve.'

'It's not.'

'Joseph wants you to live here. And he also wants you to call him Joseph.'

'*You* don't.'

'I must call him sir or Mr Young. He will not have you call him Mr Young.'

'I *wish* Mama were here.'

'Mama is in heaven.'

'You always say that.'

'Your beloved mama is watching you from heaven; she is watching over you, taking care of you. God bless you, my darling bairn!'

The conversation is repeated often, sometimes several times a day. It's not consoling that Nursey always says the same thing. And Eve is with Nursey so much now that Mama's not here.

Joseph is alarming. Sitting in the small room, he pulls her to him and looks into her face so that she turns away in fright.

'Oh you gem! Oh you child of your mother!' This is obvious, she thinks, yet his face glows like a lamp as he says it.

She looks over at Nursey, who smiles at her reassuringly, yet she can't help feeling that Nursey, too, is discomforted, knitting together her fat fingers.

But there are compensations.

'There's so much of Sarah in you, my child. As an artist I see these things, you know,' he says to Nursey. 'Eve, you will look just like Sarah when you're a woman and everyone will love you.'

She doesn't want to be a woman, though being loved by everyone is good. If only she could tell Mama.

On occasion, Joseph calls her into his drawing room. Faces in frames gaze down from pale-yellow walls, and she'd rather look out of the windows as she did that first day, in case Mama is coming along the street, but, obedient, she stands by his side while he introduces her to large men and women in furs and cloaks. Who beam and pat her head and laugh kindly at whatever she says in answer to their questions. She hopes these aren't the people who will love her. She hears her mother's name mentioned and the balloon, and the women look at her again from under their big hats and want to hold her hand. She clasps her hands behind her back, not liking the feel of their gloves.

'You must let them hold your hand, Eve. They are charmed by you,' Joseph tells her later.

When the people make their slow way, stately and swishing, to grand carriages, Nursey says coldly, 'I do believe you are useful to Mr Young,' marring the complacency Eve has begun to enjoy.

There are other, bigger compensations. Joseph commands the cook to provide Eve with all the food she likes best, which for the most part is lemon tart with a jug of cream. There are rides in Joseph's carriage to Green Park, Kensington Gardens and Hyde Park, places she's never been before. Mama always had so much to do in the coffee house they rarely went anywhere. In Green Park she runs into the great space like a freed bird, Nursey in ponderous pursuit. Cows look up, stare, move away, and Eve laughs and chases them till Nursey catches up and firmly leads her back.

A longer journey takes them up to the Heath at Hampstead. There they walk, Nursey and Stephen the coachman carry picnic baskets and Joseph breaks off from sketching to hoist Eve onto his shoulders so that she can see London set out below them. This time she lets him. He's so tall she's right up high above everybody, clings on to his head and his greasy pigtail, terrified and thrilled.

The best place in the house is Joseph's studio, which he shows her one day and where, after that, she demands to go often. More large windows, but it's the ceiling that takes away her breath: a huge glass dome which at first she thinks is open to the sky until a storm spits cracking hailstones, and she watches water stream down outside the panes. When the sun shines and Joseph longs for air, small windows can be opened with a long pole. Even on grey days there's always light above, while below the space is dark with blocks of furniture and inexplicable objects.

He wants her to sit on a chair, addresses her from his great height.

'I'm working now, Eve. Did you bring your doll?'

'I want my book.' But he doesn't hear.

Once Joseph's glance seems fixed on his easel, she drops the hateful doll, with its white porcelain face, pinpoint eyes and false smile, and slips off the chair and round into a chaos of extraordinary rubbish. Unwrapping balls of screwed-up paper she finds faces half-formed, occasionally complete. Some she flattens out, others she crumples hastily, their stern looks intolerable. There are pages and pages of hands, against which she holds her own, which barely resemble either square; chalk-reddened palms or long, tapered fingers.

In whorls of dust she discovers the thinnest curls of copper, to wrap into rings for her fingers. Or she might tease Nursey by decorating her long grey hair with them when at night she unpins it from beneath her bonnet and it falls surprisingly far down her back. In the day Nursey is old, at night she becomes a girl. It's an unspoken secret between them.

Floorboards are splattered with paint, blobs, splashes, dried pools where jars were kicked over, their dribbling trails leading into the shadowy side of the room where the 'props' live. Here are bigger objects which Joseph instructs her to treat with care, as nothing must be broken or made unusable. There are life-size heads of men whose white eyes she tries to avoid, for they stare and stare. 'They're only plaster,' he says, and eventually she learns to ignore their disapproval.

Shapely urns, broken pieces of column, an enormous, brass-bound chest. He pushes open its heavy lid for her and she strokes deep red swathes of velvet folded inside. One morning she climbs in and Nursey, finding her dozing hours later, makes a great clamour. On a low shelf there's a large shell, spiked to her touch on the outside, smooth and delicately pink within; three thick books, so heavy she can't open them, statuettes of men fighting. Cobwebs cling to her clothes, spiders run off. In gold-framed mirrors leaning against the wall she watches herself trying to hook huge glass pearls about her neck, stick curled feathers in her hair.

Tiring of this, she turns to Joseph as he dots and streaks a canvas until one side of a head emerges, a shoulder, an arm. Sometimes she recognises a face from which she's smoothed the creases on the floor, or a person who's looked down at her and smiled pityingly. Joseph paints, steps back, paints, steps back, hums, smiles in her direction, paces about the room. Daubs again.

But a day comes when he stops and roars, hurls brushes, flings the palette across the room, bawls out to Nursey to come quick and take the child away.

She's terrified the first time it happens, thinking herself the cause. Runs behind the chest to hide, where it's dark and the blank-eyed men can't see her either.

'Nurse! Take her, get her out!'

'Eve, where are you, my bairn, where are you?'

'Find her, find her! I'll kill myself. Get her out!'

'Eve, where are you hiding, my darling? If you'd cease shouting for a moment, sir, I might discover her.'

At other times he rips up his work in silence. No roaring. Rather, his face takes on a resemblance to the plaster men: she can't catch his eye, he doesn't hear her. He tears up his drawings precisely, makes piles of them, cuts canvases into squares, loads the bits into the fireplace, sets them alight. Oil paint blazes.

Subsequently, she realises that she'll always be rescued, though she must indeed get away from him quickly when he roars. Just once, he throws the palette at her, its corner cuts her cheek and he howls at her gasp of pain, apparently hurt far more by his own action than she by the missile. Beats his head against the window frame as Nursey stanches the bloody gash and hastens Eve from the room.

And there are less violent incidents, like when he stops, groans and presses his head as if he wants to crush it between his fists.

'Does it hurt?' she dares to ask. At which he groans again in reply and sits down heavily. On the first of these occasions, she tiptoes over to him.

He covers his face with his hands and lowers his head to his knees, sobbing.

'It will be better soon, Joseph.' It's Nursey's formula for pain. She gently touches his arm, strokes this big child's hand, reaches up to wipe a tear with her fingers, but he falls forward and off the chair with a massive crash and she runs out of the room calling for Nursey. It's she who's made him fall!

When this sort of thing happens he doesn't appear for two days or more and she must occupy herself dully indoors or walk out with Nursey, who's so slow. And then there he is again, apparently unharmed, and all goes as normal until the next outburst. Baffling, but she gets used to it, and as time passes she becomes alert to a pattern. Notices growing quietness, slower movements, a tendency to pick and tear violently at his fingers, an ominous dulling before the explosion. Notices, as any mother aware of her child's changing moods.

'It's not your fault. It's never your fault, Eve, when I, when I get angry like I do. I know I do though I can't always remember exactly what I say. *Don't tell me what I say!* I know you've seen and heard me. It's when the blackness comes, you understand. Please try to understand.'

'Blackness?'

'Oh, it won't harm *you*. It only comes to me. Into my thoughts. Spreading over all my thoughts like streams of acid eating into copper. Or like real streams that become a sea which swallows me up. Oh, dear God, like drowning.

'There's the little bottle, too. You've seen me whisk it out of my pocket, haven't you? Drop, drop, drop, drop, drop and more drops!'

She looks up at him. What does he mean? What is he talking about?

'The god Opium, my little one. Laudanum. Let's hope you never need it.'

'Lord? God?'

'Lord God, hah, yes! Drops of the Lord. By now I must be the holiest man alive!'

*

One hundred miles away, in late evening light, a young woman sits at a table by the window, looks out over the grey North Sea. A coast made bleak by Arctic winds. The room is respectable but meagrely furnished, the fireside rug worn and recently darned, cheap engravings of biblical scenes on the walls, uncomfortable chairs. A relentless carriage clock on the mantle competes with the sea's perpetual sough.

She's nineteen, her expression too serious, confirmed by a narrow face, hair tightly drawn back, intense blue eyes. Only her mouth is too wide for harshness.

Every so often she stops, listens, glances towards the door. A cloth-bound ledger lies on the table, closed but within reach. She's not lit the lamp, begins to write.

Sowerthorpe Parsonage
6 July 1802

My dear Sophie,

You will be surprised to hear from me. I have not written to you since

She gazes at the sea, a mirrored sky, listening for an answer, consolation.

She has never written since leaving home to be married, leaving her mother, her sister Sophie and the four younger ones.

She shouldn't be sitting down to write, for there is much to darn and mend, and on certain days the accounts to complete during evening hours. Writing now is a moment of disobedience, especially writing to her sister. Who she'll have to ask not to reply, as her husband must not know what she's done.

But something is happening that she must tell about. Must tell *someone*, for there is nobody here she can talk to, her husband least of all. She intends to post the letter without his knowledge.

A week before, a man called early in the morning, around dawn. Neither the usual begging soldier nor ragged sailor, but a collier straight off his ship. He asked to speak to the parson. It was barely light.

The housemaid, Mary Corner, told them that though it's his habit to rise early, Mr Snead was not yet about.

'I am his wife,' the letter writer said. 'What is the matter?'

They brought in a drowned woman, wrapped in sacks and tarpaulin. Drowned but not dead. A suicide, the collier man said, pulled from the sea southwards down the coast. They thought she might not live if they took her all the way to Newcastle, so they dropped anchor here off Sowerthorpe and rowed in. Didn't want a dead woman on board. A man of the cloth would know what to do for the best, the collier said.

They told the parson's wife they'd covered her in everything they had. Forced rum down her throat: they'd nothing else to give her.

Mary and the parson's wife warmed a room though they'd little fuel, for the woman was terribly cold to the touch, her skin quite blue. She was wearing few clothes and those all black with coal dust from the sacks. They undressed her before the fire, sponged her coal-smeared face and hands with warm water, pulled on a spare nightgown and lifted her into bed. She seemed barely alive, unable to move her limbs. They touched her lips with warm milk and eventually she seemed to sip some down. In the early hours they tried feeding her some broth, but she was straightaway sick. Most of the time her eyes were closed and she didn't move except to cough fearfully and painfully.

Hours later, the parson left his study.

'We shall tell no one, Hester. Not yet. Suicide is wicked and I shall not be seen to condone her action in any way. Despair is a cardinal sin and will be punished by eternal fire.'

Remembering every moment of that haunting dawn which grew to cruel summer heat, Hester has not moved from her place at the table, still stares out to sea, now a vast unending shadow.

She'd been married to Reverend Mr John Snead for a year. An angular, restless man whose gaze when it emerged from an inner world, struck icy with certainty. That his bony frame and awkward gait spoke of some distant injury, that he was unkempt, his coat maculose, cuff thrums hanging out of his sleeves, all these were perceived by some as signs of spirituality, as was the distracted way his fingers played incessantly with objects in his pockets. People said these objects were stones, but no one really knew. It was clear he needed a wife, was advised to find one. As curate in her home village near Thetford, he'd noticed Hester, even though her attendance in church was irregular, approached her and made his offer with a smile that might not have been one, she wasn't sure. Her schoolmaster father being dead, he'd spoken to her mother, who kept her sensation of dislike to herself, aware that Hester, being educated but poor, would probably have few opportunities.

When they returned to the parsonage after the wedding ceremony, John Snead admonished Hester for addressing him by his Christian name, reminded her that they would only ever address each other as Mr and Mrs Snead, most especially within the hearing of others. Sometimes, however, particularly when irritated or angry, he addresses her as 'Hester' in a belittling tone, as though she's no better than a servant.

Once, forgetting, hoping for affection, she called him 'John'. His eyes drew in, darkened and she thought he might strike her, though he didn't, not that time.

Why did he marry her? She can hear her sister ask that question, reading the imagined letter.

He'd said: 'It is incumbent upon a parson to have a wife. You have a modicum of education, can sew and add up and your person and habits are not unacceptable.'

Sophie would repeat the question she'd asked before Hester left, how *she* was persuaded to marry *him*? She answers, the conversation alive in her head:

'I wish to be useful in the world. Poor Mother was relieved to have fewer mouths to feed. That thought sometimes consoles me.

'I, too, have asked myself these questions, Sophie, but now that this has happened I see they are not at all important.'

Snead instructed her: 'Tell Bissett to call in order to diagnose the woman's condition and advise if she should be removed to the infirmary. A relation may yet come for her. Or we may discover that her mind has turned completely, in which case we shall pass her on to the parish to deal with.

'If she dies I shall not bury her, of course, since death will have been by her own hand. It will be for the parish to dispose of the body, though undoubtedly they will object that she is not of this parish, so not theirs to dispose. In which case ... One does read of bodies left to rot. In Brighthelmstone, where that notorious whore Mrs Robinson tried to have some blackguard buried and the parish refused.'

She and Mary were to attend to the woman and not trouble him with details. There was no need for more than one further visit from Bissett, for he was bound to charge for expensive medicaments which he'd made up himself out of chalk and sugar, no doubt.

Snead so dislikes the surgeon that he can barely bring himself to use the man's name. Moreover, he remarks that he'd seen the man call on occasion *without cause*. Hester will instruct him to keep silent about the woman and to stay away unless asked. And she will see to it that Mary keeps her silence, too, if the woman wishes to retain her position in the household.

Dearest Sophie, Hester thinks, looking down at the blank sheet, words and feelings crowding her mind, I dearly want to help the woman, but a sense of dread overlays all my thoughts.

And were she to actually write the letter, what good would it do? She would burden her sister with the knowledge, only a little of which could be conveyed to their mother. Burden her with the command not to reply.

She hears steps. Pushes the unwritten letter beneath the ledger, which she opens hastily to the current week.

When the surgeon comes Rev. Snead remains in his study. Cannot bear to be in the same room with him.

Edward Bissett, in his late twenties though already grey-haired, is short, compact with energy, a man of rapid movements and great stillnesses. He enters the bedroom where the drowned woman lies as though he'd been held back behind the door against his will. Strides over to the bed to examine her. Listens to Hester's account with concentration. Watches her. Of course he is fascinated by the young wife of a man who apparently delivers the threat of hellfire to his parishioners week after week. As an unbeliever, Bissett has not witnessed this himself, but has heard about it often.

'She sleeps most of the time, but she's not been sick again.'

'That's good. There's paralysis in one of her legs, though I expect it's temporary. And this right arm which trembles so much at least shows some life. Continue to encourage her to take broth whenever you can, gradually something more solid, four drops of this in warm water if she appears to be in pain, and please report whatever changes you notice, Mrs Snead.'

'Mr Snead says you are only to come one more time.'

'I see. Could you tell me, nevertheless?'

Hester bows her head and Bissett understands.

'Might she be better cared for in the infirmary?' she asks, hoping he will answer 'no', knowing it would be better he say 'yes'.

'Certainly not. I believe she would neither survive the journey there nor the place itself. She will be much better cared for here.'

Hester is relieved by his somewhat fierce smile, shows him out, and a week or more later comes across him in the main street. It is fortunate that this meeting will avoid offending her husband, which calling at the doctor's house would have done.

'The woman is stronger, Mr Bissett. She coughs much less and sits up and takes more food, though we must help her, Mary and me, for she cannot firmly grasp a spoon. But she will not speak! Oh how I wish I knew her name. If only she could tell me.'

'It is a case of *aphonia*, Mrs Snead. But be cheered, for I don't believe it will be followed by an apoplexy.'

'You mean she will not die?'

'I do mean that.'

'God be praised! But what is aphonia?'

'It is when someone does not speak. Cannot.'

'Cannot they *ever* speak?'

'If the cause is physical then probably never, but if it is not physical then they may. One day.'

'Oh.' This is hard to comprehend.

'I have no notion why she cannot use her voice. Nor could I find out without prolonged attention, which would seem impossible so long as Mr Snead curtails my visits.'

'Sometimes when I talk to the woman she opens her eyes and almost seems to speak with them. Perhaps I can learn to understand.'

'That would be admirable.'

There's an interruption: Mrs Rollesby, a woman of great size, a busybody and avid follower of Snead, a gossip and lover of hellfire. She hails Hester and Bissett hurries off.

'I hear you've taken someone in at the parsonage, Mrs Snead. What does Mr Snead say to that?'

Hester is unprepared.

'I cannot give you an answer,' she replies. Once home she reluctantly knocks on her husband's door, knowing she must tell him, even though he cannot tolerate disturbance.

'Mr Snead, they know of the woman in the village! I have just met Mrs Rollesby and she asked me.'

He looks up, twists his neck as if to shake off an encumbrance, puts down his pen, sighs loudly. His sermons are his life.

'So you have let out the secret, Hester.'

'No! That is quite untrue. I have not spoken to anybody about it. Nor has Mary.'

'How can you know she has not?'

'I trust her. They have heard somehow.'

'Mrs Rollesby is a clean-living woman. She would not listen at doors.'

Hester knows better, but will not say.

'That loose-tongued surgeon! Scoundrel! Can the woman walk?'

'Not yet.'

'Good.'

'There is still a tremor on one side. Nor has she yet spoken.'

'Good. You and Mary will say nothing to anyone in the village. And do not tell me any more about the woman unless it is a matter of significance.'

*

A quiet evening before Eve goes to bed. In due course Joseph will read to her, if he remembers. She's glad when he forgets, because he doesn't read like Mama, who chose special books and pointed out words to help her learn to read. Now he's engrossed in a newspaper, a glass of brandy to hand, his long legs stretched out so that she must mind not to fall over them when she says goodnight and goes up to her room. Nursey sits at the table mending, leaning towards the lamp, her wrinkles huge behind her spectacles. On the table is a model merry-go-round that revolves when you turn a handle at its base. From its red-and-blue-striped canopy hang three delicate boats with each a passenger, their features tiny and severe. Mama gave it to her when she was small. She's too old for it, but sometimes toys with it when she's tired.

'Boats,' says Joseph, briefly lowering his paper.

'Do you think, sir,' Nursey looks up from her work, 'do you think it's possible that a boat ... ? You know what I mean, sir.' She shifts in her chair.

'Possible, well yes. But entirely unlikely. I was told that after Jacques and I were rescued no more were seen. Besides, we'd have heard by now.'

Nursey glances at Eve, speaks in a small voice.

'It's hard not to hope.'

'Hope away, Nurse! Such hopes are futile. Full fathom five!'

'Hush!'

'The waters have overwhelmed us. You know your Bible, surely.'

'But the Holy Book says the Lord is on our side!' she snaps, blushes.

'Enough, Mrs Casey!'

Nursey mutters: 'Our soul is escaped as a bird out of the snare.'

They resume their activities and Eve, only partly understanding, yet sensitive to Nursey's anxiety, infers it's about Mama.

She returns to the story she always spins to herself as the boats sedately turn, for one of the figures is a woman and that is certainly Mama. The other two are men. She's undecided who they are, though presumes one will have to be Joseph.

Who now bursts out from behind his newspaper.

'Good Lord! Garnerin's back on his feet. Dropping from a parachute. Listen to this, Mrs Casey.'

Eve asks what a parachute is.

'I'll read you what it says.'

'There's no need to listen, my bairn.'

'Yes, there is, Mrs Casey. She *will* listen. She asked the question. It's a new experiment, Eve.

'*The parachute consisted of a case or bag of white canvas or sail-cloth, formed, by thirty-two gores, into a hemispherical form of twenty-three feet diameter, at the top of which was a truck or round piece of wood, of ten inches in diameter, with a hole in its centre, fastened to the canvas by thirty-two short pieces of rope. At about four feet from the top of the canvas, a wooden hoop, about eight feet diameter, was put on and tied by a string from each seam, so that when the balloon ascended...*'

'Oh. A balloon!' Nursey gives a moan.

'So that when it ascended, as I said, *the parachute hung like a curtain from this hoop and appeared cylindrical.* Then, Eve, once he's high in the sky, he cuts the cord, the parachute expands and he descends safely. *M Garnerin was dressed in a close jacket and a pair of trousers,* yes yes. Seems to have sailed over Mary-la-bonne and Somers Town and landed two fields away from St Pancras churchyard. All in ten minutes.'

Eve wonders if the other man in the merry-go-round should be this Garnerin. Nursey, who has stitched continuously since the evening began, momentarily rests her piece of mending.

'Would that he'd never left that accursed country.'

But Joseph says nothing, is back behind his newspaper.

Eve realises the second man on her merry-go-round cannot be Garnerin, as neither of the men is wearing a close jacket or pair of trousers. They're dressed in old-style breeches and stockings. Besides, there's something bad about Garnerin.

Her merry-go-round story has a problem. However fast she turns the handle, the boats never catch up with each other. They fly out like birds, the people's expressions unsmiling, however fast she turns the handle, however wild their flight. The woman is pursued by a man, pursues the other man. If only she could remove them from their boats! But boat and passenger have each been carved as one, and must pursue each other for ever.

Before she falls asleep she pictures the last time she saw Mama. She does this often, though as time passes the images fade.

Her mother kisses her, promises to be back soon and walks towards the balloon.

Nursey holds her hand too tightly. Smiling. Faces are smiling all about her.

'Pretty child.'

'Like the mother.'

'Eyes like the father. Did you know him?'

'Pity it's so cloudy.'

She remembers the hubbub, music, sudden singing.

Then a huge cheer. Covers her ears.

The balloon moves. Voices roar.

'See Mama can you, Eve?'

Where? Where is Mama?

The great yellow balloon moves upwards. She follows the pointing finger, can't see her mother.

'There she is! See her now? In the car underneath the balloon. She's waving at you, look!'

The day is hot. A hand waves. And floats away.

There's a trip to Richmond on a hot, late summer day. The carriage is packed with baskets and woven rugs and sets off slowly through vehicle-cluttered streets that empty gradually as houses disappear and sunlit fields take their place. Eve is charmed by so much that is new. Nursey looks green with the jolting of the wheels.

Cottages, very grand houses. 'Built from stones of the king's Palace of Sheen,' Joseph says and grunts inexplicably.

They arrive by a bridge over the river, not dense with masts and ships and shouting, but serene and smooth, small boats skimming its surface, dodging the laden ferry.

Earlier, Nursey fussed over Eve's clothing, insisting she wear a bonnet to shield her from the sun. She herself takes a parasol large enough to protect them both. Certainly it's burningly hot. The river glares. Eve would love to strip off the stockings that cling to her legs and dangle her feet in the water, especially near where a crowd of ducks and geese cluster, waiting for crumbs. But she won't demand anything yet, for she's seen the rowing boats, not so unlike those on her merry-go-round, bobbing together below the steps, their inviting wooden seats padded with pleasant cushions.

'May we not walk up the hill, sir? How fine it does look!'

'Oh no, Mrs Casey, I'm sure it wouldn't interest Eve. Distant views are not for children. And she's already been up a hill at the Heath.'

'I'd like to go in a boat,' Eve cuts into this talk.

'That's exactly what we're here for, dear child. Which boat shall we choose?'

Sometimes Joseph is just like a friend the same age, wanting what she wants, Eve thinks. She remembers what Mama said: 'Joseph thinks only of himself. He's just a big child.' She was angry with him, but today Eve is glad of his childishness. He takes her hand and discusses the terms of hire with the waiting boatman.

Eve and Nursey sit at one end, Joseph sits in the prow as he calls it and Stephen, having placed the baskets from the carriage into the boat, sits in the middle to row. Stephen is a small, wiry man with ginger hair and a pocked face who, Eve has noticed, is very fond of his horses. She likes it when he winks at her behind Joseph's back. She's fascinated by the pocks in his skin and has experimented poking holes in her breakfast roll with her finger.

This day on the river, repeated on a few more occasions in her childhood, is like a perfect dream for Eve. Everything passes as though for her own amusement: other boats, their passengers chattering and laughing, some waving to her and she waves back, trees bending into the water, cattle pondering by the edge, ducks, gulls, weed through her fingers, sprouting up from somewhere deep beneath. Stephen rows them to a small sandy spit, raises the oars, draws the boat up to the bank. He sets oilskins on the grass with rugs on top and cloths, on which Nursey lays out plates and dishes and everything is delicious like food Eve's never eaten before.

Joseph throws pieces of bread to the ducks and geese that gather beside their beached boat, unpacks his block and begins to sketch. Eve takes handfuls of bread to the water's edge and makes the fowls noisily adore her. Seeing Nursey doze, she removes her shoes, her stockings, steps into the water, feeling the heavy silt sift between her toes. Past midday the water is warm, there's weed against her legs and she peers down hoping to see fish. She will swim with the ducks, she decides, opens her arms wide, her gown spreading then pulling down with wetness.

Away from the edge the water is cooler, but lovely; she bobs up and down expecting any moment to glide on the surface among the birds, who after all do it without arms. She tries to lift her feet to paddle as they do, but her head and shoulders fall forward and she gulps a mouthful of river. Upright again, her chin touching the surface, she pushes back her dripping hair, treads the sandy, stony bottom, splashes her hands, certain she'll reach the ducks who've swum away from her into the middle of the river.

Screeching! Behind her a violent noise breaks her idyll, and the next minute she's pulled out swiftly by Stephen and Joseph to the screams and cries of Nursey.

'Quiet, Mrs Casey!' but Nursey can't stop her loud stream of complaint, of lament, her constant naming of Sarah, and Eve cries with fury at having her pleasure destroyed.

Yet the day is not entirely ruined for, dried and re-packed, they row on, turn at Twickenham and arriving in Richmond once more, buy ices and wafers before the journey home.

*

Rev. John Snead is a discontented man. The living is poor, Sowerthorpe a small fishing village of seven hundred souls on the north-east coast of Norfolk that no one has ever heard of. Without patrons or friends, it is unlikely a better living will fall his way.

Frequently he complains of his confined existence 'at the edge of the world, unrecognised'. He has set himself the task of collecting together his sermons for use by clergy who have neither the time nor the ability to write their own, and for those who like to read sermons at their fireside or to their servants. This is an unfamiliar idea for Hester, since there were never such books on the shelves in her childhood home. They did read passages from the Bible together, 'for you should know both testaments', her father said. He would always comment on the passage, sometimes in praise, more often in criticism. Fondly, she thinks of them all, Father, Mother, Sophie and herself reading *A Winter's Tale* together, the young ones listening, cross-legged on the rug.

The sermon is all in all for Rev. Snead, and he never speaks for less than an hour, twice a day on Sundays. Already a striking figure in black coat and gaiters, he rouses himself to a pitch of fieriness in the pulpit, clenching his fists, his bony shoulders agitated. At certain times of the year sunlight seems to pick him out, his hair becoming an aura. No one has told him this, though his followers in the congregation notice, exchange fervent looks.

Hester thinks he sees himself as an Old Testament prophet – Amos, perhaps, though he regards himself as better educated than Amos, who was a simple herdsman. She knows he pores over those prophets like Malachi, Haggai, Zephaniah, more concerned to tell of judgment and the horrors of damnation than of salvation. Is aware that he seems to relish thoughts of suffering and destruction.

A few people come especially to witness his ire, to hear his account of the terrors that await them all. Children sometimes cry and their mothers rush them out of the church, even though they know he will call on them later to castigate them. He declares that, as so many in the parish cannot read, the only way they will learn of the penalties of sin, of the flaming mouth of hell that gapes for them, is to be made to listen and made to hear. Sometimes he speaks for thirty or forty minutes over the hour, especially if he's heard a snore or noticed a congregant nodding. Not that many come regularly to the church, which, in itself, is a source of rage to him. They're too easily drawn when itinerant preachers make it that far, gathering the people together for emotional outpourings in windswept fields or on clifftops.

Snead writes tracts which Hester takes about the parish for him, to the few who are literate, though he delivers them himself to villages further away, for he will not let her travel outside Sowerthorpe lest she become corrupted.

'Dens of iniquity,' he says, 'where men sell their wives for ten guineas.'

One of his tracts is entitled 'Steps into the Abyss'. 'Fall Not into Satan's Temptation' is another, and with a gentler title but no gentler message, there's 'Hope for Sinners'.

He has a large library, surprising for a man of such little income, but that's because while he was at Cambridge a friend of his father's was his patron. His father is dead, the patron, too, and he refuses to speak of either. Nor will he tell of his mother.

He will not let Hester choose even one of his books to read, and perhaps it is correct that, as he says, there would be none among them to interest her. She has three volumes she brought with her from home, Bunyan, Cowper's *The Task* (her mother's favourite) and the *Common Prayer Book*, and consoles herself with Cowper and the psalms in the prayer book. He removed her volume of Shakespeare when he found it soon after they were married, and spent an hour or two inking out some of the words in her songbook. Not that there's an instrument here on which she might accompany herself, and Snead does not like to sing. Although he always sings the hymns in church, it's soon obvious to her that he cannot keep in tune.

Again Hester longs to write to Sophie. Yet she dislikes self-pity, and just as the letter begins to formulate she is overwhelmed, and knows at the same moment that she'll probably never write it.

She's glad to have kept the facts of her life from her mother, who had taught them all so well after their father died. In her saddest moments, she wonders if she'll see her or any of her siblings ever again. Her husband had pronounced her schoolteacher father ungodly. When Hester mildly protested that he was dead now, he replied that the whole household was tainted, and that in marrying her he'd plucked her from it as from the yawning gulf.

Something of this loathing for her family presents itself when he comes to Hester's bed in the night on Fridays, for he is often filled with disgust and after, falls on his knees, begs the Lord that He will subdue his flesh.

Two weeks later the drowned woman is better, though not much. Hester tells her husband that she moves little and does not speak, and when she describes one arm as trembling terribly, he says 'Good', which Hester finds unconscionable. She knows she must not judge him; tries to understand, cannot.

Mr Snead requires his meals to be served on time, and Mary complies on most if not all occasions without Hester having to chivvy her. Mary has her own opinion of her employer, reinforced by views from her Catholic childhood which she wisely suppresses. This afternoon, when he's eaten, he dabs his lips with his napkin in that precise way that Hester cannot bear to watch. His fingers are long, his nails unclean.

'Listen carefully to everything I say, Hester.' As if I would dare not, she thinks.

'We, Mrs Snead, have been chosen by the Lord. That the collier should have decided to anchor in this obscure place with its living cargo, cannot have been an accident. The Lord has answered my prayers. At last the name of Snead will become noticed. Not quite as I had foreseen it, but nevertheless there will be recognition.'

He looks hard at Hester, daring her to question him.

'The woman is a sinner. The Lord has punished her by sealing her mouth and ruining her body. She was brought to us as a suicide, and as you well know suicide is a mortal sin. No doubt she has committed other sins as well.

'My work here in this benighted world, this benighted village indeed, is to warn of the dangers of sin, to warn of God's punishments, to exhort people to save their souls from the torments of hell, and for that this woman will be of great use to me.

'The inhabitants of Sowerthorpe are lamentably ignorant, for the most part illiterate, superstitious, low-born, depraved, a rabble. I am aware that sometimes my sermons are beyond their comprehension. The woman will be a living demonstration to them.

'It is as God intended. We shall retain her here, hold her as an example. There you have your explanation to the village. I doubt not, that before long it will serve for the world outside these parts.'

Hester seeks desperately for arguments.

'You do not know of any other sins, Mr Snead,' but he waves this away. 'She may yet get better, may yet find the use of her legs. Mr Bissett thinks so.'

'Bissett! That atheist. You will close your ears to him.'

'I cannot claim she is a sinner if I do not know it to be true.'

'What nonsense. All men are sinners, women certainly are, including yourself. The Lord has chosen us to give the woman shelter and chosen me to show her as an example to the world.'

'When will you begin?'

'Soon.'

'But she is still not at all well, Mr Snead.'

'Well enough for my purpose, I dare say. You will make sure she is ready.

'The ways of the Lord cannot be explained. As it says in Isaiah: "My Ways are Higher than your ways and My Thoughts than your thoughts."'

Though it is blasphemy, Hester cannot but hear him speak of himself when he quotes those lines.

'We shall be tested. In particular you will be tested, Hester.

'The woman is to be fed and cared for adequately. You will undertake that task with Mary and of course you must needs undertake further economies.'

Hester is silent.

'I perceive you are concerned. I presume that is about the economies. Gain shall outweigh loss! In time the woman may turn her hands to simple, valuable tasks and be useful in the household as well as to me.

'Remember this is the Lord's will. He is One who Seeth not as man seeth. The Lord's Eye is upon you.'

Hester spends as much time as she can with the woman who, although she moves so little and speaks not at all, looks, in Hester's mind at least, as if with meaning. Often tears pour from her eyes, soundlessly, without sobs, as though she has no control over them.

Hester hopes and prays in the quiet of her own room that before long the poor woman might begin to speak, and then her husband's vile plan will be wrecked. Though then he would try to be rid of her, she realises, which might be even worse, for how could she survive in a madhouse? Hester had visited one once with her mother to see an old woman who'd been her mother's friend. Oh, the poor folk! It was shameful. Her mother had cried pitifully when they returned home.

No, the woman must remain in the parsonage and Hester will help her recover, even while knowing that her husband would rather she didn't.

She and Mary wash the woman's hair and once the salt is rinsed out and she's strengthened by food and milk, it is fine and thick. Hester unpacks a large shawl embroidered in green leaves that she'd brought with her upon marriage. It belonged to her grandmother, her father's mother, is out of fashion yet pretty. When Snead catches a glimpse of it he tells her to pack it away as far too extravagant and unsuitable, but Hester persists in the hope it will please the woman.

Moreover, she is herself greatly cheered for she discovers the woman's name. When Snead finds her reading Cowper to her and insists she restrict her reading to the Holy Book, Hester begins at the beginning, and at the story of Abraham and Sarah is aware of a slight jerk of her listener's head. She looks up and there it is, recognition in her eyes. Her lips flicker as though she would smile when Hester repeats the name.

'Oh! Are *you* Sarah?'

The fractional movement again, so that Hester can hardly resist kissing her on both cheeks, hugging the woman as though she'd found her own child.

At dinner she announces her discovery.

'Mr Snead, I have found the woman's name to be Sarah.'

'Oh?'

'Yes. Isn't that wonderful? It was as I read to her from Genesis chapter XII.'

'But you know no other names for her or where she's from or who her parents were.'

'I don't know who *your* parents were!' Hester can't stop herself.

'How dare you! How *dare* you! The woman's name is not important.'

'We might discover who she is one day! It is a beginning.'

'How? Nobody has come for her. Nobody wants her. No doubt

she's thought dead. We have no need to find out, for she has another purpose now, my holy purpose. She requires no name. She is not to be known by any name. You will instruct Mary. The woman is to remain nameless.'

*

Most days are the same. Eve and Nursey breakfast together and Nursey tries to dress Eve in clean clothes, though she pulls away and does it herself. She refuses to wear anything blue, since that's the colour she wore on the day Mama went in the balloon, though it takes Nursey a long time to comprehend. She brushes Eve's hair for so long that it crackles, all the while grumbling about the slovenly ways of Betsy, whom Joseph now employs to help in the kitchen and with other tasks around the house. Betsy looks sly from a squinting eye while also being small, snub-nosed and pretty, and each one of these aspects Nursey deplores. She's better educated than Betsy, who's barely literate and was thrown out of her home by her own mother in some unheard-of part of the country. For the present at least, Joseph's given Nursey the task of supervising Eve's letters and numbers.

But he seems not to have noticed that Eve can already read, taught by Sarah who, from Eve's earliest days, would sit her on her lap, read from *Songs of Innocence*, holding the child's tiny index finger to the words, show her her name in *Paradise Lost*, talk to her of her father Tom, attempting to staunch her own grief thereby.

Eve loses patience with Nursey's sluggish pedagogy, pages of ever-growing numbers and biblical recitals, wheedles a story out of her when she's had enough. Nursey's own stories stem from her childhood in the North Country, and have little enough interest for Eve, especially when a heavy moral is involved, Nursey seeming impervious or resistant to Eve's fidgeting and yawns.

There's a row with Joseph, who comes upon Nursey plodding Eve through the catechism.

'I'll not have it, Mrs Casey!'

'But I'm certain Sarah would want her child to know her catechism.'

'I doubt that. I doubt it strongly from everything I learned about

33

Sarah. I'm quite sure she did not attend church. You will cease immediately.'

Nursey does so for a month, then resumes, and one Sunday takes Eve to church. There Eve is thrilled by the sound of the organ, annoyed that everyone sings songs she doesn't know, outstares a boy peering at her from his pew on the other side of the aisle. While Nursey listens intently to the dull echoing voice of the vicar in a sort of balcony above them ('Pulpit,' says Nursey), Eve begins to plait the ribbons hanging from a large woman's bonnet in the pew in front, earning a rebuke from the woman. She turns instead to the man sitting next to the bonnet, who has a very small hole in his coat. Concentrating on this hole, she imagines tiny silverfish streaming out of it like the ones she recently discovered darting about the shelves of the pantry when she was searching for something to eat. If only he'd take off his coat she could see them all flashing up and down his back like shreds of light.

But Nursey hauls her up and there's a long and dreary song and a prayer out loud. They sit and then Nursey tugs her away from the ribbons and silverfish and into the street's dust clouds.

Now there's an even bigger row than before, which Eve creeps down to listen to, sitting on the stairs out of sight. She's surprised to hear Nursey shouting back at Joseph, though these protests don't last long.

'I forbid it!' Joseph booms, and Eve scuttles up and away as Nursey's steps approach and the woman runs into her room and slams the door. A strange silence lasts for two whole hours.

Mama certainly never took me to church, Eve thinks.

'There is a higher Being,' she remembers her saying, 'that created the world, created everything beautiful in the world. Some people call it God. But you see, Eve, it is far away from us. That's what your father and I believed. We are Deists, Eve. Many good people in America are Deists, like Tom Paine.'

*

On a hot August Sunday that won't cool till the sea breezes of late afternoon, Snead harangues his sweating congregation, before the nameless Sarah's first appearance in St Wilfrid's, Sowerthorpe. He chooses his text to suit listeners who, while oriented towards the sea, live close to scratty fields of grain.

'*For, behold, the day cometh, that shall burn as an oven; and all the proud, yea, and all that do wickedly shall be stubble: and the day that cometh shall burn them up, said the Lord of hosts, that it shall leave them neither root nor branch.*

'Thus writes the prophet Malachi. But soon, I shall show you a wonder! Here in Sowerthorpe. You will witness a woman rescued from the grasp of death, a woman completely dumb, a woman whom the Lord has brought to this very place to be an example to you.

'You, like the woman who has come to us from the sea, must emerge from the ocean of sin in which you dwell! You must pour out that ocean of sin that lives within you and strive for salvation.'

The villagers mop their brows with damp kerchiefs and pieces of rag and wonder vaguely about wickedness. The children wonder, too, for Snead instructs them similarly in his Sunday class he holds in the parsonage kitchen, where they sit on benches, bemused by his words and the lingering stink of boiled onions. They long to see this dumb woman, for Mary has let it be known in the village that she is beautiful. Those who live by the sea and make their living from it are frequently superstitious. In the past, Mr Snead has often railed in his sermons against their unholy beliefs and practices. 'The Lord shall smite the ungodly' is a favourite theme of his. (He also preaches firmly against Mr Bissett and his vaccination, saying that it interferes with the will of God. Smallpox, he says, is sent to punish the people for their iniquity. Bissett will be damned for ever.) But now, no doubt, Snead is glad of this tendency of theirs, for everyone accepts, no one questions the sudden appearance of the beautiful, nameless sinner.

Hester makes one final attempt to write a letter to Sophie. Her husband, finding her crouched over a scrap of a paragraph, eyes full of tears, rips up the sheet, having read only her sister's name.

'No doubt this is one of many, Hester. How long have you been sending letters to your benighted family?'

'I have not sent any.'

'I can hardly believe that.'

'You must! It is the truth. I have not sent a single one.'

'Whether you have succeeded or not, here you are, pursuing a life of pleasure when I toil in my great work to haul souls back from the jagged edge of the abyss. When your work is to aid mine, you waste your time writing to your godless family! You shall do it no more. I forbid it.'

To reinforce his point he comes to her bed that night even though it is not the usual Friday, to punish her. In the dark she turns away her head but knows too well the expression on his face.

2

AS THE NEW CENTURY STUMBLES FORWARD, the hopeless Peace
of Amiens collapses and war with France renews, to last another
twelve years. Napoleon is crowned in Notre Dame. In the small
sitting room of Joseph's house a scene repeats itself: Joseph's newspaper and brandy glass, Nursey peering through spectacles at her
mending, Eve playing idly, listening to the sporadic talk.

'Boney's had himself made Emperor! Did you hear me, Mrs
Casey?'

'I did, sir. I believe it was the Pope who crowned him,' she says
with perceptible distaste.

'The Pope will have had no option. An invitation from Boney is
a command. If Napoleon ordered you to forget your superstitions,
Mrs Casey, by God you'd obey! Hah!

'But listen to this. It's a full description of the ceremony and
the festivities in the Place de la Concorde, and then, where am I,
lost my place, ah yes, *many small pilotless red and white balloons were
launched, but the centrepiece was a very large balloon under which was
suspended an enormous eagle, constructed, we believe, from a light wood,
painted. It was from this that the renowned aëronaut M Jacques Garnerin
was able to pilot the balloon.* Of course! Who else? The man was in
thrall to his wretched Emperor even then.'

Stitching, muttering from Nursey.

'Sir, I do wish you'd not speak of the accursed man.'

Eve, increasingly bored with her wooden merry-go-round,
knows that the second man in his painted boat isn't Garnerin, but

also cannot be this Boney people are always complaining about, as he's not wearing a crown.

In Sowerthorpe, Snead is fired up by the figure of Napoleon:

'Now we hear that the beast that ascendeth out of the bottomless pit has done so again to make war against us, to overcome us and kill us!

'Now the angels of the Apocalypse will pour out their vials full of the wrath of God upon the earth in retribution: for ye have all sinned, all of you!'

Not many fully believe they've brought about Napoleon's hostility, nevertheless terror of invasion spreads and is spread around the country. Napoleon's forces will come on ships, on rafts, on balloons. On barges propelled by windmills. The Tyrant will build a bridge from France to the south coast, first spying out the defences with a colossal telescope. Around Sowerthorpe beacons are built ready for firing and lookouts posted on high points along the coast, though there are few enough of those on these low mud cliffs. Worse still and perhaps most frightening of all, Boney will himself land at night and be among them the next day, unrecognised, disguised as a fisherman.

There are 'sightings'. People flee into their cottages at a distant sail. An unfortunate Irish tinker is surrounded and beaten by a crowd of boys who've learned that the Irish are waiting to welcome Napoleon with their arms wide open.

Edward Bissett, sceptical, does what he can to calm local fears; employs reason to counter the horrors purveyed by Snead, but without much success. Rails to himself against the heavy hand of government, the execution of so-named traitors who supposedly plotted against the king.

It's not entirely surprising that Sarah becomes a focus for the frightened people. Anglican though they are, and certainly few Catholics think of living in this place, the only dissenters being of the Wesleyan tendency, they grant her a kind of symbolism, believe that if they treat her well, even with reverence, her grace may protect them.

At first she's carried into St Wilfrid's on a board like the wounded from a battlefield. Her legs are wrapped in a blanket, she is pale and her eyes are open yet seem not to see as she passes down the aisle to be placed at the foot of the pulpit steps. The people of Sowerthorpe stare, nod to Hester when they succeed in catching her eye, which is not often. Yes, they assure themselves, she is beautiful.

With a look of ferocity Snead surveys the congregation, these days swollen in number by the curious.

'I well know you have all heard of this woman, for gossip and rumour spread through this village like the poisonous boils of plague and affect you each one.

'Know that in his Epistle, James tells us that the tongue is a fire, a world of iniquity: so is the tongue among our members, that it *defileth* the whole body, and setteth on fire the course of nature; and it is set on *fire of hell.*

'For every kind of beasts, and of birds, and of serpents and of things in the sea, is tamed, and hath been tamed of mankind;

'But the tongue can no man tame; it is an unruly evil, full of *deadly poison.*'

Those who are listening, compelled to concentrate on their hands and laps to avoid the glare from the pulpit, know that *not* all the things in the sea have been tamed, for are there not huge whales that overturn boats? Yet at the same time their tongues seem to swell in their mouths with Snead's slow and horrid emphases on 'defileth' and 'full of deadly poison'.

'Expect to learn! For you shall mend your ways, your wicked ways! This woman, this woman without a name is here to be an example to you, and *you will learn* from her example.'

Hester flinches, her knuckles white on her prayer book.

When, exhausted and anxious, they finally stand to sing, they crane their necks to see the woman. Those in the front pews say she's made no reaction to anything the parson has said.

A while later, Anthony Thurgarton the wheelwright constructs a special chair with wheels and handles so that Sarah can be easily conveyed about. Alone among the villagers Thurgarton is known to be never ill, chewing garlic all day and washing his head in vinegar. He makes no charge for the chair, much though he needs the money, being satisfied with the villagers' praise and a secret hope of reward in the next world. More realistically, that one day the silent woman might smile at him.

Whenever Eve tries to remind Joseph that her mama had several books she now wants for herself, he forgets, or seems to mishear. She wonders if he intends to keep them for himself.

Then a carrier brings some wooden crates to the house, his great cart horses creating a stir in the street. There's hasty talk between Joseph and Nursey, during which Nursey dabs hard at her eyes.

'Come, Eve, I'll take you out to see the illuminations. Iluminations for Trafalgar, you know,' Joseph says.

'What's in the boxes?'

'Oh, this and that.'

'Why are you crying Nursey? It's Mama, isn't it? Mama's things are in the boxes, that's it! Let me see them!'

The lids are prised off and Joseph swiftly takes two smaller boxes out and up to his room.

'Mrs Casey, look through the clothes, will you? Find what you can that can be unpicked and cut down for Eve.'

The clothing smells of Mama. She holds a shawl, a gown, one garment after another to her face, scenting Mama, her very self. For long seconds she believes all is as it was before. Mama is here, has gone into the next room to collect something. Until, knocked from this hallucination by Nursey's hefty sobs, she rushes to tears herself.

For some time she's so caught up with visits from the dressmaker, with the strange, cruel task of allowing Mama's garments to be cut to pieces, to feel in these reduced gowns both the presence and the absolute absence of Mama, that she forgets about Mama's books.

Not for long. 'Joseph, in Mama's room she had many books. I remember them well because she read to me from some of them and showed me which ones were my father's. And I know she had papers in a drawer, too, which she said I could read one day. *Where are they?*'

Sighs from Joseph. 'Oh, all right. I'll show you.'

'No, I want to *have* them myself. They belong to me as much as the clothes. Please give them to me now. They're in those two smaller boxes, I'm sure.'

A small set of shelves is moved into Eve's room and on them she arranges, almost as sacred objects, her mother's books. *Lyrical*

Ballads, Songs of Innocence, Songs of Experience, Paradise Lost and Regained, A Vindication of the Rights of Woman, Lives of the Poets, Shakespeare's plays, Cowper's *The Task.* After those come her father's books.

'These were Tom's,' she can hear her mother saying. 'I read them all.'

Rights of Man I, Rights of Man II, Age of Reason, Ruins of Empires, Robinson Crusoe, Goldsmith, Voltaire, Homer.

Cross-legged on the floor, she sifts through pamphlets and papers, stumbling over words. Two copies of *Massachusetts Magazine*, one with a note pinned to it: *see Judith Sargent Murray*; Jo. Priestley, 'The Importance and Extent of Free Enquiry'; T. Day, 'The Dying Negro'.

The most exciting finds are two roughly sewn sheafs of paper. The first has a printed title page: 'Rights and Virtues in the New World by Thomas and Sarah Cranch', with an inked remark above the title, 'notes for pamphlet'. The second is entirely handwritten, its title page inscribed 'Notes for pamphlet entitled Women's Education, by Thomas and Sarah Cranch'.

She knows, has seen from a page or two, that without Mama's help she will find the books and writings difficult to fathom. But she doesn't care. One day she'll read them easily, and meanwhile they are hers. The great treasure is hers.

*

October is cold – not as cold as it will yet become, but the sea wind is harsh.

John Snead's walks through the village bring out his supporters, send off the weak and cowardly. Taller than most, his odd gait is easily recognisable. A small crowd gathers around him in the square, led by Mrs Rollesby, whose outer clothes are buttoned severely as though to hold back an overflow of bile. Elizabeth Catton at her side, pallid, ever conscious of inferiority in height and marital status. Not that anyone can remember having seen a Mr Rollesby. The fearsome Mrs Cragin joins them today. A woman of magisterial build, severe mien, she is reputed to have said, 'I confess Christ in me as Saviour from all sin; I shall never sin again,' and not spoken since.

'What do you say to the news of Trafalgar, Mrs Rollesby? I've been hearing about it all morning.'

'All morning' is the clue for Mrs Rollesby, her square face fixed admiringly on the parson.

'Too much time wasted.'

'I knew you'd agree with me, Mrs Rollesby.' He flashes her a rare smile.

'Yes, oh yes,' Elizabeth Catton hastens to join in. 'Folks should think to their own battles.'

'My very own words, Miss Catton! Our generals, our admirals must defeat Satan overseas of course. But each man, each woman, must first defeat the enemy that dwells within their own souls.'

A look of deep complacency illuminates Mrs Cragin's face.

In the parsonage, as sometimes happens, Snead does not go straight up to his study, rather he seeks out Mary or Hester for something to eat. He's ruddy from walking against the wind and, thinks Hester, chopping vegetables with Mary, from reprimanding.

'Oh the folly, the stupidity, the godlessness I encounter each day! Yes, Hester, I should like more cheese than this small piece you've given me. They think to slack and celebrate because of one victory. When the Beast is still at large!'

'It cheers them, Mr Snead, even if the hero was killed. They have little enough to make them glad, especially now winter's setting in.'

'*Hero!* You're as bad as the rest.'

'His ship was called the *Victory!* Isn't that excellent?' If only she could communicate this to Sarah.

And all the while she's listening for sounds from upstairs. The parsonage is a poor house, its ceilings and floors thin. Now that her legs are moving, Sarah has begun to take small steps around her room.

'What nonsense. I'll have some of that cold bacon, Hester, and take it with the rest of the loaf up to my room. I shan't stay to hear any more.'

He walks out. She picks up his coat which, unusually, he removed in the meagre warmth of the kitchen and dropped onto a chair. It's heavy. Well, he's a tall man. But the weight is something else. The pockets are full of stones. The rumour she'd heard before her marriage was true, then.

When Nursey asks for time off to watch Admiral Lord Nelson's funeral procession, Joseph shouts at her for a good five minutes:

'It is a bad war! We should have stopped it years ago. Look at the money it absorbs in ever greater sums, the men killed, the men wounded! Look at the streets: you can't walk a step without falling over a legless beggar with a shred of uniform on his back. Or bumping into a block of militia marching up and down. An utterly profligate government! Ignores all protest. Think of the prisoners of war housed, fed and watered in their thousands. The folly of the whole enterprise! And we're to celebrate the ruinous victory at Trafalgar with the biggest funeral there's ever been!'

Nursey, taking all this to mean no, retreats from the room.

'No, Nurse!' Joseph calls after her. 'We'll all three go. A hero is a hero, I suppose.'

'Surely a funeral is not suitable ...'

'It'll be a show, flags, drums, uniforms. We'll go.'

But first Nursey wants to see the body lying in state, and that she does on her own, two days before, delivered to Greenwich in Joseph's coach, to join thousands in their long wait.

And Joseph, disgusted at the news that the vergers in St Paul's charge people sixpence to see the scaffolding, winch and hole for the coffin, decides to limit their observation of the funeral to the barges on the Thames as they approach Whitehall Steps on their way from Greenwich.

'That at least will be unusual, at least memorable. There'll be other state funerals, but not with barges. I'll sketch it. Prints will sell. I might even paint it.'

From the window of a house close to the landing place, owned by a rich couple whose portraits hang freshly painted on the walls behind them, Joseph, Nursey and Eve watch the perfectly matched oars as black barges of admirals in mourning cloaks, of officers in full uniform, black waistcoats, breeches, stockings and crêpe round their arms and hats, approach slowly, form two lines to let through the coffin barge. Joseph turns over page after page of his sketch-block, catching details. Gunboats fire, a shudder of trumpets and drums play the 'Dead March' from *Saul*. Behind the barges stretches a tail of black-clad rowboats of the London companies, drapers, skinners, stationers, fishmongers, goldsmiths. River fencibles, harbour masters. Only the procession moves, yet when Eve looks hard she sees decks, yards, rigging, masts of the boats and ships that fill the river massed with silent spectators.

Suddenly the sun goes, clouds darken the day and hail beats down. Nursey automatically puts her arm round Eve, who shoulders her away, for she is not perturbed. She is enthralled by the piece of drama that follows: the moment the body is brought on land the sun appears. A unanimous sigh of amazement, of contentment arises from the river, the shores, the room in which the watchers stand, loud enough to hide Joseph's gruffness as he makes to leave. He mustn't have his patrons hear his views, he has plenty of useful material and he can't bear a moment more.

Eve doesn't need Nursey's protective arm. Sounds, images take their place deep within her mind.

*

Hester keeps the information about Sarah's movement from her husband as long as she can, but in the awful quiet of the house Snead eventually perceives new sounds as the two women, even with the greatest discretion, help Sarah to walk from her bed to a chair, from chair to the window.

He bursts into the room one day and there together stand the three of them, for all like a new representation of the Three Graces, whose smiles die from their countenances.

He points a long finger. 'This woman cannot walk!'

'You must leave, Mr Snead. It is unseemly.'

'You will not order me in my own house, Hester. This woman cannot walk. She *will not* walk!'

Hester dares to continue. 'By God's will she has begun to. God be praised!'

'You tell *me* what God wills? Shameless woman! God has commanded me to use her as an example to the ungodly sinners of this parish. She cannot speak. She cannot walk. You will bind her legs!'

He storms out and Hester, fearful of upsetting Sarah, unsure how much the woman has understood, needing, too, to stand firm in front of Mary, swallows her desire to cry.

Later, reasoning to herself that her husband didn't stipulate exactly *when* Sarah's legs should be bound, she arranges with Mary, after first swearing her to total silence on the matter, to tie them together with ribbon only on Sundays, when Sarah is wheeled into the church, but to continue to encourage her to walk about her bedroom. Moreover, Mary is never to mention Sarah's name, except to her and to Sarah herself.

'Let it be our secret, Mary. We must protect Sarah. Swear it now on your missal.'

Hester talks to Sarah when no one's about, explaining what they will do on Sundays, but that they'll keep her legs wrapped on other days. It seems to her that Sarah does not understand what is happening, how or why she is being used. Her expression hardly changes.

'Please, Sarah, I beg you to go along with this charade. If my husband were to face discovery, I think he would resort to a terrible action to prevent the destruction of his character. I think he would declare that you are mad. He might even declare us both mad. Do you know what this would mean?'

It's hard to tell if she does or doesn't.

'You would be taken away to bedlam. It would be terrible. Like prison.' Hester looks desperately at Sarah's face, searching for the slightest indication of understanding. There seems none, yet she cannot believe this woman's mind is blank, feels a certainty that however deeply concealed she is now, the person who is Sarah will one day emerge.

*

Joseph takes Eve to see 'old friends' near the huge cathedral of St Paul's, where they get out of the carriage.

'Look, Eve, how great it is, a masterpiece, a monument to the glory of man.'

Nursey draws in her breath. 'For shame, sir! To the glory of God!'

'Eve, I'll tell you a marvel. We flew so close to the dome I almost touched it. We flew, your ...'

At her elbow Nursey is pushing her away. It's about Mama again. Like so much of what Joseph says, it makes little sense.

They come to a narrow street with shop windows of nothing but books, pamphlets and engravings, stop at one whose many panes contain a print in each.

'Look at Digham's work,' Joseph says. 'He's still a master.' They walk in and straight through to a back room.

'At last!' A fair-haired woman and young boy sit at a table, a book open before them, the boy's finger on a page. 'Joseph. I knew you'd bring her eventually.'

'Eve, this is Matthew and this is Mrs Digham.'

'No it's not! It's Matthew and Lucy, Joseph. I know her.' She walks round the table to them. 'You used to call on Mama sometimes.'

'It's Eve,' Matthew says, and they look at each other uncertainly. The woman draws her into her arms and kisses her.

'My dear child. I have wanted to see you again so much, since, since … It's been a few years. Goodness, how you've grown! I wrote, but received no reply. Joseph only acts when he wants to. But finally he's brought you. And Eve, he's right, I am Mrs Digham now, though of course you should call me Lucy. Your dear Mama and I were friends. She was so kind to me when times were hard. Nurse, sit you down. Mrs Casey, isn't it?'

'It is so, madam. Mrs Digham.'

Joseph interrupts. 'I thought she might sometimes come here, Lucy. She has nobody but Nurse and me for company. I see you are teaching the boy, that's good. Nurse, here, has taught Eve her letters and numbers.

'No, Joseph! Mama taught me to read. And I have all of Mama's books at last.'

'I read to you sometimes, Eve. But, Lucy, as you'll remember, my patience is poor. Perhaps she could learn a thing or two with you. I'm reluctant to send her to some worthless school for young ladies where they spend all day covering screens and sewing silk landscapes.'

'Like the one I went to.'

'Exactly so! Her mother would have wanted something better than that, no doubt. But you have some education, at least, from that dismal father of yours I suppose, or your mother. Ach! It doesn't bear to think about *them*. I'll go up and see William.'

Eve is amazed to hear Joseph speak in this way about Lucy's mother and father, but Lucy seems to take no notice.

'Come, sit by me, Eve. Matthew and I are reading a history of England. Mrs Casey, please find tea things in the kitchen through that door. There's bread and butter and a fruit cake.'

Matthew bursts out suddenly: 'We used to read together! Tiny books.'

'Yes, you did. They were called *The Infant's Library*. Pretty little books, but it was pretend reading, for you were hardly more than babies. I used to take you to Battle's, Matthew, you still in petticoats and the two of you sat on a rug on the nursery floor together while Sarah, oh, dear Sarah.'

Eve has seen so many faces peer at her and weep that she's quite inured to it. Sometimes tears are succeeded by surprise when she doesn't cry, too, as though she should weep just because they do. Lucy Digham is not one of those.

'Do you remember sitting on the floor together?' she asks Eve.

'I'm not sure.' She doesn't, though she does remember a room with her cot next to Mama's bed, Mama stroking her cheek. Singing. 'Jack Sprat', 'The Cuckoo is a Merry Bird', 'London Bridge is Falling Down'.

She remembers not so long ago, sitting with Mama before the fire in the office at the back of the coffee house, reading and talking. When Mama stretched out her feet she did the same to see if her own would stretch that far.

'Not yet,' Mama said. 'But they will.'

'Tell me about Papa again.' If she concentrates hard she can just hear Mama talking. Has a sense of her face in the firelight.

Joseph comes ducking through the doorway.

'Here she is, Digham! Isn't she beautiful? Isn't she like her mother?'

An old man in a round felt hat of many colours smiles at her until his eyes, made huge at first by the lenses of his spectacles, almost disappear into the folds of his face.

'Ah Eve,' he says, taking both her hands and kissing her on the forehead. 'Yes. Your dear mama.' He smells of ink. 'But, Mrs Digham, let us shut up shop and be more welcoming.' He touches his wife's shoulder and they look fondly at each other.

Eve thinks how odd that Lucy isn't an old lady, for he's certainly an old man, his face is all creased. And shouldn't Matthew be much older if he's their child?

Upstairs there's a small room with comfortable chairs, a narrow fireplace and engravings on every inch of wall. A window casts shadowed light. The old man heaps coals on the fire and warms the others with his geniality. The children sit side by side, unsure how to proceed. Lucy is subdued, Nursey silent. Joseph, compelled by the low ceiling to sit down, dominates.

'My interests have changed, Digham, old man.'

'Oh yes?'

'I'm giving up engraving altogether. Lithography, let others do it. I'm concentrating entirely on painting.'

'You were always ambitious, young man Young, even when you were my apprentice. I knew then that you'd go far. But what of the Nelson funeral? You published a series of prints of that.'

'Westfield did a reasonable job. They sold of course. Who hasn't made money out of Nelson?'

'True enough.'

'But the painting brought in the most.'

'I saw it at the Academy. We both went, did we not Mrs Digham? Paint so thick I wanted to poke my finger into it. I doubted it was dry. The drama of the disappearing sun, storm clouds, darkling sky. Rain smearing the coffin's black lines. Mirifical! I should say you've become a thorough-going Romantic.'

'Yes! I knew you'd understand, Digham! That's my direction now. The sea calls me. Mountains, lakes.'

'You must take yourself to Italy then.'

'Perhaps I shall.'

'And the portraits. What of them?'

'How sick I am of the rich! I must always be on my best behaviour, cannot say what I think.'

'You were quite the radical when you were a lad and worked with me. I think of those cartoons of yours and the meetings you went to.'

'That's all gone. I can't concern myself with the downtrodden. I need time to follow my new path. Portraits bring me money. So, I've learned to flatter, William. It disgusts me to hear myself.'

'Oh, really? Surely the rich have made you rich.'

'Almost rich enough to cease painting their portraits. To tell the truth, I'm sick of people.'

Eve sees Lucy watch him closely, notices a slight smile dart over her face. Eve is bored hearing Joseph boast so loudly in this small space. But she likes the old engraver, feels sure Mama liked him, too. And the cake is good.

*

A fisherman's wife knocks on the back door of the parsonage.

She brings her boy, sick with fever, in the belief that the sight of the dumb woman will distract him. She says she can't afford to have him bled, though in fact Edward doesn't ask payment from the poorest and he's against much cupping. It's clear to Hester that she just wants to gawp, but Mary lets her in. Sarah, half asleep in the parlour, her legs tucked under a shawl, happens to open her eyes wide at the child, and that night, according to the mother, the fever leaves the boy and he is perfectly well. The following day she goes about the village telling everyone and the news that the nameless woman in the parsonage has healing powers is soon known by all.

Hester cannot think but that Snead will hate this eruption of superstition, and for her it means a move yet further away from the curing of Sarah for which she so longs. If people believe that she has the power to heal then they, too, as well as Snead, will require her to remain dumb if not paralysed. It will be even less possible to coax Sarah into normal life.

Snead is silent for a day, and Hester awaits his reaction with dread.

Four meals pass without comment, but she must speak.

'Mr Snead, villagers have begun to call. They want to see Sarah. Some believe she may heal their ills.'

'Godless imbeciles!'

It's as she expects. But he pauses, dabs his lips firmly with his napkin. Takes up his knife and fork again. Chews. She waits. Looks at the stringy meat on her plate without relish.

'Let us see.'

'Shall I not turn them away, Mr Snead?'

'Not yet. Let us see.'

They come, a straggle at first, timid, gaping at the strange, pale, unseeing woman. The sick, weak, hypochondriac bring their little gifts of thanks or of hope, halfpennies, farthings, tokens, small treasures long hidden in drawers. A silver pin. A metal button. Some bring small offerings of food: three eggs, a handful of apples, a griddle cake, in summer a saucer of samphire. Hester thinks it right that Sarah should eat these, Mary, too, since she works hard enough. She tells Snead that whatever's left should be taken to the most wretched in the parish.

'No. We must eat what we are given. Anything that remains after that may be fed to the woman.'

Hester feels sure he enjoys the food more than this saying implies. She suspects that all the offerings are part of the 'gain' that he anticipated.

A box in which the people place their tributes stands by the door. Mary is enthusiastic, Hester embarrassed. Snead remains silent, but one day removes the box and returns it empty.

And Sarah? No longer trembling but physically confined, too deeply removed within herself to speak let alone protest, sits, according to those who stand humbly before her, in quiet seren-ity. An acute observer would note how blankness alternates with alarm that flickers in her eyes.

Hester talks whenever she can in the hope that one day Sarah will reply. She tries to explain.

'These people who come believe you have the power to heal, Sarah.'

Surely *this* will provoke a response, but no. 'One look from you and they think ill folk will be well again. Oh, you will think it strange. Or wrong. You will think it wrong, just as I do.'

Sarah looks hard at Hester.

'Perhaps we need to see it like this. If people are really cured just through your existence, it cannot be a bad thing.'

So odd this dialogue with only one voice! Yet Hester feels sure that *something* of her words is understood; as though they *almost* converse with each other, though Sarah says nothing.

Eventually, Sarah turns away, looks about her, puzzling, as if she cannot understand where she is or even who she is.

Nursey tells Eve a surprising thing. The old man, William Digham, is not Matthew's father. Joseph is his father.

'But he never called Joseph Papa!'

'That's surely so, my dear. Indeed they didn't speak to each other at all, did they.'

'Why doesn't Matthew live here?' Eve asks, hoping her question won't somehow make this happen, as she's not inclined to like the boy, certainly doesn't want another child in the house.

'Because Mrs Digham is Matthew's mother and it's better for Matthew to live with her. Mrs Digham, before she was Mrs Digham, was once, er, in a manner of speaking, married to Mr Young.'

'Mrs Young!'

'So to say.'

'But Joseph loves Mama. Is Joseph my father, too? Then Matthew is my brother!' This is unbearable.

'No, no, certainly not. Your father was Thomas Cranch. Come now, *Eve Cranch*!'

'You've said that before.'

'Of course.'

'Where *is* he? Why is Joseph *not* my father?' Everything is wrong. Everything.

'I'm sure your mama did tell you often. She told you about Tom Cranch even when you were a bairn. I overheard her many times. Remember now, your father was a printer and bookseller and he died in America.'

'But Joseph does love Mama.'

'I know nothing of that. You mustn't fret so, Eve.'

Mama would answer her questions. She always did. But Mama is dead.

She thinks of black boats, men all in black, guns booming, music, slow marching. A big box, the coffin, black, carried slowly, placed on the strangest carriage.

That was Nelson, not Mama. Dead means 'gone'. For ever. Will she really *never* come back? They say she's in heaven. Heaven is somewhere else. It's not here.

Everything is wrong.

Everything. Hate wells up like feeling sick. She hates them, Nursey, Joseph. Nursey always says the same things. Yet Nursey thinks Mama is alive, she's picked up that much, for Nursey drops little hints now and then while always telling her that Mama is in heaven. Joseph says Mama is dead, but Joseph says many inexplicable things or won't even listen.

She boils with rage, her body will burst if they don't bring Mama back. Hate, she hates them. That ridiculous doll! She grabs its legs, swings it against the washstand so that its head smashes and its stupid expression is destroyed. Runs out of the room, slamming the door, down stairs and more stairs straight into Joseph's studio, charges at him, punching, knocking the brush from his hand, the palette, pushes over the easel, shouting. She's seen him do it himself, she knows how to roar and rage, to howl, to throw things about, to hurl things down.

He grasps her wrists, she kicks out at his shins and all in a moment he slaps her face and himself bursts into tears.

'Oh Eve!' The blow shocks, stops her. He falls on his knees.

'I'm sorry. I will never do that again. Never. What is it? Dear God what *is* it that angers you so?'

Suddenly silent, she touches her cheek as if she might find blood like before. She doesn't cry.

'What *is* it?'

'Why are you Matthew's papa? Why aren't you *my* papa?'

'Because Tom Cranch was your father! And dear Sarah, your mother, told me your father was a much better man than I. She didn't want me, told me that herself. Tom Cranch was a good man, a wise man and she loved him. She wouldn't marry me even though he was dead.'

'Why is he dead?'

'He caught a disease that was rife in Philadelphia. Called yellow fever.'

'But why? And why did Mama die? Why does nobody tell me anything?'

'I have no answer for you, Eve. None.'

'Where *is* Mama?'

'Oh, she is dead even though we don't know where her body is. You and I, we mourn her.'

'But I heard Nursey say ...'

'Your nurse is a foolish woman. Simple-minded. Superstitious.'

'Well, that's what she says. Why *did* God take her to heaven?'

'Ask *her!*'

'Is my father in heaven, too? He can't be if he's in America.'

'Oh, I've no patience for this!'

That night she dreams she's on a hill so high it's almost in the clouds. It's like being up on the Heath only higher, and no one is there except God, who gradually becomes more and more like Joseph.

Before, behind, all around her is the world, the whole world. She knows Mama and her father are somewhere near, but she can't see them, and as she peeps over the edge of the hill God pushes her and she falls, falls and falls until she starts awake.

*

It is not hard to imagine how the 'healing', inadvertent though it is, increases, together with the gifts; how the village begins to blossom in its local fame, how Snead's name flickers in the clerical world, though his work on the book of sermons proceeds slowly. Sarah, so recently emerged from degrees of physical paralysis, remains deeply withdrawn, silent.

A visit from the newly established *Eastern Post* infuriates, though later pleases Snead. The report reads:

> An extraordinary phenomenon is to be seen in the village of Sowerthorpe on the north-east coast of the county of Norfolk. A dumb and paralysed woman is healing the illnesses of the villagers.
>
> It seems that the woman, who is aged about 30 years, was pulled from the sea by colliers returning to Newcastle from London after delivering their cargo of coal. The colliers are unknown, the place where she was found remains unknown also, but your correspondent has seen the woman with his own eyes.
>
> She has been given a home with Reverend Mr John Snead and his wife, Mrs Hester Snead. Mr Snead's *A Year of Sermons* is eagerly awaited by clergy throughout the country, we are told.
>
> The first remarkable event that took place was recently, when a

seven-year-old boy was cured of his fever and sickness by a glance from the woman when his mother took him to the parsonage. Since then, many others have been healed by the woman, who, despite attempts by Mrs Snead to encourage her to speak, remains quite dumb. People bring small gifts for the woman, though, it is said, she is quite unaware that they do this.

Your correspondent can vouch for the beauty of the dumb woman, though being in good health himself upon his visit, cannot claim to have felt the effects of her healing power. Readers can be assured of further reports in the forthcoming months.

There comes an occasion when Snead is called to an interview by the bishop's secretary, concerned about events in Sowerthorpe, the details of which have scuttled some few miles south to Norwich. The cases of healing by a dumb, paralysed woman on the north Norfolk coast have reached the bishop's notice at last. Does it not smack of practices of the Church of Rome, the Scarlet Woman, statues weeping tears, exuding milk, that sort of thing? And yet they say this Snead is methodistical in his preaching, full of ire. Must be one of the new lot in the Church. Evangelical rabble! Who is the wretched man? Who was his father? Unheard of! What in heaven's name is going on?

While he's away, Edward calls on Hester and takes the opportunity to fully examine Sarah.

'It's nonsense, Mrs Snead. The paralysis has gone. Yet the story is *still* that she cannot walk! The illusion is being maintained. It is an illusion. It's false.'

Hester's shame prevents a reply.

'Her legs seem firm: you've been letting her walk about, haven't you?'

'Of course.'

'That's good, very good. Without use, her leg muscles will cease to work. And you say she's called Sarah?'

Hester takes Sarah's hand, smiles at her. The surgeon has been talking to Hester alone, as though Sarah were not present. At last he turns to her.

'Sarah? Tell me who you are.'

She looks at him but is silent.

'Sarah, I feel sure you understand my question. Mrs Snead, if you have some paper and a pencil, let her write her answers. Her hand is not trembling. You say she holds a cup?'

Hester places a pencil and paper by her.

'Where do you come from?' he asks firmly, but not unkindly.

No answer.

'Is your mother still alive? Your father?'

She looks down. Hester strokes her hair.

'What can you remember?' He waits, giving her time, but she doesn't look at him.

'Amnesic. She's amnesic.'

'How can I help her? How can I help her remember? Is there any way?'

'I don't know. Her case interests me greatly, however without Mr Snead's agreement I can attempt nothing. But look, I'm sure that whatever you do will help her, Mrs Snead. I shall try to think of some means of bringing this business to an end.

'Yet I have no power. Cannot ask for help from the big house, since Wyke's never there, nothing to interest the man in this god-forsaken place. Anyway, he'd brook no disturbance to authority: bring in the militia!'

He laughs, running fingers through untidy grey hair and, aware of Hester's close observation of him, dares to ask if he may call her by her first name.

'Yes. Of course, yes! I should much prefer it. But only when we're …' She blushes at her disloyalty. Presses on, is shocked by what she hears herself say, '… when there's nobody else present, Edward. Mr Snead must not know. He is so irritable.'

'Splenetic, from what I've seen. And how much money has he made from her, I wonder?'

'I don't know. He takes the box and empties it himself.'

'Do you not hate this ridiculous business, Hester?'

'I can hardly bear it. But what can I do? I am bound up in it. I am part of an unholy sham.'

*

Lucy takes Eve up to see William's room, which is dominated by a huge printing press with a great star wheel on one side and lines of drying prints pegged from the ceiling like washing.

'Here by the window I engrave the copper plates,' he tells her. 'It's where Joseph learned to engrave when he came here as my apprentice years ago.'

In his round felt hat William is a benevolent king in a magical, inky kingdom. Eve watches as he rolls ink over an engraved plate until the grooves are filled, places it on the bed of the press, fixes a sheet of damp paper over it and turns the great wooden wheel which creaks musically as the press lowers. And pegs up the wet sheet: a river scene, a ship, boats.

She wonders if William would help her understand some of Mama's books. She recalls a day when Mama had an argument with Joseph and came into their sitting room at the back of the coffee house quite red with fury.

'Why should a woman not journey in a balloon as well as a man? Why is that a cause for laughter?

'So often he is *wrong*! Would rather speak of his ambition than reform. Oh, of course we must be careful what we say!'

'Why, Mama?'

'Because the government is looking out for those who want to reform it. Radicals. But I know which men are spies, like Lynam and Tolfrey. We must uphold our beliefs, encourage those who work for reform, even though we do it in hushed voices.

'Don't worry, Eve. You will understand more when you're older. Soon we'll read Tom Paine together, my darling, and Judith Murray, a clever American woman. We'll have to do it in secret!'

Eve remembers the excitement she felt at that prospect, can still feel it. But there's a dread that she may not understand these books that her mother and father both read. She's peeped into *Rights of Man* and found it hard. Who can help her?

She suspects that Lucy won't, because she has other ideas about what she and Matthew should be learning. She wonders about William, though, whom she strongly likes, even if his eyes do disappear into the folds of his face when he smiles at her. He seems wise in his inky workshop.

But now Nursey is crying. Her deal box stands in the middle

of the room. With fat fingers she folds pieces of clothing, weeping over each one. They must all be quite wet by now.

With extra care Nursey wraps her Nelson plate and cup in layers of cloth, packing them round with worsted stockings. Recently Eve asked what food Nursey would eat from a plate with a very black funeral car on it. Surely cake would taste nasty.

It's a while before Nursey will explain the packing, but eventually she pulls herself together enough to say:

'Mr Young has told me to find another position.'

Eve won't believe it.

'It is true, my darling bairn.'

'But you can't leave. You can never leave, Nursey, never.' She flings her arms around her, forgets how annoying the old woman often is. She's the nearest to Mama, so she must stay. Tears start then she flames up. 'I'll tell him you must never go!'

Again she hurtles through his door ready to kick, to strike, even to bite, but his head is in his hands and she senses the blackness descending. Sniffs it.

'Joseph, tell her to stay. Nursey is not to leave, ever.'

'Her influence on you is too great. She fills you with her claustral views. I'll not have it so. Sarah would never have spoken as she speaks. Such stuff, such rubbish.'

'Don't send her away! If Nursey goes, I shall go with her.'

'Nonsense,' he says without conviction.

'I shall. You can't stop me.' She wonders where they'll go. Does Nursey have a mother? Perhaps in a house in Richmond where they could go boating every day. She'll take Mama's books and Stephen will come and drive them out sometimes.

Joseph groans.

'If I stay here I need Nursey. Think when your black mood comes, Joseph. She gets me out of your way. Who will do that if Nursey's not here?'

Undeniable. Joseph says nothing. Eve senses her advantage.

'Mama wanted Nursey to look after me when she was busy. She liked Nursey. She *chose* her. Mama'd hate me to be without Nursey.'

Joseph groans again, Eve strokes his sleeve, presses her face against his coat, hears his heart. Not quite a cat whose master is her slave.

'Can I tell her she can stay? Can I?'

'Yes,' he growls and she runs from the room.

*

Snead returns from his interview with the bishop's secretary. Not long after, Edward Bissett calls.

'I shan't see him. I shall have no dialogue with an atheist.'

'He do insist, sir,' says Mary.

'Tell him to go away.'

She goes, but is back again shortly.

'He say he have some'at important about Sa— the dumb woman, sir.'

Snead is irritated, yet still affected by relief that his interview in Norwich resulted in merely a mild reprimand. 'I can spare five minutes.'

Edward, pushing through the door, wastes no time.

'I have examined the dumb woman. She is able to move her legs and must be allowed to walk if she is not to become crippled for the rest of her life.'

'You are telling me "must", Mr Bissett?'

'Certainly.'

'And so you have entered my house and inspected her while I was away. That is trespass. For all I know it was breaking and entering.'

'What nonsense. Your wife let me in.'

'Of course! A viper in the nest.'

'Oh, for heaven's sake, Snead!'

'Do not you dare call on heaven in this house!'

'Mr Snead. The woman has survived some grievous accident. She has recovered well from her paralysis. I'll put it like this: if she is not allowed to use her limbs in the normal way, to walk, the muscles will waste. Her legs will waste, she might well die and you shall have her death on your conscience, to say nothing of your reputation.'

'Leave! I have had enough. And if you have the impertinence to send a bill for your intrusion I shall hand it straight to the magistrate.'

Snead says nothing to Hester, who gathers much of the exchange purely from the heightened tones not stifled by thin walls.

The following day he questions her closely about Sarah's speech, is gratified to learn that there is no progress. No words, no sound, seemingly no understanding of what she hears.

'I have decided,' he announces over mutton sunk in bland white caper sauce, followed by a slice of bread pudding left by a villager in Sarah's box. 'I have decided that the woman may now walk.

'Thurgarton will wheel her into the church this Sunday and then she will stand. I shall speak of it, use it in my sermon. But hear this, Hester. She may walk, *but she will not say a word, and she is to remain nameless.*'

The news that the woman's paralysis has gone speeds around the village well before Sunday. Mary feels no need to ask Hester's permission; it's too important a matter for scruples. The people are astonished, pleased. More than that, for the notion soon ignites, that it is *they* who have made her walk. It is *their* gifts, *their* thanks that have caused her legs to strengthen, so that now she moves and soon will walk among them.

*

On four days a week Joseph Young's carriage sets off for Paternoster Row and deposits Eve and Nursey at *William Digham, Engravings, Prints.* There, while Nursey sews and potters in the Dighams' kitchen, Lucy guides Eve and Matthew through elementary stages of arithmetic, introduces them to maps, perhaps a little vaguely, and tells them fine stories of King Alfred and Queen Mathilda. Of Boadicea and Richard the Lionheart. She gently encourages Eve in her enjoyment of poetry, especially Cowper, which Eve reads with the fluency of one who loves the sound of words while understanding only ghosts of meaning.

It is apparent that she is more able than Matthew, who is slow and embarrassed, and, keen to impress pretty Lucy, Eve surges ahead.

'I want to read Tom Paine, Lucy.'

'I don't think you're old enough yet, Eve, besides I don't have any copies of his books.'

'I do. *And* Mary Wollstonecraft. Mama said *then* she'd start reading some with me soon. Matthew doesn't have to read it if it's too difficult for him.'

Lucy is kind to her, as she is to both children, while she's disappointed in Matthew. Eve would be happy with an alliance against the boy if only she could achieve it.

'Oh let me read, *I'll* read it,' she says too often. More heartlessly, she describes outings with Joseph, sitting next to him in his carriage, picnics under trees, choosing comfits and ices at Parmentier's, numerous days on the river at Richmond, a visit to Kew. She claims to 'help' him in his studio, though it's pure invention.

It becomes necessary for Lucy to point out the unkindness of Eve's triumph. She admonishes her in private, reminds her, too, of the thoughtlessness of Joseph's treatment of his own son. Eve is shocked at being criticised by someone to whom she has become strongly attached, someone seemingly so different from herself, delicate, calm, whom she admires. It's a betrayal. Lucy should love her for *everything* she does.

Lucy is patient. 'Dear Eve, I realise you have no father of your own, for which I am so very sorry. Nor, my poor child, do you have a mother living, whereas Matthew has. But please try to imagine the cruelty of being barely noticed by your own father, of having another child preferred by him to you.'

'He has William! Your husband.'

'William is the kindest man alive. How well I know that! He understands everything. Yes, you are right that William is very good to Matthew, but he is not his father.'

Eve finds it impossible to pity Matthew. Fair-haired like his parents (and would that *her* hair were fair!), his dark eyes are downcast. It doesn't help that Matthew is a quiet boy who has capitulated entirely to her brilliance. I'm much cleverer than he, she thinks to herself. He should try harder, he is so stupid.

There's to be a visit to Barker's Panorama.

'Where's Nursey gone?' she asks Joseph, waiting for the return of the carriage.

'She's collecting the boy.'

'You mean *Matthew*?'

'Yes. He will come with us. The weather is perfect and we'll arrive soon after midday when the light will be at its best for viewing.'

William Digham has spoken to Joseph about Matthew. While Joseph is much more famous than William, there is still a residue of their long-ago master–apprentice relationship. Joseph cannot help but respect the old engraver, though he'll certainly not admit to Eve that William has talked to him. Eve suspects her life may never be the same again, but decides to wait and see, bites back her disgust.

By popular request, Barker's Panorama is displaying the Battle of Trafalgar once again, even though that event took place a year ago. The large, double rotunda is surprisingly hidden behind Leicester Square and Cranbourne Street, its entrance inauspicious, confused by an overpowering smell of roasting coffee from the adjacent shop. Shillings paid, they walk down a darkened corridor and Eve, unwilling to discard tetchiness, asks:

'Where *is* the panorama? It's too dark to see anything. How stupid!'

'Be patient, Eve. Enjoy the dark,' Joseph tells her, to which she snorts in reply.

The corridor leads up a dim stairway and all of a sudden it's bright midday light and there they are in the centre of the battle, the whole viewing platform railed off like the upper deck of a ship, huge masts and sails towering over and all around them, the sea apparently heaving. The dramatic effect is superb. Even Eve gasps. Painted smoke clouds force them to peer into the scene to find sailors and redcoats as they fire their muskets, haul ropes, fall, die. Over all, daylight shines through the enormous dome, discreetly diffused by thin cloth. Only Joseph thinks of the enfolding scene as paint, great quantities of it, thousands of brushstrokes, immaculately planned perspective, the toil of erecting a colossal circus of canvas. Men, ladders, platforms, winches.

Two fiddlers and a man with a flute play 'Rule Britannia', 'Heart of Oak', 'Britons Strike Home'. Spectators talk quietly, hushed by the brilliant realism of this famous battle at which, amazingly, they are present.

Matthew is galvanised. 'Look, Papa, a Spanish ship. There, there's the tricolour, look! And here's the British sailing straight through the enemy line! But the *Victory*, where is the *Victory*?' He sets off round the room and Joseph, despite wincing at Matthew's 'Papa', is caught by enthusiasm, goes with him in search of Nelson, curious to see if the artists, Robert Barker and son Henry, have presented the admiral alive or dying.

Eve is tossed between thrill and pique. Matthew knows all about the battle, whereas she knows nothing. How can he possibly tell which ship is which? He's probably making it up. She leans over the railing, wondering if there might be whales beneath the waves, but sees only blackness below. If a whale came up and swallowed her like Jonah *then* they'd be sorry.

Nursey is almost speechless at the experience, like so many spectators: the panorama is the best entertainment in London.

'Oh, what a marvel!'

'Where are they? The others I mean. Where've they gone?'

'Oh, Eve, will you look at that ship going down! How dreadful!'

'Where are Joseph and Matthew? I can't see them anywhere, there are too many people here. Why don't they come back?'

Nursey clutches the railing and stares at the boiling sea. 'Oh dear Lord, but I feel quite ill.' Holding her hand over her mouth she plumps down onto the floor.

'What is it, what are you doing? *Nursey!*'

A woman hurries over. 'Is it your mama, dear? No, she can't be, she's too old. Here, I'll remove her bonnet. Dry her forehead with this kerchief while I fan the lady. Poor thing, she's overcome.'

'It's the sickness,' says the man with her. 'Panorama sickness, it's well known. Happened to Queen Charlotte, don't you know, so she's in good company.'

Eve kneels next to Nursey, who's turned a terrible white, and whose eyes are closed. She wipes Nursey's brow with the woman's kerchief, feeling how cold and wet the skin is.

'They oughtn't to sell tickets to people as gets seasick,' says another man.

'It's not just the *sea* making her sick, is it!' a woman retorts.

A desire to blame simmers in Eve's mind: it's Matthew and Joseph's fault. If Matthew hadn't come with them, then ...

Matthew bursts through the little crowd surrounding the slumped woman, crouches down. 'What's happened, Eve?'

'Go away! Nursey's fainted, can't you see? She's ill, go *away*!' She shoves him violently against someone's legs. 'Get away! You shouldn't be here. Shouldn't ever have come!' And shoves him again so hard that this time he falls backwards and his head bangs against one of the cannon placed here and there together with coils of rope to aid the illusion of battle.

'Eve?' Nursey opens her eyes with a start as a woman waves a bottle of sal volatile under her nose, but sees little she can comprehend.

Joseph appears. 'What's this, not well? We'd best return. Can you stand up, Mrs Casey?' He's had enough of this outing.

'I'll try, sir,' she says, and is helped to her feet by the first man and woman while the other onlookers cluck, commiserate and advise, dust her down and hand her her bonnet. Hold her by the elbows as she gradually steadies her stoutness towards the stairway.

'Get up off the floor, Matthew!'

Eve is not with them. As soon as she hears the crack of Matthew's head on the cannon and sees his dark eyes close, she pushes through the standing legs and runs from the room, glad if he's dead but knowing they'll come after her. Holding up her skirt, she rushes down the stairs and then, unsure which way, takes the shadowy corridor that's empty, at the end of which there are different stairs going upwards. She rushes up two flights, pausing on a dimly lit landing, puffed with the effort. When she hears voices below she starts up the next flight. Yet another flight.

Too much darkness. Too many steps. And annoyance that Joseph has not come to fetch her back even if he knows what she's done. He'll forgive her, won't he? He doesn't even *like* Matthew. If Matthew hadn't been there it would never have happened. Nursey will forgive her.

A short stairway down, another up, yet another murky passageway. By now she doesn't know where she is, up or down, but she must pass through this door if she's not to turn back, and suddenly a huge sky dazzles her so that for a moment she shields her eyes. Opening them, she's surrounded by sky and before her is a great stretch of river. Over the water are blocks of grand buildings, surely royal ones. The wide river is calm, shining, stones show through the shallows. Small boats seem to skim past the palaces. She stands in the centre of the room, turning slowly. Up here there are very few spectators, so she can drink in the scene without interruption. By one embankment she sees a woman sitting on the dry stones, a small dog on her knees, the sky above blue, the great buildings on the opposite side of the river doubled as if another city lies quietly beneath the still, blue water.

'Oh, if only I were there!' she thinks. 'I'd call out to that man in his boat and he'd take me and my dog, for I'd have a little dog like that woman does, he'd take us out into the wide river and we'd look at all the different places and the people strolling along. And perhaps I'd see Mama looking out of a window and I'd go in and find her at last.' She rarely allows herself such daydreams about Mama. Tells herself they're childish, foolish. And yet.

'Good God, Eve!' It hurts where Joseph grasps her shoulders. 'Thank God you ran up here and not into the street: then I'd *never* have found you.' He's panting, sweating.

'Is he dead?'

'What?'

'Is he dead?'

'*Dead*? Who?'

'Matthew.'

'Of course not. Why should he be?'

She says nothing.

'Here you are in St Petersburg,' he tells her, gazing around him. 'What do you think of it?'

'I wish I could live here.'

'Well the czar is our friend at present. You might live in the Winter Palace. I think it's that building on the other side of the river. I have to admit they're skilled, the Barkers.'

'*Could* I live there?'

'Don't be silly, Eve. Come on. Nurse had better know I've found you.'

She bursts into tears. Shocked by the wild storm within herself, she sobs as if broken-hearted. Joseph, unsure how to deal with this exasperating girl in a public place, a few people turning to stare, draws her to his chest, which is soon damp.

*

Snead's sermon with the dumb woman, paralysed no more, has less effect than he'd expected, because everyone already knows what has happened. When she suddenly stands up before the congregation and Anthony Thurgarton rushes to support her, firmly, tenderly holding her arm, the people are less impressed by the 'miracle' than by the wheelwright's quick thinking, his kindness.

But Snead is unaware that people have been informed. They are always sluggish.

'Open your eyes and see! The Lord has made this woman to walk! She has paid her penance for past iniquity. The Lord has raised her up like Lazarus.'

But she wasn't dead like Lazarus, thinks Hester and a few others who know their Holy Book reasonably well.

A couple of days after this, Hester, a basket of tracts to deliver, sits behind a low wall of the churchyard. There are no funerals today; her husband is in his study, but there's nowhere in the parsonage where she might not be interrupted. She feels safe here. The grass is dry. Soon I'll bring Sarah with me, she thinks. Though no, a churchyard might distress her. I shall walk into the fields with her. But now she needs some peace in which to think over recent events. The tracts can wait. There are not many: so few villagers can read.

Because of the lack of surprise in that first appearance of the no longer paralysed Sarah, Rev. Snead decided to confront the villagers in his own parlour, gathered to gaze with hope at the dumb woman. He can't quite remove the memory of the bishop's sneering tone when he asked this unknown, increasingly notorious parson about the healing woman.

'Do you seriously believe the common people are leaving your house *cured* by this dumb cripple of yours, Mr Snead?' he'd asked.

'God hath chosen the foolish things of the world to confound the wise, my lord.'

'It does not confound *me*, Snead!'

'No, no, of course not, my lord. I must tell you that the parishioners of Sowerthorpe are simple almost to the point of idiocy. They are illiterate, superstitious, depraved, easily taken in by wandering Wesleyans. While I certainly do not believe she has curative powers myself, I do know that they learn from the example before them. The woman is a living lesson of one who cannot sin because she cannot speak. I can instruct them better through her than I can through all my tracts,' Snead says, immediately regretting the folly of dousing his own powerful pamphlets with such cold water.

Worse even than the bishop's sneers, that foolish declaration aggravated like a deep splinter. He'd intended to *promote* his tracts! At the very least he must reassert his purpose, the instruction of his illiterate parish.

Hester recalls that there were many in the house that day, taken aback when the parson, shaking, burst into the room, something he'd never done before.

He began by pointing a long finger at the nameless woman, once more declaiming her sinlessness, her dumbness; her blank mind free from error. How Hester longed to contradict him, for she's sure Sarah's mind is not blank.

'Like her, like this woman, we should all wipe clean our minds and mouths from foul corruption. Remember this: *Every idle word that men shall speak they shall give account thereof in the Day of Judgment.*

'Think on that! Think of the idle words you all have spoken. Today. Yesterday. Last week. What account will you give when you tremble on that Great and Dreadful day? Remember, also, that the Great Day of the Lord is *near*. It is near and hasteth greatly.

'If God smiteth those he loveth, think on how much more he *smiteth* those who deny him.

'*What idle words* have *you spoken*?' his sermon voice enormous in a room so much smaller than the church, his shoulders jerking with passion.

'You!' he said, 'You!' addressing each person in turn, pointing at their shrunken limbs, club feet, their scabrous skin, weeping ulcers and widows' humps, each infirmity like a hideous growth of idle words and its own punishment from the Lord for their sins.

Nobody dared move while he strode about the room, glaring into faces, so that wasted limbs seemed to shrivel yet further, palsied hands to shake, coughs to rack more deeply, pustules to exude ever more pus.

'Now you will kneel, all, all and confess your sinfulness aloud so that everyone can hear.' He looked pointedly at an old man with two sticks who groaned, then fell, in a hopeless attempt to kneel. 'Leave him!'

Sitting peacefully among the gravestones, Hester remembers each moment of this scene with deep dismay. How some went red with shame, others white with shock. How they fled the house as fast as they could hobble away the minute Snead left the room.

And Sarah was frightened. Her face contorted and though voiceless she yet seemed to scream. Screaming without sound: it was strange and terrible, an image hard for Hester to banish from her mind.

She told Snead that the woman was ill, though that was strictly untrue. When Sarah continued to resist going downstairs, she insisted that Mr Bissett be called and Snead reluctantly agreed. Of course Hester talked to her, tried her best to soothe her and Edward took her hand and was kind and gave her drops to calm her.

Nobody dared come to the parsonage for more than a week, and gradually the disadvantage this brought about occurred to Snead. An empty offerings box. He told Hester to let it be known in the village that in future he would confine his sermons to the church.

Meanwhile, Hester thinks, leaning up against dusty ivy that grips the churchyard wall, he is urging Mrs Rollesby, Elizabeth Catton, Mrs Cragin and others in Sowerthorpe to establish a branch of the Society for the Suppression of Vice. Looming over them, striking his rarely given smile, he fires their malice with his absolute certainty, persuades them easily. Hester knows it will give great encouragement to those who like to spy on their neighbours. She must be careful, must warn Mary, who, she has inferred, has notions of her own about the parson, conveying her dislike by action rather than words, such as letting her rosary hang noticeably from her pocket when he sees her, placing the dish of fatty meat almost out of his reach at dinner, 'accidentally' spilling gravy, or chopping vegetables with sudden noisy violence when he enters the kitchen.

And she worries about lying again to her husband, telling him that Sarah has a fever. She's disobeyed him in several small ways, but never lied in her life before now, and thinks she may again. 'God help me!' she murmurs, wondering momentarily which corpses buried in this place had never lied when, fleshed and uncorrupted they'd lived their humble, difficult lives.

With Edward's drops and Hester's constant assurances Sarah has at last come out of her room and sat for two days with no visitors. Hester has a feeling that she misses them, that she likes to have people to look at.

She sends word around that Mr Snead will not intrude any more, and expects that people will begin to return. For all the horrible falsity, for all that she is part of it, she finds that she is glad at the prospect of people returning to the parsonage. She herself has become used to the presence of others, some sick, some sad, all touched by an idea of hope.

If only Edward would come and find her sitting here. She would talk to him. He would say something wise.

She knows she should not have such thoughts.

3

LUCY THINKS HER WORDS have taken effect, for Eve is quieter, no longer seeking triumph. In fact, Eve's reticence conceals reluctant guilt as well as relief, and an odd annoyance that Matthew has told no one of her action at the Panorama. His silence renders him superior, she is obliged to feel grateful. It's a secret that she doesn't want to hold with him, but one which she cannot forget whenever he's present. Sometimes she suspects him of nurturing it, flashing looks at her from his usually downcast eyes, to remind her.

Perversely, she stops trying to impress Lucy, is even tempted to stumble over words when reading aloud, to become stupid herself. That, of course, is more hurtful to Matthew than anything else she's done.

Joseph emerges from another period of desperate gloom, which for Eve entails even more hours at Paternoster Row. He stops eating with her and Nursey in the evening, and perhaps is not in the house at all.

Then one day shouts of joy are followed by a call to Eve to join him downstairs.

'Today we're celebrating! Eve, you must meet my dear, dear friend Gilbert Downs. Gilbert, meet my ward Eve Cranch.'

'Ward? What's a ward?'

'Oh, don't worry about it! Gilbert wants to greet you.'

An elegant bow from a man even taller than Joseph and black as few men she's ever seen.

'Glad to meet you, Miss Cranch.' He smiles, shakes her hand and then she remembers seeing sketches of him among the drifts of faces crumpled and thrown about the studio floor.

'And this is my wife, Ann,' he adds, bringing forward a short, brown-skinned woman who's been standing, waiting.

'I've heard about you, Miss Cranch,' she says, taking Eve's hand and patting it.

'Gilbert and I have been friends for years, Eve, and in addition he was my Othello. You've noticed this, haven't you?' He takes down a small watercolour from the wall which no, she hasn't really noticed before, there being so many paintings on his walls. She supposes it must be the same man, though in the picture he's swathed in a white cloak edged in gold and has a great sword at his side. He stands next to a bed on which a woman is lying.

'It's only a small, preparatory sketch for a much bigger painting that I sold years ago, but the essential parts are there. Do you recognise the woman, Eve?'

'It looks like Lucy.'

'Yes, that's right, it is. And by the way she and Digham will be here to dine with us at four-thirty. To celebrate freedom!'

'And Matthew?'

'Yes. He, too.'

It's rare for Joseph to entertain like this. Eve has heard him occasionally through the closed door dining raucously with one or two friends, but this is the first time she has been present. She's impressed by the table, laid elaborately with wine glasses and silverware for eight. Apparently she and Matthew will drink wine with the rest of them.

Joseph sits at one end of the table, with William Digham and Eve on either side of him. Eve likes sitting opposite William, his eyes squeezed up in his wrinkled, smiling face, his colourful round felt hat never removed. It's hard to think of him as Lucy's husband. She suspects he's really Lucy's father. People aren't what they seem.

Down the opposite end sits Gilbert with Lucy and Ann to his left and right. He's looking pleased. In the middle, facing each other, are Nursey and Matthew, Nursey next to Eve.

Joseph is in grand mode, leaning back in his chair as though it were a throne, his tone alternately pompous and polite, loud then abruptly quiet, as though responding to an inner reprimand.

'They've done it at last! They've seen sense!'

Lucy tells him to explain, for Eve and Matthew cannot be expected to understand.

'Yes, children. The government has abolished slavery. Let's drink to the liberty of all slaves!' He wrests the bottle of wine from Betsy, the snub-nosed housemaid waiting at table who isn't pouring fast enough, pours everyone a glass, raises his and declares again, 'To the liberty of slaves everywhere!'

Momentary quiet as all drink, Matthew and Eve imitating the adults, each choking and spluttering at the wine's sharp shock.

'What is slavery?' Eve asks, recovering first.

'Slaves are men and women who have no life,' Joseph replies.

'You mean they're dead?'

'In a manner of speaking, so they are.'

'Mr Young, let me explain to the children. May I do that?' Ann Downs, impatient, speaks up.

'Of course.'

'Slaves are living people, not dead, Miss Cranch, Master Young ...'

'Oh, for heaven's sake, Ann, call them Eve and Matthew!' says Joseph.

'Living people who belong to a master. He *owns* them. Men and women, children too, they do everything the master makes them do. They work all day, have no money, never escape. They're never free, you see.' She looks at the children intensely, though her eyes smile.

'Why? What for?' Eve asks.

'The master buys them to work for him. They're bought and sold like cows and sheep. Children are bought and sold to work. Sometimes they're beaten.'

'*Oh!*' Eve gasps. 'They must be stopped!'

'Hush, Eve.' Nursey squeezes her arm firmly but not unkindly. 'Slaves are black people.'

'Oh, why?'

'And,' says Joseph, keen to get on with the toasts, 'Gil's and Ann's mothers were slaves.' Eve is aware that she is gawping at Gilbert and Ann. How horrible. Beaten? Like when she saw a carter beat his horse in the street?

'But they were lucky. Their mothers were both set free. They came here from America and got their children some education. A toast to your mothers, both of them!'

'My dear mother,' Ann says and wipes away tears.

Eve thinks: 'Oh, Ann is like me. Her mama is dead.'

Glasses are drained, glasses are sipped.

Gilbert intervenes: 'No more slaves are allowed in this country ever again, and that's why we're celebrating, Eve and Matthew.'

'No one's permitted slaves in England or the colonies, Gil, but Boney has brought back slavery for the French, you know.'

'Leave him out of it!'

'I will. But it's a pity they couldn't pass the bill here without the damned Pious Party.'

'Forget it, Joe, and *rejoice!*' says Gilbert, they raise their glasses and drink, the children again with caution. The adults begin to flush; even Ann's pale brown has reddened, thinks Eve, though she can't tell with Gilbert, he's so black.

'Listen to this story I keep hearing,' Gilbert says. 'A parrot is overheard in Kensington, having just returned from the West Indies. First it laments and weeps, quite shocking to hear. After that it laughs loudly, coarsely. First it mimics the slave, you see, then the slave's mistress.'

'Shortly Kensington will be *full* of such parrots,' laughs Joseph, though he and Gilbert are the only two that find it amusing.

Gilbert says: 'They could use them as evidence in court: "Now, Polly, put your right wing on the Holy Bible. Do you swear to tell the whole truth ..."' The two men can't stop laughing.

William Digham speaks: 'I should like to raise a glass to those who are not present, who cannot be, but who certainly would have celebrated with us.'

Two more bottles are opened, Gilbert pouring at one end of the table, Joseph at the other, Betsy ignored. William holds up his glass first in Eve's direction and then towards Lucy and finally to Matthew.

Nursey blows her nose. Because of Mama, thinks Eve, yet Lucy is dabbing at her eyes, too. Must she do the same?

William leans across to her. 'Eve, we drink to your dear mother, Sarah, and to your father, Thomas, who, by repute, was a good man, too radical for this country.'

'Radical!' That's what Mama talked about. It's something good, secret, something to do with Tom Paine and those other writers.

'Alas, no one around this table ever met your father, but reliable friends tell me he fled to America because of his belief in liberty and democracy. In America they've shed the monarchy, have written a constitution. Even for an old stick-in-the-mud like me it does seem the only place in the whole world where real liberty flourishes.'

This is rather more than Eve understands, though it sounds right. She feels as though her father, who's existed through a few books and the loving tones of her mother's remembered voice, is standing in the doorway. Shadowed but present.

'We drink to Tom Cranch!' shouts Joseph too loudly, and rapidly empties his glass. 'And we drink to Sarah Cranch, who went with him to the land of the free!'

Eve, daring to drink the wine in tiny sips, unsure why she feels vaguely happy, watches Joseph push back his chair and stumble heavily out of the room. There's silence at the table, a loud sobbing through the wall. Gilbert goes out and soon after returns, his arm round Joseph, who splashes wine into his glass and downs it without a toast, once, twice, three times.

But William hasn't finished. 'There's someone else we shall remember. Matthew Dale, Lucy's brother, young Matthew's uncle.'

What's this? Matthew has an *uncle*, also called Matthew, of whom she's never heard. Does Matthew *himself* know about this person who's never been mentioned before?

'Mama?' Matthew turns to his mother, his dark eyes raised, searching.

'Yes, I named you after him, Matthew. When you are older I shall tell you.' She is trembling.

Joseph says: 'Matthew, your uncle believed in revolution. His convictions were absolute.'

'Is he dead?' the boy asks. He has gone white.

'Unfortunately yes, Matthew,' William replies quietly. 'Let us drink to him and to Sarah and Tom, and to all our departed friends.'

The mood of the party has plunged. Gilbert tries to pull it back up.

'Here I sit with two wives! My real wife on my right and my half-a-day Shakespeare wife on my left. Ann and Lucy Desdemona, please shake hands!'

Lucy, still tearful, blushes at the memory of herself as Desdemona on her deathbed when Gilbert, dressed as Othello, stood over her, both hardly daring to move, while Joseph painted their likenesses. At a time when she lived with Joseph in continuous unhappiness, always uncertain of his moods, dreading news of her hunted brother. Nobody knows how miserable she was then, certainly not Joseph himself, impervious to his effect on others. Only William Digham, on rare visits to his ex-apprentice, perceived something of Lucy's suffering. And Sarah, when Lucy took her despair to Battle's.

Ann reaches over, takes Lucy's hand in both of hers. 'I'm no longer jealous!' she laughs and Lucy smiles wanly.

'Let's eat, Joseph!' shouts Gilbert, and the gloom lifts.

This night both Matthew and Eve have been told something important, but each is quite unsure what it means. Confused by this, by wine, by the adults' inexplicable emotions, they resort to eating everything that's offered them. As do all around the table, for Joseph's cook is excellent.

*

People come from yet further away, bringing their ailments to the healing dumb woman. Bandaged, inflamed, sweating, pale, bruised, infected, they limp, stumble, hold trembling hands, push each other in barrows. Not all at once, but often several at a time, so that Hester and Mary make room in the kitchen and hand out water in summer, bread and broth to the more obviously starving in the cold months, with a copy for the literate of Snead's tract 'Escape the Dreadful Gulf'. It's the condition for allowing the handing out of food he claims they can ill afford to give away, though Mary often 'forgets' to ask who can read.

Sarah, dazed with unknowing yet regarded with desperate respect, gazes at each person with such benign sadness that they leave, if not cured, at least brushed with hope. After all, folk memory still tells of the King's Touch, last used less than a century before.

Of course few are cured, and those that are, only by coincidence. Despite Mr Snead's unkindly expressed belief, Edward's practice is little affected by his 'rival', for always there are births and the sawing of limbs, cauterisation, drawing of teeth. But many feel uplifted by the mysterious experience and help to spread the word.

Moreover, the morale of Sowerthorpe greatly improves through the influx of visitors who require beds for the night, food, drink and souvenirs: carved driftwood in the shape of a woman's head with closed lips, for instance, or crude outlines of a woman scratched upon pieces of supposed whalebone with the month and year beneath. Sowerthorpe Cakes are particularly popular, sweet biscuits roughly formed like a woman's head with a straight line marked in the dough for a mouth, currants for eyes. Three a half-penny. Even the begging sailors, limbless and homeless from endless war benefit occasionally from an increased flow of coins.

Little grows in the garden behind Sowerthorpe parsonage, and only a few hard-hearted bushes dominate the front, so when Hester takes Sarah outside for the first time, they walk down the nearest lane that turns off the main road on which the parsonage stands in search of something green and pleasing.

She tells her husband that Sarah needs fresh air and exercise. He appears barely to listen, but insists that when out with the woman Hester should stop and talk to no one. She's reluctant to promise him this, but finds that, in any case, the people they come across stand back, regard Sarah with awe, make hesitant, polite greetings, at best grin as though handed an unexpected gift.

Each time the two women go a little further, sit on the grass, sometimes on a rug and look about them, freed from the sight of worn parsonage furnishings, the louring presence of the parson. Gaze up at thick-leaved trees, flowers along the hedges, all of which Hester names. She has brought a fold of paper, a pencil stub in her pocket hoping to encourage Sarah to write, but that she still seems unable to do. There are no words to speak, none to write.

Sometimes, momentarily, Hester wonders if Sarah is almost content with her silence. Sealed into herself, safe. Yet, in gentle sunshine, Sarah runs her fingers through rough tufted grasses, and when Hester picks a field pansy her eyes light, and for a moment Hester thinks she really will speak. Together they assemble a bunch of unassuming bindweed, mayweed, shepherd's purse, storksbill, even mugwort. Holding them, Sarah breathes a tiny gasp of pleasure, barely heard in the sea-blown wind, but for Hester as clear as a bell, distant but certain. She kisses Sarah on the cheek, bursts into tears.

It's at about this time that Rev. Snead's preaching shifts its feet, as it were, in an apparently positive direction. Although hell is ever present for sinners, the word 'salvation' begins to be heard; the fierce voices of the prophets less often.

Of course he can never resist a direct threat to his congregation. There's the sermon, in which he quotes Zephaniah:

> Woe unto the inhabitants of the sea coasts, the word of the Lord is against you.
> And the sea coast shall be dwellings and cottages for shepherds and folds for flocks!

which results in a physical attack on one of the few shepherds in the area, the thin mud walls of his hovel holed by lobbed flints.

But Snead begins to speak of the Spirit.

> The natural man receiveth not the things of the Spirit of God: for they are foolishness unto him: neither can he know them because they are spiritually discerned. But he that is spiritual judgeth all things, yet himself is judged of no man.

Those in the congregation not too occupied keeping an eye on the woman lest she suddenly speak, are puzzled by the missing, more usual, more easily perceived horrors spelled out by the parson. Here is a different failing for which he's castigating them, their lack of spirituality, whatever that means. The Spirit of God. Is that the same as the Holy Spirit – what *is* that, anyway?

It is also around this time that Hester, coming from the kitchen to offer Sarah toast and tea before bed, finds her husband in the parlour, standing over her, staring with that ambiguous smile.

Sarah sits at the table with a small piece of embroidery, attempting to reproduce something in silk threads like the field flowers in the small jug before her, but now alarmed, unmoving as if expecting a reprimand.

'Mr Snead?' Hester, too, is taken aback.

He clears his throat, skews his neck away from her, but offers no explanation.

Hester puts a plate of toast before Sarah, the teapot on a trivet. Snead leaves the room.

It happens again, soon after, and Hester catches a look on her husband's face that she's never seen before. She has no name for it, knows only that it disturbs her as surely it must disturb Sarah, its recipient.

Hester has always perceived her marriage as a thing of duty and sacrifice. Her duties are to keep house efficiently so that her husband, Rev. Mr Snead, may carry out his holy work smoothly. She has sacrificed her family, her leisure to write letters, to read freely. Although she struggles not so see it in this way any more, it seems as though she gives herself up like a sacrifice to Snead on Friday nights, in darkness. The shock of physical pain has gone, but her teeth and fingers clench and tears run at the loathing expressed by Snead's assault on her body and then the disgust he invariably proclaims aloud afterwards.

There comes a Friday when, lying in bed waiting, steeling herself, the night cloudy, no moonlight seeping through thin curtains, Hester hears his latch click, his footfall pass her door.

Her heart beats, she dares to hope, waits for his steps to come back, the latch to lift. She sleeps. Undisturbed.

The following day Snead announces to Hester that the woman will eat with them in future rather than in the kitchen with Mary. Hester is happy with this until she sees how *un*happy Sarah is under Snead's glare. Only it's not the glare he uses against his parishioners. It's not a glare at all, rather it's more like what she remembers seeing on boys' faces when she was a child, as they contemplated a nest to raid up a tree.

Sarah looks down, eats little. And that's how it is at every meal.

'Mrs Snead, I do think Mr B ...' Mary says to her one morning.

'We are short of eggs, Mary. Please buy a dozen from Mrs Mundesley when you take the jug for milk this evening.'

'Mrs Snead, I shall speak.'

'Mary, I know Mr Snead is a testy master to work for. I know, too, that your mother was of the Roman persuasion, which makes it hard for you to accept what he preaches.'

'Mr Snead have a fancy for Sarah, Mrs Snead.'

'Mary!'

'I see that before my eyes. How he do look at her.'

Hester hesitates.

'Poor, harmless body, she be. You do make him stop that, Mrs Snead!' She rushes out, relieved to have spoken, sorry to have attacked the mistress to whom she is devoted.

Another Friday. Tired but alert, Hester hears his feet pass her door, the click of another latch, pulls on her dressing gown.

Snead, kneeling by Sarah's bed, has hold of her hand.

'John! What are you doing?'

'Ah! Ah, Mrs Snead, yes!'

'John, you must not do this.'

'Her spirit is innocent.'

'Exactly!'

'I am a man of the spirit.' He pushes past her out of the room.

Sarah sits up. Hester puts her arms round her.

'Oh Sarah, how can I protect you? How shameful! To protect you from my *husband*.' She feels helpless, but must not despair. For Sarah she must not.

'I'll have Mary help me move the day bed into this room. I'll sleep on it. He'll surely not dare touch you if I am here.'

For a while this scheme works. Sarah and Hester, closer than ever, continue their walks while the weather is clement, reaching the lane's end with its stunted, wind-beaten trees, its crumbling clifftop, mined from below by the waves. At this time of year there is no turbulence, the sea, too often grey, is nevertheless calm, its lapping and withdrawing like sighs.

They climb down to a ledge above the beach and pick short twigs of samphire into a basket. Later they'll make pickle with it, and Mary will help gladly for, she says, it's St Peter's plant.

Hester thinks of Sarah's attempt at suicide. Will she ever find out what compelled her to take such an action? Such a terrible action. Perhaps she was married to a man like Mr Snead. For a moment she understands how it might have been, even though suicide is a cardinal sin, the sin of despair.

But how can Sarah look at the sea, be so close to it? She was rescued by a passing ship. Did she wander out into the waves, fully clothed? Had she thrown herself off a cliff? Yet she seems unperturbed. When they sit together on the clifftop she looks out into the distance as if she might somehow reach the horizon.

'I'm keeping an eye on my watch. We should be back by three. I do find that I lose my sense of time when sitting by the sea. I think it is the light from the sea that burns out all unimportant things. Or it's the continuous breaking of the waves. Do you agree?'

Sarah looks at her, not speaking, yet Hester senses an answer. So often now this is the form of their communication. Hester says something, Sarah replies with her eyes.

'It consoles me, this great space. It consoles me for all I have lost.'

Tears pour down Sarah's cheeks. Hester cannot know for whom she is crying, whether for herself, or for her, Hester. Or for them both.

*

Snub-nosed housemaid Betsy Toft is frightened by Joseph, his outbursts, his difficult demands, his apparently criticising silences. Like all young women in her position, she knows she's in danger from the master of the house, that either refusing him or becoming pregnant could mean dismissal. And *that* would mean trudging back to the mother who'd expelled her from home, saying she was possessed by devils. Shan't go back *there*. *Witch*. And some say her's *holy*!

It is said of Mr Young that he finds his pleasure elsewhere in the city. Nevertheless, her anxieties nourish resentment, and she is pleased to deliver a letter to Eve which probably ought to go to Joseph or at least be read first by Mrs Casey, whose superior mien she also resents.

'*Term*agant!' she likes to call her, a word she once heard used of her mother. Barely appropriate for Nursey, it nevertheless sounds good to Betsy.

79

'A old fellow give me this letter, Miss Eve, from the coffee house he come. He say I can give it you straight if I want and not the master.' She nods knowingly at Eve.

'Oh! Is the man still here? Let me see him. Quick!'

'No, miss, he be gone. All knobbled and gnarled he were and his head leanin' and his eyes runnin'.'

'Thank you, Betsy. Please go away.'

Miss Eve Battle
c/o Mr Joseph Young
6 John Street
Off Strand

Eve hides the letter, wonders if she might feign illness in order to avoid Paternoster Row so as to read it, but Nursey will fuss and that'll mean she'll have even less of an opportunity to treasure it on her own.

When at last she is alone she rips it open. It's come from Battle's. That it's addressed to Eve Battle means it's something to do with Mama. Its cover is crumpled, smudged, brought by some old man. Oh! Was that the old man Dick?

Battle's Coffee House
3 June 1807

Dear Miss Eve,

We is writin to tell you good bye. The new man whats bought Battles dont want us no more. Dick and me.

Please will you come and say good bye to us Miss Eve?

Your fond friends,
Hezekiah Trunkett and Dick

As the years have passed, five now since she left home, she's thought less and less about Battle's. Somebody has bought it and is getting rid of Mrs Trunkett the cook and Dick the arthritic 'boy' who put himself to all the tasks in the coffee house. Who once *was* a boy there.

Of course she'll say goodbye.

It's remarkably easy to persuade Stephen Merry, Joseph's ginger-haired, pock-skinned coachman, to take her to Battle's Coffee House, for she simply tells him Joseph wants her to go there immediately, and he doesn't question the command. She feels pleasingly grand seated alone in the carriage as they make their slow progress, jammed behind drays, hackneys, gigs and drags whose passengers perch on top like owls. They pass fine buildings, shops, fashionable people. She sees a woman in a beautiful gown followed by a black boy in livery carrying several boxes. 'You're not allowed to have a slave!' she wants to shout out. But then a cart has toppled at the side of the road, the horse fallen. Men try to right it, a woman desperately wrings her hands. They move along Poultry where, though Eve doesn't know it, her grandmother, Sarah's mother, was killed, shot by militia in 1780, mistaking her for a Gordon rioter.

''Ve alley's too narrow, Miss Eve, I'll stop ere and walk wiv you to Battle's.'

Other coffee shops and tall houses darken the street, and Stephen must shoulder his way through the people to reach the end of 'Change Alley.

'Is you to meet a particler person, miss?'

'Mrs Trunkett and Dick.'

'I see.'

Inside, the huge room is crammed with solid noise and smoke, as it always was, she recalls. She's aware of men and more men sitting at tables as Stephen leads her to a central counter and asks something, but she can't hear what in the racket of voices and clinking. She had forgotten this scene, and suddenly here it is again. Smells are like Joseph multiplied a hundredfold. Coffee, tobacco, brandy, meat, men's unchanged clothes.

She is taken to a room near the kitchen, from which, soon, the gnarled and knobbly man appears, definitely Dick, and with him Mrs Trunkett, her round face red from the kitchen's steam, who clasps her to her large body like a person long lost.

'Oh, Miss Eve! Oh, I'm speechliss! You 'ev come just as we esked! Oh the picture of our dearest Miss Battle when she were a gel! Did I nivver think to see such again! Let me look on you!'

The gnarled man, whose contorted hands resemble knobs of

uncooked dough, stares at her with his head on one side and his eyes running, exactly as Betsy had described him.

'Dick, Miss Eve. Does you remember me? We all did love yer muvver, Miss Battle. We miss 'er so.'

'Of course I remember both of you. But my mother was Mrs Cranch, and I'm Eve Cranch.'

'Ah. It's compli ... It's 'ard to say.'

'Let me explain to Miss Eve, Dick, you nivver do tell a story straight. I been cook 'ere since Sam Battle's day. Yer granfer that is, what run it after 'is father. Your dear mother were Mrs Crench in America, so I do believe, but when she come beck, Mr Crench 'avin' gorn and died, she did want to be Miss Battle agin. She were borned and growed here in Battle's you see. And so was you borned 'ere, o' course.' She gives an enormous sigh.

'You got the letter from the gel what I give it to, then, Miss Eve?'

'Yes. Thank you for bringing it, Dick.'

Dick begins to wring his sad hands. "E don't want us no more. Where'll we go?'

'Us'll be on the parish if us don't look sharp,' Mrs Trunkett adds.

'Perhaps you could come and live with Joseph and me in John Street. We've got plenty of room.'

'Ooh now, that'd be a miracle.'

'I'll ask him. I'll persuade him,' she says, thrusting away the certainty that he'd never agree. 'And can I ask you for help, too? Dick, did you know my father Tom Cranch?'

'Oh, deary me. I don't know nuffink abart all of vat. She didn't tell nobody much abart im, not as I know of. I don't s'pose none o' ve drinkers know of Mr Crench neiver.'

Eve feels tears coming, frustration. *Why* doesn't Dick know about Tom when he's worked here all his life? Surely somebody must have known Papa.

Mrs Trunkett, her eyes unmoving from Eve's face, speaks up brightly. 'Dick, that man Mr Thynne is 'e 'ere today eatin' 'is dinner? Take Miss Eve to talk to 'im.

'Let me give you a kiss afore you goes, my pretty gel.' Mrs Trunkett clasps her again and Eve feels the heat from her cheeks, tastes salt from her skin. 'Oh, dearest child, I did 'old you in my arms when you was just borned!'

'I shall ask Joseph,' Eve says in parting.

Dick leads her back into the large room, its boom of voices, thickness of smells. Her eyes prick with smoke, let alone annoyance.

A table of men, apparently immensely old, turns at Dick's approach, and shortly they begin to crow and smile, to raise their glasses and try to stand.

'Miss Eve, we welcome you, fair daughter of our much lamented Sarah Battle!'

Eve, not knowing what to do, bobs a minimal curtsey. Notices men dabbing their eyes.

'We lament her loss and, let us not deny it, the loss of the past!'

'Mr Thynne sir,' Dick speaks up, his eyebrows rising and falling with significance, 'Miss Eve 'ere 'ave come 'ere all by 'erself from John Street. 'Er do vant to know abart Mr Crench.'

Mr Thynne, appropriately, seems all bones and spikey parts. But he looks at her fondly. 'Now, my dear. Thomas Cranch, printer and bookseller in Berwick Street, if my memory is true. While no one at this table was an acquaintance of Mr Cranch, we can most assuredly call upon someone who knew him, can we not?' The men nod their heads and mutter to each other.

'Yes, oh please, can you?'

There's a sudden shouting from a nearby table, two men scrape back their chairs and grab each other by their neckcloths. 'But you should return to your home, I think, Miss Cranch. For surely they'll be worried by your absence? Even Mr Young will be, whom we once named the Conquering Hero. Remember, my friends?' The whole table laughs. 'Marching in, demanding to see Miss Battle.'

'*Some* say he should be took off to Hackney. Old Bissett's madhouse,' a man calls out. More laughter.

'I heard Young's father was there till he died,' another voice pipes up. 'Lavender water factory. Bankrupt. Went mad.'

'Oh well, then. There you are.'

Eve's hope is slipping away again. 'No, I need not return there. Certainly not. I can live here, can't I. It's Mama's house. I was born here! I used to live here and I should really live here once again. It's my home!'

'Alas,' says Thynne, whose face is all prickles like a hard brush, 'the house no longer belongs to your mama. It was sold, my dear. And now Mrs Trunkett and Dick will leave any day.

'We still come to meet and drink and eat of course, for the time being, but no, Battle's Coffee House belongs to Pollen now. Mr Jeremy Pollen. A lawyer who has done very well for himself.'

Nodding round the table, more muttering. 'Miss Cranch, I can see you're not pleased.'

'I shan't go back, whatever you say. I *shan't*. Joseph and my nurse, Mrs Casey, won't help; they don't know anything about Mama or about my papa, Tom. They know nothing! They won't help me! *I shan't live there!*' It's as if she's slipped back into being the girl she was when she lived here last. Wants to stamp her foot.

'There really is nowhere for you to stay in this place, my dear. Besides it's so loud and smokey, is it not? But, look, I can most definitely help you. Go home now and I shall ask a certain person to call on you. He's called William Pyke, a good man, an apothecary and an old friend of Tom Cranch. He will tell you everything he knows, and that's probably a good deal. There now! Look out for Mr Pyke in John Street.' There's a scraping of chairs as the men struggle to their feet again, bowing stiffly and smiling as Dick leads her out.

There's nothing she can do. But Mr Thynne does seem wise. She thinks she can trust his promise. And it's true that, for all her protestation, the coffee house is not at all a place in which she'd like to live, doesn't seem at all like home. Her room and Mama's were upstairs, away from all of this. But it's no good without Mama.

On the journey back, the carriage gets stuck when a crowd of people pours along the street. Through the windows she sees blue banners with yellow words she cannot understand:

Burdett & Independence!

and

Sir Francis – a plumper!

As they pour past they're shouting *Form! Form! Reform! Reform!* And they mouth *Reform!* at her, pressing their faces against the carriage windows, flattening their noses. They're in great humour, laughing, so she laughs back, wishing she were one of them, whatever they mean. If they shout *Radical* she might open the door and jump out. 'My papa and mama were radicals you know,' she'll tell them.

A small group with a placard reading COOK THE REPUB-LICAN GOOSE! is speedily pushed out of the way, the placard stamped underfoot, its bearers howled down with *Reform! Reform!*

Eventually Stephen is able to persuade the horses forward, and Eve longs for some of the roaring people to come home with her to face the wrath of Joseph and Nursey.

*

Snead preaches from St Paul to the Romans:

'*They that are after the flesh do mind the things of the flesh; but they that are after the spirit the things of the spirit. For to be carnally minded is death.*'

From which Hester takes a small comfort.

Sarah is calmer since Hester began sleeping near her on the day bed. The room is narrow, barely holds them both, and looks out onto wretched scrubland at the back of the house, though sea-light infuses even the dreariest parts of Sowerthorpe.

The day bed is not comfortable, but Hester finds a way to sleep on it, and each woman becomes used to the night-sounds of the other as they turn, sigh, cough, start out of a dream.

Hester wakes to a stirring. Sarah moving. At the moment Hester utters her name she's certain it's worse, strikes the flint as rapidly as she can for a candle and sees Snead kneeling, pull the cover from the bed. She leaps out, hurls herself at her husband. The candle falls, goes out.

'Get out! Get *out* of here! *Vile!* How can you, how *can* you?'

She grasps his shoulders but only tears his nightshirt. Beats his back, his face as he turns, but he grabs her arms, rises up, shakes her.

'Ah, I'll stop you! You know nothing, woman! *Now it is high time to awake out of sleep: for now is our salvation nearer than when we believed.*'

'Salvation? This is *damnation*. I too can quote scripture: *to be carnally minded is death.* You preached it yourself last Sunday!'

85

She struggles, kicks his legs, his groin as he staggers and he releases her, retreats and she places a chair at the door, its back under the handle, there being no lock.

Sarah is terrified, shaking, though not much harmed: Hester awoke in time. She holds Sarah to her, then wraps herself in her blanket and sleeps on the covers next to her. Except she cannot sleep.

In the morning she goes straight into Snead's study without knocking.

'You can see I'm busy.' He looks up at her, calm, dismissive.

'How can you explain yourself, John? To be carnally minded is death. Remember? You are worse than a common criminal.'

'I did nothing. There was no crime.'

'You pulled the covers off her bed. Your intention was clear. I shall go directly to the magistrate.'

'You cannot know my intentions, woman. And what if you do go to the magistrate? What folly, Hester. Why should he believe you? A whining, complaining wife! I am a man of the cloth and you merely a woman.'

His sneer-smile is triumphant. His angular shoulders seem to rise; he throws back his head. The strength Hester felt in herself when first she entered the room falters. She knows what he says is true.

'Don't try quoting scripture at me, Hester. You know too little of it. Besides, *the letter killeth, but the spirit giveth life.*

'Now understand this: she is a woman of the spirit. Perfectly suited to me, a spiritual man. That is clear. Cannot be denied. She was sent to me by God, a bride of the spirit. We are a union of spirits. There can be nothing closer to God than a spiritual marriage.'

'A *spiritual marriage?*'

'Yes, spiritual marriage. Harken to the angelic beauty of those words!'

'And me, your wife?'

'You will remain a concubine, so to say. The real marriage, the only marriage of any significance will be my spiritual union with the woman, for her spirit is perfect, she is brimful of grace.'

'That was not spiritual, last night.'

'What a heathen you are, Hester! Such a vulgar mind. You broke what would have been a pure symbol of our heavenly union.'

Hester is aghast.

'Of course you will tell no one at this stage. Like you, the people's thoughts dwell in dust and dirt. I must needs prepare them and later, the congregation will accept our union. I shall make them understand.'

His fingers, clasped together, are white. His nails black.

'Then, in the fullness of time, others pure of spirit will join us and we shall live together, girdled about by grace.'

'Mary will let it be known. I'm sure of that. And it would do no good to dismiss her. She'd only find more listeners.'

'You will pay her for her silence.'

'We have no money!'

'You will pay her all the same. Use the money that the people bring. I forbid you to run to that atheist surgeon! I see *that* idea forming on your face.'

A spiritual marriage! Hester feels lost. What he says is ludicrous, and yet he means it. There seems nothing she can do to protect Sarah, and in the meantime she must persuade Mary not to blurt the shameful facts all over the village.

'I beg you not to speak of Mr Snead's actions, Mary. Please think of me. Think of Sarah: how we should both suffer were a great scandal to break over us.

'He is right: he has authority, a supposed holiness. Who would believe anything ill of him?'

Mary bows her head. Her tears are of rage.

And that Sunday, as if to reinforce his commands, Snead takes as his passage on which to preach to the people, St Paul to the Corinthians:

'*Let your women keep silence in the churches: for it is not permitted unto them to speak. Indeed it is a shame for women to speak in the church.*'

*

It's ages before Mr Pyke arrives. Eve has a birthday, and feels too wise to regard herself as a child any more, even though Nursey still insists on brushing and pulling back her hair into a knot, and actually she couldn't do without that daily soothing. The old man says he's been ill, and she imagines him that very morning stepping gingerly out of bed in his nightshirt like the engraving of a skeleton she's seen in a book. He coughs terribly and winces whenever he sits and stands. But a smile cracks the lines down his face as he greets her.

'Of course you want to know about your father! I'll tell you what I myself knew of him, and I can repeat what your mother told me of her time in America. I can also tell you that I see Tom's face in yours, as well as that of your mother.'

She would fling her arms round his neck and kiss his hollow cheek. Instead, she asks:

'So my papa was really your friend, Mr Pyke?'

'Most certainly. There was a group of us radicals, members of the Corresponding Society: Hadfield, Harley, Baldwyn, Cranch and me. Tom was our idealist. He worked out ideas more thoroughly than the rest of us, and he'd more courage and energy than all of us put together. We missed him greatly when he left, even though by then the society was banned, and it was hard to meet without being spied upon.'

Pyke is melancholy. His sad tone pulls Eve with him, yet his talk of radicals and spies has great power. Radicals – there it is again! She begins to etch fine lines out of a barely perceived world in which her mama and papa played a part. A world in which Tom was important: 'courage', 'energy', 'idealist', the words thrill her.

'I came to see your mother shortly before you were born. I knew she would want to talk about Tom to a friend and I, too, wanted to hear everything she had to say.'

'Oh tell me, Mr Pyke, please tell me! Nobody here knows anything about America.'

He smooths down thin strands of white hair. 'They worked for a publisher and bookseller, a friend of Baldwyn's who'd emigrated from Edinburgh years before and had a shop in Philadelphia. They lived in an upper floor of his house and for a while got on well, for he was a believer in democracy. Sarah told me that Tom wrote pamphlets and walked the streets talking to whomever he came across, telling, teaching them about votes for all people, a free press, even the ownership of the land, for he thought everything should belong to all the people. Not everyone agreed with that.'

'Oh.'

'Am I going too fast? There's a lot to absorb.'

'No, no! Please don't stop. I've never been told anything like this. I want to hear everything. *Everything*. Please!'

'They were going to set up their own press, your parents, publish books and pamphlets. They'd begun writing a pamphlet together, she said, when Tom became ill of yellow fever and died. They loved each other dearly, that was clear to me, and his death was a bitter thing for Sarah.'

He looks down at his hands. Eve wonders if, like so many others, he'll cry.

'Mr Pyke, is Mama really dead?'

'Good heavens, my dear! It was said that she drowned when the balloon fell into the sea, even though the two men survived. I've always held that to be true.'

'Sometimes my nurse, Mrs Casey, says things ... I think she believes Mama's still alive.'

'I expect she has a strong sense of hope. People will often believe the oddest things when they allow hope to out-voice reason.'

'Mr Pyke, I have all of Mama's and Tom's books you know. I made Joseph give them to me.'

'That's good.'

'And I have some notes they made for pamphlets. Look! Here they are.'

He hooks on some spectacles, holds the sheafs almost absurdly close to his eyes. An amazed expression lights his face.

'Eve, these are wonderful. A treasure.'

'Yes.'

'I'd ask to borrow them, but they are too precious to take away. Keep them safe and one day we shall read them together.'

'Oh yes, please let us do that.'

'But now I should also speak to Mr Young, my dear. It would hardly be courteous if I did not.' He stands up stiffly, wincing at a pain somewhere.

Joseph insists on speaking to Pyke alone, so Eve listens from the other side of the double doors. She likes Mr Pyke, but perhaps he knows more than he's said, that he may now tell Joseph. They all keep things about Mama and Tom to themselves. They do what they want, think what they want without asking her, and yet Mama and Tom were *hers*, not theirs. Why should she wait until she's a woman to find out everything?

'It's good of you to tell her of your memories of Tom and Sarah, Mr Pyke. But I fear she will dwell upon them too much when her life is here now, my ward in this house.'

'Your ward?'

'Yes, I had her made a ward. The money from the sale of Battle's is in a trust for her when she reaches maturity.'

'That's wise.'

'Eve should inherit what was Sarah's. However much people may disapprove of me, they cannot accuse me of being a thief. I never stole prints from the British Museum! Not like Robert Dighton. I can't understand why he did it. Didn't need the money; was a famous singer, you know.'

'She will be a rich woman.'

'Perhaps. Except that the war is ruinous.'

'I must tell you, Mr Young, that Sarah was concerned about Eve's education. She told me she'd teach Eve all she knew, and after that I was to help her find good teachers for, she said, "I would have her taught as men are. Tom would have wished it." *Those were her exact words.* She spoke of a Philadelphia academy for girls that she admired, and wished there were such a place here, where they taught the students philosophy, geography and mathematics.'

'Ah. Well at present she's learning with Mrs Digham, whose own education was, admittedly, modest. But in effect she's a private tutor for the child, since the boy now goes to school. I am about to travel to Italy, so can do nothing further until I return.'

'That seems unfortunate, I should say. Eve is intelligent beyond her years and would benefit immediately. Can I look into it for you? I have the time, being little in demand now that certain druggists have become so successful, supplying all manner of physic. I promised Sarah.'

'No, Mr Pyke. I'll deal with the matter myself when I get back. I'll see you out.'

*

'You will eat with Mary, Hester. My bride will sit and eat with me. It is appropriate to make this distinction between my spiritual marriage and the worldly arrangement.'

He forbids her to sleep in Sarah's room, threatens 'punishment'. Hester has no idea what to do. She longs to talk to Edward. Yet what could *he* do? Even he would not be believed by any authority. He could hardly walk into the house and lock her husband in his room! Her head fills with hopeless fantasies. Might she travel to Norwich to speak to the bishop? Snead would easily discover it. Bring her back. Deny everything.

For several nights she lies awake, tense with listening, hears nothing. It seems her husband remains in his room. Exhausted during the day with lack of sleep, she must keep her vigil nevertheless.

A night comes when she hears the latch, his footsteps, Sarah's door open and close. With great caution she creeps along the corridor, lifting Sarah's latch slowly; peers through, watches him pull back the covers, gaze down at Sarah, who at first doesn't move, then wakes, sits up, backs away from him and Hester hears:

'Fear not, woman! My love is of the spirit. I shall not defile you. God tells me that you and I shall be one in spiritual union. I hear Him! He speaks to me. And you, too, must open your ears to Him.

'For you shall love me as I love you: there can be nothing closer to the Holy Spirit than our union!'

Hester cannot see Sarah's face, and no sound comes from her.

'I shall come again and again until God leads your spirit to fully love mine. And then! Ah then! Then shall we consumate our spiritual marriage!'

He backs from the bed, turns and a board creaks beneath Hester's feet.

'The Devil spies upon us!' He closes Sarah's door. 'It is *you* who are carnally minded. There can be no surprise in that, knowing your origins. Father no better than an atheist.

'My union with the woman is pure. Her beauty is the outward and visible sign of an inward and spiritual grace. Whereas you, Hester, for you hell is waiting.' His hand over her mouth, he pulls her into her bedroom to adminster punishment.

After this he locks her in her room each night. Each day Hester observes Sarah closely. She thinks, hopes that after what she heard him tell her, he will not yet do her physical harm. She searches for signs, can find no bruises like those on her own limbs. The worst is Sarah's fright at his wild words.

One night he hammers on Hester's door, forgets that he has locked it himself.

'Open up, you viper in the nest! You have locked her in there with you!'

Would that I had, she thinks. 'I am alone. You turned the key.'

'Where have you hidden her? Where is she?'

Sarah's bed is empty.

'Oh! Dearest Sarah, no! She's run away! Of *course* she has, poor woman. But when? I must have fallen asleep, I heard nothing.'

'The Lord will return her to me.'

'How stupid, how *wrong* you are! She'll be in danger out there, alone. I shall rouse up the village.'

'You will say that she has been stolen away. That someone has taken her.'

Hester says no such thing to those whose doors she knocks upon, but it's not long before a group of busybodies, led by Mrs Rollesby and Elizabeth Catton, the monumental Mrs Cragin striding behind them, are at every house and hovel with their lanterns and prying eyes, longing to search under beds and in cupboards, under upturned boats and piles of nets in need of mending.

The moon is amost full, the night like a cold, white, heartless day. Hester worries that Sarah, inadequately dressed, may fall and freeze. That she's in a state of confusion and fear is certain. It occurs to her that Sarah might try to make her way to the cliffs, which though not that high could still be perilous. That she might try to repeat her desperate action from before. Is the tide in or out?

She runs to Edward's surgery, and he, used to being called from his bed in the middle of the night, lights his lantern immediately and goes with her, rousing Anthony Thurgarton along the street as a practical man of some sensibility.

'Of course she may stumble and not know where she is, Hester. But let's imagine that she's gone where you tell me you've been together. There's enough moonlight to have helped her find the way. So you must lead us.' He has a further thought: 'And it will show us that she can remember new things even if she cannot, will not, remember her past.'

They rush down the lanes where the two women have walked, across a handful of small fields, Hester's panic rising as they near the sea, tonight becalmed, strangely silent, an infinity of whiteness. At the same time she feels a confidence in these two men, particularly Edward, a man driven neither by hideous thoughts nor obsession. Whose actions seem always rooted in reason. Whereas her husband ... has he become mad?

Their shoes, trousers, Hester's long skirt are soaked by heavy dew in the tall grass. They push on towards the edge, saying nothing.

She's there above the samphire ledge. Standing. Trembling.

'Come, Hester!' Edward says. 'You talk to her. It must be you.'

Sarah turns at her name and the two women hold each other, cry together while the men hang back.

Edward wraps his coat about the shivering figure. 'Sarah, we must warm you up. Come with us to my house. You will be safe there.'

Hester rubs Sarah dry, Anthony Thurgarton makes up a fire in the parlour, Edward finds blankets and calming drops. Hester heats milk gently in a pan on the last embers in Edward's disorganised bachelor kitchen.

No longer shaking, Sarah's face yet seems stretched with suffering. Once more she appears to weep without noise, her mouth turned down, a tragic mask. Hester holds both her hands or strokes her hair and talks soothingly to her until eventually her distorted face relaxes.

It's a night that ends well, though Hester dreads what may come in the following days.

Edward turns away the gang of prying women from his garden gate. Thurgarton goes home by the back way and over the wall as soon as he's lit the fire and seen it blaze. Hester remains all night with Sarah.

'It is best for her that you stay, however much Mr Snead will complain.'

'I fear so greatly what action he may take.'

'Don't think about it now. Try to sleep. I shall support you however I can. Even if it comes to fisticuffs – and you know, I rather wish it would!'

For Edward the night is more than a successful rescue of a possibly suicidal woman. It gives him an opportunity to see Hester.

He's said nothing of his feelings to her. If she hardly dares admit what she feels to herself, he certainly knows what *he* thinks. But what can be done? Why imagine that she'd leave her husband? She is critical of Snead and certainly is frightened of him, perhaps even hates him, he rather hopes, but no doubt she's a good Christian woman who wouldn't countenance divorce. And just suppose she did feel able to break her marriage vows? Divorce was only for the rich, and elopement was for the rich or the foolish, and he was neither of these.

His father had been a mad-doctor, though he'd preferred the title *Antimaniac Physician*. After a spell working in Bethlem Hospital, old Bissett established his own private asylum in Hackney, and it was there that Edward grew up, familiar with the calls and cries of lunacy, aware, through childish curiosity and utter lack of privacy, of the mechanical nature of treatment: the strait-waistcoat or English camisole, the maniac's bed, the swing, the spouting boat. Wondered, too, even at a young age, why all were named 'lunatick'. For instance the large, ungainly man called Young, who wept incessantly and would not be consoled. What was lunatic about *him*? All his clothes smelled strongly of lavender water. His wife had died, his son suddenly parentless. He was just incurably sad.

For a year Edward was apprenticed to his father. Then, when his mother was found behind the door with a kitchen knife, waiting for her husband, and was removed from the Bissetts' quarters to sit restrained by leg and wrist among the melancholics and deluded, Edward learned revolt. He defied his father, that gaoler of minds, refused to work in the asylum and took himself to Edinburgh to study for an MD.

His work is all important to him. Despite his qualification, for which he attended lectures on medicine and chemistry, anatomy, physiology, surgery, theory of medicine and experimental philosophy, he prefers life among the lowest to a lucrative hospital appointment, which would have made his father boast. He is compelled to differ from his father.

The inhabitants of Sowerthorpe suffer grievously from the hardships of sea-dominated life, when they survive at all. The sea provides their living, takes their lives. Even in a place so miserable he can aid existence a little. Medicine has taken the place of easily lost faith in Edward's mind. New ideas and practices stimulate him beyond enjoyment. He holds up his box of ivory vaccination points before the population of Sowerthorpe almost as a priest raises the host.

As to the 'dumb woman', the exploitation of Sarah's inability to speak, it is absurd, wrong ('unholy sham' – how well Hester had expressed it!), he longs to expose it, yet to do so would be to bring disgrace upon Hester as well as Snead. He must bide his time. There might come an opportunity yet. At worst, when his father dies he might inherit enough money to move from this wretched place, though it would seem like cowardice, and he'd lose Hester for ever.

4

———

ORDER IS UPENDED IN PREPARATION for Joseph's journey to Italy and further afield if the whim takes him. It's essential travel for a man whose mind has grown in its own turmoil since boyhood, and for whom Romantic thought in all its forms is a perfect match. Mountains, lakes, brilliant light, remains of the ancient world still standing. Works of the great artists, the living tongue of Dante, all this is experience Joseph must have if his painting is to meet his ambition.

He's going at a remarkably bad time. Napoleon dominates Spain, is at war with Austria, annexes the papal states and imprisons the Pope. British victory at Cintra in Portugal ends in scandal, followed by defeat at Corunna. He takes advice to avoid Spain and Portugal, rather to sail to the Mediterranean and then to Sicily.

'No one shall prevent me seeing Italy, not even the Corsican himself. Why should he care about an artist he's never heard of? I'm hardly likely to make sketches of his infantry! If necessary I'll give him some paintings to keep him quiet. He's said to be carting stacks of paintings back to Paris.'

Gilbert, who's been recommending caution, says:

'Mightn't that be treason, Joe, giving your work to the enemy?' They laugh.

His mood is intolerably high. He rushes from room to room, heaps equipment into piles, searches for clothing, bawls commands, takes the carriage several times a day to buy something from 'the only shop in town', often passes Eve without noticing her. He seems not to eat. Nursey and Eve agree that probably he doesn't sleep.

When, finally, his boxes and trunks are packed and loaded, ready to depart, he's forgotten to give them his addresses in Palermo and Naples, and must hunt for details, sit and write them down.

Suddenly he remembers Eve.

'Now Eve, dearest girl, you must be good while I'm abroad and not get angry. Don't think about Sarah and the past, and do everything that Mrs Casey and Lucy tell you. Behave with honour and restraint, as did your dear mother. No running away!'

He gives her a quick kiss on the forehead on his way to the carriage and hardly knows what he's saying. How can she *not* think of Mama and Tom? And didn't Mama run away? Tom had run away from spies, Joseph once told her. So Sarah ran away with Tom to America. *They both ran away.*

The quiet in the house is a relief for all at first. Then for Eve the silence becomes deadly. On Saturday, glad not to be at Paternoster Row, she goes to his studio, in even greater disorder than usual because of the recent rummaging in search of a particular palette knife, small oilskin-bound sketchbooks he remembered having once bought, his spectacles with the hinged sun lenses and a pocket telescope, both of which miraculously survived the downing of the balloon in the sea.

In a stab of guilt she remembers that she never asked Joseph about Mrs Trunkett and Dick. It's too late now. She wanders around the room, picking up papers, prods blobs of paint to see if they're wet or dry, idles by his now rarely used engraving table. She opens a long box containing tools, lined up like so many model mushrooms with long stalks, tries out the thinnest, sharpest point against her thumb, digging, squeezing drops of blood onto a block of wood. Cuts another line, causing a proper stream of blood this time, but it hurts and she sucks the cut, smears bloody fingers onto a pad of paper, wraps a rag around the wound and moves away.

She holds up huge smocks, gaudy as if daubed by a large child, envisaging Joseph inside them, smelling the linseed oil, smoke, his staleness. It's an act of love but not of worship, of love but also fury and insubordination.

She lingers until there's little light, is suddenly aware that the entire house is silent. Where is everybody? She tiptoes into the small drawing room where evenings are spent. Nursey's pile of sewing is on the table by the lamp. Nursey herelf is snoring lightly on the sofa where Joseph usually sits, her head resting on two cushions, grey hair coming loose, her stockinged feet at the other end, unlaced boots placed neatly on the rug.

Eve quietly closes the door and makes for the kitchen, hungry, since no one has called her to supper. No sign of cook, no sign of cooking. There's food in the pantry and she stuffs her mouth at random, bread, a lump of cake, cheese; she gnaws at a bone of mutton, swallows a handful of jelly and is now sticky and must wash her hands. Voices from a distance, probably cook and Betsy, she can't tell, but then a scuffle and running feet which she wants to find, to see.

She looks in store rooms, along passageways leading to unused cubbyholes, a region built for a much larger retinue of kitchen servants than Joseph cares to employ. Opens doors to cold stone shelves, to racks of bottles, empty wooden boxes, a stinking privy, returns to the dairy for a mouthful of milk, but Stephen Merry has got there first. He's standing with his back to her, one candle on the floor illuminating the breeches round his ankles. How large his buttocks are! Doesn't he realise there's a privy nearby, she begins to think, but there's someone's knees and legs sticking through his arms and the voice of Betsy groaning and grunting like nothing she's ever heard before.

'Oh, Lord!' she hears. 'Oh, Lord, Stephen, Oh Lord!'

*

The rumour is soon put about that the surgeon *stole away* the dumb woman from the parsonage.

Early next morning Mrs Rollesby, Mrs Cragin and Elizabeth Catton, egged on by Snead, gather a crowd that marches to the gate of the surgery. For a time they stand outside, inciting each other, the bolder ones and those wanting to impress Mrs Rollesby, shouting loudly.

'Bissett, give back the dumb woman!'
'Kidnapper!'
'Give her back!'
'Monster!'

'Hand over our dumb woman! Bring her out!'

Mrs Rollesby thumps repeatedly on Edward's door. Sarah still sleeps, Hester dozing beside her. Edward has remained awake all night in his room above, fascinated by Sarah's situation, tantalised by the presence of Hester in his house. He doesn't open the door, and inside the house he keeps the shutters closed.

About midday the magistrate calls. Sir George Cludd is a man of limited understanding, but not fond of Snead, much preferring a Sunday of hare-coursing with friends and faithful dog-handlers to fire and brimstone among a cowed congregation.

'Bissett, they say you kidnapped the dumb woman. Kidnapped her. Is it true? Is she here in your house?'

'She is here. You may look round the door, though I'd prefer you not to disturb her by speaking, for she is still distressed.

'But of course I didn't *kidnap* her! What rubbish. She escaped from the clutches of our gentle parson. You will have to believe something entirely distasteful of Snead.'

'I am no friend of Mr Snead, as you may be aware, Bissett. No friend. Between you and me, can't stand the man. But the law does not allow the removing of other people's property. Does not allow it, you know.'

'She is not his property!'

'That might be disputed. And the law certainly comes down heavily on kidnappers. Heavily, Bissett. Besides, I see you have Mr Snead's wife here. You have kidnapped two women! Kidnapped two of them!' He's tempted to laugh, but merely goes red around his purple nose.

'I came of my own free will, Sir George,' Hester says. 'This dear woman, whose name I shall not reveal, fled from my husband. *Please consider what it is for me to tell you that.* When we found her she was in danger of her life, and had to be brought here for Dr Bissett's medical attention.'

'You must believe Mrs Snead, Sir George, but you cannot expect her to recount all the details. This is not a court of law.'

'Even if I accept your explanations ...'

'How can you *not* accept my word and the word of Mrs Snead?'

'All right then, I accept what you both say by way of explanation for the presence of the dumb woman in this house. Her presence in *your* house, Bissett. To think about the behaviour of Mr Snead, as you imply it, is another matter. Another matter, you know.

'However, at this very moment, I don't know how I can clear the crowd from your gate, Bissett. I can't very well read the Riot Act. They are not exactly rioting. Yet they are a determined lot and a damned inconvenience.'

Hester speaks up: 'I shall talk to them. They will surely believe what I say. Yes, Edward, I shall do it.'

'Let me stand with you.'

'In view of their attitude towards you, Bissett, I think it better Mrs Snead address them alone. Alone, you know.'

There's an immediate quiet when Hester walks down the path to the surgery gate. They have not expected her. Their blood is up for Bissett. What can they shout at the parson's wife?

'Good morning.'

A few sheepish greetings.

'Because you know me, you will realise that everything I am going to say is the truth. I've come out to tell you that the dumb woman is safe. We found her last night on the clifftop, cold and very unwell, and brought her to where she could be given help.'

Muttering from Rollesby and Catton.

'It is painful for me to tell you, though I must do it: she ran from the parsonage yesterday because of danger to herself.'

Drawing in of breaths.

'I cannot say more. Mr Bissett will care for her until she is well enough to return.

'I say again that everything I have told you is the truth. Now please go home. I beg you.'

Murmurs by those who see the welling of tears. Mrs Rollesby clears her throat, moves forward, but with an unexpected gesture Mrs Cragin holds her back.

Hester would run into the house. She feels sick from lack of sleep, from excess of emotion. But Sir George comes out and stands next to her, watching as the people disperse.

'You did well, Mrs Snead.'

'I ... please would you speak to Mr Snead, Sir George? I think it will not be safe at home until he knows he must desist.'

'He neither likes nor approves of me, so will not be inclined to listen to what I say, you know. But my authority may have some effect, of course. Let us put trust in my authority.' He puffs slightly.

Hester and Sir George return to the house and Edward, pushing back his hair, cannot resist taking Hester's hand as Cludd warms himself before the fire, but drops it quickly when the magistrate turns to toast his other side. He longs to embrace her.

Cludd blows out his cheeks.

'While, as Bissett said, I cannot ask you to tell me everything, Mrs Snead, not *everything*, could you perhaps, at least, give me some notion of what has taken place, what we heard you describe as "danger" to the woman in the parsonage?'

Edward looks questioningly at Hester. Will she now betray her husband? He knows she would do anything to help Sarah.

'I shall tell you what he himself will announce to the congregation before long. He told me he will. He believes he has a spiritual marriage with ... with the woman.'

'Good Lord! *Spiritual marriage!* Whoever heard of such a thing? Bissett, have *you*? Good Lord. Say nothing more, Mrs Snead. We must keep an eye on the man, and I shall endeavour, I shall endeavour without actually using that very phrase, perhaps, to calm the man down.'

'*Calm him down?*' Edward envisages a ridiculous scene.

'Well, I shall tell him of the danger to *himself* were he to make himself a laughing stock. That's what I shall do. And ah yes, I might mention my relation to the bishop. The bishop's wife is a cousin by marriage to my own wife. A distant cousin. But that is enough. It will do, it will do for my purpose.'

*

Nursey takes to Joseph's sofa every evening; Eve wonders what she'll do when he returns.

'I'm so tired by the evening,' Nursey says. 'All this mending Mr Young has given me to do while he's away. He says he'd rather go on wearing his favourite coats, for he likes the stuff they're made of and will never find it again. Such nonsense, a man with his money!'

She's also trying out Joseph's brandy, Eve notices. A little glass before she unlaces her boots and puts up her feet.

Eve doesn't tell her about Stephen and Betsy, though she does ask her if Betsy hates Stephen, which Nursey doesn't think is so, not at all, she'd have noticed by now. In fact she rather thinks ... but her sentence trickles away.

Mr Pyke calls, asking to speak to Eve.

'I thought you might like to write to the man with whom your parents worked in America, Robert Wilson. Baldwyn has given us an address: 8 Zane Street, Philadelphia. I suggest you simply ask what he remembers of Tom and Sarah. I'm a little worried that Wilson's character may be unsavoury.'

'What do you mean, Mr Pyke?'

'Baldwyn says Wilson claims to be a widower, though it's not clear that his wife is dead. He has a mistress who was once a slave and it seems he may be the subject of blackmail, for mixing of the races is much frowned upon, you know.'

'What exactly is blackmail, Mr Pyke?'

'It's when a person extracts money from someone for keeping quiet about them, for not telling anyone. The person who pays up has something to hide, you see. Really you have no need to know such things, and Wilson is hardly likely to write back and tell you all about it!'

Eve begins her letter. Nursey is reading a newspaper, has yet to undo her boots and nod off. Sips her brandy.

'Oh, such a story here as I must tell you, Eve, child. I did mean to tell it before, but Mr Young had not yet left and I know what he would say. There's a woman healing all the ill folk in the county of Norfolk. What are you doing, my dear?'

'I'm writing a letter.'

'To Mr Young?'

'No! To a friend of Mama and Papa's in America. Mr Pyke gave me the address.'

'Oh dear, oh Lord, but Mr Young did say you were not to think on the past and Sarah and your father. You'd better stop immediately. Give it to me.'

'He won't know. He's not here. I'll do as I like. Read about the woman, Nursey.'

'The dumb and paralysed woman about whom we wrote five years ago, still lives with Rev. Mr John Snead and Mrs Snead in Sowerthorpe on the north-east Norfolk coast.

'I do believe that hussy Betsy comes from thereabouts. Chased out by her mother, I heard.'

'Read *on*, Nursey!'

'The woman, whose name remains unknown, is not deaf, but it is not known why she cannot speak. At some point her paralysis disappeared, which was either a miracle or, as your correspondent has heard it claimed by people in the village, was the result of their copious prayers for her and their many gifts given in tribute. For this dumb woman has healing powers and has cured numerous illnesses with her Beneficent Glance.

'Your correspondent assures his readers that she remains as beautiful as she was when he first encountered her, though still completely dumb. The people of Sowerthorpe are justly proud of her existence among them.

'Rev. Mr John Snead's A Year in Sermons is still eagerly awaited by clergy throughout the country, we are told.

'Oh think of that, Eve! Such a wonder!'

'Why is she dumb?'

'They don't know, it says.'

'Is it true she heals people?'

'Why of course. Nor would it be in the paper if it wasn't.'

'I suppose Joseph would say ...'

'Mr Young would say it's *not* true, I suppose. Most everything's not true for him. But he doesn't know about such things. He doesn't know about a lot of things.'

Eve could easily imagine Joseph's explosion: 'How gullible you are, Mrs Casey! Take no notice, Eve. Absurd story! Obviously fraudulent.'

Nursey turns back to her paper, searches for more remarkable information. Eve writes her letter.

6 John Street
Strand, London
3 October 1809

Dear Mr Wilson,

Mr Pyke has given me your address which he had from Mr Baldwyn.

I have been told that my parents Tom and Sarah Cranch lived and worked with you in Philadelphia before I was born.

I never knew my father, and my mother died seven years ago. Please can you tell me what you remember of them? I intend to travel to America soon and hope that you may be able to help me. I shall write again when I have made arrangements.

Yours in hope,
Eve Cranch

For a while Eve keeps up her spirits by envisaging her letter, which she secreted to Betsy to post, sailing in a packet boat over the sea, imagining Mr Wilson's reception of it, far too soon, even half expecting the man to appear in John Street, friendly and smiling, come to whisk her away to America. He'll be a bit like Mr Pyke, tall and thin, but with eyes like William Digham's, squashed up with love for Tom and Sarah.

Such fantasies make lessons at Digham's ever more dreary, for although Lucy and Eve are fond of each other, they've also seen too much of each other, and there's no longer even the distraction of Matthew's presence. Eve instructs Stephen to turn the carriage away from Paternoster Row and instead take her to Parmentier's, where, recognising her from frequent visits with Joseph, the shopmen treat her with exaggerated respect. She chooses a selection of macaroons and rout cakes, two of every kind of fruit drop, making a kaleidoscope too pretty to eat, so she ups the number to three of each, and finally orders pineapple ice for Nursey, orange for herself.

No money is paid, for she has none, and in any case it can all be added to Joseph's account.

Nursey is amazed when Eve returns at midday.

'Lucy is ill,' she lies easily. 'A bad cough, she can't speak.'

'You surely should have bought lozenges for her then. And we must send round some broth and blackcurrant cheese.'

'Oh, she'll manage quite well, I'm sure. William will look after her. He wears that felt hat all the time. Do you think he even wears it in bed? And there's Matthew too.'

'I thought Matthew was at school now.'

'He's not well either.'

'Mr Digham is devoted to Mrs Digham, that's not hard to see.'

'And look, I've brought your favourite ice as well as some crystallised pineapple, Nursey. I know you're mad for pineapple. And I think it's time I stopped calling you Nursey. I'm too old to talk about my "nurse" in shops. I shall be thirteen this year. I was so embarrassed in Parmentier's. I shall call you Casey instead.'

'I see. Why not *Mrs* Casey?'

'Oh no, Casey is best!'

Nursey is hurt, but she enjoys her ice and candied fruit. For a day or two she's taken in by Eve's story, but the next early return so soon after the first is more troubling.

'Mrs Digham still unwell?'

'Yes, it's pneumonia now. She cannot teach me for weeks.'

'Dear Lord! I shall go there directly!'

'No, no, Casey, she is well looked after. Besides I have brought you morello cherries in *brandy*, Nursey dear. I thought of you.'

Annoyed that her tippling is known, Nursey gathers her things together.

'No, Casey, don't go! You've no need. Lucy said she didn't want any visitors. She said I was not to let you come. Let's go to Hyde Park. Call Stephen, Nursey!'

Eve increases her power over Nursey by using the two names, sometimes one, sometimes the other, depending on what exactly she wants Nursey to do. A sort of pull and push. Nevertheless it's a dull stroll and when they return for dinner in the late afternoon they find a letter addressed to Mrs Casey.

'Mrs Digham did bring it 'erself,' Betsy says, wiping her snub nose with her hand since there's no master at home to notice, and she'll certainly ignore any disapproval from that termagant Mrs Casey.

As well as revealing her perfect health, Mrs Digham writes that she has perceived Eve's discontent, acknowledges humbly that the girl is bored, and that there is little she can give her to improve her mind, to increase her learning, for she only attended a silly girls school herself, learned more from Joseph when she lived with him. A better-educated tutor than she is needed, but Joseph would want to arrange that himself, would most likely be angered if she or Mrs Casey found one themselves.

Nursey feels how threadbare her authority has become. What neither she nor Eve knows is that, at the same age, Sarah, suddenly motherless, was forced to take on the woman's role in her father's smoke-thick, all-male coffee house, thrust into early womanhood. Eve, though she's experienced a kind of responsibility for erratic Joseph and longs for more than her life gives her, is still, at times, wilfully childish.

Nursey is aware that she must retain some control before Joseph returns if she is to keep her position. Imagine him returning to find Eve running about like a wild thing! The prospect of losing her position is terrible, for where on earth would she go? But it's also the one effective threat she has, for Eve still needs her presence, if only to defy it.

*

Sir George Cludd has 'words' with Snead, Hester returns home with Sarah and reluctant restraint is maintained in the parsonage. Hester sleeps in Sarah's narrow room once more, and the two women both eat their meals with Snead, who keeps up an offended silence, pressing his dry lips ever harder with his napkin after each mouthful as though to prevent an eruption of spite.

In the village there's much talk initially, with details hatched by the prurient, though nothing is confirmed by Mary, who keeps remarkably silent. The size of the congregation swells for a few Sundays, but Snead reveals nothing in his sermons, which sound oddly bland. Someone notices that he's not speaking, but reading from a book: another man's words, not his own. The sharp-eyed watch him jerk his neck uneasily, see his fingers grip the lectern; keen listeners hear the voice made smaller than usual through gritted teeth; many observe how he sometimes stops and looks up as if expecting a signal from on high.

When Sarah's paralysis wore off she'd begun to use her hands, helping Hester and Mary in the kitchen, seeming to know how things were done. Hester had quizzed her:

'Sarah, have you made samphire pickle before?' or 'I can see you know how to make pastry or at least have watched it being made. Do you remember?'

Sometimes she opened her mouth as if to speak, gave a meaningful look, yet what was the meaning? Did she remember? Did she not? Did she not want to remember? Hester's thoughts have stumbled this way and that.

In the presence of Snead, Sarah is tense, flinching at the slightest move towards her. Sits as far from him as she can at meal times, barely eats until he's left the table, starts if she hears his voice outside the door. Hester encourages embroidery, gives her pieces of mending, pillow cases, tablecloths. She mends her husband's clothes herself, the frayed cuffs, stockings holed by uncut toenails. She tries giving Sarah the one book she thinks might interest her, her copy of Cowper's *The Task*, but Sarah's eyes glaze, then fill with tears.

Folk ask to see the dumb woman at odd times, in dribs and drabs. Now, even more than before, Hester wants to protect Sarah. She cannot be unsettled every hour of the day. She tells them to come back later, or sits them somewhere until there are enough of them. She's noted that Sarah has never minded encountering several people at once, thinks she must have been used to numbers in her past, not led a secluded life.

The man from the *Eastern Chronicle* visits Sowerthorpe again but hurries off as soon as he's jotted down a note or two, driven off by biting salt winds. He misses the tattle with which Mrs Rollesby and her fellow gossips want him laden, such as Mr Snead's abandonment of his ambitious book of sermons, his plan for a Community of the Pure. His report is based entirely on a rapid inspection of Sarah and an interview with Snead himself, who dismisses him after five minutes with the puzzling words: 'You live in time; I do not.'

The *Eastern Chronicle* is read outside Sowerthorpe of course, and some reports sold to newspapers further afield. How amusing for those in towns to read about occurrences in remote regions! Soon, news also having passed by word of mouth, the sick and halt are back as before, hobbling along the lanes to the parsonage, muddy, travel-tired, dropping gifts warm from clutching into the box, fixing Sarah with their hopeful eyes.

Mary complains about the mess they bring into the house, dropping rags, often bloody, stony clods, particles of food, some chewed.

Worse are the rank smells of those who cannot wash the only clothes they have. The stink lingers of recent and ancient urine, putrid odours of rotting teeth and innards. A constant hazard is caused by random shitting in the front garden.

Despised, misshapen men and women heave their odd bodies into the parsonage parlour, lug puling children, cuffing their resistance.

Sarah is bemused, sometimes distressed. She pats the head of a small child and a miracle is pronounced the next day. If rashes reappear after a 'cure' their owner simply comes back to the parsonage a week later, sits again at the feet of the strange dumb woman with the mouth that looks as though it might utter a word but never does, that contorts and sometimes almost smiles.

November dusk and Hett Toft, a woman with eyes that swivel in her puffy, soft-skinned face, sits in the middle of the only sofa in the room, opposite Sarah, poking back a sheaf of white hair that falls forward over her snub nose. Her mobile eyes try to fix on the space above Sarah's head.

'I see it!' she bursts out. 'There! There! Above the lady.'

'What's it ye see?'

'It hev gone there now!' Her eyes range left, right. 'Now *there*, d'ye see?'

'I see it,' a voice calls out from the back.

'Feathers. Under them feathers!' The woman's eyes seem at last to stop moving.

'That's wings, you do mean, that is,' a man remarks.

'A *angel* that is!'

'A angel do fly above the lady.'

'That be her *garden* angel.'

More people see the angel, its wings hovering over, protecting the dumb woman.

'There it is! There!' They follow it as it moves about the room.

'That do fly over us all.'

'There, in the corner. That have big wings.'

'Noo. Small wings. A cherubim.'

'*Noo*. Niver is. That glows, lights up. Above her, look!'

The people gaze as one at the space above Sarah's head. They're inclined to believe Hett Toft, who is known for her great sensitivity to the presence of good and evil. Who, years ago, expelled her own daughter for being possessed, she claimed. Of course some say she found the girl in the hedge with tinkers too many times, but it's known that the daughter, Betsy, made off to London, which really just proves her mother's point.

At first Sarah is calm, but as the pleasure in the room turns to excitement then to something more like hysteria, she rises, frightened, backs behind her chair.

The shrieks reach a pitch. The door flies open. Snead.

'What noise is this?'

Screeching slowly ceases. A small voice says: 'A angel. The lady do hev a angel with feathers.'

Seeing Sarah cowering in the corner of the room, he moves towards her with open arms, but she cowers the more.

'Get out, you dupes of Satan. Angels care not for you – look at you, disgusting imbeciles!' They run as from the Devil.

*

Nursey's anger and disappointment soon fizzle out into a tearful prophecy of her banishment and exile, and Eve promises to keep to the old arrangement in Paternoster Row. Lucy tries to construct a reading programme for Eve, remembering the books in Joseph's lodgings when she first met him. She picked them out of the squalor and disarray of his room and arranged them on a shelf. Some of these were books for the radical he was then, a follower of Tom Paine, and she thinks not suitable for Eve.

It works for a while.

'I'll bring some of Sarah and Tom's books,' Eve suggests. 'Will you help me read and understand them, Lucy?'

But Lucy is often unable to answer questions or explain words, and Eve must control exasperation. She tries not to think of strawberry ice and chocolate drops, but the dullness of life offends and the lack of a reply from Mr Wilson distresses her.

Suddenly she remembers that Ann and Gilbert's mothers were once slaves, came over from America. *They* will know how she can get there.

'Stephen, I should like you to take me to the home of Mr and Mrs Downs. I don't know their address, though I'm sure you do.'

'But, Miss Eve, I've strict instructions. I must only take you to Paternoster Row. Not to no place else.'

'That's only Casey, Stephen. You've no need to obey *her*! And you're not to *tell* her, either!'

'I must keep to ve orders I'm given. What would Mr Young say if he come 'ome and found out?'

'What would he say if I were to tell him what you do to Betsy, Stephen?'

'Oh, Miss Eve, what *are* you atalkin of?'

'*About you and Betsy*. I *know*. I've *seen* you, Stephen, and I've heard Betsy cry out and grunt like a pig. In the dairy, at night with your clothes all down and Betsy's clothes all up. Nursey says Betsy's a hussy out of Norfolk.'

'"ave you told 'er?'

'No, she just says that about Betsy anyway. But I'll tell Joseph when he returns and what do you think he'll say *then*?'

She watches redness creep over Stephen's face, remembers his buttocks fleshy and yellow in the candlelight, thinks of subsequent nights when she went down again, these times not daring to enter the dairy but listening beside the half-open door. Cries and groans from Betsy, shouts from Stephen puzzle and excite her, unsure what pain is taking place. She waits, flattens herself against the wall as they emerge, sees Stephen's arm around Betsy, who's pulling down her skirt.

The blackmail works perfectly, and they arrive one morning in a narrow, dismal street where there's no reply when Stephen knocks on the door. An old woman scuffs out, curious about the smart carriage and groom.

'Not in, o' courst. Vey's art. Beck lite.'

'How late?' Stephen asks.

'All 'ours. Try agin Sundy.'

This is a blow, for not only are there no lessons on Sunday for her to miss, but Nursey insists that Eve go to church with her, now that Joseph isn't there to stop them. Eve calculates carefully, thinks if she goes to church *and* tells her, Nursey will do what she wants and let her go by herself.

'I want Stephen to take me to Gilbert and Ann's house after church on Sunday, Nursey dear.'

'Have they asked you to visit them?'

'I'm certain they'll be glad to see me.'

'I shall accompany you.'

'No need, Nursey! They are so friendly and kind. You remember! I can't possibly be in danger.'

'I shall come all the same. You're not nearly of age, still only a child. Besides they're not English.'

'They're Joseph's friends, Casey! So they're my friends, too.'

'Just because you've been gallivanting about, getting Stephen to take you wherever you want, to anyone you fancy, you can't expect to keep doing it, my girl. Who knows when Mr Young might return.'

'He's not said he's coming back yet.'

'Doesn't mean he won't turn up all of a sudden.'

Ann Downs answers their knock and beams at the sight of them.

'Miss Eve, Mrs Casey, this is an honour! Come in, come in. You're lucky, I'm only just back from church.'

She takes them into a room shabby and poorly furnished by contrast with her pretty, white, sprigged-muslin dress, Eve can't help noticing.

'Sit you down now. I'll bring you something to drink. Gilbert's not back yet. He has to help his master change his clothes after *he* been to *his* church. A fine big one.'

'Who is his master, Mrs Downs?' Nursey asks.

'Oh, Lord Somethinborough, I'm never exactly sure. I'll make tea. And a sandwich, Miss Eve?'

'Yes, please!'

'It's not necessary to give Eve anything, Mrs Downs, and we must go home shortly,' Nursey says stiffly.

Eve would retort at this point, but is subdued by the surroundings. She has never been in a house with so little furniture, where the boards are bare, where the occupants live on one floor only, where the bed, she suddenly notices, is in the drawing room. The Dighams' place is hardly grand, but this is miserable. There are a few books on a shelf, a bunch of flowers in a jug on the table where Ann has placed her bonnet. How can Ann and Gilbert be so poor when they are friends of Joseph's? Eve notices three sketches pinned to the wall and recognises Gilbert with the cloak and sword.

'Miss Eve, I'm sure you've come with a purpose. What can I do for you?'

Eve is hampered by Nursey's disapproving presence. 'I'd like to talk to you *and* Mr Downs. When will he return?'

'Today he's back about five. Will you come later?'

'No, that's quite impossible,' Nursey says rapidly, 'we shall be at dinner. We'll drink our tea, thank you Mrs Downs, and depart.'

On the way home Nursey says: 'I thought it wrong to accept food when most like they have none to spare. And we don't know what black people eat.'

'Oh, same as us, of course! But they're so poor. Why?'

'Many people are poor, black people especially. Mr Downs works for a rich man. The rich are often mean. I don't know where Mrs Downs works but I saw she takes in extra work, stitching. Did you not notice the huge pile of linen? I expect she works on that at night.'

'Oh. But Joseph is their friend. He should give them some of his money.'

'It's not for us to say. Still, he could at least have had those sketches of Mr Downs framed.' She tuts and knits together her gloved fingers.

Eve's plan is simple. After dinner Nursey takes her tipple, somewhat more now than when she first began, and snoozes on Joseph's sofa after she's seen Eve off to bed. It's fortunate they no longer share a room.

In the kitchen Stephen is finishing his meal, Betsy is in the house somewhere and the cook is out.

'Stephen, please take me back to Mr and Mrs Downs, for Nursey wants me to give them some food.'

'Would she not wish to take it herself, Miss Eve?' he counters.

Betsy comes in with a sacking bundle that clanks, hides it behind her back on seeing Eve.

'Betsy, I need you to get me some things for Mr and Mrs Downs. Stephen is taking me there. He knows he must do as I ask, Betsy, lest I tell Joseph about you and him. You and him *together* in the dairy. Because I've seen you, you see, and heard you too, making a lot of horrible noise.'

Betsy claps her hand over her mouth and Stephen nods a frowning confirmation at her.

'So, Betsy, you are to make up a basket of good food from the pantry.' Eve enjoys this greatly. 'I'll take them a ham, a loaf of bread, some of those lemon pies. They'll want butter and cheese. Bottles of wine, too. Wrap up that currant cake.'

Betsy doesn't move from shock till Stephen gruffly tells her to 'gi' me that, silly,' and to 'get on wiv what Miss Eve says'.

Stephen takes the clanking sack. 'I'll drop you at their place and be back in 'alf an 'our,' he tells Eve. Ten minutes later they're off.

'Miss Eve, I think we must ask your groom to take you back home. You're a young girl. And all this food!'

'Ann, Ann!' Gilbert says. 'Joseph's not there, so he can't know about Eve coming here and can't miss her. And I think he wouldn't mind at all. He'd be pleased about this basket. I know Joe so well. We've been friends since all those years back in Wych Street.'

'Oh that place, Gilbert Downs! Before I married you I *rescued* you from Wych Street. I'll certainly not let my daughter go about at night if I ever get a daughter. If ever I do.'

'Don't you start complaining, Ann.'

'I'm quite safe, Mrs Downs, please don't worry about me. Stephen will wait and Nursey, I mean Mrs Casey is asleep. She doesn't even know.'

'Oh dear, worse and worse.'

'I understand Eve, Ann. Eve, you're a good girl from a good mother and you want to *do* good. Isn't that so? And Joseph, he'd never be angry if he knew. If he ever does find out we'll laugh about it together.'

'Share the food with us, Eve. I'll make a sandwich at last!'

They sit at the table, Gilbert slices ham, Ann makes up the sandwiches. Sandwiches will never taste as good for Eve after watching their construction on this day.

'You say what you want to say, Eve. And call us Gilbert and Ann. We can't do with the Mr and Mrs even though we are.'

'Please tell me how to get to America. Can you help me get there?'

'Dear Lord! The other side the world! Why do you want to go *there*, my girl?' Ann looks up from her making. 'They still keep *slaves* in some places there!'

'Oh.' Eve's put out by Ann's tone, but persists. 'Mama and Papa went there. They lived in a town called Philadelphia.'

'And your poor papa died there, too. Still, I understand what you're saying.'

'It's not simple, Eve.' Gilbert is suddenly serious. 'Where would you live? Your mama and papa are no longer there. You don't know anybody in America. A child can't turn up on her own and just find a house. Even if you are a young lady now.'

'Oh yes, I do know someone. The man they worked for, called Mr Wilson. He was a radical, too. I've written to him already.'

'Has he replied to you?'

'No.'

Ann rushes to hug Eve. 'Oh my dear girl! I wish I could take you there myself!'

'Could you, really?'

'No, no, now stop this, Ann.' Gilbert finishes his sandwich. 'Don't raise the girl's hopes.'

'Only I feel so sad for her.'

'Of course! But Eve, you must wait until you're of age. That's hard I know, but unless you can persuade Joe to take you himself it's impossible for you to travel alone. And this Mr Wilson. He might well not welcome you.'

It's not what Eve wants to hear. Together Ann and Gilbert exhort her to be patient until she's old enough to take her life into her own hands.

'It's not so long now.'

'Oh, it is, it is,' Eve cries on Ann's comforting breast, loved, soothed and altogether miserable.

'Come and call on us when you can, Eve. Trouble is, every day we're out working. But I'll talk to Mrs Casey if necessary,' Gilbert says. 'She knows we're Joseph's friends.'

Eve can't sleep that night, her mind's too full of warring thoughts. The Downs are so kind and so poor, the sandwiches unforgettably delicious, her disappointment extreme. She really had believed they'd promise to pack a bag and take her to America, where all would be well.

Even the prospect of continuing to blackmail Stephen and Betsy palls.

5

———

THE STRANGE TRUCE LASTS A considerable time in Sowerthorpe parsonage. Daily routine remains unchanged but a hush descends. Snead rarely speaks at all, and awed by this uncharacteristic self-control, Hester and Mary talk more quietly. For the moment it seems that Snead is not constantly irritated by petty failings around him, nor feels the need to hector all those within hearing about the sins of the world. Napoleon's onslaught in Europe passes him by. Even the Corsican's imprisonment of the Pope doesn't move him to comment.

In this atmosphere Sarah eases a little, though Hester is on guard. For her it's more like living with a barrel of gunpowder in the basement, likely to explode with the smallest spark. She has heard of such things.

Although Mary's natural tendency would be to make herself popular by telling all, she now enjoys her special role as holder of unspoken information. Villagers look at her as a person of immeasurable value. Of course the more she refuses to answer questions the more might be inferred about the parson. And this pleases her greatly, for she's always hated Snead, and would dearly love to see him toppled.

Her loyalty to Hester demands that she imply nothing even by the slightest raising of an eyebrow or pursing of lips, must allow the common Sowerthorpers to breed their own maggots. Perhaps the timing of her silences becomes indicative. But she fails to take into account the Sowerthorpe Society for the Suppression of Vice, who would in any case suppress the *discussion* of vice where they refuse to believe it exists. After all, it was Rev. Snead who'd set them going in the first place. In him their faith cannot be shaken, and for Rollesby, Catton and Cragin, it's so easy to see who the real culprit is.

Prevented from bringing about the arrest of the atheist surgeon by her verbal accusations and initially popular attack on Edward's surgery, Mrs Rollesby returns to her usual method, which together with Mrs Cragin's terrifying looks, aims darts of venomous gossip at wavering villagers. The weak fall.

Yet in time even those living in backwaters experience boredom. The villagers are more interested in Sarah than in Snead, in whom Sarah might 'cure' next. Those who set store by miracles wonder what she might do for menfolk returning maimed from abroad, Sowerthorpe men who'd been pressed for the Royal Navy. Thousands of men died of the fever in Flanders at some place you couldn't pronounce, but 'them as be not too badly cut about from retreat in Portingal or Spain or one o' them places 'ave got back 'oom, and mebbe our dumb 'ooman can do a miracle for 'em?'

Edward's powerful part in the rescue of Sarah breaks open a closed door in Hester's mind. Of course she is grateful. More, she is fascinated and touched by the order in his surgery and waiting room, the disorder in his kitchen and sitting room, where the floor is strewn with books and papers. But it's the intensity with which his grey eyes search her face that tell her what she has long perceived yet dared not articulate to herself. A gust of longing sweeps through her.

They meet by chance as she takes her basket of tracts to the literate few. Though in a hurry, he stops long enough to ask how Sarah is, pushing overgrown tufts off his forehead.

'We are very quiet in the parsonage these days. My husband ...' She'd rather not name him, wishes she might not mention him to Edward at all. 'He says little to any of us and so Sarah is more at ease.

'Every day I think she might begin to speak. And yet she does not.'

'Every day you hope, Hester.'

'I do.' She smiles at him. Understanding opens.

A sudden wind blows several 'Steps into the Abyss' out of the basket and down the street.

'Oh no!' Hester cries out, but before she can run after them Edward puts his hand on the hand that holds the basket.

'Leave them.'

She looks at him, momentarily alarmed. Pleased. Notices how the corners of his mouth curl up with amusement, that they always do, even when he's serious.

'By the time you reach them, they'll be too muddy to read. The gutter's the best place for them.'

He checks her face for any sign of dismay. Finds none. 'I must hurry away. Jane Ann Newby's taken a turn for the worse, her mother says. Goodbye, Hester.'

'Goodbye, Edward,' she says, thrilled by the warmth of his hand. How she still feels it after he's gone.

From now on, though compelled to inaction, awareness of mutual delight informs every meeting, however brief.

Hester witnessed the affection of her parents before her schoolmaster father died of consumption, leaving her mother to bring up six children in poverty. Something of that affection, firelight, stories told, sounds in her memory, nourishes longing. Though she never allows herself to imagine a life with Edward, the certainty of his presence, so close, enriches her bleak existence.

*

The year Joseph decides he must travel to Italy sees the 'total downfall of Imperial Rome', as the papers put it. Yet Joseph *must* go, has reached that stage in his development as a painter in which he *must* see Italy. And after all, Nelson has re-opened the Mediterranean. However, the only ship available, a merchantman, the *Lavinia*, is loaded with armaments, part of a convoy sailing to southern Italy after King Ferdinand's retreat from Naples.

Captain Ormerod is intrigued. In his diary he records the large quantity of laudanum bottles Joseph brings on board, the plentiful supply of brandy and rum, the famous artist's daily activity – *doesn't eat much, is alternately morose and cheerful* – how often and how frequently Joseph remains in his tiny cabin, *this very large man in a space*

not much bigger than a cupboard, cluttered with books, paints, crates of
bottles, heaps of clothes.

Well into the voyage Joseph becomes ill and the surgeon is called
to administer an enema, a sure sign of the overuse of laudanum, he
tells Ormerod. As weeks pass, the squalor in the cupboard-cabin
builds up, and *although I have made numerous suggestions, offered help to*
clean and order the place, he informs me that he never notices mess. 'Years
earlier,' (these are his words), 'I lived with a woman who attempted order
and cleanliness and said she wanted to turn my lodgings into a home. She
doted on me,' he recalled.

From the Bay of Biscay the *Lavinia* and its convoy sail at a safe
distance from the coast of north-west Spain and Portugal, the scene
of the recent Corunna disaster, anchor briefly at Gibraltar and then
move on into the Mediterranean.

Mr Young is beside himself with joy at our arrival in the Mediterranean
Sea, writes Ormerod. *He told me, 'This is where my life begins', and then*
he gave me the very first drawing he made of the Rock, 'as a mark of our
friendship'. Yet only yesterday he would not come out of his cabin, appar-
ently replying to knocks on his door in the gruffest whisper.

He is an extraordinary man, unlike any I have met before, alternating
warm friendship, amusing stories of his life, enthusiasm for many aspects of
the voyage, with the blackest gloom, during which he hardly acknowledges me.

Piling up in Joseph's cabin are quantities of pocket books containing sketches in watercolour, pencil, charcoal. For a painter
consciously working in the Romantic mode, the sea is one of the
best subjects. There's the significance, too, of his own nightmarish
sea-landing when the balloon came down eight years ago. And of
course it was the sea that took Sarah. Sarah Battle, for whom he'd
experienced the most ecstatic love on that aerial journey. So there are
seascapes and skyscapes from all times of the day and all weathers,
and nightscapes, too, tabulating the gradual darkening of the sky, the
awakening of stars. There are endless drawings and painted sketches
of clouds using almost every colour cake from his box, gamboge,
ochre, burnt umber, raw sienna, brown and purple madder, carmine,
crimson lake; reflected or shadowed on calm or turbulent seas; the
moon appearing behind or within them, its own disappearance,
pages of almost complete darkness, bone black worn thin.

However much Joseph is ruled by his erratic state of mind, by the physical dictates of the drug, he retains a solid gob of arrogance mixed with knowledge of what patrons desire to display on their walls, how much they'll spend and what else they'll buy.

As a young artist he soon discovered that what really earned well were erotic drawings and engravings sold under the counter or hired out in portfolios for a night or a week. He produced hundreds of sheets of penises, buttocks and breasts, all huge, lively, pink-tipped, boisterously engaging with each other in carriages, carts, on and off sofas, behind hedges, on gates, more or less anywhere. Shirts up, breeches down, large feathered hats, oddly, still in place. Faces unimportant except to express surprise or lust. Rumpled, crumpled, a hearty disorder, satirical, funny, a series of cheerfully enthusiastic fucks.

With age, becoming almost respectable, he improved his reputation by painting a series of Shakespeare's women and then the portraits of those who yearned to pay and boast about it. He certainly made a lot from the dramatic paintings that recorded Nelson's funeral, and the hundreds of engravings of them for the less well-off to hang in their parlours. His youthful, radical ideals faded and his opposition to fighting against France mutated as Napoleon strove to rule the world.

At some point, Joseph discovers that the *Lavinia*'s convoy is not just delivering crates of ammunition to southern Italy; the presence of warships is not simply protection for the *Lavinia* and the other merchantmen, but is actually a war convoy, with a large contingent of marines and other infantry on board the warships. Obviously, paintings of naval battles, of triumphant British forces, will sell well back home, and so the foreign sky, the huge Mediterranean moon become mere backdrops against which he pitches the stirring sight of massed sails and British flags sailing towards the enemy.

Then, as the coast of Calabria nears, he draws page after page of smoke, rendered in pencil, thin watercolour or black and white chalk on blue paper, as British and Sicilian boats exchange fire with the batteries on shore and British troops land. Smoke, streaks of fire, glimpses of obscured sail and mast. Sometimes he manouevres Etna smoking magisterially in the background. There are scenes of French prisoners of war boarding ships from Calabria. With great vividness he renders the extraordinary episode of British troops hauling cannon from the sea at Scylla where they'd been thrown from the castle by Napoleon's defeated men. It's as if the exertion of power and destruction, present only in his own mind until now, at last becomes real.

Ormerod advises him to delay embarking in Italy until Napoleon's defeat, and writes him letters of recommendation to the British authorities in Valletta. In fact the defeat of Napoleon is not imminent. It will be four years yet before he overreaches himself in Russia, five before Waterloo. Joseph never experiences Italy.

Instead he spends several months in Malta, where he is welcomed by both British residents and Maltese, eager to see themselves in oils. Morale is high on the island, whose people so recently rebelled against the garrison Napoleon left behind on his way to Egypt. Who, with the help of Nelson's blockade, entirely rid themselves of the French after only two years. Joseph paints portraits, lists all his sitters, the dinners, balls and invitations to the governor's palace. He also travels round the island finding exotic scenes to build up into what he's sure will be his best work. He envisages enormous canvases filled with huge edifices in brilliant light, sea-struck rocks, glittering heat, great heights, great distances. The Napoleon of painters, sweeping away all opposition.

In his Maltese journal he uses a code with two frequently recurring symbols. A crude cross indicates a purchase of laudanum, the cross being a pun on lord/laud, from a conversation he once had with the young Eve which has stuck in his mind.

The other, a small rounded letter w, resembles a pair of breasts, which he occasionally embellishes with dots for nipples, indicating the days on which he sleeps with a woman. At first it's little more than collecting, pleased to find himself desirable to so many women. Given that he's never kept a journal until now, noting these facts becomes a compulsion in itself to impose a kind of regularity on a life that continuously threatens to disintegrate.

Many of the women are prostitutes, who make good business from all grades of the visiting navy, and demi-reps, too, those hovering within the limits of respectability, expecting remuneration in style, like their sisters in London. In London previously, with Eve in the house, he'd almost abandoned his need for women, a need connected in his earlier years to his changes of mood. In Valletta he returns to the pattern from which Lucy had eventually fled: the periodic quest for immersion in the lowest life.

There are other, more or less disastrous relationships with socially superior women from the island's ruling set. Frequently courted, he can hardly resist these flattering, idle wives, though his instability guarantees disaster: elaborate flirtation, often cancelled assignations. Typical is the note he receives from Mrs Henrietta Benningham, previously of Hampshire:

Valletta, 18 December

My dearest Joseph,

I must complain! I am Neglected by you.

    First you charm us with your lively tales of London, about which we all long to hear of course, and your description of the Ill-Fated Balloon Flight (how we hate the Beautiful Woman you had in the basket!). You accept my invitation, but come the day, do not arrive for dinner, and Maria later informs me that you've been seen at a Particular House in the lower district the same evening.

    A week later you call and apologise rather Too Profusely (believe me, it is so), claiming <u>illness</u>! Of course it was then that you invited me to your studio to see your latest work and Entertained me, <u>dear</u> Joseph, in such a way that I do <u>not</u> complain! Except for the interruption, which surely you could have prevented!

    Now comes the invitation to myself and Mr Benningham to see your portrait of Colonel Henry Buller and Mrs Buller, which you deem a Most Remarkable Likeness to them both. In case we, too, should desire to be portrayed as a contented couple (Ha ha!). But of course Benningham has Got Wind of you and has insisted that he accompany me on <u>any and every</u> visit to your studio (so conveniently attached to your apartment). He says you are Not a Man to be Trusted.

    And now the worst: I am <u>not at all amused</u> to hear of her experiences from <u>Amelia Brine</u>. I am abused by you!

    Reply and <u>tell me she is lying</u>! Else I remain for ever wretched.

Yours until I hear from you,
Henrietta

In fact the illness Henrietta Benningham mentions is not feigned, nor are several other occasions when Joseph lies in the darkness of his shuttered apartment, groaning, vomiting, ordering his man-servant to refuse all callers. Sickness often follows his bouts of drug-taking or else his attempts at withdrawal. And then there are the attacks of pox for which Corbyn's Blue Pills, the mercury cure, are not easily available in Valletta.

After several months, Joseph realises he must scrap his grand plan, and although he's accumulated much material, later to be converted into paintings which will enhance his artistic reputation, in his own mind the trip is a failure, as he says on many occasions when back home, admitting that despite all his boasting before he left London, Boney *had* prevented him from seeing Italy.

He makes money while in Malta, and thus has plenty to spend on laudanum and spirits, especially since the price of laudanum is less than in London because of the cultivation of opium poppies in Sicily. But he spends prodigious amounts on objects to take home, many pieces of antique Egyptian and Syrian furniture and copperware, painted ceramic bowls and platters, exquisite cotton clothing for himself, countless shirts, embroidered waistcoats and bales of cotton cloth, some of which he thinks can be made up into gowns or blouses for Eve. And all of it must be packed into crates and transported to John Street.

He has dozens of sketchbooks from which to produce paintings on patriotic subjects, and with dread can already hear himself pouring out enthusiasm for sea-battles in over-excited speech to galleries and potential buyers. Knowing that at the same time the failure of his original plan and the physical consequences of desperate excess will drop him into deep gloom.

By 1810 then, he's had enough, feels a longing to escape the growing talk about him and return to London, which is embroiled in its own much more entertaining political and royal scandals, particularly the widely satirised folly of the Duke of York and his mistress, the beautiful, brazen Mary Anne Clarke.

He sails from Valletta on the *Dryad*, another merchantman, but this time loaded largely with Sicilian hemp. On this voyage his friend and confidant is the ship's surgeon, Arthur Pickmore, an understanding, humane man. Pickmore is clear that Joseph's addiction to opium is no help to the disorder of his mind, and so he begins the gradual reduction of laudanum by minute amounts, recommending a colleague in London, Dr Henry Sessions, with whom Joseph can continue the cure upon his return. Whenever Joseph's mood begins to stumble, Pickmore holds off the reduction but refuses to be kept out of Joseph's cabin, patiently engaging him in conversation to prevent the darkest pessimism and keep Joseph's hands off the green bottle.

The journey takes twenty-seven days. By the time the *Dryad* makes its way through the flat estuary marshland of the Thames, then past stinking riverside works towards Wapping, Joseph's earlier elation and relief at the longed-for return are fast transposing into despair.

*

Hester is astonished when her husband agrees to see two men who call one day. He usually lets no one into his study except her, and then reluctantly, with sighs of impatience, shoulder twisting and much clearing of his throat as though he'd cough and spit her out of the room. It surprises her, even in his recently quietened frame of mind.

Dressed in striped waistcoats and garish jackets, the men sweep their hats off their heads so elaborately as to suggest performance. Hester has never been to a fair or a circus, though as a child she stood outside the school-house door to watch fair folk pass along the main street with their trumpets and drums, shambling chained bear, shaggy and smelling bad, jugglers, bearded lady, and huge, honking elephant. These two men remind her of the colourful characters she saw strut and shout along the street, promising glorious entertainment.

They tell Mary that they must speak to Mr Snead, that he is expecting them, and when he doesn't shut them out of his room, Hester does an unusual thing: she listens at the door. Unusual, but many things feel different because of Edward. Her awareness of him, even when he's nowhere near, gives her courage.

'We was given yer letter, dahn ve coast, yer 'oliness.'

'If you are who I think you are, it was a considerable time ago that I wrote to you.'

'Too busy to call, yer 'oliness. Folk vant us, yer see. All year rahnd.'

'It would be preferable to address me as Mr Snead. And let me be assured that you are indeed the man to whom I wrote back then. Give me your name.'

'Tonks, Stringer Tonks of Tonks's Famous Sights. You 'eard of us, didn't yer. And this 'ere's me bruvver 'arry. We read it, what yer wrote, and we fought a man of ve cloff don't 'ave a lot o' shiners, specially not vese days, so we fought as 'ow we'll offer you a good sum. It'd suit us dahn to the grahnd.'

'How much do you have in mind?'

'Vere's free ways, Mr Snead, yer 'onour, sir. We give yer a sum for the 'ole lot, say fifty, or we show 'er for yer, in fairs all rahnd abaht and share the takin's evens stevens. Look 'ere, read vis avertisment fer a woman dahn Gloster way. Deaf and dumb. Famous.'

There's quiet as Snead reads. Later, darting into his study, Hester opens a screwed-up ball of paper that reads:

Ann Stanley, who by divine favour, has naturally an extraordinary Genius and Conception, can cure most curable distempers belonging to the eyes. She also cures deafness and thickness of Hearing if the Drum of the Ear be not hurt or broke; can cure broken Bellies in Old & Young; Gravel, Scald Heads, Rickets in Children & has a peculiar method in curing most Calamities incident to Women & Children for which she is famous.

'Somefink like vat, writ on a board fer yer woman, yer 'onour. Better'n a magic lanthorn she'd be. And we'd bring 'er beck in time for your own show when wevver turns bad.'

'And the third way? You said there were three possibilities.'

'Vat's sumfink extra. We get er to *do* a bit o' magic.'

'What do you mean?'

'Ah, we're not givin' away no secrets, are we 'arry?'

'Jus' fer you, yer 'onour sir. A man of ve cloff no abaht words, eh? You got a lot of words 'ere, a'n't ya? 'ere!'

What Hester can't see, of course, though she eventually finds it stuffed into a pocket of some trousers she takes to mend, is a piece of paper with this inscribed on it:

ABRACADABRA
ABRACADABR
ABRACADAB
ABRACADA
ABRACA
ABRAC
ABRA
ABR
AB
A

'She waves it over people, see and fings 'appen. See?'

'I need a little time to consider this. Please come back in an hour, Mr Tonks.'

'We can do vat, 'arry, eh?'

Hester darts away, busies herself in the house for an hour, and when the men return she tiptoes up again, after they've gone in. Again stands outside Snead's study, ear pressed against the door. Ready.

'What's yer answer yer 'onour?'

'I believe letting you show her and bring her back would be, shall we say, awkward, and might be misread. However, I am willing to accept a good sum for her, so long as removal is rapid and at night. Tonight preferably.'

'For the 'ole lot then.'

'Yes. Only it seems to me that fifty pounds is far too little. She's worth twice that much.'

'Ooh now! We couldn't never run to vat much, could us, 'arry? We'll say sixty pound all done, Mr Snead, yer 'onour, sir. Yer 'oliness.'

Hesitation. 'I'll accept nothing less than ninety. Think what you're getting for that amount. She's not just for looking at. As you realise yourselves, she *cures* people!'

'Well, I s'pose us could creep up to sixty-five. What d'yer fink, 'arry?'

'Ooh, I dunno. Vat's a lot o' shiners.'

'I'll take eighty and there's an end to it.'

The door bursts open: '*There's an end to it, Mr Snead?*' Hester finds herself shouting. 'You're *selling a woman! Bartering!*'

'A *dumb* woman, Hester. A dumb healer who draws crowds. But, how dare you come in like this. Leave us immediately! *Now!*' His voice rises. 'Get out! *Get out!*' He is already standing, and begins to move round his desk towards her, twisting his neck, picking up a large book as he comes.

'The Lord will smite the ungodly!' Hester hears herself continue to shout as she never has before.

'Think as 'ow the folks'll love 'er, my lady! All vem miracles. Folk linin' up all dahn ve streets.'

She is at the door.

'Mr Snead, if you do not send these men on their way immediately, I shall run out now and tell everyone that you've sold the dumb woman for eighty pounds. That intelligence will spread like fire in dry stubble.'

Running from the room and out into the street before she can be stopped, Hester unties the Tonks' gaily painted cart, slaps the pony's rump till it skitters off, runs back into the house and up the stairs.

'Your cart has set off down the road,' she tells the Tonks brothers, 'you'll have to hurry. I am delivering tracts now, Mr Snead. Shall I inform those to whom I give them of the sale?'

*

Any authority that Nursey once had evaporates completely. Eve still needs her presence, if only for the purpose of treating her badly. Everyone else ignores the old nurse, which she barely notices, protected in a pleasant glow of brandy.

The king being too mad either to reign or to celebrate his birthday, the Prince of Wales puts on a grand event to mark his regency. Although Joseph's not here to allow or refuse the visit, Stephen delivers Nursey to Carlton House on the last day of the fête, when the public are allowed in to admire the rooms, or to slake their prurience. Here is an opportunity to view the splendour of the truly rich, thinks Nursey, especially the abode of the wonderfully notorious man who, before long, will be king.

All morning crowds pour through the gates which frequently must be shut against them. Pall Mall and St James's Street fill up with vehicles unable to move and soon frustrated people leave their carriages and rush forward to the next opening of the gates. They press greedily, uncontrollably, and such is the crush that clothes are torn off, lost, and women wander about the gardens, dazed, without shoes, gowns, or, so reports insist, completely undressed, their hair hanging about their shoulders.

Nursey and those others in the first line of that crowd are less lucky. They are quickly felled, trampled on, their limbs bruised and broken, and Nursey herself is asphyxiated, her face and body blackened.

When she doesn't return, Stephen is called to identify her, later blurting out the news to Eve, who experiences a curious sensation. For a long time she despised almost everything Nursey said or did. Now she is horrified by his brief report, more so by the detailed description of Nursey's body she overhears him giving to Betsy. When Betsy expresses pity at the death of 'the old termagant', Eve is shaken into a slowly unfolding sorrow for her faithful nurse.

*

It seems that Snead is avoiding Hester. When Mary places food before him he takes it to his study and shuts and locks the door. It's peaceful without him and Mary sits and eats with Sarah and Hester, but Hester fears a quiet before some awful explosion.

She wonders if she should take him a bowl of broth as a conciliatory offering. They surely cannot live entirely in silence.

It's late in a long summer day, dusk already present. Approaching his room, she hears his voice within. Surmises he thinks she's gone to bed. Perhaps she should leave him be.

But it's not speaking she hears; it's low, throttled cries, sounds, not words. And there are bangs and thumps. She puts the bowl on a table, moves up close to the door.

Hard things are hitting the floor and walls. 'Ah! Ah!' he's rasping. 'Ah! Ah!'

She listens, mesmerised, hears the tone of loathing he so often expresses, and rage too. But there's something else that makes tears start in her eyes. Anguish. The deep-sunk anguish of an abandoned being. Like the cry of a creature she once heard, unseen among the river reeds, drowning. And suddenly she knows it's the stones she found in his pockets that he's hurling onto the walls, floorboards.

What is wrong? What is it? She's standing, rigid. But dare not go in, for his frame of mind is terrible.

'Oh! Oh! Ah! Father!'

Surely *not* the Our Father. She creeps downstairs. Hastens to bed. Doesn't sleep all night.

At about this time Edward's father dies, wealthy, unlamented. With great relief, Edward sells the Hackney asylum at a low price, the economy weighed down by war. The buyer is an apparently humane doctor with whom he discusses the treament of the insane at length. The man seems to share Edward's concerns, or rather, readily agrees with everything Edward says.

'I have editions of all our great British psychologists on my shelves, of course, but I intend to follow only the latest thinkers,' he declares, smoothing a wrinkle in his claret-coloured velvet jacket. Probably he thinks the increasing number of bankruptcies in and around the City will guarantee plenty of patients, omits to calculate that the relatives of those who are completely ruined might well not pay for treatment.

With the sale money, Edward buys a practice in a Yorkshire village not far from Wakefield. He's never been to the North Country, but has heard of an interesting experimental asylum not too far away outside York, which he thinks he might visit. The Retreat, set up by the Quaker William Tuke, apparently uses methods as far removed from those employed in his father's asylum as can be imagined. How good it would be to see if their methods might have been used to help Sarah, though of course he can hardly take her with him.

There's a good-sized house with the practice, and it's miles north of Sowerthorpe, which he's longed to leave for years. He tells no one exactly where he's going, knowing that a complete break from everything here would be best. He completes his notes for every Sowerthorpe patient, wondering how much to tell his successor about the situation at the parsonage. No doubt he'll soon find out.

He makes arrangements for removal of his furniture, clothes and books in numbered boxes. Of course he must leave medical equipment for the next incumbent, but takes what he feels he cannot do without: who knows what primitive ideas the old doctor he's replacing may have had!

That he'll lose Hester is extremely painful, yet there's no solution short of kidnap. As a rational man he allows little time for dreams of taking Hester with him. An inner voice tells him that he'll find a wife soon enough in a more populated, less impoverished area, and forget the past. Beneath the reason another voice reminds him that he'll never replace Hester in his heart.

*

A fine June day. Shoals of ferrymen shift crates from the line of masted ships mid-river to the wharf. As the sun begins to burn on the water, activity slows. Lightermen sweat and swear, tars row dozing officers ashore, passengers await their luggage, unsteady, feeling the ground still swell and roll beneath their feet. Joseph is impatient, surrounded by every size of wooden packing case, travelling bags and baskets, and no sign of Stephen, even though he wrote to him and Mrs Casey giving clear instructions about his return.

He waits until after midday, tanned from the Mediterranean sun, not troubled by this heat, but aware of his mind dissolving at the edges, gratings that hold back terror beginning to melt.

He pays two carters to take the wooden crates, a porter to help him to a hackney with his numerous possessions. The journey from Wapping is long, made worse by the slow progress of the two carts, making his notion of a convoy impossible. The workshops and warehouses of Wapping High Street don't interest him, he grinds his teeth and then there's more delay as they pass the Tower. Crowds of people. Militia. Banners. The people in jovial mood, not a mob propelled by hunger and hatred like those he remembers from a few years back. This is celebration, and for a moment a thump of joy in his blood makes it into a great public welcome home for the prodigal artist.

The hackney is stuck, the carts who knows where. He gets out and hears the odd sound of a speaking trumpet: 'He is gone by water!' it calls, 'He is gone by water!' again and again from somewhere in the Tower.

Cockades are blue, ribbons are blue, and blue silk banners read:

The Constitution!
Trial by Jury!
Burdett and Freedom!

The cabman jumps down. 'Been away, 'ave you, yer 'onour? Banged 'im up in the Tower. Sir Francis Burdett.'

'Of course, I know of him. Heard something of this in Valletta.'

'Where's 'at ven?'

'Malta.'

'Shockin' business. Power of ve Commons! Got to be stopped it 'ave. Look at this: the 'ole city's behind 'im, see?'

'Wonderful,' says Joseph, a younger self cheering somewhere in his memory. The citizens of London can always be relied upon to protest against authority.

It's hours before they reach John Street, for the Strand, off which John Street runs, is not so far from Burdett's house in Piccadilly, and the entire route from the Tower in which the Member of Parliament was disgracefully imprisoned is lined with ebullient people of all ranks crowding the streets, clustered in windows and wagons, standing on tables, chairs, up ladders.

Eve is among the crowds in Piccadilly with Stephen, Betsy and the baby. Not that Stephen and Betsy are particularly radical, or even know what is meant by the constitution, but everyone is here. Eve's fear at the press of people, thinking of Nursey's death, is soon forgotten, for it's a holiday, better for many than a hanging or riot, though anyone whose fingers itch for a brickbat will be disappointed.

It's a good day for street sellers, of strawberries in particular, saloop that Eve's not tasted before, ices, cherries on sticks, winkles. Stephen finds a gin seller, and when the baby becomes restive, Betsy gives him sips on her finger. He's called John. John of John Street. Betsy thinks this may help him get on in life.

Eve enjoys their company. Her threat of blackmail still holds, of course, and there's the matter of the clinking parcels, about which she's informed them she also knows. But Stephen and Betsy are neither tedious like Nursey was, nor earnest like Lucy. Nor do they bring out the bully in her, as Matthew inadvertently did, and bullying can become tiring. She's happy that Stephen has plenty of money to spend today, and anyway there's no sign of Joseph.

She wishes someone would explain the reason for this celebration, but Stephen says little about it, and she would never have got any sense out of Casey, even when she called her Nursey. She'll ask Mr Pyke, but by then it'll be over. The crowd's mood is raucous, she gives into it, gladly accepts the offer of a place on a table on top of another table to increase her chance of seeing the hero, ignoring the winks of the men who help her up.

Great cheers when Sir Francis arrives, not in the expected vast procession of carriages and walking supporters, because he's been taken by boat from the Tower to avoid possible accidents with such huge numbers of people, accidents for which he might be blamed. Piccadilly is crammed with people, there's scaffolding for an elevated view for those who'll pay, and poles with blue ribbons stick out from houses all along the road.

More cheers and shouts as he climbs out of his carriage, and in a moment he's gone. She doesn't see him, doesn't know who to look for, there's just a bundle of people rushing into the house.

The day is over. Except it's not, for already it's a species of fair, and jugglers and musicians stroll up and down, helping the crowd prolong the fun, especially since it's almost midsummer and the night will be short. Plates spin on sticks, a whole family in torn stripes tumble and stand on each other's hands in a pyramid, a one-legged black fiddler plays the songs everyone knows until a hurdy-gurdy man moves in to the cries of 'Humstrum!' and dancing takes off.

Stephen grabs Betsy, and before she knows it Eve has the baby thrust at her and must hold it tight while they jig about with the rest. She doesn't much like the baby, which has wisps of ginger hair, often cries and now feels wet, and really she'd like to drop him. When he begins to bawl she barges her way through dancing couples and pushes him at snub-nosed Betsy.

'The baby is wet. I can't hold him any more. I want you to buy me a goldfinch, Stephen. One that woman's selling over there: she's got two in cages.'

'Why'd you want ...'

'Just buy it for me!'

Betsy says she must take John home to his cradle. On their way there are gingernuts for sale, and they brush aside begging sailors with empty sleeves or on crutches, swinging their stumps.

Nearing the Strand, Eve notices a girl about her age standing, staring at what, Eve cannot tell, or perhaps she's listening out for something. Ragged, but not begging. A sudden sadness knocks her, perhaps in recognising the girl's complete aloneness.

'Take this!' she says, giving the girl the cage with its pretty bird, and then the gingernut she was about to eat.

'Come on, Miss Eve! Leave the beggar,' Stephen steers her by the shoulders and she shakes him off but goes along all the same, being weary.

'What you do 'at for?' he says.

When she turns she can't see the girl among the crowds. She'd cry, only then she'd be no better than baby John, who's howling and all blotchy.

It's late. They're eating hot rolls, which are selling well now the night's become chilly, and are astonished to see two carts outside the house in John Street with men unloading boxes and carrying them inside.

'Oh Lord,' says Betsy.

'Go round ve back,' Stephen tells her. 'For Lord's sake keep ve baby quiet.'

'Joseph's here!' Eve rushes forward, and there he is, wild-looking and dirty, brown-skinned and bearded, supervising the men.

'Joseph!' She runs up, hugs him and he pulls her to him, squeezing almost too hard. She realises she's missed his huge presence all this time.

'Eve! *Dear* Eve.'

'Joseph, it's been so dull without you.'

'Where have you been tonight? No one in the house; that's no welcome for me, is it?'

'In Piccadilly. We saw someone called Sir Francis get out of his carriage there. Stephen took me.' She'll leave Stephen's misdemeanours until tomorrow. Not mention the baby yet. 'There was dancing and jugglers and singing and lots to eat.'

'*Not* dull then.'

'Well, not tonight, no. But all the other days were.'

'So that's where Stephen was when he should have met me from the ship. Taking you about when he should have been ...' He starts to splutter. 'I've stuff for you somewhere in these boxes but, Eve, oh Eve, I'm so tired.'

The carter and his men leave, the entrance hall is piled with wooden crates. He looks gloomily about him, and Eve senses the wave of blackness pour over him. Sees tears creep down into his beard.

'Tomorrow,' he says. 'Tomorrow,' and stumbles on the way upstairs.

Eve goes to her room, washes her hands with cold water, tastes salt on her lips from Joseph's coat where her face pressed against him and where, too, she couldn't help noticing the smell of his unwashed clothes.

She lies in bed exhausted, unable to sleep, scenes from the night and Joseph's unexpected appearance flicking randomly before her closed eyes. The still strange silence, no snoring from Nursey's room. She thinks she hears the baby crying in the distant basement, but the hurdy-gurdy plays the same tune over and over in her mind and she can't stop wondering if the girl crushed the gingernut and fed it to the goldfinch.

*

After the shock of Hester's brief rebellion and the exertion from meting out nocturnal punishments to her, Rev. Mr Snead gradually becomes himself again, that is, the self he was when he'd begun to hear from the Lord, when his desire for spiritual union with Sarah began before she'd run away. He fills his sermons with phrases about the fruits of the spirit, frequently stops mid-sentence, staring down at Sarah, who is still placed by the pulpit steps, or, looking upwards, declares that he is listening to the words of the Lord speaking to him *now*. Such moments of sudden silence certainly make the congregation attend.

One Sunday he begins his sermon: 'How often have you heard me warn you sinners of the abyss that awaits you, of the ease with which you may slip into it. How often have I warned you to amend your ways and your doings! How often reminded you that the very hairs of your head are numbered, each one! *Forget these things at your peril!'*

His glare is familiar; they know what to expect.

'Today, however, I take for my text the First Epistle General of John: *He that loveth not knoweth not God; for God is love.'*

He stops in the way more recently familiar to the congregation, twisting his neck and shoulders, listening, it seems, to the voice of God. Looks down at Sarah seated at the foot of the pulpit. Hester feels dread. Nothing has changed. Her husband will have his way.

'This woman was struck dumb by the Lord. First He struck her so that she could not move her limbs. Then, He took away her voice so that she could not speak *and never will. He struck her for her sins as he will strike each one of you!'*

As usual, Sarah sits with head bowed. Does she listen, does she hear? Hester hopes she does neither.

'You all know this woman, know her for the purity of her mien, of her soul, you know her for the healing effect of her presence. For although she cannot actually cure, that being the work of the Lord, who alone both cures and kills, yet in her have people felt goodness, abandoned sin and begun to heal.

'She is a being whose spirit is utterly pure. White as the driven snow.

'*Today let you witness a marvel!* For the Lord, the Lord God of hosts, has spoken to me. He has told me that on this day Divine Grace shall descend into *this very church*, yea, even into St Wilfrid's here in Sowerthorpe.'

A general shuffling of unease, murmuring. Hester's whole body tightens.

'Yes! Today you, sinners all, shall be blessed by the Divine Grace that descendeth into this holy place, girdling us about. Today, the Lord in his glory shall honour you, yea, even those within whose hearts lurk sin and doubt.'

He cranes upwards; his shoulders seem to rise.

'For this day you will be as witnesses to the union of myself and this nameless, dumb woman in Spiritual Marriage!

'In the name of the Lord, I do take this woman to be my spiritual wife!'

With a look that's almost beatific, Snead slowly steps down towards Sarah, his hands held out to her.

The scraping of her chair on the tiled floor is the first sound. But then, as she stands, backs away from him, they hear a cry of terror.

Her voice. Distorted by despair, no words decipherable.

In a pinpoint of silence, no one breathes. Then comes a gasp, more gasps that run through the congregation. Voices call out:

'She speaks!'

'She speaks! Not dumb! She speaks!'

A hubbub as people turn to each other, amazed.

'What *did* she say?'

'No matter what words: we did *hear* her!'

'She is not dumb!'

'It be a fraud! A fraud! She speaks. It be all a lie!'

Hester, mortified, faint, sees the turmoil as people rush from the pews, some straight out of the church to spread the news, some towards Sarah. At first Snead turns to them shouting, his angular body quivering with rage.

'Woe unto them that call good evil! *He that is not with me is against me!*'

Hester rushes over to Sarah to protect her, and Mary, in church because she'd sensed a coming disaster, runs towards them both, triumph in her face, jumps onto Sarah's chair and bawls at the crowd as loudly as she is able.

'It be a fraud! Yes! Listen to *me* now!' Gradually they hush.

'Though I be loyal to Mrs Snead, who's innocent as a babe, *this be fraud*. Nor's the woman nameless. She be Sarah. *Sarah be her name.* She too's innocent as a babe.

'It is the parson you must blame. Keep from the parson! Snead be a wicked man!'

'*The dog is turned to his own vomit!*' Snead screams, backing rapidly, awkwardly, from the gathering crowd towards the vestry. Where pursuing congregants are astonished to find themselves pelted hard with sharp stones. Before the door shuts some follow him as he rushes through the room and out at the side of the church. Among these, Hett Toft retrieves a stone in each hand, but her throw is hampered by her unstable vision and, in an odd loping run, Snead quickly outstrips them all.

An unexpected, painful sensation of pity for her husband afflicts Hester, seeing him stand, at first as though he himself were struck dumb and then shriek in terror and hatred, his features seemingly askew as the people turn towards him. The sound of stones falling on the flags of the church floor! Had he always anticipated such a scene? Carried stones for just that purpose? She remembers what she'd heard, listening outside his study. And all the while she thrills at hearing Sarah's voice.

The congregants are not sure what to do. Can a parson really be wicked? Mary is known to have been brought up a Papist, so can she be believed? And is the woman, Sarah, despite what Mary says, is she part of the fraud? Perhaps she could speak all along. What *did* she say? Did she say anything?

But spiritual marriage – what's *that*?

After a while they cease to shout, leave the church, used only to experiencing guilt and boredom there. They mutter and whisper, puzzling. Swear there really were stones thrown. Just like being in the pillory! They stand in knots on corners. Argue, look behind them, jostling on the path home. No sign of Rollesby, Catton or Cragin. Gradually they disperse.

Their lives call. There are nets to mend, boats to caulk, weeds to hoe, cradles to rock.

News reaches Edward with a request that he attend at the parsonage as soon as possible.

Snead, pale, jittery, punctured, sees only one way out.

'Bissett, the woman's insane,' he says urgently. 'She has perpetrated a deception upon us and must be incarcerated in bedlam. Will you be so good as to certify her condition and effect her immediate removal?'

'Indeed I shall, Mr Snead, though I cannot imagine that anyone will believe it possible that such a fraud was perpetrated upon you *in your own house without your knowledge*, let alone without your connivance.'

'Lies! Insanity displays itself in many ways. The Devil is subtle.'

'Have you thought how you and Mrs Snead will endure the pointing fingers, the delight of the press, the shock of your superiors in the Church?'

'Mr Bissett. What I require of you is to effect the removal of this madwoman as soon as possible. I shall not enter into further discussion, especially not with someone who strives to interfere with the will of God.'

'I shall be pleased to take her from here, Snead. As it happens I am on the point of moving to a practice at a considerable distance south of here in the vicinity of Cambridge and can with ease deliver Sarah to ...'

'Don't tell me! I know nothing of "Sarah". However, that is satisfactory.' He doesn't ask what Bissett will charge, knows he'll pay whatever is demanded, however much it pains his purse.

There's more to Edward's plan than he says. He's not going south at all, of course. He feels fully justified in lying to Snead, indeed likes the idea that the man might set off in a fury in the opposite direction to him. And although once in the North Country he'll certainly visit the renowned Retreat outside York, he wants, above all, to treat Sarah himself.

With passionate urgency he explains this to Hester, putting it to her that he can only run his new practice with her by his side and that Sarah's recovery, which he intends to bring about himself, will only take place if she herself is present during it. Sarah will *never* recover without Hester, and they both know it to be true.

It's hardly a romantic proposal. And it cannot be a proposal of marriage. Yet Hester hesitates not a moment, believing that whatever she abandons in Sowerthorpe, including her faith and her reputation, will be richly replaced by love. Love that has been missing ever since she left her childhood to be a parson's wife.

With less difficulty than she expects, she persuades her husband that she must act as chaperone for Sarah on the journey to the asylum. Seeing that he can hardly bear to speak to her, that in a frenzy of agitation he acts with unnerving rapidity and rushes up to his study, locking the door behind him, she gathers together clothes for Sarah and herself as quickly as she can, together with her three childhood volumes. It is more escape than elopement. They leave in a closed carriage, Edward's belongings and sticks of furniture having been taken by carter beforehand.

'The charge will be calculated upon our arrival,' he tells Snead, though he never sends an invoice. Hester is the largest amount he'll ever charge anybody, he's amused to recount to his closest friends.

'You should have posted a receipt, Bissett,' his old friend Sessions remarks later, on a visit from London. '*Received with Thanks, one Excellent, Unappreciated Woman.* In your very best script!'

Snead's ingrained meanness, his pleasure at apparently never paying a penny for the removal of the wretched dumb woman, certainly makes it easier for him to stomach the removal of his wife.

Fury at failure spurs his retrieved disgust at the congregation. If the deep wellspring of misery that so moved Hester is never completely held back, there is no one to overhear it.

Desire for Sarah still lingers. Some nights he rises from his bed, his head pushed back against some visualised restraint, tiptoes along the corridor to her room, where he slowly pulls at the cover with long fingers in case her night-clothed body should be there, awaiting their spiritual union.

Edward's tendency has always been to look forward, and his prospects now are very good. When he stops to look back, if ever he does, he congratulates himself on freeing both Hester and Sarah, as well as securing the love he's harboured for so long. Nor is he troubled by the use Mr Snead may make in recounting the flight, as long as it doesn't reach his new patients. Whenever he can, the parson does tell how outrageously he has been abused, the object of a long-planned conspiracy between his adulterous wife, the atheist surgeon and a lunatic woman. But his connections are few; the story, doubted by most who hear it except for his still faithful supporters, laps around the nearby hamlets and coastal towns, drying up before it gets any further.

It's no surprise that the Sowerthorpe people do worst out of the situation. The villagers' local importance, their entertaining existence, all briefly illuminated, are dimmed by notoriety, their increased incomes cut off. Deprived of their dumb healer they welcome ever more itinerant preachers who trudge to the bleak mud-cliffs of Sowerthorpe. By way of consolation they never lack material for gossip with each other, vying for stories both true and invented about the doctor, the parson's wife and the dumb woman, even years after it's over. Mary, given notice to leave but not immediately replaced, so that Snead dwells in squalor for several weeks, provides the best details, and for a modest amount will allow her visitors the sight and even the touch of a nightgown supposedly worn by Sarah when Snead crept into her room and drew back the cover.

*

Joseph doesn't come out of his studio for three days, which gives the household time to pull itself together, to recall how things were or ought to be.

The place is wholly disorganised. Since giving birth, most of Betsy's daily tasks have fallen away, and Stephen increasingly stays clear of her recriminations and demands so that his household tasks, sharpening, polishing, are abandoned, too. He keeps the carriage in good shape, the horses well fed and groomed, ready to take Eve wherever she demands to go and his clinking parcels to the dealer, who gives him a fair price. Cook has kept up supplies in a dilatory way, driven by her own appetite, and now has none of the master's required foods to hand and has run out of money.

The Dighams, separately and together, have visited every so often, especially after Nursey's death, and tried to persuade Eve to live with them during Joseph's absence, but of course she'll have none of it.

Now Betsy takes the baby to a sluttish friend to tend while she rolls up her sleeves and cleans the most noticeable parts of the house. Stephen sharpens knives, cleans windows, polishes the silver he hasn't sold on. They all hope the master will be so absorbed in himself that he'll notice little. Cook borrows money from Stephen's considerable supply to find at least some of Joseph's favourite fish and meat. No one dares tell him about Nursey's death.

Days are given to unpacking crates, and since Stephen is Joseph's main help, there are no opportunities for Eve to report his activities, for which she's so usefully blackmailed him. Thinking about it, she realises she might squeeze still more out of Stephen by having *not yet* told Joseph. And Joseph finds he has to abandon his fury at Stephen failing to meet him with the carriage at Wapping when the letters he wrote to him and Mrs Casey turn up in the pocket of one of his expensive summer coats last worn in Valletta.

Dismantled boxes and their contents fill the gound floor of the house, and Betsy wonders why she bothered to clean up. For the moment there's so much noise and activity that she thinks baby John's crying won't be heard, but her friend, who's found herself more lucrative employment, is refusing to tend him any more, and sooner or later Betsy'll have to face Joseph. Most masters would throw her out with her baby, Stephen not having married her and not intending to. But she's working on convincing Stephen to pretend. She only needs a little ring and his willingness to lie.

For a week Eve and Joseph breakfast together. Eve feels her world is restored, as does Joseph. Pleased by his reappearance, Eve is barely hungry, prefers to feed on every word, drink in his enthusiasm. He talks, talks, shows her sketch after sketch to illustrate his points, describes, amuses, expatiates then rushes off to see patrons, leaving her dazzled. No doubt he'll dazzle them too and return with lists of commissions. She recognises the explosive energy that hurtles break-neck through the day, compelling all to go with it until the blackness returns. Perhaps it won't return, she hopes, and indeed soon he begins rising even earlier, leaving the house before Eve is awake, taking a plate of chops with him to eat in the carriage. And comes back late.

The carriage is occupied all day, Eve won't remind Joseph about her education with Lucy, but eventually Stephen plucks up courage to tell him of Nursey's death and remind him of the arrangement with Paternoster Row. Eve is whisked there by hackney.

She entertains Lucy with retold tales of Joseph's travels, some-times carefully exaggerated, sometimes carelessly. William Digham comes to listen, drawn away from his engraving by Lucy.

'May we persuade Joseph to call on us and tell us in his own words, do you think, Eve?' he asks gently, his smiling eyes squeezed in the folds of his face.

Eve is offended.

'Oh, he's far too busy. Out all day. Indeed I hardly see him,' she has to admit.

'Lucy, write him a note, my dear.'

Matthew returns from school and speaks up. 'I should like to see my father myself. I should like to call there.'

'I cannot imagine when you will find him at home.' Eve's tone is imperious, hearing Matthew's determination, his new confidence since removing from her orbit. 'In any case I don't suppose he wants to see you.'

It's not long before she tests the hackney driver's pliancy, takes a trip to Parmentier's and several to Gilbert and Ann's, though they're always out.

There's a day when Joseph's at breakfast again, opening his letters.

'Bill after bill. Dammit, they choose *now* to claim payment before I've the money. Haven't *begun* on the commissions yet. Look at them all! Rumball's, Brailsford, Pickett, Fogg, Richards queuing up for their pennies! They'll have to wait, make their threats and wait.

'And what's this? Parmentier's? Haven't been there since before I went away. Remember, Eve, I used to take you to choose peppermint drops and ices? How dare they! Or they've made a mistake. I'll ignore it.'

Eve stays quiet, then protests: 'But you're rich, I know you are, Joseph! You could buy me a pianoforte.'

'Oh, I was rich, I was, but it's mostly gone, and travel's expensive you know. Still, I shall be rich again, and *then* you can have your pianoforte. Clementi, Tottenham Court Road. Thirty guineas at least, I should think. No, I *shall* be rich once I produce the big paintings. Yes, I ought to begin, I know I should. Enough people are interested. But this war is losing money for everyone, they haven't the money to buy. I always said it was a folly, and I wasn't the only one. Everything's lost its value. The papers are full of bankruptcies.'

'What's bankruptcies?'

'When people have no money left and are sent to the Fleet. Or worse. Sometimes they shoot themselves.'

She doesn't ask about the Fleet, but obviously it's a prison. Then when Joseph spends all his time in his studio she's pleased that he must be painting and soon will be able to pay Parmentier's bill. But cross, too, that he's gone again, that she doesn't see him, that he has no time for her at all. Once more the days are dull.

She gets Stephen to drop her in Piccadilly instead of at Lucy's. Joseph will hear about the outing before long, she hopes, and take notice of her again. Stephen says he'll do it just this once and drive all the way round and meet her on the corner of Piccadilly and Haymarket in an hour. Secretly she thinks she'll spend much more time than that, but he'll just have to wait for her.

She enjoys walking along the street, despite having vaguely

hoped there'd still be music and hilarity left over from the night when Joseph returned, knowing there couldn't be. The pavements are crowded, the road, too, but she can choose where to go, whether to walk fast or slowly, what to look at and no one will tell her to hurry or come on. She feels superior in the gown made from an exotic material Joseph brought back from Malta. Exults in her freedom, turning all ways to glance at fashion and frumpiness, servants in wigs and tails, ladies with parasols and muddied skirts, beggars, painted carriages with gaudy crests. Locks and watches, boots, shirts, cabinets, she stops at shops with strange objects behind their panes: leather pipes, leather pots, boxes and buckets or extraordinarily real flowers of silk.

'Pretty clo's, my gel!' A hand on her arm, gravelly voice. Two women, not too clean, paw her dress, her shawl, her bonnet.

'You on yer own, young lady? Come wiv us, we'll show you somefink, shan't we?' The other woman nods. They haven't many teeth.

'No! I don't want to.'

'*Come* along. We'll give you even better clo's, stead o' vese. Vese is *rags* compared wiv what we'll give you.' They jostle her against a shop window, push her towards a doorway. They're strong, but Eve's used her fists before.

'Go away! Go away!' She hits out, people turn to look and the women disappear through an alley between buildings.

'Not hurt, miss?' a man asks her. 'They was after your clothes. To sell in Rag Fair.'

'I'm not hurt, no. Thank you.'

'Truly? You were wise to fight them off, I must say. They'll leave a child naked once they've taken the clothes off it.'

'I'm not a child.' She wishes he would go, wants to move away herself. 'I'm quite unharmed, and in fact I'm in a hurry. Good day.'

She's taken aback by the incident, by the women's clawing hands, but presses on, mustn't give up now, keeps further away from buildings, while avoiding the hoofs and wheels showering clothes with dung. A dog stands in the road, barking incessantly, a rare sedan chair forces her to move from her path down the centre of the pavement, its liveried carriers bouncing up and down, its passenger surely shaken.

She reaches Green Park, would go in, away from the crowds, but remembers hearing something about danger from thieves. She'd like to cross to the other side of the road, but can't see how to do it without being knocked down, let alone miring her shoes and the hem of her gown completely.

Turning back, she finds a quieter side street with houses and a large building in the distance, perhaps the king's palace. She noticed people looking at her in Piccadilly, but here they all stare. Is she dirty, she wonders, but no, of course it's because there's nobody with her. The other girls she's seen were shopping with their mamas or else they were obviously beggars. No one could think her a beggar, and probably they'll think her mama is visiting a friend.

'Well, young lady, you *are* a fine one!' She's aware of a gold watch chain across a stomach, a smiling face. 'Are you off to the palace?' He laughs.

'Certainly not. I'm taking the air.' She's heard the phrase before, likes the sound of it.

'I see. And you would like some company, I'm certain.'

After the horrid women, this man is pleasant, and will perhaps protect her from anybody else who might attack her. 'For a little while. Until Stephen picks me up.'

'Stephen. I see. No need for him. Let's leave him out of it. So, you're taking the air, seeing who comes along?'

'Yes.' She won't explain. He might demand to take her back to Joseph.

'And your name, my pretty one?'

'Eve Cranch.'

'Well, I don't know about Cranch, but Eve will do well enough. Do you dwell in the Garden of Eden?' He laughs rather a lot at this.

'Of couse not!'

'A wise answer. A straightforward young lady. Very good. So will you tell me your price, my young beauty?'

'Price?'

'Good heavens, girl, yes! You're from round here, are you not? St James's Place, I suppose. I'll walk with you. Mrs Dobell's. Surprised I've not noticed you there before.'

'No, I live in John Street near the Strand.'

'Aha! Trying new fields. Oh my, you'd better beware. There's a lot of competition in these streets. Good thing I've come along: we don't want any hair-pulling or eyes scratched out, do we?'

So he *will* protect her from danger, whatever it is. 'No.'

'Well, we shall take a cab to your place then. It's not far.'

Eve's tired. Her shoes pinch. Although the morning's been preferable to Paternoster Row, she's had enough of it and would like to go home, where, if she's lucky, she might come across Joseph. If he takes her home it'll be quicker than standing on a busy corner looking out for Stephen.

The man is not poor, his clothes are those of someone well-off, he seems more or less kindly, though he's an older man than Joseph and smells strongly of tobacco and a sweet, greasy perfume which disturbs her inexplicably. He grasps her upper arm hard and she realises she must get away from him.

She hears a rasping bark as he shouts after her, takes steps towards her, but, skirts in one hand, she runs off rapidly the way she came.

Quite unsure how to meet up with Stephen, the attraction of Green Park is too great to resist. She remembers the cows there once, when she was little. Nursey lumbering after her.

Through the gates, the great stretch of green lies before her, but she remains on the path. The next minute she's in a crowd, pushing and pummelling her along. Are they after her clothes again, but no, they're not trying to drag her away, rather knocking against her, bumping into her, forcing her from one side to the other so that she nearly falls, young men and women about the age of Stephen, only dirtier.

'Come on, miss. What yer got fer us?'

'Wery nice vat gownd o yourn!'

Hands finger it, jostle and jog her on both sides.

'Don't mind 'im, miss. We'll look after yer, keep yer compny all ve way.'

'Goin' 'ome is yer?'

Then there's Stephen himself, of a sudden, barging through the crowd, whip in hand and the people scatter.

'They'll 'ave robbed ya, Miss Eve. Oh God, what'll ve master say to vis? Come on back to ve carriage.'

He's right. Her purse has gone, her pockets entirely empty, hanging inside out.

Back at the house she tears off her clothes and orders Betsy to stop her work, and fill a hot bath. She scrubs herself with desperate vigour, orders the water thrown out and the bath filled again.

Stephen reports as much as he saw, and Joseph reprimands Eve. He is annoyed, and Eve is even more convinced he's only concerned about himself. He seems to take no notice when she stalks from the room, slams several doors, refuses to eat, cries herself to sleep. She becomes a very young child again. Hunger and boredom soon take over. Now that Joseph is back Pyke calls, and it is only he who has patience. His presence calms her.

6

_____

HESTER WORRIES THAT THE JOURNEY from Sowerthorpe will disturb Sarah in some incalculable way. She explains to her as simply as she can, and stays close to her.

'We are going away from that wicked man, Sarah. You will be safe. We shall both be safe.'

Sarah looks at her; surely she is listening? Her outburst in the church, almost speech, is not followed by anything more, but that she uttered a sound at all fires Hester with hope.

How extraordinary it is to hear herself speak of 'that wicked man' when that man is her _husband_, and to know that she is _escaping_ from him. While she appears calm for Sarah's sake, she is elated. She might faint. She might shout aloud for joy.

'We shall live in Edward's house, Sarah. All will be well there.' She understands how it might be possible to die of happiness.

At first she'd feared that Snead might follow them, make them turn back, but Edward assured her that Snead would not dare send the law in pursuit since he'd want to save his own skin. Besides, Edward told him they were going south. A worthwhile lie. He sits up on the box with the coachman, looking in on the two women whenever the coach stops. As the day cools he joins them inside. They must stay the night at an inn, where he tells the landlord he is accompanied by his deaf sister and her companion.

He asks Hester what her name was before she married.

'I was Hester Fulbeck.'

'Use that name which will not be completely false. And in your own mind it will underline your separation from Snead. Just for the journey. Once we're in Hawkswith it will be different.'

His thoughts race ahead of her. She must catch up.

'You are right, Edward. I have not stopped to consider. I am confused.'

For Edward there must always be clarity. 'It is true you are breaking the civil law in leaving your husband, and I am breaking the law in taking you from him. But the cause is great! Neither of us can ever forget that. Together we shall help Sarah recover, help her to find herself again.

'I congratulate myself on removing two vulnerable women from the clutches of an evil man. I am certain God would approve of what we do.'

'You are not a believer, Edward.'

'No. But if God exists he would agree. I know I'm right.'

It is not arrogance. It is confidence whose strength draws her.

They set off early the following day and Hester, although fascinated by all that passes outside the carriage windows, has time, while Sarah dozes, to attend to her conscience.

She is breaking the law. It is an offence against God to break her marriage to John Snead, a marriage consecrated in church. No doubt Edward could help her argue away her anxiety, yet she must work out how to reconcile herself without him, for as an atheist he would have no problems with God.

For a long time now she has hated the Church, in permanent taint from her husband's vicious preaching, his hypocrisy, his madness. Why did the bishop not stop the terrible abuse of Sarah; had he not called John to interview? Surely he questioned him. Here she is, a parson's wife hating the parson, his church, the whole establishment.

Yet she could not abandon God, in whom she's been brought up to believe, if without dogma. With a rush of joy then dismay, she realises she can at last write to Sophie. What shall she write? What can she tell her mother?

God will forgive me. I shall tell them the truth. They will understand and they will forgive me, too.

This, like a prayer, repeats itself whenever guilt tries to pull down sheer delight, when in dark moments Snead overshadows her memory.

Holly Lodge is a large, symmetrical stone house on the edge of a sparse village among wooded hills and moorland, a landscape that could hardly be more different from Sowerthorpe. There's a low front hedge with too many holly trees, but behind the house good-sized flower and kitchen gardens, a small orchard of apple, plum and pear trees. A coach house is attached for a horse and a donkey trap, both of which will be vital, for Edward's patients are spread around for miles. He'll need to buy a sturdy, reliable horse to take him up steep ways in all weathers, at all times of day and night. He only used a donkey trap in Sowerthorpe, and that rarely.

The house is on three floors, with a surgery downstairs in which Edward can examine the lesser sick, a long hall with two benches and a dispensary. The previous incumbent, old Mr Carnforth, too often found dozing at the bedside, leaves his furniture which, archaic and fusty, will do until they've time to replace it, though they remove the moralising watercolours from the hallway.

The three of them look round the house together. Hester begins to talk as she's not done for years, even to chatter, pointing out how they might improve this room and that, what colours would go well in certain rooms with more or less light. She opens windows.

'Sarah, would you like this for your bedroom?' she asks, ever hopeful of provoking speech.

No answer, but Sarah has clearly heard, for she nods, and in a small flash there's a smile, gone a second after.

'We'll make new curtains. You can choose material.' Downstairs, in a back sitting room looking out onto the garden, Sarah reaches for some paper, a pencil.

'Write something, yes!' Hester almost shouts. Edward puts his hand on her arm in gentle restraint.

He finds a book of blank sheets for Sarah small enough to keep in her pocket with a pencil.

She writes:

Is this America?

'No, Sarah, it's England. Hawkswith, in the county of Yorkshire.'

I don't live here.

'You do live here! For the present, until you are well. Edward and I shall look after you.'

Later Edward warns her not to excite Sarah too much.

'I love your care and enthusiasm for Sarah, Hester. But we must be cautious. The state of her mind is fragile. That she hasn't spoken for so long except for the outburst which, you say, wasn't even speech, tells us how deeply submerged she is.'

'You are right. I shall calm down.' But he'd said 'I love'!

'Not with me, though.' He holds her. For the first time kisses her.

*

Eve takes time to recover from her experiences in Green Park. Massive August thunderstorms assault the city, bombard it with hailstones, inundate sewers that swamp the streets with stinking sludge. Lightning kills at random. All of which confirm to her the evil nature of the world, and she can take no pleasure in her fifteenth birthday.

Kindly, precise Pyke has two strategies to aid her. Now that Joseph has finally agreed to it, he'll begin her tuition soon, introduce her to subjects that will engage her intelligence, distract her from herself. Meanwhile, he talks to her about Sarah and about Tom.

'I never saw them together, because their decision to go to America was made at the last moment.' It is not yet time to tell the girl her mother was already married then, to a man whose deception affected the lives of many, including his own.

'Why did they go there?'

'It had become hard, almost impossible to hold the views Tom held, Tom and us, his friends. It was certainly impossible to express them aloud, for you never knew who was listening. We thought the government corrupt, that there should be suffrage for all. We were inspired by Tom Paine, whose matchless writings we'll read together, Eve. We wanted all to change. But a new law prevented meetings in large numbers, so that we crept into corners in which, even there, there were spies.' The husband, one James Wintrige, a man without conscience. A spy playing the plausible fool, whom the whole Society failed to detect.

'You see, Eve, it was safer to flee. More importantly, in America there was a real prospect of democracy.'

'But *you* didn't go there.'

'I hadn't Tom's courage. Besides, I could work here; apothecaries are always needed. We're physicians to the poor. Tom was a printer and bookseller who sold pamphlets attacking the government, and wrote them too, so he was constantly watched, constantly in danger of arrest and imprisonment.'

'Why did Mama go?'

'It's true she had plenty to do in Sam Battle's coffee house. She worked so hard I wonder she had any time for thought. But she said Tom came there sometimes and talked to her, and it became clear that she held the same views as he. Then all of a sudden they knew they loved each other.'

Eve wonders about this; will dwell on it often in years to come. Sudden love.

Pyke says: 'I wish I'd seen them together.' He pauses, thinking back. 'He was not a tall man, Tom, but dark, his eye held you. Sarah was rosy-faced, that's what one noticed first about her.'

Eve is entranced. She'll tap Pyke for every drop of memory.

'What did Mama wear?'

He smooths thin strands of white hair. 'I am quite useless when it comes to describing women's clothes. She was a handsome woman, everyone said so.'

'And Papa, what did he wear?'

'What can I say? He dressed as we all did. Except that, oh yes, he wore a red neckerchief. Yes, always a red one.'

It's as Pyke hoped. She occupies her mind with the reconstruction of her parents. Easier than recalling appearances, Pyke tells her about Tom's ideas, what it was to be a radical, how before the government bore down on them, the Corresponding Society would meet and debate, and how sometimes there were huge meetings in places like St George's Fields and Mary-la-bonne when whole families gathered, the men with their wives and children, and listened to rousing speeches. How the crowd laughed and wept as one.

His own pale melancholy lights at these memories, delights at stirring the girl's imagination. For he is certain they'd be talking to her like this, Tom and Sarah, were they alive now.

'I remember Mama telling me about the big meetings, Mr Pyke, even when I was little.'

'I'm not surprised.'

And gradually her father takes on a presence and her mother lives again in Eve's mind, so that one day she even thinks to address them, to question them. Although she struggles to recall the sound of her mother's voice, her interior monologue, recently so bitter, becomes a tentative dialogue.

'I like Mr Pyke. He is a good man, isn't he, Mama?' She feels an answer.

'I used to think he looked like that engraving of a skeleton in one of my books, but I was quite wrong, he's just thin, isn't he?' Senses agreement.

It's much harder with Tom, yet somebody is there, behind Mama, nodding firmly.

Pyke is an atheist, not that he instructs Eve in his way of thought, but he will turn a sceptical eye on notions, particularly those that originated with Nursey.

'Mama said she and Tom were deists.'

'Ah yes. Many people in America are deists. They believe in a God who is remote.'

'What do you think, Mr Pyke?'

'I cannot believe, and yet it is true I do not know God does not exist. And, to anticipate your objection, that means I'm not an atheist after all. I'm agnostic.'

Such distinctions are not interesting to Eve. She dares to ask, 'Do you think my mother and father are in heaven, as Nursey used to say they are?'

'Heaven is a human invention, as is hell; there are no such places. People like poor Mrs Casey, and there are many of them, like to think in terms of reward and punishment. The good go to heaven, the bad to hell. We can make our own lives heavenly or hellish of course.'

'Where are they, then?'

'There are those who believe that all our souls are part of one great soul.'

'Oh.'

She tries this idea, but Pyke's re-creation of Sarah and Tom cry their individuality to her. Not that they are revenants. Nor is it ancestor worship. They are her father and mother, alive to her if to no one else. She feels them watch her, provide comfort and fortification for her. Which she needs, for Joseph is hurtling downwards.

*

There are signs of progress in Sarah. Those almost-smiles appear more often and she cries less, the strange, soundless weeping that has always been so disturbing, ever since the collier brought her into the parsonage. Book and pencil are with her always so that she can write wherever she is in the house. Edward and Hester catch her looking intently at their faces, fathoming them, unable to comprehend why they are together, why they are no longer in the place they were before, even though they have explained. There are episodes of grief when she shakes her head, writing *I don't know* on her pad. One day there is something almost like laughter but soundless, though they soon realise it's probably in imitation of them.

Comes an early autumn evening, Sarah goes to bed, Edward is not attending a patient for once and he and Hester read, knowing that in an hour they too must go upstairs each to their separate rooms. A tense awareness unsettles the air which has cooled rapidly through an open window.

'Hester, I must ask you.'

'Yes, Edward?'

'Hester if you were a spinster I'd ask you to marry me. Would you accept me?'

'Why yes!' She laughs.

'I'm serious. If we are to pass as man and wife, as we've agreed we must in order to be accepted here, then it were best we were as married as possible even without some parson's blessing.'

All this while they sit demurely in wing chairs opposite each other.

Hester is serious, too.

'Yes, that makes sense. But I ...'

He is ready to burst. 'Oh Hester, cast aside these old rules! I love you. I've loved you for years.'

Without hesitation she says, 'Edward, I love you as I have never loved anyone.'

'Then surely that is enough! Were Snead to die we should marry immediately. No, no! I don't mean murder. Don't look horrified!

'God knows what we feel for each other and knows that it is good.'

'It is easy for *you* to say that.'

'Deny it, Hester!'

'I can't. I can't know God's mind. I can hope what you say is true. And I can pray.'

'Begin tonight! May I come upstairs with you, or would you rather pray down here?'

He reaches for her hand, they climb the stairs in the quiet house, open the door to Edward's room and Hester's prayers must wait till the following day.

The Hawkswith practice is almost too widespread for Edward to handle on his own. Typhoid breaks out frequently in the district, his constant attempts to inoculate people against smallpox meet the usual resistance, and now that the war is almost over there's an additional burden of the returning wounded, patched up abroad, yet still in need of attention. Far more of them than just the ragged-beard beggars everybody has stopped noticing for years. Shoals of maimed and dazed.

There are wounds closer to home, too, for disturbance is alive in the north: men threatened by machines, rioting by day, breaking in, breaking up by night, shooting, shot at. They terrify with the cry 'Ned Ludd', sudden in the dark. Or scrawl it on scraps of paper nailed to the shards of smashed machinery. The 'General' is extolled in songs sung out, or murmured sotto voce.

That his patients are sometimes cured, mended, helped to live, give birth, continues to satisfy him, even when he must ride a difficult path, then sit for hours by the bedside, returning home after daybreak. Of course they die, too, frequently endure acute infections, pain, occasionally amputations, but he avoids the awful burden of the supposed incurables with whom he was raised. He sends those few deemed mad, when he's sure they really are, twenty miles to the Retreat, run by the Quaker Tukes, a place of much greater enlightenment than his father's madhouse.

He's never shaken off a fascination for the mind. The new theories, about which he heard so much as a student, intrigue him; the new practices which point up the inhumanity of his father's coarse methods, employ reason, calm, even humility.

Edward watches Sarah discreetly but often, aware that at any moment she might reveal a thought, a movement that would help him know how best to treat her. He becomes somewhat obsessed. He's sure she's not insane, though no doubt others would diagnose her as such. She has a nervous disorder. For a while he wonders if it might be *nostalgic melancholia*, for she seems to long for something out of reach, but no, that is inadequate. Melancholia is a large category.

'It's always possible that it might have been caused by a hallucination, you know, what's known as *hallucinatio maniacalis*. And that would make care very difficult.' It's not that Edward wants to impress Hester, he can't help wanting to share his thinking with her after all those years when they were hardly free to exchange a greeting, let alone talk. When they glimpsed each other down the street and hastened forwards with desire and trepidation.

Hester, untrained in anything, much less categories of lunacy, has her own view.

'No, no, Edward. I'm convinced that something actually happened that made her stop speaking, made her forget her past life. I'm sure of it.' Of course Hester knows Sarah better than Edward, and he trusts her judgment, her common sense.

After a while Sarah begins to help in the house, especially in the kitchen, where cooking is apparently familiar even if she barely knows who she is.

Hester asks: 'When did you learn how to cook and bake?'

I don't know. Then. In that other time.

They are fond of her. Of course Hester has been for years, and however strange her silence, Sarah is a woman of grace and affection. Finally together, Edward and Hester are not disturbed by her constant presence. It is enough that they *are* together.

*

The results of Joseph's frenetic activity away from the house all day are good for a short while, as the naval battle scenes sell well. Galleries, loyal clients are swayed by his patriotic enthusiasm, his reasonable prices, and engravings of the paintings bring in income, too.

But his new, huge, Romantic oils are more than people can take. Critics sneer:

'Mr Young's new work is indeterminate, marked by vagueness of brushwork, considerable oddity of palette and lack of a recognisable subject.'

'Standing before the huge painting with its grandiose frame, one longs for a figure, a building, something to tell us that this is the work of a human being. Even a mule would do, but one can discern neither bird nor bush.'

'We dare to speculate whether the heat of the Mediterranean may not have turned Mr Young's mind.'

Patrons drift away.

The clamour for debt repayment grows. Since he's not followed Arthur Pickmore's advice for addiction treatment from Dr Henry Sessions, opium in its dilute form, laudanum, is ever needful. Indeed, he takes to brewing his own dilution, infusing opium with quince juice and a handful of bruised spices.

By strange coincidence, Henry Sessions calls one day to arrange for a double portrait of himself and his new wife, Laetitia. The name seems familiar, yet Joseph cannot remember why.

The discussion takes place on a bad day, too early, before Joseph has broken through night's crust. Nevertheless he's blearily aware that Sessions is watching him closely. He quickly forgets the whole episode when, shortly after, a letter arrives cancelling the commission.

Desperate for money, he decides to produce a book for students and that class of young people with no pressing need to work yet with sensibility, for whom drawing and painting might occupy idle hours. This will raise money surely because of his past reputation. He calls on the publisher/printer Thomas Tegg opposite Bow Church in Cheapside, who draws up a contract demanding Joseph cover every possible aspect of the subject in a way that will strain Joseph's patience to the limit. It will be a pocket edition and not sell for much. He grinds his teeth, is intolerably bad-tempered for several weeks.

Drawing, designing, painting with oil, watercolour, landscapes, portraits, engraving, everything needful is present, prefaced by the words: 'Genius is absolutely necessary, yet it will not alone suffice.' The first phrase is obviously true, and he groans at the need to write the second.

He provides examples throughout, but those of English country scenes and fashionable figures against architectural backgrounds are dull, whereas those showing how to draw the Passions are much more striking, particularly the faces of Fear and Weeping and the female face of Love, which for those who knew her, looks remarkably like Sarah Battle.

Ploughing through everything required by Tegg, he details methods of making paint, for example King's Yellow, using powdered arsenic and sulphur, or burnt hartshorn by burning horn. He warns how to detect when there's adulteration of vermilion with red lead. How in making ultramarine, you 'take the lapis lazuli and break it into very small pieces'. *Young's Guide to the Fine Arts* sells modestly, mops up a few debts.

But the dwindling of his fortune seeps into the household. There are fewer ices, meat is fattier, less frequently served, there are too many pies with almost nothing but fragments of potato lurking inside, no sign of a crystallised fruit. Where's Betsy? She's only there on a Friday, helping in the kitchen, and it's not because of her troublesome infant, for Joseph waved away the presence of Betsy's child and her lack of marriage to Stephen as beyond his caring. Betsy is taking in laundry in the room she shares with her sluttish friend to make up her lost earnings and Eve realises this from the strangely puffy, bleached-white hands that clear dishes hastily, carelessly from the table once a week.

The grand carriage is sold and Stephen, still employed, takes over many of Betsy's tasks instead. The loss of his pride and joy, the missed company of his fine horses, renders him quite stiff with shock, far less genial, the smallpox pits in his skin somehow deeper. He's relieved to have employment at all, of course, since he's gone through most of his gains. There's little left in the house worth selling, but in any case filching seems wrong now the master's actually at home.

Joseph takes hackneys when he needs to go any distance, or when carting around his unwanted canvases. A year after his return he 'celebrates' the sale of carriage and horses, for which he gets much less than he paid, with a loudly miserable meal in the dusty dining room where Gilbert, Ann and Eve are present.

How different this meal is from the night they toasted the end to slavery! Although that's not an event Eve recalls with unmixed happiness, this is simply a drunken rant by Joseph accompanied by many bottles of wine and slightly more food than usual. A rant unstoppable except by the occasional interjection from Gilbert. The best thing about it is the exchange of looks between Eve and Ann, silently acknowledging their meetings while Joseph was away. Though Gilbert is reluctant to betray his friendship, glances between Ann, Eve and him share recognition, pity, tried patience.

Ruddy with too much drink, frequently thumping the table, Joseph bawls: 'Year after year of hopeless war. We even fired on Copenhagen, dear God! And who is winning in the Peninsula, I ask you? They tell us we are, but why believe papers in the pay of the government? The Portuguese, the Spanish smashed to bits by Boney, *we failed them*!

'But *everything's* corrupt, so what else can we expect? Fat York snuggling all day with his Mrs Clarke. Such a pretty nightcap! Rowlandson's cartoons are the best, oh how I wish I'd stuck to caricatures. Think of the money he's making! Oh, why didn't I? Oh *why*?' Tears gather, but he pulls himself together.

'At least I'm not a failure like that lunatic William Blake. What a wretched thing his exhibition was before I left! Trash!'

Eve would shout a protest. Blake was a friend of Papa's, she knows. But Joseph probably wouldn't even hear her.

'The king's mad, Fox is dead, Sheridan's disintegrating. Perceval, that *evangelical skull*! Imprisoned Frenchmen escape and laugh at us. Everybody's bankrupt, unpaid workmen riot and destroy: who wouldn't do it? *I* would, wouldn't you, Gil, smash the frames, *smash* them!'

He stands up, looming over his frowning guests, glass in hand, shatters it on the edge of the table. 'Fire on mill owners, Gil. *Gil?*' But there's no moment in which Gil, shifting in his chair with embarrassment, can respond. 'The world's vile, everything's vile, vile, vile!' Joseph slumps, dropping a second glass onto the remains of the other, lays his head on his arms and sobs loudly.

Neither Lucy nor William Digham are present at this dinner, nor is Matthew, who, adopted by William and endlessly disappointed by his father, now calls himself Matthew Digham. He is beginning to learn the skills of drawing and engraving from William when his school hours are over, and the results are promising.

Of course Nursey is not there.

'And that Great Royal Ape! Bloated by excess, stuffing himself in every possible way and bailed out from gross spending *time after time.* I drew his monstrousness way back when I was still selling satires, we all did, who could resist portraying that hideous mountain of flesh! *His* debts are paid off while everyone *else* plunges into the abyss of bankruptcy and the poor live ten to a room in houses that daily tumble into heaps of rubble, that's *if they survive being trampled underfoot first!*'

Eve leaves at this point. She has her own guilt to smother, her treatment of Nursey which grew from impatience and impertinence to disobedience to sheer unkindness to completely forgetting the woman's existence. The remorse Eve feels extends to her dead mother, who chose Nursey for her in the first place.

'I'm sorry, I'm sorry, Mama,' she murmurs over and over, hoping Sarah's still there, wherever 'there' is, to protect her.

Pyke, whose acquaintance with melancholy is lifelong, detects the complex sadness that wells up in Eve and doubles his drive to educate her. They work together at quadratic equations, read through *Elements of Chemistry in a New Systematic Order Containing All the Modern Discoveries* ('This was still in French when I was young,' he tells her), and plan to tackle the new translation of Linnaeus, attractively entitled *Animal Kingdom.*

He borrows a friend's telescope and his copy of the Royal Society's Herschel star catalogue.

'You will be pleased to hear that this was not written by William Herschel but by his sister, Caroline. There's an example for you! Your mother would have liked that.'

He brings his small table spinet to the house, tunes it, plays her a Purcell corant, a saraband, begins teaching her the names of the notes so that before long she masters a simple minuet.

Concentration banishes all other thought.

*

Edward and Hester are happier than either has ever been. But they have two main concerns: Sarah's recovery and the possibility that their unmarried state will be discovered. They are optimistic about Sarah's recovery not least because the terrible threat of Snead has been removed. Hester dares to think that affection and kindness may be enough to encourage the return of speech. However, exposure is a constant worry, for it could damage Edward's practice. So in the house they dare employ only stolid, incurious Margaret to clean and wash. They inherit Peter, a stooping, sour-faced bachelor who doubles as groom and gardener. After Edward pulls three throbbing teeth with little pain, Peter develops a fierce loyalty to the new surgeon, employing his miserable expression against all outsiders.

There's no communication with Snead since the escape from Sowerthorpe. As there's no possibility of divorce, they have no option but to pass themselves off as married and hope the painful past remains hidden, including the dumb woman fraud. As in most parts of Britain, public interest is parochial, and apart from the Duke of Wellington's victories in Spain, or scandals among the rich, renowned and royal and, briefly, the assassination of the prime minister Perceval, it tends to fix on the segment of a county, the town, the village where the readers live. They may yet be safe.

It's not easy for Hester to lie, even if she likes the sound of 'Mrs Bissett'. Her upbringing taught her to be scrupulous.

'Oh, of course we should avoid lying if we can,' Edward agrees. 'But if the cause is good, if it is the best thing to do then we should do it. You and I shall do well here. Together we shall help the people of Hawkswith, and together we shall care for Sarah.'

'Yes. Now, Edward, how often do you find good causes for not telling the truth?'

'Oh, who knows? But Hester, I lied to my own mother when I left home. Poor, dear Mother! She tried to kill my father. Or rather, she was found with a knife. He manacled her with his own hands 'lest she harm herself'. What nonsense! A man completely without feelings. From our private quarters in the asylum she was taken down to live in misery with the insane.

'I had to get away. I was going to tell her I was leaving and say goodbye, but instead I said I would come back that afternoon. I didn't. Her mind was so disturbed. That was not good. It was cowardice.'

'Poor woman.'

'I shall always regret it.'

'Did you not try to see her another time?'

'She died not long after. I received a terse note from my father.'

'I hope you will not lie to me.'

'I haven't yet. But if I ever do you can be sure it will be for a good reason.'

'That's not entirely consoling, Edward.'

There is so much to learn about Edward. For Hester the new life is hard, but at the same time joyous in ways that she finds constantly astonishing, after a childhood constricted by death and poverty, and an early adulthood oppressed by marriage and unwilling connivance in a shameful deception. Now, she and Edward share the ambition to retrieve the person Sarah was. Not that they knew her before, can only guess what she might have been like. In all those deadened years in the Snead parsonage Sarah had been half a woman, a body with an apparently empty mind, lost. Nameless to the outside world. Now, surely they might find her, might discover, among other things, why she tried to kill herself, why she threw herself into the sea. They are careful, delicate with her. One day she will speak, they hope, one day remember her past, but it is hard to help her.

She writes in her careful hand:

It is not America
I was in America

'Did you like America, Sarah?'
Her eyes fill. She writes no more that day.
Another time she writes:

You say this is England
was it England then, in the other time?
but not here

'Before you came here you lived with me and ...'

'Sarah, you lived with Hester and a bad parson. And before that you lived in America, so you tell us, but also somewhere else in England I am sure.'

She takes this in slowly, wondering.

Where was the other place – where?
That place
There is someone – someone
someone I must find

Time and place float indistinctly. They cannot answer her.

Light
I dreamed of light
Where I lived was dark

Everything she writes suggests that her memory remains in turmoil. Yet despite that, she recognises mundane objects for what they are, washes, dresses, eats and drinks with her two friends, operates a kind of mechanical existence. Only her fragmentary smiles, her quizzical looks, her tears, make her something other than an automaton, though Edward does not use that word to Hester who, he knows, would reject it.

Partly through necessity Edward suggests that Sarah help in the dispensary, where liquids must be measured into clear or brown glass bottles and corked up, those 'not to be taken' with ridged sides to alert fingers fumbling in the dark, powders and pills weighed or counted into small boxes. He's reluctant to prescribe much, yet patients will insist on having something to swallow or rub on. Since he'd rather they didn't buy the offerings of quacks, he makes up simple, often anodyne mixtures, charging little, unless the patient is rich. In the dispensary the large storage jars are labelled, a chart of clear instructions is nailed to the wall. Sarah must match directions on Edward's prescriptive notes, measure out the required drugs with precision. At first he guides her closely then notices her absolute accuracy and concentration; wonders if she once did similar work.

She shakes her head when he asks her, pauses for some moments, writes:

I did pour from bottles. In that place.

'Was that America, do you think?' Edward asks Hester.

The people of Hawkswith take to Mr Bissett, once they accept the fact that Mr Carnforth really has gone away to live with his widowed sister in Northamptonshire, and once they hear that people of the *highest standing* have agreed to let their entire family be inoculated by the new man. Mr Bissett is an MD from Edinburgh, they say; can turn his hand to every kind of medicine, unlike old Carnforth.

They like Mrs Bissett, too, though at first she seems to have little medical understanding when they come calling at the house, so that they suppose the marriage to be a recent one. Of course they can't know that she's seen great numbers of ill people who hobbled or were carried into the presence of the 'healing dumb woman' though without ever knowing how they might be treated. Now, she learns rapidly when to help Edward into his greatcoat and boots and rush him to his horse, when to protect him from demands for physic that can wait till morning.

As to the other lady, apparently deaf and dumb, though she's said by the Bissetts to be a friend, the villagers are not fooled and know she's obviously a sister of one or other of them. An unfortunate woman though handsome in a way. Seems to be helpful about the house, but it's of no use trying to talk to her for she just looks blank.

*

Joseph careers towards collapse. He's plunged so often in his life, but now with actual disaster threatening, he judders downwards by a different route, through an extended recollection so vivid that most of the time he keeps it deeply concealed within himself. When he lets it surface he is stricken.

Over clear and cloudless land, the moment in the balloon's basket when Sarah, her face alight from within, seems a divine being. He knows he must catch that look on paper, tucking the sketch into his pocket book which he wraps in oilcloth against contact with sea-water.

'It's the best thing I've ever done,' he tells himself.

Then all is swept away by the violence of wind hurling them out of the sky, dragging the balloon along the ground, suddenly throwing it up again hundreds of feet into the squall. The vital valve rope slips from the aëronaut's hands, there's nothing more he can do and they hurtle towards the sea.

Ships that might rescue them are still distant and Jacques makes them throw everything out of the basket to lighten the load, delay landing. Paints, sketchbooks recording the whole journey, Battle's picnic basket with its plates, cutlery, orgeat bottles and wine glasses, boxes of equipment, telescopes, barometer, all, all must go.

Lower, lower, they're just above the water, he's already soaked by spray. Huge, heavy, knowing his weight to be greater than anything else they've carried, rejected, driven by despair, Joseph climbs over the basket edge and drops into the waves.

In fact it is too late. Deflated balloon, basket with Jacques and Sarah crash down soon after and while Joseph swims towards a nearing boat he sees Sarah come up and sink, up and sink. He grasps some floating debris, remembers nothing else.

Always in the same order, always the same details, but too terrible to be recalled often, Joseph throws himself out so that Sarah will be saved, Sarah, the woman he loves. He will lighten the basket of his great, clumsy, unwanted body and she will be rescued. He throws himself out to die, knowing that the woman he loves loves someone else.

There is little point in breaking out of this waking nightmare once it has begun, for there is no relief. The worst is that he survived and she didn't. That his action, the one courageous act of his life, made no difference.

7

___

WHILST DEFEAT HAS YET TO COME for Boney in Russia later that year, constant news of battles won by British forces in Spain brings cheer to the streets of the city. After a severe winter, cheer is needed, but there's none in John Street, where Joseph exists in shameful self-pity. Rising in the afternoon, he demands Eve sit with him at his breakfast. Since he won't tolerate Pyke's skeletal presence ('like sitting at table with a death's head!'), Eve is up hours earlier and she and Pyke leave the house before Joseph appears, walk the quieter streets, discuss the morning's work or begin a new idea. On warm days they take a book to Lincoln's Inn Fields, where sometimes passers-by hover and listen.

These scenes are charmingly picturesque. The thin old man, whisps of white hair stirring with every passing vehicle, his clothes a decade out of date, bending towards his companion, the precision of his speech counterpointed by darting smiles of affection. Eve, on the ledge between girlhood and womanhood, serious, grateful to this man who cares for her, has so much to tell her. Her earlier rebellion is held in check.

Sometimes they sit in Pyke's small physic garden where rosemary, foxgloves, rhubarb and lettuce grow among poppies, horseradish and pilewort. As an apothecary he doctors the poor, sells medicines from an equally small shop attached to his house. He is riven by honesty. Needing money in order to live, he yet will not sell false cures, and whenever possible persuades a patient to chop a handful of dandelion leaves with her bread or dose herself with a draught made from camomile or nettle.

'It can't compare with Chelsea of course. I once brought your mama to my garden, gave her a sprig of rosemary to sniff. Here! And she took St John's wort flowers to simmer in wine, against melancholy.'

On other days they walk further afield; on one occasion, past rubble of collapsed almshouses to Great St Bart's church where sick people used to be cured by miracle.

'I come here to remind myself how far people's beliefs may take them, how I must continue to counter superstition by what I do.

'Besides, I was born in Cloth Fair.'

Pyke avoids political matters except when he can link them to Sarah and Tom. When there are no listeners in the street, he explains how it is there's open glee about the assassination of the prime minister and unconcealed sadness when the assassin is hanged. Moves easily and with fervour to the welling-up of revolt throughout the country, the bravery of those working men who claim allegiance to Ned Ludd.

'Your parents would have been stirred up, like the rest of us,' he says, 'though no doubt they'd have baulked at the violence. Radicals will never be silent, however much the government tries to smother them.'

Someone passes by. He reminds himself that his role is to teach, not indoctrinate. Not long ago someone was imprisoned for a year and fined £500 for persuading a young man to emigrate to America.

And he won't tell her that Sarah, whose lover, Tom Cranch, was on the point of arrest when she fled with him to America, was undoubtedly watched on her return.

Eventually Joseph realises that Eve is keeping herself away deliberately.

'You're never here. You're always out, Eve! Since when were you so keen on walking? And with Pyke, Stephen tells me! I suppose I should be glad you're not alone, at least, putting yourself in danger again.'

'Mr Pyke is my friend *and* my teacher. He was my father's friend and knew Mama, too. I like him very much.'

'You're avoiding me.'

'I learn so many things from Mr Pyke. We don't like to be disturbed.'

'Oh, *we* don't like to be *disturbed*! But you don't mind disturbing *me* with your *absence*! *And* I'm paying Pyke for his services.'

This is not true. He owes Pyke weeks of pay, but the old man needs little on which to survive and tutoring Eve pleases him, for something of his dead friend Tom lives on in her quick intelligence, the sometimes fervent intensity of her dark eyes.

She must turn this dialogue with Joseph before it goes wrong and he begins to shout.

'Joseph, show me what you're painting now. I haven't looked for such a long time.'

'And all of a sudden you care about my work, do you?'

'I *wonder* about it, what it's like. I wonder what you're doing when you've shut your door for hours and there's no sound. Though occasionally you do yell out. When you were away, now I'll tell you, I went into your studio several times and looked around.'

'*Did* you indeed?' He is pleased, lurching from misery to hope in a moment.

In the glass-domed studio that so astonished her as a child by its size and dazzling light, he unlatches the shutters, but daylight is dulled by grime on the windows and on the panes of the dome. Years of London smoke and Joseph's failure to pay for cleaning cast the room in shadow yet cannot conceal a chaos of objects and furniture, the pile of bedding from the many nights he has spent there, unemptied chamber pots. There's the sourness of slept-in clothing but also a powerful smell of cloves and cinnamon as Joseph pours himself a glass from the laudanum decanter.

'Please open a window, Joseph.'

He fusses about, pushing at window frames, winding levers for openings in the dome.

'They're all stuck. Won't move. You'll have to put up with the fug.'

On the easel is a very large canvas, and several more of similar size stand along the wall. At first she cannot tell what it is she's looking at. She goes up to the painting and sees paint so thick she wants to scoop it with her fingers to test its depth but doesn't. There's a golden yellow and red, so the sun is shining somewhere, though from where she doesn't know, and if that is sea it seems to merge into sky which itself burns off into whiteness. And it's not sky that she's ever seen before.

'This is the first time I've seen the sea,' she says. Honest, but aware of his dry-kindling mood.

'Ah, well.'

'But it's all manner of colours: blue and green and black! I thought sea was blue, but no, Joseph, don't get cross with me. This sea takes my breath away.'

'Good! That's good.'

'And the sky is green too, there and there. It's not like Barker's Panorama, is it. That was a trick, wasn't it? Pretend sky, pretend sea. Mind you, I liked it then. I thought I was in St Petersburg, do you remember?'

Joseph grunts.

'But I was a stupid child. This is not a trick at all. You were very hot when you painted it, weren't you, I can tell that, and I think your head was hurting.'

'Yes, that's true. How do you know? I thought I would go blind with pain.'

'Did you paint it when you were away, Joseph? Were you ill? Who looked after you?'

'No, no, not ill when I painted it, though I *was* ill there at times. I brought back sketches. Books of them. Notes for which colours to use, written on each sketch, you know. They're all in my head anyway. I painted this yesterday.'

'*Yesterday!* Did your head ache yesterday?' She knows the answer.

He shows her other paintings, skies and sea, skies and sea, black, red, brown, colours merging into each other, painted on top of each other, daubed, brushed, scraped and scratched. Done behind his locked door in sleepless hours in a silent city. His secret self which yet she recognises: the man inside the blackness she's seen so often descend on him like sudden night. She is shocked, fascinated. Wants to stay and look but at the same time get away. Two years ago she'd have run out of the room.

'Do you like them?'

'*Like* them? I, well, they frighten me. Especially this one. But I can't stop looking at it. I think I see things in it: are those waves, is that a bird, but no it's not, it's something *in* the sea. Or *is* it? I must look again.'

'I *knew* you'd understand them! No one else does. No one but you. How limp and feeble they are, while you, a mere girl, you *read what's there.*'

'I think I'm gazing into a deep pool or, no, I'm staring into the far distance. When we went to the Heath the first time, do you remember? We had a picnic, Nursey was there and Stephen carried the basket. I was nearly six and you put me on your shoulders and said, "There's London," and I could see distant buildings and smoke but I didn't know what was meant by 'London' except that I felt it drag me towards it. I held on to your head, probably I pulled your hair, because I thought you might hurl me over and down into it. Your paintings, these, they're like that.'

'Other people say, "I've never seen sky that colour, it's impossible," and they turn away. They don't understand. They're not interested. They know nothing. Ach, God! I despair!'

She watches him hold his head with both hands as though he'd lift it off, then lurch forward and collapse on the ground onto all fours, this large man who so easily dominates others, his sun-browned features contorted by his old misery. And as she did when first she witnessed this in him, she strokes his hand and wipes his tears. Except that in those days she acted as one child to another, whereas now she feels herself infinitely older than him, for she has changed, if he hasn't. She imagines her mother, hears her own voice as Sarah's as she helps him up off the floor and onto a chair, soothes him, passes him the decanter when he asks for it.

That night she dreams she's standing by a weed-filled lake. On the other shore is Mama, waiting for her.

The sky is green, the water black with dense weed. A warm wind blows. She begins to cross, running lightly over the surface.

The firm certainty under her feet gives way, soft, it will not hold her. Mama seems to call, but Eve cannot hear, cannot reach her. Halfway there she sinks through the weed.

*

Sarah strolls in the garden with Hester. Unlike Sowerthorpe days, it is not escape. There's no sense of desperate need for air and space, for the other life of grasses, wind-blown trees and weed flowers found when they walked as far as they dared from the parsonage. Beyond these garden walls the ground slopes up towards the tops; the beck pours lavishly over rocks, coursing through the village, unending. The garden is only steps away from wildness; yet it is also an extension of the house. It pleases, will grow: they can enjoy and improve it as they wish.

Peter is there, preparing seed beds for vegetables, rooting out weeds, raking, sieving soil. He is reluctant to take orders from Hester, having been used to masters only and putting his trust entirely in Edward, who cannot be faulted. He doesn't address Sarah at all, won't look at her. His down-turning mouth is disconcerting, but Edward tells the two women not to mind, and that Hester must persist in giving instructions.

'Will you grow potatoes this year, Peter?'

''appen.'

'I think we should have other vegetables, too: onions, parsnips, spinach, cabbage, celery.'

Peter grunts.

'What else do you suggest, Sarah?'

Another grunt, in a different mode, implying the utter absurdity of talking to a deaf and dumb woman.

Sarah writes: *Green beans.*

'Green beans, Peter.'

'Rumph!' A shoulder indicates a wooden and string structure in a further bed that means he *always* grows beans.

'Oh, that's good. Did Mr Carnforth grow cucumbers in these cold frames?'

The man stomps off, the answer too obvious. The woman's wasting her breath.

'Well, *I* shall sow sweet williams. My favourites at home. I shall beg some windflowers and forgetmenots and michaelmas daisies from Mrs Cliffe. I've seen them all in her garden. Old Carnforth was obviously not interested in flowers. Which flowers were your favourites when you were a girl?'

No garden, Sarah writes, and Hester regrets her question.

They wander through a wooden gate into the orchard, where trees are just beginning to bud.

'This is a plum, I can tell from the leaves. These are apples. I wonder if they're cooking or eating. This one's a pear, I think, looking at the bark. I remember them all from the trees that grew behind the school house.'

She stops herself in time from asking Sarah again about her childhood. So excited about the richness of this new life, her pity for Sarah fails to make her downcast.

'We can watch the progress of the blossom each day, as the buds gradually open. Plum will be first. Let's hope there isn't a frost.'

Soon, Sarah walks out into the garden on her own. Hester watches discreetly, seeing her drift apparently peacefully, bending to flowers, gazing at trees. In particular, as herbs put on strength in the sun, she sees Sarah occasionally picking a leaf, smelling it. She avoids Peter, but that's not difficult, since he avoids her.

Hester tries to understand what it must be like for Sarah, but finds it hard to imagine a childhood in which nothing grew. What *can* it have been like?

The two women sit on a bench near the house one afternoon. Daffodils and narcissi fill a bed on the other side of the path. Earlier they planted sweet pea seeds in small pots lined up on a kitchen windowsill. A Hawkswith woman, herself deaf, gave them to Hester in a screw of paper. In a few days they expect a visit from Hester's sister Sophie, who has promised to bring seeds collected from last year's flowers.

They are silent for a while. A thin late afternoon sun warms them.

It was dark where I lived in that time.

'When you were a child? When you didn't have a garden?'

Yes, a child. And a woman. Then.

Hester dares to ask: 'In America?'

No.

170

This time the mention of America doesn't draw tears.

'It was dark, then, but not in America?'

She has asked too much. Sarah covers her face and Hester puts her arm round her, rests Sarah's head on her shoulder. Asks nothing more.

Sarah writes:

There's someone in the dark. I long for her.

But Hester can't ask who it is.

*

The city will celebrate victory, Wellington's Spanish successes, in particular capturing Salamanca from the Tyrant. And it's the usual form, illuminations. Public buildings are lit from top to toe, private houses show lights in every window if they want to avoid brickbats and mud from the crowds surging past.

'Let's go and see the illuminations,' says Joseph; anything to avoid making those first steps back to portraiture, to escape the bitterness rising in his gullet. Eve, recalling the night with Stephen, Betsy and her damp baby, the night when, later, Joseph returned, familiar and strange, agrees readily.

'Dammit, we might have gone to the Hindoostanee Coffee House, Eve, and eaten Indian curries and I'd have smoked a hookah, that's a kind of pipe, you know, but Sidi Mohammed is bankrupt. Like everyone else!'

No matter, however, for once more there's food and drink to buy in the street, jugglers, acrobats, a fire-eater, though a sharp edge to the crowd's mood. It's not long before a hue and cry is raised, someone rushes past and pursuers knock people into the road, pushing Eve hard against Joseph's side. There's bawling, shouts, roars of support for the thief and soon after, the satisfying shattering of glass, then thumps of iron on wood as others take up the call to destruction.

They dodge into a tavern, where Joseph drinks three brandies, and out again when Eve insists. She remembers Nursey snoring deeply, a brandy bottle on the floor at her side, and by now she wants Joseph to get them both home. He takes her hand and they push into the crowd, falling against puny beggars, stepping over low wheeled trays on which the limbless skim to offer themselves for pity. Shutters in great houses are pulled back, their windows alight. At street level and beneath, doorways make dark homes for the homeless.

While Eve feels threatened, Joseph is buoyed by the crowd's hearty impertinence, incipient riot, for defiance is alive in the whole country. He, like them, can rise above oppression, kick failure in the teeth.

'Come, dear Eve, come into the studio. It's cleaner than it was, you know. I had Stephen remove all the offending articles.' He laughs inordinately. 'Come on. Said the spider to the fly!' Laughing more, he guides her in with one hand, swigs straight from the decanter with the other.

'I'll not give you any of my delicious diabolical concoction, but you could sip a little wine, my dearest girl.'

No, she says, does not explain. She's relieved to be indoors, but a sense of menace lingers, shouts carry up from the street as though the house is surrounded. Would Joseph protect her if they broke in? His eyes glitter, he strides rapidly about the room. At any moment he might jump up onto a table or scramble to the top of the window shutters and grin manically at her. He might swing on the pulleys that open the dome's panes, knocking over his easel with his feet.

He stops before her. 'Dearest Eve, each day you look more like your dear, dear mother!'

He hasn't mentioned Sarah for a long while, and in any case she's never worked out what to say when he does.

'How I loved her! *Oh, Sarah, how I loved you!* You do know that, Eve, don't you?'

'You've said it before.'

'So beautiful, so noble. Would she have loved me eventually when time had passed, when the memory of Tom had faded?'

He doesn't want an answer.

'I would have waited. Quietly. Waited any amount of time.'

Eve can't bear to hear more, walks towards the door.

'Oh, but you needn't be jealous!'

'*Jealous?* Stupid! How can you say *that*? Stop talking like this,

Joseph! *Mama loved Tom.*' Sarah and Tom are indissoluble in her mind, mother and father, whose images she has struggled to create, vital shadows.

'Stay! Stay! Has old Pyke told you we're now at war with America?'

'No. At *war*? Why?'

'Oh, more folly. On both sides. Good thing your parents aren't alive. *They'd* have been upset.'

'Don't say that! Don't!'

'Come back! Don't run off, Eve, come back. I've something important to say to you.'

'*Not about Mama!*'

'No. Don't worry. No, Eve. My paintings. My paintings and you. You have understanding. How clear that was when you looked at them and spoke about them. That is so good, it cheers me so much I feel I could give up this devil that mingles with angelic spices and juice of the quince tree fruit. I *could*.'

He reaches for the decanter, but doesn't take it, plumps down on the nearest chair, stands up again.

'Eve, knowing you're here in this house is good, very good. But I need you here *always*. You're still young, you have yet to reach womanhood, though you're not far off it. This is what I want to say. This.' He takes a swig. 'I want to say, I want to ask that you'll marry me when you are of age. Of course not yet. But I'll wait, oh I'll wait until you're twenty-one.'

She gasps. Gapes at him, rigid.

'I know what you're thinking. That you're a substitute for Sarah whom I love and yes, I do still love her, yes! But you're wrong, you're not a substitute. Not a reincarnation. You're *Eve*.

'Think how long we've lived together. Most of your life! I've *always* loved you, first as Sarah's child, now for yourself and for the woman you'll shortly be. You may grow to love me in time, Eve. And then we shall be happy. Live happily ever after! I'm *sure* of it!'

Astonishment, dismay, make her rush past him, dry-eyed, out, up stairs and the further stairs to her room. Where she locks the door but knows not what to do with herself, stands fixed with tension and horror until, feeling she might break open, she begins to pull at her hair, roll her body from side to side, then runs from wall to wall beating her knuckles and head against them until they hurt too much and finally, as tears release her, covers her face, throws herself onto her bed and howls with outrage.

The almost animal sounds of her fury disturb her terribly, as though she's been entirely changed, but in a while these settle into sobs. She cries until she can no more, but her mind is dense with wild thoughts, underneath which lies the realisation that there is no one who can help her decide what to do, no one. Pyke would of course be kind, would *want* to help. He and she are close enough for him to be a sort of confidant. But he's an old man, even ancient, and she's a young woman. He *couldn't* comprehend her feelings. And she's well aware that he dislikes Joseph, disapproves of him. Would see this as a problem with a solution like algebra, which he might even try to impose himself, and then Joseph would be furious at his interference.

'Oh Mama! Oh, Tom! Help me!' she thinks, waking from exhausted sleep in ashen light. Having never known a father, she finds it easier to address him as Tom.

Could Mr Pyke ever understand, could Mama and Tom in her head understand as she does, that Joseph cannot be ignored, cannot be abandoned? That one refusal will not be enough. Could they understand that for all her revulsion at the thought of marriage, her attachment to Joseph is too deep to be yet unlatched?

*

Sophie comes to Hawkswith, bringing jars of bottled pears, raspberry jam, hollyhock and nasturtium seeds and a songbook. She's also brought two fine blouses sewn by their mother for Hester and Sarah.

Nothing for Edward. Hester has not dared tell her sister and mother that she is living with him, thought by Hawkswith people to be a married couple. That they *are*, to their own minds, married.

The likeness between the sisters lies in blueness of eye and a certain movement of the head when listening that suggests a desire to analyse. Otherwise Sophie is rounder and rosier, though Hester's face is no longer as taut and thin as it was.

Edward shakes her hand warmly, is on his horse and out of the house for most of that first day so perhaps his relationship with

Hester is not immediately obvious to Sophie. But the situation must be explained.

'You must know, Sophie, that Mr Snead was a cruel man, with ideas that should never have been countenanced.'

'You told us as much in your letter, Hester, and that he treated Sarah disgracefully.' Sarah listens.

'Edward and I are trying to help Sarah recover. Although Edward is a doctor in the usual way, he is also especially interested in the mind, and he believes there are methods he can use to help Sarah remember her past.'

'That's wonderful.'

Edward is good. You are good.

'*Dear* Sarah! Sophie, I *had* to get away from Mr Snead. Sarah and I both had to. Did Mother understand that?'

'She did. In such circumstances it is the only thing you could have done, she said, despite breaking the sacrament of marriage.'

'I have abandoned the marriage. It is a broken thing. It should never have taken place. Sophie, I must tell you that Edward and I live together as man and wife. The people here know us as Mr and Mrs Bissett.'

Sophie's red cheeks redden. She is shocked, for a few moments speechless. But, as a reader of novels, she is thrilled. She liked the look of Edward this morning, and it is obvious that Hester is happy. But oh, *she* will have the task of persuading their mother to accept something she will dislike terribly.

'Can you accept this, Sophie? Do you condemn us?'

'*Of course* I don't condemn you. Of course I accept it. But Mother, you know. I'm not sure how I can go about persuading her.'

'Can you refer to me as Mrs Bissett without blushing, Sophie?'

They laugh, knowing how often Sophie has been thought blushing when it's merely her high colour.

'If only Mother could meet Edward,' Hester muses. 'If she could see how good he is, how right is our decision.' She can hear Edward speaking as she says this. 'I can help him in his work and together we can care for Sarah. I never did any good for anybody in Sowerthorpe. Snead certainly never did.'

'Oh Mother, Mother, what can I *say* to her, Hester? You must help me work out what to say.'

Sarah, agitated, hastily begins to write:

My daughter. Where is she?

Her eyes are suddenly wild.

I must find her. Must find my girl.

'Oh my goodness, Sarah. You have a daughter! That's wonderful! But yes, where *is* she? What was she called?'

Eve. I named her Eve.

'A lovely name!' Sophie is charmed. 'Is she like you? Where does she live?'

In that place. She was my baby. My child.

'A daughter. Sarah, where do you think she is? Let us send for her.'

Hester is anxious. Too much disturbance and Sarah could retreat into herself again. 'We shall do everything we can to find Eve.'

Edward, returning later, says: 'All the talk of mothers and daughters must have spurred her memory. That's very hopeful. But we must take it slowly, must not over-excite her.'

He is tired. Ever since he'd become aware of the injustices and humiliations meted out to inmates in his father's lunatic asylum, Edward had been alert to the sufferings of the lowest. Life in Sowerthorpe confirmed and increased his awareness, though there the impoverishment of fishermen depended more on natural misfortune than human maltreatment. Snead's hideous sermons were maltreatment of course, but of the mind, for he offered no hope to the oppressed.

But Edward is soon made aware of quite different sufferings particular to Yorkshiremen, those workers of cloth, not men of the cloth, whose livelihoods are under threat as mill owners and those running finishing shops seek with new machinery to produce in eighteen hours what was once done by hand in eighty-eight. Although as doctor, Edward's position is ostensibly neutral, having learned to defy authority in his youth, his sympathy leans towards the men. Today he has his first encounter.

Hawkswith is not a large village, but included in its parish are homesteads spread out among the hills and moorland slopes, where weavers have made good livings for years. Before their houses stand tenters, the newest pieces of woven cloth stretched out on hooks. Their gardens are spiked with bean poles and pea sticks, bushy with soft fruit, bright with sun-facing flowers. Some miles down, the river bends westwards, is joined by streams and surges into the valley towards a mill and nearby finishing shops. To the south is the town of Wakefield.

Everyone knows of 'troubles' rumbling around the country, gatherings of discontented men and women in Manchester and Stockport, potato riots, smashing of stocking frames in Nottingham, starvation in Liverpool.

Although the parish doesn't extend as far as the town, Edward's rounds cover miles. Today, following a visit to check a leg-splint, he is stopped and asked to ride to a cottage far up the hill to see an unnamed man who's 'cut 'isself'. Encouraging Dolly, his mare, with oats from his pocket, he plods up the steep track. When he arrives, the man, sitting beside his weaving frame, not at it, is young, sullen. His equally young wife continues with her spinning, but tells him her husband:

''Ad a fight wi' a bottle. 'E'll tell you nowt else.'

Unwrapping the man's bloody rags, it's clear to Edward that the lacerations can only have been caused by his inadequately protected fist and arm smashing through a window and pulling out again too rapidly against jagged glass.

The young man closes his eyes when he questions him, so he cleans up the wounds, bandages him properly, and in parting tells him:

'The cuts could have been worse. You're lucky the "bottle" missed your artery. You'd have bled to death faster than you got away. Take three of these drops in warm water against the pain. You should be able to work again soon.

'Wear your coat and nobody'll see.' He trusts the man compre-
hends this reassurance that he'll not report him. That he's on his
side.

*

In John Street there follow months of silence, an impasse, during
which nothing is said about the proposal. Predictably, Joseph's
peak of enthusiasm and optimism plunges, and he withdraws,
burned. When he surfaces, opens doors, appears again, still no ref-
erence is made, and they continue existence as before. Except that
Joseph is either out, touting for patrons or ensconced with them in
the studio, dabbing at the canvas, stifling his sighs and yawns, sup-
pressing groans of boredom.

Eve feels the weight of secrecy, the weight of responsibility. For
she has it in her power to cheer Joseph or to depress him, notices
how her presence lightens his mood, how an angry tone or momentary impatience stings him. Sometimes she's careless, wounds him
with a word, but regret comes too late and she doesn't know what
to say. Takes herself off to the spinet and plays a slow ground by
Purcell over and over again, a sad piece that seems to suit contrition.

Lessons continue with Pyke. Time spent with him is like gulping
fresh air, which doesn't exist in the City, only in high places such as
the Heath or Highgate. The old man is aware that something has
happened, but suspects that, because of Eve's age, it has a physical
cause.

And all the while, wherever they are, they hear the constant
firing of guns from the Tower and the parks for every important
event: the restoration of the king's government in Hanover, Wellington's victory at Pamplona, the surrender of Dresden.

One day they turn the corner towards home and there's a com-
motion further down John Street. It's only after they've seen the
wagons, big pieces of furniture carried out of the house and heard
the shouting and roaring between Joseph and a man yet larger
than him that Pyke rapidly guides Eve back to the Strand to find
a hackney.

'Is it Mrs Digham that you know, Eve, and is it Paternoster Row?'

'What's happening, Mr Pyke? Are they taking Joseph away?'

'No no. But it's bailiffs, I fear. He must owe money. They will take what he owes in furniture and household goods. It's better you're not there while it happens.'

'Oh, I'm sure it's my fault! I ran up bills when he was away. I didn't care.' She covers her face.

'It can't possibly be just you, my dear. Cheer yourself now. It's Joseph's concern and the bad times in which we live; evidently he has not managed things well and he will have to deal with it somehow. And you will need to brace yourself for empty rooms when you return. For all we know he may be obliged to move house.'

'They may take the spinet! It's yours, Mr Pyke, they shouldn't take it away.'

'Quite right, it *is* mine, though I'd rather hoped you'd keep it yourself. Wait here.'

She watches him urging his old legs to hurry down the street, take the huge man aside and make him listen.

'That's settled,' he tells her, coming back breathless.

'Did you talk to Joseph?'

'I told him where I'm taking you.'

'But I must console him.'

'No. Far better that we don't interfere. Mr and Mrs Digham will agree with me.' He instructs the cabman.

Eve is convinced she's helped cause this terrible outcome, whatever Pyke says, and soon after their arrival at Digham's Lucy realises that she must close the shop for several hours to comfort the girl. For girl she still is, despite her awkwardly elongated limbs and emerging breasts.

Lucy tells Eve something of the life she once led with Joseph so many years ago, herself barely older than Eve is now, the daily uncertainty that eventually led her to leave him, taking her baby Matthew with her. That being married to William Digham has shown how it is *not* usual to have such violent changes of mood. Neither usual nor endurable for those who live with it.

Eve listens, calmed by the pretty, fading woman whom she once adored, strove to impress and then disliked, kicking at Paternoster tuition, playing and eventually hating to play the bully towards Matthew. They've seen little of each other since that time, and Eve appreciates freshly Lucy's quiet certainties. Before long she tells Lucy of Joseph's proposal, and then, whispering it, of the dreadful bleeding she had a few months ago.

'I was unkind to Joseph, I know I was, you see he demanded I take breakfast with him at three o'clock in the afternoon and I wouldn't and lost my temper with him and told him I hated him and I saw his face sort of crumple and I said I didn't care if he never sold any paintings ever again. Why did I say that? I marched out of the room and banged the door and that very night I had the dream again in which I try to cross a weedy lake and when I awoke there was so much blood. Oh Lucy, it was punishment for how cruel I'd been! And they're taking everything out of his house and Mr Pyke says Joseph will have to live somewhere else.'

*

Now that Sarah has revealed the existence of her daughter, Hester feels able to gently question her, asking about the place where Eve was born. To which Sarah writes one word:

Battle's

'Oh, was that a shop, Sarah?'

There was coffee.

Hester asks nothing more, for those two words, 'coffee' and 'Battle's' may yet yield something firm. Surely Edward's friend Henry Sessions can find an address for Battle's which most like is in London or at least nearby. The colliers said they'd delivered their load of coal to London, after all. Battle's coffee shop or coffee house or coffee warehouse.

Edward, distracted by growing disturbances in the district though he is, writes a quick note to his friend, and when there's a reply Hester goes to sit with Sarah in the quiet kitchen drinking tea and talking gently.

'I have an idea, Sarah,' she says. Sarah seems to her calm enough. She'll try.

'Look:

Battle's Coffee House
Exchange Alley
London

Is that the correct address, Sarah?'

Yes

'This is my idea. Write to Eve. Ask her to come and live with us here. Wouldn't that be wonderful? I should love it so! I know Edward would, too.'
Sarah starts, smiles. Then shakes her head.

She may not forgive me.

'You have been ill, Sarah. You certainly could not have written before now. You knew not who you were. Of course she will forgive you.'

I should not have left her.

'Write to her, Sarah!'

I have been dead for a long time.

'Not so!'

Alive but not alive.

'Write!'

My darling Eve,
Come and live with us here. The people are good.
Your loving Mama

The letter is addressed to Miss Eve Battle with a return direction c/o Mr E. Bissett, Holly Lodge, Hawkswith, Nr Wakefield. A dark vision of Battle's comes to Sarah as she writes, along with sharp spurts of memory: her own mother pulling her by the hand to church, her father's black looks. The blank misery of her marriage to – to? They pile together, unwanted, yet needed.

The waiting is bad enough, but the letter is returned unopened with this message scribbled on the back:

> *The Coffee House no longer belongs to the Battle family. It was sold some years ago. No one of that name lives here. No one who worked here then works here now.*

It is hard to tell Sarah; to retain hope.

'Eve must be living somewhere else. Who would have taken her when you – when you ...?'

> *Her nurse. But she has no money.*
> *Everyone is dead. Joseph is dead.*

'Joseph?'

Sarah snatches back the letter, crushes it, throws it in the fire and sobs soundlessly.

*

Eve stays overnight in Paternoster Row, for it takes Lucy hours to explain things to her, to encourage her to accumulate a store of rags to use each month and to disassociate what will happen regularly to her body from anything she may say or might have said to Joseph.

'This happens to all women, Eve, though you have begun late. Mrs Casey would have helped you, had she lived, poor thing.'

She plays down the matter of the proposal, stressing Joseph's erratic behaviour, how one moment it's one thing, another the next.

'Years have yet to pass, on his own reckoning, before he'll think to carry it out, Eve, and who knows that he mightn't drop the idea, even find someone else to marry.'

In fact Lucy is more shocked by Joseph's proposal than she will say. When Joseph took up with her years ago, it was an impulsive action. Impulsive and quickly disastrous. It's not impossible that he might go abroad suddenly, take Eve with him, marry her, under-age, in some obscure country. And her own miserable 'marriage' to Joseph would play out all over again, but this time with Eve. She discusses it all with William, who has known Joseph longer than any of them.

'I'll talk to him, my love. Of course I've talked to him before, not least when he first met you. And look how I failed to make him change his mind then! It's hard to influence him, but I must try, certainly. Sarah, that fine woman, would be shocked, had she lived.'

Matthew returns from school, greets Eve, who colours with embarrassment, but keeps out of the way while Lucy gently mothers the girl and prepares her to go back on the morrow.

'You must be sure to come straight here if ever you're unhappy, Eve. I shall never forget Sarah's help to me when I was quite desperate. I owe a great debt. Besides, William and I are fond of you. You must always remember we are your friends.'

Eve marks Lucy's omission of Matthew's name, but guilt is swept away by increasing anxiety at her return to John Street.

*

They piece together an incomplete picture, reluctant to tire her with too much writing, but years of Sarah's life remain undescribed, and still she does not speak.

Hester says: 'Something prevents her from speaking, some knowledge. There is something more that claws at her heart.'

In Edward's view, a nervous disorder could be cured by discovery of its source, even in Sarah's case, where the root seems too deep for easy revelation. But how to discover it? What method is there that causes no harm to the patient? Certainly not by the ridiculous use of magnets, baths of water, convulsions, hysteria, for Mesmer is discredited now, although gestures and mumblings of mesmeric cures are still practised by physicians and quacks all over the country. That will never be Edward's way. If the root is not known, he thinks, perhaps it can be uncovered through gentle persuasion.

He is inspired by what he's read of new practices in France, where there is much talk of the Marquis de Puységur, who, he's pleased to discover, treats both rich and poor. Edward has never turned away a patient too poor to pay. De Puységur apparently speaks of 'artificial somnambulism', and the obscure Portuguese priest Abbé Faria of sleep and quiet suggestion. These are the simple techniques he'll use. If, somehow, Edward can speak to Sarah while she's asleep or at least half asleep, she might respond, recount the thoughts that overcast her mind.

Hester has admired Edward's skill as a doctor for years; all the time in Sowerthorpe she would hear praise for his effective treatment, his kindness.

''Tis a wonder 'e doon't marry 'e be so good wi' bairns,' people used to say.

Recently, Hester's even experienced a new sensation of ambition for him, wanting his successful methods to be recognised by important physicians in London. But, to try out something new with Sarah, somehow that's different.

'Please don't, Edward. Let her recover in her own time.'

'But not being able to find Eve is making her worse.'

'I know, I know, but you can't risk using a method you've not tried before. Not on our dearest Sarah.'

'Hester, you must trust my judgment. But, all right, I'll ask her what she thinks herself.'

Sarah, sensitive to disturbance between the two, looks timidly at him.

Yes, I do want to speak. But I cannot. I can't.
How can I find Eve? I must find her. Please help me find her!

'Of course you must find Eve. But first you need to learn to speak again, to remember more, to become well again. I cannot let you go anywhere in your present condition. It would be far too dangerous. We must hope that Eve is well looked after, is safe until you have recovered. We shall help you as much as we can.'

I think I shall never speak.

'I believe I can help you with that. I have an idea.'

How? I know I can't.

'This is what I want to try. I should like you to fall asleep, here in this room.'

Fall asleep! How can that help?

'Don't worry. I shan't use any medicines, no leeches!'
She's stopped writing, is unsure.
'I shall talk to you when you are asleep and maybe you will reply. That's all.'
'I'll be here,' Hester says. 'I shan't leave the room.'
Edward extinguishes all except one lamp and places two small mirrors at different angles on the table at which Sarah sits. Asks her to gaze at them.
No sound. Their breathing is imperceptible, as if they dare not. Only two clocks tick, unsynchronised.
They wait. Five minutes. Ten. Nothing happens.
She writes: *I can't fall asleep!*
They leave a day before the next attempt. Edward abandons mirrors, instead places a candle about ten inches away from her and asks her to gaze into the flame.
Her eyelids droop, her hands relax in her lap. Hester dips her pen, ready to record.
'Sarah, can you hear me talking to you?'
No reply.
'Sarah, tell me about Eve, about when you last saw her.'
There's a long silence. Sarah's mouth opens, closes. Her lips move slightly.
She opens her eyes and tears pour down.
Soon she takes Hester's pen and writes for herself:

I was asleep. Did I speak?

Edward says: 'No, you didn't speak, but your face looked as though you were remembering in your mind.'

I waved to Eve. So many people. Then she'd gone.

'Shall we try again another day? Do you want to remember what happened before, Sarah?'

Some parts perhaps.

Hester says: 'There are parts of my past I certainly don't want to remember, Edward! Sarah, can you tell me where Eve went?'

No

Later, Hester takes Edward aside.

'The experiment makes me feel uneasy. It's like prying. But also there's a frightening uncertainty about it.'

'Of course there is! Experiments are always uncertain. But the risk is worth taking.'

Even if she lacks Edward's education, this relationship with Edward, compared to that with John Snead, is equal, unoppressed. Unlike then, she can tell him what she thinks.

'What if she does recall and it's somebody or some time she'd prefer to forget? I meant what I said about my own past. I couldn't bear it if some of those days came back vividly into my mind.'

'But what if it helps her recall something good, Hester? Besides, she's said herself we could try once again.'

'Yes. I suppose that makes it better, because she said so. But she may not realise how much risk there'll be. It worries me greatly.'

More than a week passes before the next candle-gazing session. Although many in the village have been won over, Edward must spend hours riding round outlying homesteads trying to convince ploughmen and kitchen maids that vaccination with cowpox will prevent them from becoming disfigured with smallpox, not turn them into cows.

The room is darkened as before, Hester has pen and paper and Sarah, though apprehensive, sits at the table, stares at the candle flame. It takes longer, but in time her eyelids droop and she sleeps.

'What did you see, Sarah, when you waved to Eve?'

They watch her face, still at first in the low candle glow. She says nothing, but her features begin to move in slight shifts, her mouth tightens, she frowns, her eyebrows rise, her eyelids seem to stretch though her eyes remain closed, her lips move almost as in speech, smile, purse, smile again. She laughs without sound, her body sways, her hands grip the edge of the table to steady herself. They understand she's experiencing every extraordinary detail once more.

Her face lights, her eyes open, lambent with inner exultation.

Astonished, Hester bursts out:

'What is it, Sarah?'

The question breaks her trance. A mask, her face falls, she covers it with her hands and cries.

8

———

THERE'S NO SIGN OF JOSEPH when Eve and Lucy arrive the next morning.

'I should stay here with you until he wakes, Eve.'

'No need to worry, Lucy. I'll be quite safe.' She surprises herself with this sudden accession of calm, but despair in Joseph is not new; surely it can't be worse than anything she's already seen so often. And her home is here; where else can she live? She's also heard too much of Lucy's previous life of misery when she lived with Joseph and can't bear to listen to any more.

She wanders through half-emptied rooms, boards carpeted only with dried mud cakes from bailiffs' boots, patches of bright wallpaper where paintings have been removed. She is not shocked, not even sad, since most of the furniture was huge, and when she first lived here she thought of the pieces purely as obstacles to circumvent. Besides, some of them were in rooms into which she rarely went, kept to impress patrons, particularly the carved cupboards and inlaid tables brought back from his travels. The dining room has been completely stripped, and in the middle of the small parlour where she'd spent many boring hours with Nursey, she's annoyed to see Mr Pyke's spinet on the floor, a folder of music flung into a corner.

'Ah, Eve, you've returned!' Joseph says, filling the doorway. 'I thought you might stay away for good. Was sure they'd keep you. Lucy will want you to remain with her, no doubt.'

'Please help me lift the spinet onto this small table. Aren't there any chairs? They left the music, that's something.'

He picks up the instrument with ease. Looks at her resentfully.

'I would not have stayed away, Joseph. I live here.'

'Come with me to the kitchen then. Cook has left. We must fend for ourselves. Can you cook?'

'No, of course I can't! No one's ever taught me.'

They find bread, butter, cheese, enough for a few days. In the meat safe a piece of fatty mutton going green, but the range has gone out. They cut the mould off the bread and Joseph makes tea.

'I shall soon get everything back, don't you worry, Eve.'

'Mr Pyke said you might have to leave this house.'

'Damn Pyke! Oh it could happen, but no, no, we'll stay. Don't fret, we'll not move. I'll soon make plenty of money again. I'm thinking of reviving my series of Shakespeare's women that was so successful fifteen years ago. Your mother loved them, you know. And there's one person coming to see me about a portrait tomorrow. Or is it Friday? Did I write down the date? In any case I'll have to take him up to the studio, shan't I, since all the other rooms are empty. They didn't bother with unframed canvases. No idea how priceless they are, only interested in pictures with frames. But why should I care that bailiffs have no taste!'

Eve is barely persuaded by Joseph's outpouring of optimism, but at least he hasn't dropped into one of his black moods. He ought to be depressed and gloomy in the circumstances, she thinks, and no doubt he will be sooner or later. Meanwhile he's buoyed by enthusiasm for his latest project.

'I painted all the principal women in Shakespeare: Ophelia, Juliet, Cordelia, Lady Macbeth, Desdemona. Gil was Othello: you've seen my sketch in the studio, haven't you? People bought the oils, then hundreds bought engravings. I painted a whole new set for Sarah to hang in Battle's Coffee House.' He sighs, then notices Eve's frown.

'And your lessons must continue, of course. I'm sure Pyke won't mind my owing him a bit of money for a week or two, will he? Don't worry, Eve. You look unhappy.'

'I've remembered something. I once listened behind the door to a conversation you had with Mr Pyke.'

'Did you? Well, what about it? He was probably annoying me when I was busy.'

'He was telling you how Mama wanted me to have a good education, that she had told him so herself. You wanted me to carry on with Lucy.'

'Oh, don't hold it against me! He's teaching you now. Isn't that enough?'

'What I also remember was that you said Mama's money was put aside for me when I came of age. And Mr Pyke said I would be rich. Where is that money, Joseph, and can I have it now to buy back your furniture?'

'Oh sweet, good child. Oh sweet young woman. How generous, how like Sarah! O *matre pulchra, filia pulchrior!*'

'What does that mean?'

'It's Horace, I think.'

'But I don't know any Latin.'

'O more beautiful daughter of a beautiful mother.'

'Where is the money, Joseph?' She hates these outbursts about Sarah, dreads a repeat of his proposal, then at that same moment she realises that of course, any money of hers will pass to him if they marry.

'It's in the hands of a lawyer with instructions to hand it over when you are twenty-one. It came from the sale of the coffee house.'

'Let me have it now!' To herself she thinks: and then he'll not want to marry me, as I'll spend it all and there'll be none left.

'It's not so easy. The legal arrangement would have to be broken and the lawyer would charge money for doing that.'

'I'll pay him from the money that he's holding. My money.'

'No good! You see, there's the matter of what it's worth these days. Everything has lost its value because of the war; even very rich people have gone bankrupt. Everyone except the damned Prince Regent! You've heard me say it, haven't you? You are kind and good, Eve, but there's no point my even asking Mr Wigram how much is left. I know already what his answer will be: it's dwindled to nothing.'

*

There's hammering on the door late at night after Sarah's gone to bed. Edward and Hester are reading by a late autumn fire.

Edward, worn out by riding up and down dale all day and sitting all the previous night with a dying patient, keeps shaking himself awake.

'Edward, wake up! Will you go? It's someone needing you or your pills!'

She hears voices at the door and in a moment Edward is pushed back into the room by three men with blackened faces, two pistols and a bludgeon.

'Where's t'oother 'ooman?' Voice muffled beneath a tied scarf.

'She's in bed, asleep,' Hester says. 'Please don't get her up. She must suffer no more harm.'

'Us knows abowt 'er. Been reckinised. She's roon awa'.'

Edward speaks up.

'I understand what you want. You need my silence. Well, you have my word for it. Though you can't expect me to swear allegiance to King Ludd.'

'Yer word's nor enough. Swear on t' 'oly book. Us's no need fer t'dumb 'ooman if she be *truly* dumb.'

Hester reaches down the bible.

'Say after: I do swear to keep all I hears and knows tonight secret on pain o' death. I do swear I shall ne'er say nowt abowt t' working men in future on pain o' death.'

Edward holds the book, repeats the words.

'And missus 'ere.'

Hester swears, trembling, words she can hardly bear to say.

The men turn to go and, last out of the room, the masked spokesman makes a gesture of doffing his cap to Hester. Is he sincere or is he ironic? She cannot tell.

Edward rushes to her when the men have left. Holds her to him until she stops shaking.

'Who can blame them? They're working men beneath the blacking. They stand to lose their work, their living; their wives and children will starve.

'Before they left, they told me to hand over all my guns and weapons. They suggested old Mr Carnforth had left behind a blunderbuss. I had to insist there's nothing in the house.'

'I've heard they force people to give them their muskets, even swords.'

'That's true.'

'I dread harm coming to Sarah.'

'Yes, of course. And we'll keep our word, my love. Did you notice the leader's wrist? The hoof of skin on it?'

'Now you say so, yes. It looked strange. When he raised his hand to me.'

'He raised his hand to you?'

'Only that he almost raised his cap.'

'I see. He's a cropper, Hester. The handle of the shears rubs when he crops the cloth, makes a hard welt. Croppers are always recognisable. I doubt either you or Sarah will be troubled further. But I think they'll come again for me.'

*

Eve tries hard to be cheerful. While her body grows in fits and starts, enlarging, lengthening, she feels her self within it shrink. Wonders at that person she once was who ordered people about, Nursey, Stephen and Betsy, who spoke harshly to Joseph. She finds herself suddenly tongue-tied buying fish, unable to remember which vegetables she'd planned to cook, drifting from the mathematical task Mr Pyke has set her as she daydreams about America, knowing it to be futile.

The news for which she's half prepared, that Joseph will sell the house and move somewhere smaller, cheaper, depresses her further and frightens her, too. For finally Stephen must find another employer, and she will be completely alone with Joseph.

'And I've certainly no more money for Pyke!' he tells her with a kind of black triumph. He's kept up the pretence that he pays Pyke for months, and Eve retains hope that somehow the old man will still be there, whatever else happens.

'Damned New River Company is threatening to cut off our water because I've not paid the rent. So they say. But why are you crying, Eve? It's I who should be in tears, not you! I'll fix somewhere for us to live, you won't be homeless.'

She's hunched with her head down on the kitchen table.

'You should comfort *me*,' he says, not that he's making any attempt to comfort her.

She raises her head. 'When I was younger I used to think everything was wrong. Now I *know* everything's wrong!'

'Never think of the past. It's what Garnerin said in the balloon, and I rather agree with him. Except when you remind me of Sarah, I never think of my past.'

'Never? Don't you like to remember when you were a boy? Don't you think of your mother and father, Joseph? I know nothing about them; you've not spoken of them once. Did you have a brother or a sister?'

'No siblings. My mother died when I was a boy.'

'Like me, then!'

'No, I was fourteen. Weren't you almost six when Sarah died? And I had a father, unlike you. But for a while everything did go wrong, I suppose you could say. For my father seemed to break up when my mother died. Went to pieces and sent me away. Apprenticed me to William Digham.'

'But that was good!'

'Yes. I soon grew fond of him.'

'Did your father die?'

'He had a lavender water factory in Catherine Street. He sold it when my mother died. I think he went mad. Nobody told me what happened, except there was mention of a madhouse in Hackney, where I suppose he lived the rest of his days, for I never saw him again. Not so long ago somebody said I should be sent to that same madhouse!'

'Didn't you miss your mother?'

'I stopped thinking about either of them. I thought only about my future. Like now! Enough of this going backwards, making yourself miserable! Look here, Eve, I've decided, before we move to a smaller house, I shall call on all the patrons I've ever had, every one. Humble myself. Well, no, I shan't do that, I'll flatter them. I'll creep and crawl, it'll be disgusting but someone will bail me out! Good idea, eh? Now what have you got us to eat?'

How can he be so loud when everything's bad, she thinks. Soon he'll tumble down again, of course; soon she'll have to soothe him, not see him for long hours until he appears again. But when he's ebullient, unfeeling, she finds it hard to like him. Longs to escape, knows it to be hopeless, impossible.

'We *must* find out about her daughter,' Hester says to Edward. 'But how?'

'Her memories may not all return. We know there's no physical injury: she's completely recovered from the early paralysis when she was pulled from the water. If there's no longer any physical damage, the injury can only be mental. We can encourage her, prompt her.'

'But not distress her,' Hester says, 'and yet now we know there's a daughter we must do what we can to find the child. It seems urgent to me, and yet the information comes so slowly.'

Edward thinks frequently about treatment for Sarah, wonders about electric shocks which, had he been living in London, where they are often used, he might have considered trying. During his medical training, while freezing in barely heated rooms and drinking too much with his friend Henry Sessions, he'd been impressed by particular ideas, not least Alexander Crichton's stipulation that the first step in analysing mental derangement should be *self-analysis*, to return to his own childhood and see how the mind 'is modelled by instruction'. This Edward has tried and wonders why, given his boyhood experiences (the hideous madhouse, his heartless father, desperate mother), he is not himself deranged. Mostly he's gripped by the recent ideas from France he's read in the best medical journals. Yet how can he use any method to treat Sarah when she will not speak?

Hester has her own theory.

'Something bad has happened to her, as I've said before. I'm sure of it. And it's as though she has locked up the memory of it. She must have reached a point of depair to have tried to drown herself,' she says. 'If only we could find out what caused her to try.'

'But what then, Hester? What could we do if we did find that out?'

'Perhaps that depends on what actually happened.'

'And she said there were so many people when she waved to Eve. That doesn't sound like suicide.'

'Yes, you may be right. Meanwhile I have faith in kindness and patience. Eventually we'll encourage Sarah to speak again.'

Then Sarah writes:

Sarah Battle. I am Sarah Battle.

'But are you not Sarah Cranch?' Hester asks tentatively. 'Once, you wrote ...'

Tom Cranch. I loved him.

She covers her face.

Hester surmises a love affair, an illegitimate child, rejection by Tom. Once more she thinks of attempted suicide, perhaps with the child. All enough to shock a person into silence, surely! But the story is broken the following day.

My darling Tom is dead. We lived as man and wife.

'Ah, we have that in common, Sarah. A husband to whom we are not married.'

I came back from America.

'And Eve?' Hester asks tentatively.

Eve was born in that other place.

She sits back, exhausted by resurgence of the past.

*

Joseph makes up the range, Eve broils the mutton in a heavy pan on the red-hot coals. The shrivelled result is mostly too black to eat, but in desperation they pick out scraps, smear them with mushroom catsup and press them between pieces of bread.

Pyke arrives and postpones mathematics in order to instruct Eve in the buying of fish, meat, vegetables and fruit, and then in some basic rules of cooking. Joseph begs an advance from printer Tegg against a new edition of *Young's Guide to the Fine Arts* to pay for food and his even more necessary supply of opium.

While Joseph remains absurdly buoyant, Eve begins to sink. Or rather, she retreats into herself, even though she's obliged to keep a constant check on supplies in the kitchen, to thrust sticks into the range, walk out with a basket and a purse containing not many coins, lug back the purchases like any kitchen maid. She recalls Parmentier's with self-conscious bitterness. At times she soothes herself at the spinet, picking out all the pieces she can find in minor keys.

Occasionally, playing a particular Purcell ground over and over leads to a kind of joyful grief, but away from the instrument she wonders endlessly about Sarah and Tom and what they would have done if they'd been her. Wonders whether she resembles either of them, and if so, how much. Regards herself in the mirror, turning her face from side to side:

'Am I handsome like Mama? But oh, I can't remember how she looked. I've only a vague sense of her. I can *feel* what she was like, but what did she really look like? Perhaps my eyes dart like Tom's?' She tries to make them do so.

At night she searches through her memories: has she done anything that's noble and wise like Mama? She's mortified to think of her treatment of Matthew, of Nursey; consoled, slightly, by her action of giving away the caged goldfinch to the beggar girl. Sifting through the past is dangerous, leads to self-castigation. Perhaps she should be punished. What would that be; would she stand in the pillory for an hour while people threw rotten eggs and garbage at her? Oh, but once she'd heard how two men were killed in the pillory when the crowd threw stones. What could they have done for people to have hated them so much?

She thinks of Joseph. Is *he* noble, is *he* wise? No, he's not either. He's ... What is he? He's strong, he's clever at painting, very clever. His paintings are like dreams. They amaze her. But *he* was unkind to Matthew, too, and very bad to Lucy. And sometimes he's like a huge child, shouting and sobbing, when the blackness gets into his head.

She poses two questions to herself: What if Tom isn't dead? What if Mama isn't dead? The first leads to a pleasing fantasy that is soon dispelled by the certainty that Mama would never have returned to England if Tom had lived, because she loved him, as Mr Pyke said. Oh, if Tom had lived, she'd have been born in America, an American girl! If *only!*

She allows herself longer to dwell on the second question. Joseph has always said that Sarah is dead and Mr Pyke, too, says that she must have drowned. Nursey seemed to think she might still be alive. Yet Nursey was ignorant and superstitious, and for all the guilt Eve feels about her treatment of her old nurse, she *must* agree with Joseph and Mr Pyke. With her increasing knowledge, her sharpening reason, she cannot believe what Nursey hinted at; yet she wants to, badly wants to. If Sarah *were* alive she, Eve, would stay not a moment longer in this house with Joseph. Would go to her mother immediately.

But how on earth can she find out if Mama *is* alive and, if so, *where* she is?

*

Woken by a boy one night to go to his injured father, Edward saddles Dolly, sits the puny lad before him and arrives in a bleak spot far beyond his usual round.

Hardly through the cabin door, he's grabbed by the throat and pinned against the wall.

'We know you do live in sin. Your "wife" by rights be parson's wife. Mend my friend's wound or we spread news all over like muck.'

Here it is, then, finally, the exposure he and Hester have been dreading.

He recognises the voice, feels the hoof of hard skin against his windpipe. Have they forgotten the oath he swore?

His eyes adjust to a body on a table and a surprisingly large number of shadowy men, masked with kerchiefs, jammed into the squat room. When he gently pulls back the blood-stiff garments, sees the shape of the wound, he surmises a bullet deep in the left thigh.

He asks three of the shadows to hold lanterns high over the body, another to dose the wounded man with brandy or whatever spirit they have to hand, as much as they can make him swallow, another to ensure a red-hot fire, the pot hanging over it full of water.

'I'll need clean rags.'

'Us've plenty of rags,' a voice calls out ironically.

A man strips off his shirt. 'You'll git nowt cleaner'n 'at.'

Luddites, each one. He knew they'd come for him again. He notes pistols in belts.

'Let him finish the bottle,' he instructs. 'Easy, easy!'

Someone cradles the man's head.

'I'll try to remove the slug. Hold him down. By the shoulders, arms, the lower part of the bad leg. And you there, the whole of the other leg. Give him your belt to bite on,' he says to the man who pinned him against the wall.

There's much damage to muscle and bone: healing will be slow. As if she can read his thoughts, a woman's voice from the back of the hut cries out, 'Oh let 'im not lose 'is leg!'

A sound of men hushing her.

He probes for the slug as carefully and swiftly as he can to lessen the agony, yet minutes pass before he finds it, picks it out gently, staunches, cleans, sews up the gashes, bandages the limb which yet may need amputating, though he doesn't say so. The man's muffled groans cease as he loses consciousness and they lift him gently to a straw bed. Edward cleans his instruments as far as possible, packs his bag.

'We must see how it heals,' he says. 'Destroy his breeches, burn them, lest they come searching and find the bullet hole. Remember: the wound's from falling drunk against tenterhooks. I'll tell them if they question me.'

And as he turns to the door he says:

'I'm disappointed you should think it necessary to use blackmail. You heard me swear an oath. Why did you imagine I would not treat your friend without conditions?'

Murmuring, muttering, resentful tones.

'Who was it told you about my wife? A local man?'

'Away off,' says the leader, waving his hand vaguely.

'I'll come back in three days. Let me know before that if he worsens.'

*

'Do you know where the balloon came down, Mr Pyke, where my mother died?'

'Ah now. I heard it was blown very much off course, east, north-east. Ended up somewhere east of Colchester, though I'm not sure.'

But where is that and how would she begin? People would think her mad looking for a dead woman, they'd refuse to help her, and if she only half believed in it herself she'd never find out anything. Oh, a foolish notion altogether!

And yet there's no stopping her thoughts. For a while she convinces herself she'll encounter Mama when she's out with her basket buying a loaf, a handful of cheap vegetables. She takes to shopping daily, looks about her like a bird as she goes. Hesitates, suddenly speeds forward, lingers, shades her eyes to stare across the road, wondering if she might plunge across.

Then she realises that she'll probably pass her mother in the street without recognising her. How can she recognise her since she no longer knows what her mother looks like? Worse still she may have passed her already! Now she dreads going out at all, lest she fail to see Mama, lest she miss her one chance for ever.

On a day when she tries to cook sprats, boiling them in water until she has a disgusting fish-oily soup of bones and scales, Joseph, drinking wine to celebrate the completion of a painting and blot out the vile stink, begins to talk of Sarah.

'Please don't speak of Mama, unless there's something you've not told me before.'

'Oh there is, there is, and you are old enough now to hear about it, I'd say.' Eve invariably winces whenever Joseph mentions her age, seeming to hint at a reiteration of the proposal.

'She was married, you know, your mama.'

'I know that! She and Tom were married.'

'No, no, no. They were not married. Sarah thought of Tom as though he were her husband but they were not Mr and Mrs Cranch. They couldn't marry because Sarah was married to someone else already.'

'But she was Sarah Cranch and I am Eve Cranch!'

'Look, Eve, I heard they were known as Mr and Mrs Cranch in America. They passed themselves off as married.'

The smell of sprats is bad enough: she's had to put the pan out in the yard for cats to find. There's bread, but no more butter, and she's hungry.

'Oh.' It's as if she's falling down a well. At the bottom she will be sick.

'She had a terrible husband. I saw him, you know. A huge, fat man who raised bets on how much he could eat and drink. Monstrous quantities of food, quarts of port. His meals were like performances, really, and men would watch for hours, his audience. I wanted to draw cartoons of him by way of advertisement for Battle's Coffee House until I discovered he was Sarah's husband. James Wintrige, he was called.'

'But Mama couldn't possibly have married someone so horrible.' She wants to cry. Asks in a small voice: 'Am I this Wintry man's daughter then?'

'No, no, a thousand times no! You are the daughter of Sarah Battle and Tom Cranch. Sarah couldn't bear the name Wintrige and reverted to her unmarried surname, Battle. You should ask Pyke about him, he knows much more than I do.'

And Pyke is indeed her best source. Best and kindest.

'Ah, dear girl, I had hoped to keep these disagreeable facts from you somewhat longer. Why Mr Young should want to tell you now I can't understand, but there it is.

'Wintrige was not always vast, in fact at first he was tall and thin. He and Sarah married when she was very young. I suspect she thought by marrying him she might escape her tyrannical father, Sam, a crotchety, gruff man with few words and even less humour who became worse when his wife, Sarah's mother, died. But he insisted she continue to run the coffee house, married or not. (He was your grandfather, my dear Eve, however I must tell you the truth.)

'Then when Sarah returned to England after Tom died, and you were born there in Battle's, Wintrige began making public spectacles in Battle's out of his eating and drinking and Sarah hated it, but couldn't stop him. I tried to help by arguing with him but it was hopeless, and quite soon he died of a surfeit. I do believe he determined to eat and drink himself to death.

'Rather worse was that he'd spent years spying for the government. He posed as a member of the Corresponding Society in the '90s, and I and my dear friends were taken in by him. He reported all our meetings directly to the minister in charge of the government's secret service and we never realised it. How blind we were!'

'Please stop a moment, Mr Pyke. When Mama went to America with Tom, was she running away from this terrible husband?'

'She went to America because she wanted to be with Tom and because she believed it to be a place of freedom. I expect she was indeed getting away from Wintrige, though she told me she'd had no idea that he was a spy when she married him. However, just before she and Tom fled to America she did find an incriminating letter.'

'Oh poor Mama. Poor dear Mama.'

'Eve, these facts are unpleasant. But they should not affect you. Your mother and father were both innocent. As well as brave in their attempt to make a new life. Be of good cheer! Concentrate on learning, and that way, honouring your parents. It was wrong of Mr Young to worry you. Please will you tell me if he worries you any more? Strictly speaking I am his employee, of course, but ...' She knew he'd not been paid for months. Joseph was never there to hand over any money. 'But I think of teaching you as an act of friendship. To Tom and Sarah and to you.

'Still, we mustn't forget that you are his ward.'

'Ward, what does that mean, Mr Pyke?'

'It means that legally he takes care of you. He is your guardian. There'll be a document drawn up by a lawyer setting it all out. It also means you can do nothing without his permission until you come of age.'

'Nothing?'

'Nothing.'

She gasps at this. It's like when the crowd in Green Park jostled her, wedged her between them, rifled her pockets. She can't breathe. Must struggle to be free.

9

———

AS THE YEAR PROGRESSES the temperature drops. With each
fiercely cold day, for there's no money for fuel, Eve anticipates
Joseph's next collapse. The signs are there: staring at the wall, unable
to work, tears, self-pity. She's with him too often, for they live in
the kitchen, eating bread to keep warm, hovering in the meagre,
infrequent heat of the range. Only the previous week he'd brought
down an armful of old engraving woodblocks to burn.

'Might as well, since William says there are better men than me!
Haven't done my own engraving for years, anyway. Getting old!'
He glares at Eve.

Her own mood alters within a day. Often she's amazed to find
herself cheerful, ready with a sense of almost parental concern for
Joseph. The smallest thing turns content into contempt, then dejec-
tion and longing for the mother and father she will never see.

She's poking disconsolately at two thin chops she's broiling for
Joseph's afternoon breakfast when he bursts in, filthy dressing gown
pulled over a shirt and trousers, waving a letter.

'Eve!' He grabs and hugs her so that the fork clatters into the
fire. 'We're saved! Saved! Wauchope Browne is shocked,' he reads
from the letter, 'to learn of "the situation of a man of such genius",
and in short, he's arranging a banker's order for six months in the
first instance until I can get on my feet again. "I am too much of
an admirer to allow destitution even in these hardened times," he
writes. Sir Wauchope Browne, you remember? It was his house in
Chelsea where we watched Nelson's funeral.'

'Yes, I remember that day.' Endless black-draped boats, black-coated men, black boom of guns, shudder of drums, trumpets. Death. Clouds, hail, day turned into night, sudden sun as if by command.

'Well, that's good,' she says, pulling out from under his arm, glad at the news, perturbed by the great change of mood, both his and hers.

'We'll go out, Eve!'

'Your chops.'

'Oh *them*.' He picks the blackened bones out of the pan, sucks the thin mouthfuls of meat. 'We'll eat well again. You can buy us coffee at last! Now, where shall we go?'

'We don't need to go anywhere, do we?'

'What nonsense. We must! Come on! I'll hunt for some change.'

He scrabbles through pockets, crawls among the debris in the studio, finds a handful of coins and off they go.

Joseph is uproarious all night. Eve's gloom infuriates him, but she doesn't want to smile.

*

'If only someone in London could seek out Sarah's daughter. Could Henry, do you think?' But Hester has never been to London; her notion of the city is vague.

'Hester, no one could just find a young girl in London. And Henry's far too busy. He has a practice and extra patients. The city's full of wandering girls.'

'Pray God she's not one of those. I do wonder what she's like. I see her as a young version of Sarah, quiet and pretty. A gentle girl.'

'Well, Sarah can't possibly go to London on her own. One of us would need to speak for her, prevent further shock. But in any case her mind is still too fragile. Imagine if she found out something dreadful. It could do her much harm. She might never recover.'

'What if she wrote to every girls' school in the city, Edward?' But when, timidly, they make the suggestion to her, Sarah flies into a sort of silent rage, clutches her hair as if to tear it, scribbles frantically:

No! Girls' schools are bad.

She writes nothing for Hester and Edward for several days, and when she does she asks that they do not try the falling asleep experiment again.

When I wake there are nightmares.

Edward is disappointed. Hester too, though she won't remind Edward of her earlier warnings. He has kept a detailed account of Sarah's state, his ideas about treatment, her progress, hoping to add notes on successful experiments. Now he must put it aside, not knowing when it will be completed, if ever. He'd hoped to contribute something to the new psychological ideas, even send a paper to Paris. He takes down his student copy of William Battie's *Treatise* and finds the stricture to 'not dwell too long on endeavouring to remove the causes of Madness, which perhaps are only imaginary'.

'But,' Edward would argue, were Battie to emerge, suddenly, from the pages of his book, bewigged, lace-cuffed, 'just because it's imaginary doesn't make it any less of a cause. It simply means the cause is more difficult to find.' Battie's riposte to Edward would probably be his statement that Madness 'oftentimes ceases spontaneously'. Lunatics even become well when treatment stops.

Of course, Edward reminds himself, Battie had as target the hideous methods Edward's own father carried out. But Battie's approach was undoubtedly striking fifty years ago, well before he was born. Can he bear to let it determine Sarah's case when he's been so inspired by the new wisdom? He reminds himself there's no point in novelty for its own sake, recalls the complacent fellow to whom he sold his father's asylum, concerned only with the latest thinkers. There seems so much sense in Battie's view.

The problem is that Sarah's case is urgent: there's her daughter to find. They cannot let more years drift by. But amnesia lingers and still she cannot speak, cannot bring herself to speak. With only splinters of memory, without speech, they'll not find the daughter.

Worst of all is the possibility that his experiments may have put back Sarah's recovery, may have caused things to be exhumed in her mind that will make her even less likely to speak. He acknowledges this to himself, though his optimism tends to quash the notion.

Perhaps one day I shall suddenly speak again.

She looks doubtful.

I have been lost. Lost to myself.
<u>And Eve is lost</u>.

Edward says: 'When your voice comes back you will be able to travel to London to look for Eve.'

Perhaps it sounds like admonition, for Hester adds quickly, 'I shall go with you, Sarah, we'll go together and search for Eve.'

But rather than encourage, their words seem only to depress her.

Out of Sarah's hearing, Edward says:

'After she waved to Eve on some occasion when there were "so many people", as she told us, there must have been an accident in which she fell into the sea and was rescued by the collier who took her to be a suicide. And anyone else involved didn't see her picked up, thought she'd drowned and made no further search. We know it was 1802, because that's when she arrived in Sowerthorpe. Perhaps she was boarding a ship. She may have been returning to America.

'I'll write to Henry and ask him to seek out old newspapers for the year 1802 for lists of sailings or some public event in which she might have taken part. At least that's easier than actually searching for Eve.'

'Remember that she said everyone else was dead.'

'We don't know if what she thinks is correct. We don't know how much may be imaginary.'

Edward decides to discuss Sarah's case with a physician he knows at the Tukes' Retreat outside York. He's away for two days, risking the health of Hawkswith, but no one is seriously ill at that moment.

He's struck, as all visitors are, by the serenity of a place in which the insane are treated with kindness and respect, where warm baths and plenty of food are important parts of treatment.

'I know it seems foolish for you not to see the patient, Mark,' he tells Mr Fenner, 'but I can give you a full description.'

Mark Fenner listens carefully, comments: 'Very unlike most of our patients, Edward, but evidently you're treating her well just as we try to do here. Seeing her as a rational being.'

'Of course. Besides, my wife and I have become extremely fond of her. The problem is how to persuade her to speak, for despite the calm and warmth of our life, she will not.'

'You'll be familiar with Crichton's aphasic attorney? Unlike your case, the man could speak, but his memory was so faulty that he used all the wrong words. His life became nonsense.'

'Yes, yes, and supposedly the man was cured with huge doses of valerian. In my opinion it's conceivable he developed aphasia through severe guilt about the mistress he was keeping despite being happily married. We never hear whether the valerian helped him give her up. But, good Lord, the man was seventy: it must have calmed him down! My wife is convinced that some event, not necessarily one that involves guilt, unlike the attorney, but some event has driven Sarah Battle to withdraw her speech, to prohibit her memory. And I'm inclined to agree with her. But how on earth can I discover what this event was?'

Towards the end of an hour Mark says: 'Edward, I fear our talk has been more useful to me than to you. I can think of nothing other than what you have already tried. Nothing more than that she may suddenly speak. Inexplicably. We could do with you here, you know.'

'The Retreat has an excellent reputation, Mark, and it would be an honour. The best regulated institution in Europe, they say!'

'Yes, that was Duncan from Edinburgh, two years ago.'

'The fact that I'm overworked in Hawkswith doesn't prevent my being content there.'

'Look, before you go, Edward, may I ask you a personal question? Was your wife married before, to a Reverend Snead?'

'Why do you ask?'

'I've begun a small study of those whose childhoods were overcast by notoriety.'

'Oh yes?'

'We should discover more about our patients' childhoods.'

'Must we?'

'The child is father to the man.'

'Oh, but that's poetry, not psychology. However, yes, you're probably right.'

'Well, you'll know about Snead's father, I expect.'

'No, I don't. Yes, Hester was married to Snead, most unhappily. And look here, Mark, she and I are not married: he will never give her a divorce. It's vital that no one should know.'

'Of course. You have my word.'

'What about his father, then?'

'He was killed standing in the pillory. Stones thrown at his head.'

'Good God. And his crime?'

'Detestable practices, as they like to call it in the newspapers. Sodomy.'

'How extraordinary that he was not hanged.'

'A *lenient* judge! Who undoubtedly knew the man would be badly wounded at least. Condemning someone to the pillory especially for that crime: it's simply lapidation. His death was shocking, but he's not the only man of such inclinations who was, in effect, executed in the pillory by a vicious public.

'I heard he had a son, a parson, and thought to call on him when I was visiting a friend in Norfolk, but he refused to see me. And discreet enquiries suggested a bitter man of violent religious tendencies. Preaching to a shrunken congregation. Perhaps no surprise.'

'But he's not a patient of yours.'

'Indeed he's not, yet when I read about the father I couldn't help thinking the son would be a perfect case for my study.'

'We talk as little of John Snead as possible. He is indeed a man of extreme religious views and quite possibly insane. Hester did say that he would not answer when once she asked about his father and thereafter never mentioned him.'

'There are questions to ask: what age was he when this happened? Was he still a child? How much did he know? Did he even witness it? What about his mother?'

'Yes, you're right. There must have been humiliation at least. Probably he was tormented by others as a boy. It wouldn't surprise me if you find you're treating him in a few years' time.'

Edward will tell all this to Hester before long, for the information about Snead certainly helps a kind of understanding of her husband. He comes away from the Retreat with little advice on how to help Sarah, instead with a quite unexpected pang of pity for a man he'd always thought both cruel and ridiculous.

*

Joseph is out all day buying furniture, Stephen driving him in a superior gig instead of a carriage. Stephen is pleased to be re-employed and not just for the pay, which is little enough. Mr Young is an odd master, erratic in his demands, apparently unaware of the freedoms Stephen enjoys and exploits and the gig, well, it's a more modest vehicle than before, but smart, fast, almost racy.

For the time being Joseph avoids despair, but his restlessness clashes with Eve's new tendency to severity, her longing for solitude and independence. She snaps at him often, or forces herself not to.

Mr Pyke is ill. He always coughed a lot and winced with pain when standing up or sitting down. Now he writes that he's taken to his bed, but only for a few days, he's quite sure. Eve misses the diversion of his lessons but is glad she can think about herself without interruption.

She wonders if Joseph was telling the truth when he said her money was entrusted to a lawyer. If he was, then somewhere in his studio from which the bailiffs only removed a few framed paintings, there'll be a letter or document with Mr Wigram's address printed on it. She could go to him and find out everything for herself. Today, with Joseph not at home, she'll search through his things. Most likely it'll be difficult in the disorder, the mess, the smells, for though she's not been there since she looked at his huge sea and sky paintings, she doesn't expect it to have changed.

The shutters are closed, though brightness presses through the grimy dome. She lights a lamp. Alone, she can observe the room more carefully than when it is filled with his overbearing presence. There's order of a sort in the centre where the easel stands and paints are set out on nearby tables. An ornate chair for the sitter is raised on a small dais with a tall drape of red velvet suspended from a pole behind it. Objects that she knew from the days when she wandered about while he painted are arranged on a long table, presumably for the sitter to choose for inclusion in the portrait to suggest fame, intellect or aristocratic background: small busts, huge books, pieces of broken column, a sword, a leather folder of manuscripts. She runs her fingers over the enormous shell, knobbed and spiked on the outside, smooth and delicate pink on the inside. Just as she did as a child.

All around the centre lies chaos: years of discarded paper, paint jars, rags stiff with linseed, ripped canvas, rusted knives, encrusted palettes, hundreds of candle ends. She ignores the engraving table, where she pierced her thumb and left her blood on wood blocks and paper. It would have been dry by the time Joseph returned from Malta and he wouldn't have noticed. And probably it was burned in the kitchen range the other week. Against another wall is a large chest of numerous drawers. On it the sweet-smelling decanter and glasses of many sizes containing dead flies, pinned by sticky residue.

She opens drawer after drawer: papers, papers. At first she reads every letter, but soon learns to detect which to discard immediately. Letters, contracts, bills and more bills, odd posters and cards he engraved for all manner of businesses years ago. Unused sketchbooks he must have forgotten about. A box of coins and paper money he also must have forgotten. Nothing with the name Wigram inscribed upon it.

There's even a couple of drawers of clothes, smelling musty and unwashed, hastily stuffed away from the sight of sitters, she imagines. Underneath, a folder, which, kneeling on the floor, she pulls out and opens.

Her first thought is that it's her, a sketch of herself. 'Me! He drew me, but *when*? Where was I? I never noticed him doing it. And it's not me now, it's me older.' He's imagined what she'll be like when, old enough at last, he'll marry her.

'Of course not! How stupid I am. It's *Mama!*' Moreover, with a rapidly coloured blue background, it's her mother in the balloon. 'Oh Mama!' She bursts into tears. 'Mama, it's you!'

And yes, there's the date: *SB, 28 June 1802.* The last day of her life. Yet here she is, her mother, here in her own hands, glowing, her face uplifted, her expression one of certainty and a kind of glory, *alive*.

'Dearest, darling Mama! This picture should be *mine*, not hidden in this drawer, under all these horrible clothes. It *shall* be mine. I'll keep it.' She holds it to her, looks at it again, the details that soon will be committed to memory, the upturned mouth, cheeks reddened with chalk, rosy with life, eyes that seem to see into a far, unclouded place. Presses it against her half-grown breasts. Stands up to leave, though she must return everything to its place. 'He probably won't find Mama missing. I expect he's forgotten it under all these things.'

She hears the street door slam, Joseph's unmistakable footsteps crossing the hall, stuffs papers into drawers, hastily picks up the folder and kicks it under a table. She'll come back later and replace it properly. Rushes out of the room with her treasure.

*

A letter arrives from Henry Sessions.

I've got it! Think this must be the event you're after, old man. A <u>balloon flight</u> marking that hopeless peace of Amiens that lasted less than two years. I suppose it was a sort of gesture of amity welcomed by people already tired of war. Not knowing war would last another thirteen years! The aëronaut was a Frenchman, one Jacques Garnerin, and the English were represented by Joseph Young, an artist who was to record scenes from the air.

No sketches have ever been seen. I suppose they were lost. French and British flags hung from the balloon's basket and anthems from both countries were played. Here's the important bit: <u>A handsome woman, Sarah Battle, accompanied the men, to show that balloon travel could be enjoyed by women as well as men.</u>

I take it this is your patient, Bissett?

The reports all agree that the balloon was caught in a sudden violent storm, was blown eastwards and came down off the coast of Essex. The two men were rescued but the woman was never found, so it was presumed she'd drowned.

I've discovered that Garnerin has been flying balloons for Boney since then, though given the French defeat and <u>real</u> peace, surely no longer. As far as I can ascertain he's still alive, as is Young.

*In my opinion, Young is not a man who'll be of any help to you at all. I
must tell you that a while ago, just after our wedding, Laetitia had the notion
that Mr and Mrs Henry Sessions might be portrayed together in oils to hang
in an elaborate frame over the mantlepiece. She'd heard that Joseph Young
had painted many well-known people, so I called on him to commission the
portrait. I found the man to be chronically addicted to opium and brandy, all
ill-disguised by desperate friendliness. Since it was probable that the painting would never be completed, or even begun, I cancelled the commission and
put an end to Laetitia's absurd pretension!*

Edward puts the letter aside. He'll read it to Hester later when
they can both absorb its contents more carefully and decide what
to do with the information, if anything. He's too busy to deal with it
now, administering, among other things, to householders rendered
hysterical after visits from black-faced, threatening Luddites. And
far too distracted by worries about the machine-breakers themselves and his own dangerous involvement with them.

*

Eve takes her first opportunity to replace the folder in Joseph's
studio. He's out for the afternoon after a snatched breakfast: there
should be enough time. She goes straight to the table under which
she'd kicked it.

Pulls it out, picks it up too quickly, it slips out of her hands and
sheets of sketches pitch onto the floor. She kneels to retrieve them,
sees faces, enormous animal-like faces. Monstrous bodies. Mad
eyes of a massive bird stare right at her, its beak immense, its head
covered in matted hair, not feathers. A vast hog on bird's legs grins,
leans out from behind a jagged mountain. Half-human bodies with
bat wings as big as themselves shriek through toothless human
mouths. Worse, featherless birds stagger under the weight of huge
erect penises. She's aghast, can't bear to touch the sheets lest they
clap her in their wings, swallow her. Pages and pages covering the
floorboards. Hideous shapes. It's as if Joseph has roared and they've
gushed out all over her, flooded her, for she'll not rid her mind of
the grotesque images for years to come. For some moments she's
mesmerised by a colossal whale on the surface of the sea, then

realises that it's a collapsed balloon, its ropes and basket disappearing beneath the waves. She forces herself to gather up each page, catching sight of sinking ships, desperate claw hands sticking straight out of the water, before she shoves them all back into the folder then under filthy cravats and shirts in the drawer.

And yet the portrait of Sarah was with them!

In her room she spends an extraordinary night, sleepless, alternately joyful and terrified. She contemplates her mother, weeps. Studies every line of Sarah's face like children never do, except as babies learning their mother's features. The face is in half-profile, looking forward and half upward. What does her mother see, Eve wonders, sky, the sea, the world set out before her, below her? What is she thinking? She thrills at her mother's strange, exultant smile.

Then like devils the vile creatures surge into her memory and only shouting aloud disperses them: 'Get out! Get out, get *away*! *Away from me!*' So exact and powerful were the drawings, black ink on white paper, that they move and sound in her head, jostling, grasping, squawking, howling. Stinking of unemptied pots, dead air.

How can she live in the same house as the man who created those monsters? His mind is full of horrors. Her reason tells her they only exist when the blackness descends, at those times when, desperate, he curls up in misery like a child and then disappears into his room for days. She's tried to console him so often, to mother him before the worst happens. But as the images swarm into her own mind they merge with Joseph himself. Joseph who wants to marry her! He might burst in. She locks her door.

Mr Pyke would be calm, she tells herself. He would explain. But no he could not, for, disliking Joseph, disapproving of him, he would be disgusted, would steer her away towards further study of the planets or the stirring good sense of Tom Paine, whom they've been reading together at last, the writer who so inspired her dear mother and father.

Towards dawn, when her lamp is empty of oil, she looks out of her window. It's not the direction in which the sun rises, yet gradually brightness emerges from the ashes of the night.

She remembers the tale of Proserpina that Lucy read to her and

Matthew. How Proserpina's mother nearly went mad with despair at the loss of her daughter. In the end the mother was miserable one moment, cheerful the next, and she'd certainly understood *that* at the time. But now, how well she understands the story, even if it's she, the daughter, who must search the whole world for her mother.

She must leave. She must find Sarah, or at least see the place where the balloon went down, where her mother died (didn't Ceres find the place where Proserpina had disappeared?). She must leave Joseph, his horrible drawings, his great, shambling body that demands so much from her, for soon it will be too late.

If she asks them, Ann and Gilbert will prevent her. Ask Lucy and she will insist she move to Paternoster Row with her and William and Matthew. She can hardly live with Mr Pyke. Stephen might take her some of the way if she can persuade him. After that she'll be on her own.

*

Cavalry is billetted in the Hawkswith area, tension is high and soon the authorities, searching everywhere after an attack on the mill, call on Edward. There's a magistrate, Josiah Hartley, a special constable and an officer from the militia.

The Luddites are disciplined. Before the attack, large bands of men, workers and a few masters, are observed drilling on common land outside nearby villages. Their leader, the cropper Edward encountered, is admired, obeyed. Yet this time something goes wrong, a fault in the usually well-planned strategy.

Armed with muskets and pistols as well as pikes, hammers, axes, mauls and Great Enochs, the men are unprepared for continuous firing down onto them from high up in the mill. Several are seen to fall, illuminated by flames from outbuildings they'd set on fire, are carried, dragged away by the others as they all flee.

'Mr Bissett, you will have heard of the attack on the mill.'

'I have.'

'Several of the attackers are known to have fallen, wounded by musket balls. Have any wounded men been brought to you?'

'No.' The truth. None were *brought*.

'Have you attended any of the attackers in their homes?'

'No.' I don't know if it was *that* man's home, Edward quibbles to himself. He saw the weaver with the severely cut arm in his cottage *before* the mill attack.

Josiah Hartley persists.

'Mr Bissett, would you give the same answers in a court of law. Men will be brought to trial you know.'

'I don't know *what* I might say in a court of law.'

'That hardly inspires confidence!'

'Mr Hartley. I am a doctor, bound by oath to treat all who are sick whatever their occupation, however much or little they pay.' He'd charged Hartley 4gns for smallpox inoculation, when others paid the usual 10/6, the poor nothing. 'You may know that recently I have given aid to several families in the district suffering from the effects of terror after masked Luddites threatened them in the night.'

'Yes, I have heard. However, I have also heard that you ride all over the area, calling on remote livings.'

'Of course! How else am I to deliver babies and attend the dying? My poor mare is often as exhausted as I am. Has anyone *seen* me attend a wounded machine-breaker?'

'Mr Bissett, I must ask you where your sympathies lie.'

'I am against injustice.'

'Who is not? Would you defend your house against criminal attack?'

'Of course.'

'I warn you, Bissett. Militia and cavalry are here in force. You may be called as a witness in court. Special constables are well primed. You will be watched.'

*

At the end of the year the Thames freezes over. 'Frost fair!' Joseph shouts to Eve as he rushes downstairs. 'You know how I love fairs!'

'No, I don't know.'

'Well, I do. Come on! Put on all your outdoor clothes or you'll freeze.'

'There are overturned carriages in the streets.'

'But it's no distance to the river. Come *on*, Eve!'

She'd much rather not go. Has tried to keep away from Joseph. Wants to begin thinking about her escape, how she can persuade Stephen to take her. But she has no hope of resistance. They set off down to the frozen Thames.

The river is dotted with ramshackle tents and plentiful flags, smoke from numerous fires, and there's a smell of roasting mutton so much more inviting than anything Eve has cooked over the past weeks. Boarded ways lead down onto the ice, and paths have been shovelled through snow.

'No, I don't want to go,' Eve says, turning, that recurrent dream of walking across the weed-thick lake alive in her mind. 'Let's go back!'

'Oh, come on! There's no danger, none at all. You can hold my arm.'

She clings to makeshift rope rails, then to Joseph's arm and once on the ice, which feels nothing like the dream weed, she's unable to resist a quickening thrill, similarly felt by those around them who express it in shrieks and shouts.

'Lapland mutton! Now's your only chance! Won't niver 'appen agin!' a man yells, sharpening his knives. A whole sheep strung from a pulley over a fire smokes, drips, hisses its fat into the flames.

'Two pence to watch, four pence to eat!' A woman takes money: who could watch without wanting to eat? Joseph pours out pennies and neither one can resist gobbling the singed pink meat.

If it's too expensive for some, there's gingerbread and gin and enticing tents labelled 'Moscow' and 'Wellington', within which men sit on boxes around fires, smoking, drinking, singing, as though it's just another tavern.

Joseph leans into Moscow and shouts: 'What are you calling it Moscow for? The place was burned to a cinder!'

'Aw! Get away, fizzling snudge!' someone yells, and the rest look at him, bemused, drink on, cuddle their women to keep warm.

There's screeching from boat swings tossed high above the ice, men bowl at nine pins, couples caper and hug each other to a shivering, black fiddler; books for sale, toys for sale, gambling booths, it's like any other fair except that people slide, slip, fall about and gape at two horsemen galloping along the solid surface of the river.

'You missed ve elephant, las' Tuesdy,' someone tells them in a confidential tone.

The wind bites, a fight erupts and sudden screams of "E's fell in!" cause a slithering rush to rescue.

'Look, Joseph,' Eve points at a booth with the sign: 'The Thames Printing Office: Copper Plate Prints'. They join a queue at the heavy printing press for a souvenir poem, itself of little worth, but invaluably inscribed:

Printed on the River Thames, 27 January, in the 54th year of the reign of King George III. Anno Domini 1814

Eve feels additional pleasure, musing that her father Tom was a printer as well as a bookseller. Wonders if he would have done this, heave his wood-and-iron press down onto the ice, risking its loss, even if the ice really is many feet thick, all for the sake of money? Mr Pyke implies that her father was more interested in ideas than money; nevertheless might he have enjoyed the banter and hilarity, sharpened by the sense of danger? And if he'd lived, might she have printed and sold books and pamphlets with him: Thomas Cranch & Daughter, Berwick Street?

'For the lovely lady, is it?' the printer's assistant breaks her dream. 'Lucky man, eh, sir. Wish I 'ad a pretty little wife like yours.'

'She's not ...' Joseph begins.

'Oh, ooh, not the wife, eh? 'ear vat?' a man behind them sniggers to his companion.

'Enjoyin' ve ice, pretty miss?'

'Vere's gents jus' waitin' for ladies to tumble and show us veir petticoats.'

Joseph puts his arm round Eve and guides her away.

'They're right, of course,' he tells her, 'you get prettier by the day, Eve,' but she doesn't want to hear this from him of all people, ducks out from under his arm, inevitably slips, loses her balance, falls to the sound of roars and laughter. He helps her up and now she must hold on to his arm, though she doesn't want to, and they make their slow way back up to the street.

She's not hurt, only slightly shaken, but angry. To be seen as Joseph's wife! It will encourage him. She wishes they'd never come.

10

———

THE HAWKSWITH BECK BEGINS TO FREEZE, air cracks with tales of arrests, of men not found, hiding over yonder, wounded, re-arming. Rumours circulate anew each day. Nervousness touches everyone.

Hester is shocked when she hears about Snead. Talking to Edward, it all comes back to her: the stones in his pockets, how he must always have kept them there, rattling them with his fingers; the stone-throwing she heard when she listened outside his study; the pelting of the congregants in the church.

'Mark Fenner is right,' Edward says, 'we need to know about people's childhood lives to understand why they behave as they do.'

'A time to cast away stones, and a time to gather stones.'

'What is that?'

'Ecclesiastes, Edward. How ignorant you are! It speaks of the vanity of everything. He was haunted, don't you think?'

'That's a good way of putting it.'

'Reminded every day of his father's terrible death.'

'Reminding himself. And before that, arrest, a trial, no doubt.'

'Oh Edward, I've realised something else. He had a way of some-times jerking his neck, sort of wrenching it from side to side. You saw him too rarely to notice. I think ... oh, too dreadful ...'

'Wresting himself from an imagined pillory?'

'Yes.'

'The power of the human mind. It fascinates me.'

'But I never thought! What would I have done if I had known? I should have been kinder.'

'I doubt more kindness would have made any difference to him. You must not blame yourself, Hester! You did your best in a profoundly difficult situation. You and Sarah suffered badly because of his disturbed mind.'

Hester's remorse about her husband is superseded by anxiety about Edward. He has not told her the details of the two breakers he's attended, but she opened the door to the magistrate and knows that Edward is under suspicion. The house becomes quiet. Sarah, sensitive to moods in both her companions, stops writing, works silently in the dispensary.

Several men who took part in the mill attack are apprehended, despite a general refusal to help the authorities hunt them down. Cottagers are silent, turn their backs on the militia. But someone lets on, and they're taken to Wakefield House of Correction and thence to the cells of York Castle, where it will go hard with them now that winter is setting in. When snow arrives it's heavy, roads become impassable all over the country and mail coaches are delayed for weeks. An occasional letter gets through only when mail coaches are exchanged for horseback or because men plunge in and out of snowdrifts with sacks over their shoulders.

'Henry says the Thames is frozen, and he and Laetitia have had an immensely good time at the frost fair in town,' Edward says, reading the latest from his friend, unamused by its frivolity. 'He wrote this more than a week ago.'

Henry also sends an address for Joseph Young. They could write to him, perhaps? He won't offer to call on him himself because of the unfortunate business over the cancelled commission. When she eventually gets to London Sarah should approach him herself, he suggests.

Edward takes no pleasure in freezing conditions. He and Dolly are sorely tried getting to accidents caused by snow: old roofs caving in under its weight, burns from those snuggling too close to fires. Nothing can be done for those who steal liquor for warmth, tumble down in drunken sleep then freeze to death, or those whose employment is cut, whose families begin to starve.

He's no longer followed: spying's too visible in this weather for the special constable assigned to trail him. Doorways are blocked by snow; hills and fields show up every figure except sheep. Unwatched, Edward is approached furtively in a barely cleared street by a man with a brief message.

''E did die.'

'Oh God. I have thought so much about him.'

'But they did niver *arrest* 'im!'

'That is something.'

His decision not to amputate the Luddite's leg was wrong. He should have done it immediately, saved the man's life. Yet he might not have survived the shock of amputation. And then what life would he have had? Regret is balanced by relief that the man had never been apprehended, chained in some frozen cell, questioned for hours and ultimately hanged, a man with a stump. For that's what is due soon, hangings in York.

Relief is reasonable. Yet he goes over that night again and again. Why did I not? Why? I had the instruments; there were plenty of men to hold him down. It was the cry of the woman. The man's wife? His mother?

'Oh let 'im not lose 'is leg!'

It's not an excuse. He just knows the cry had clutched his heart.

Hester and Sarah do what they can tramping around Hawkswith in heavy winter pattens along channels of shovelled snow, taking bread and broth, pears and apples from their attic store, clothes, especially worsted undergarments. It's no matter that Sarah doesn't speak. It is enough for her to look a greeting, recognising the face of others' desolation.

*

Eventually thaw comes. The streets are pooled with melted, filthy snow.

Eve sleeps with the drawing of her mother next to her pillow so that the first thing she sees each morning is her mother's face. There comes a day when she wakes after having slept little and in a moment is elate with determination. Senses a force within herself that seems new, though it's also a resurgence of girlhood rebellion. Nothing will stop her. But unlike when she was younger, she'll not just run off, will be careful, will plan.

She washes in cold water; there's been no one to bring warm water since Betsy left. In the kitchen she eats bread, drinks black tea as the milk is souring, but at least she can sit peacefully, for Joseph will sleep all morning.

Mr Pyke said somewhere east of Colchester. That is where she must go, to the place where the balloon fell, though now there's the image of a whale floating on a heavily turbid sea that she wishes she'd not seen. But she *must* find out what happened to Mama, and *someone* will know, surely. If Sarah lives she will go to her. If not? She will not think of that. Her mother is alive in her mind, more vital than ever.

Can she make Stephen take her to Colchester? The snow has gone, the roads are clear. He *could* take her, she thinks, without having any idea how far away the place is, even *where* it is. Can she bribe him? She has no money, though already she intends to take that box of coins and paper notes from Joseph's studio.

She'll need fresh clothes. Tries packing several gowns, but the travelling bag is soon full, and she imagines that once Stephen has left her she might have to carry everything herself. Two changes then, only one bonnet box. It's spring, winter's cold is now over, so she won't need much.

She finds Stephen brushing down the horse.

'Stephen, I never did tell Mr Young about you and Betsy. Or the baby.'

'No, Miss Eve.'

'And I never told him about all those silver things you took away and sold.' Better not to use the word 'stole', she thinks.

'No, Miss Eve.'

'I still could.'

'Yes, Miss Eve. What is it you'd 'ave me do fer you?'

'I'd like you to drive me to Colchester. Soon.'

'It'll eat up three days or mebbe four wiv stops to give me beauty a rest. Not much room fer boxes and bags in the gig. You'd best be takin the dilly. Take the stage, Miss Eve.'

'Oh. But I've not much luggage, and I don't want to travel with a lot of other people.'

'D'you mind me askin' if Mr Young 'ave agreed?'

'No, Stephen, I haven't told him, and you'll say nothing, please.

But in any case he'll be away for at least two weeks when he goes to wherever it is to paint all the Wauchope Brownes in their country house. He doesn't *want* to go, but he's got to.'

'I see, Miss Eve. And they're sendin' their barouche for him, 'e says. *Very* grand, I'm sure. No need fer me.'

'Exactly! So you *can* help me, you see. I *could* still tell him all those things, you know. I could leave him a letter.'

'You wouldn't want to do that now, Miss Eve. P'raps you 'ave a little somefin' that'd help me show I'm willin'?

'Oh yes.' She removes a silver bracelet from her wrist, a present from Joseph years ago. 'Seeing that you're so fond of silver, Stephen. You could give it to Betsy, couldn't you. How *are* Betsy and baby John?'

'Very kind of you, Miss Eve, I'm sure. I spec they're in good 'ealth.'

*

A man asks to see the surgeon and waits for him an hour or so. Sarah is at work in the dispensary, Hester elsewhere in the house, though glimpsing the roughened, ruddy face, she thinks she's seen him before, oh years ago.

'What can I do for you?' Edward asks. The machine-breakers have gone to ground – those who have not been executed. A wave of disgust strikes him when he thinks of the injustice of the punishment. The futility. The leader, that cropper, a man of twenty-eight, able, self-educated, respected by his men, surprisingly well travelled. A life wasted.

But surely this is not more blackmail; and a local man would be pale, not like this one.

'I'm not come for the physic. I'm sent on. Place called Sowerthorpe.'

'Well?'

''Tis a long way.'

'There's a surgeon there. No need to see me.'

'I do need to see you, sir.'

'How did you find where I live? Nobody in Sowerthorpe knows I live here.'

'Young woman goes by name of Mary Corner. I wanted parson.'

'If you wanted the parson, why trouble me?' Edward replies, impatient, hungry for his lunch, having only pocketed some bread on his way to a breech birth in the early morning. 'Unless you've come to tell me the parson's dead, of course. That *would* interest me.'

'Please to 'ear me out, sir. I called on parson to tell 'im somethin about the woman I did bring 'im from the sea once.'

'Oh, yes?'

'I did think to tell my part, see. I did think to confess to parson, but 'e did say it had nowt to do with 'im and 'e knew nowt. Then I did come across this Mary, 'oo did say the lady do live here in this village. I been walkin' more'n a week.'

'*Confess?*'

'Conscience, sir. My conscience it have pinched like crabs these years, but then I did hear say the balloon man and the painter did live.'

'Please sit down and explain, Mr ...?'

'Niver mind my name. Us did see the balloon come down, see? Boat's a collier. *Whitley Queen*. Sold the load down London. Us was comin' 'ome.'

'And you were the ship's captain? If you won't give me your name I shall call you Collier. Where did this take place, Mr Collier?'

'Off the Naze. Colchester way. Boat were near. Us'd room below wi' coal gone. It were comin' on night, mind. They was in the water, two men and a woman. We heave to, see, to pull 'em out. Balloon skin, ropes was sinkin'. Basket gone.

'Then Barnabas were shoutin.' 'E did see the Frenchies' flag floatin.

'"Frenchies, they's Frenchies!" he shout. We did often think of invasion in them days. Boney's men comin' in balloons and rafts were all the talk.

'So I did tell them get the woman. "Us cannot let a woman drown afore us very eyes." So we did. But the rest of the men did set about the others, push 'em back off the boat, push 'em down in the water, damn Frenchies should be drownded.

'So then we take the woman and sail on soon as we could, but she were very sick and then we did leave 'er in Sowerthorpe and say we pulled 'er out from killin' herself, so's nobody'd know about the others.'

'What made you admit to this after so long?'

'I did hear someone say the men did niver die. One were French certain, but he were the balloon man, not a soldier. T'other were a Englishman, a artist. Not drownded, see, we'd not done it.

'But the woman, she did think we had, do you see, for she did call out to stop even while she swallowed water. When we was pullin 'er out, she were chokin' and callin' the while.'

'When did you learn that you and your fellows had not succeeded in drowning the two men?'

'Oh a time since.'

'And so you've decided at last that the woman might like to know you didn't kill them after all?'

'Yes!'

'How *thoughtful*.'

The battered face looks pleased.

'It never occurred to you that she has lived with that false horror all these years? That she has suffered terribly?'

'She have? I be sorry for it.'

'Or that in telling a lie about how you found her, she was never identified?'

The collier has already spoken more than it's his habit to do.

'It was easier not to think about it, was it, Mr Collier?'

'It were.'

'I have not asked your real name. However, you will wait here while I write down everything you have told me, and then when I fetch my wife to read it back to you before you sign it. While it would be fruitless to report you about an event so long ago in which you tried but failed to murder two men, I do need to have the exact account for the woman's sake.'

The collier can neither read nor write, but *Bill* is recognisable in two circles and three vertical lines.

*

Impatient though she is, Eve must delay her flight, for there's so much going on in the city. Boney abdicates and Europe congratulates itself by coming to London in force. Even while houses fall down in Lombard Street and Luddites smash warp lace frames further north, Louis XVIII, the Czar, the King of Prussia, Metternich, Russian and Prussian generals Platoff and Blücher arrive in waves with all their retinues to celebrate.

Crowds jam every street, wild to see the great people. Windows cost fifty guineas to rent for the procession to the Guildhall. There's little bread, milk and washing, for bakers send only to the royal visitors, laundresses prefer royal clothing and cows in Green Park take fright at the constant huzzaing.

Boney may have abdicated, but the country is still at war with America. Yet celebration remains in the air, and can't be stopped. A huge event is planned in all the parks, Hyde, Green and St James's. Joseph wants to go.

'You *must* come, Eve, for stupid though it is to celebrate peace while a war's still on, there'll be fireworks and a mock Battle of Trafalgar on the Serpentine. We don't have to go to all the booths and swings or buy any trash, but I'm not missing fireworks on any account – *and* there's to be a balloon flight!'

Eve shudders. 'No, I don't want to see it. I don't want to go.'

'Oh, come on! Stephen will take us.'

'I especially don't want to see the balloon.'

She's glad to be alone in the house. In any case since her discovery she cannot look Joseph in the eye, knowing what might occupy his mind. Turns away whenever he appears, though probably he doesn't notice. She longs to leave. In two days he'll travel down to his patron's country estate and she will go as soon as she can after that. Her bag is packed; well, it's two bags and a bonnet box, but there'll be room for them next to her in the gig. She stuffs Joseph's money into four purses, there seems so much (how *can* he have forgotten it?), returns the box and feels only the slightest guilt, promising herself to pay it back one day, though she's not counted it and has no idea how much there is.

Joseph and Stephen return late, so that it's not until the morrow that she encounters Joseph, sour-faced when she snatches a look at him.

'The fireworks were no good,' he says, 'and there was a blaze.'

'A blaze?'

'Chinese pagoda. Went up like paper, fell into the lake. Two people killed.'

'Oh, what a poor celebration, then.'

'There were swans killed too. Balloon didn't stay up long.' He says no more about it and Eve doesn't ask. His face is grey and she feels a jab of guilt about her plan.

'Damned portraits!' he growls, thinking of his forthcoming journey to paint every one of his patron's family. 'We were better off poor, weren't we, Eve?'

'But you were going to have to find somewhere else to live, Joseph. Have you forgotten? There wasn't much to eat either.'

'That's because you couldn't cook.'

'How unfair you are!'

'Going back to bed. Head's a weight of lead. Drank too much last night, Stephen and I. What else could we do? Ridiculous event.'

*

There's a tension over lunch that's hard to keep from Sarah, though Hester does her best to give nothing away, however excited she and Edward feel. He is silent despite his hunger, barely able to eat, trying to work out exactly what to say and when. Sarah must not hear it all at once.

At last, the solution to the puzzle of her state of mind! The cause of her disorder was witnessing the apparent murder of her two companions while she herself was drowning and then rescued. No wonder she couldn't speak, had wanted to forget! This is the event she's locked up in her memory, the event about which she cannot speak. Hester was right.

He'll tell Sarah as soon as possible, yet must do it gradually, for the shock will be great, nor will the aphasia be cured immediately. He prepares himself. Reads Sessions's letter again, recalls Sarah mentioning the name Joseph Young at least once before.

'Sarah, Hester and I have something of very great importance to tell you.

Sarah writes rapidly: *Is it Eve? You have found her!*

'No, not yet. But the information given to me by the man who came this morning should help us do so before long.'

She's disappointed, though Hester looks at her encouragingly.

'The end of your balloon flight was not as bad as I believe you have thought. M Garnerin and Joseph Young were not drowned. They are both alive.'

It is as he feared, Sarah gasps, slumps forward fainting, he catches her before she falls and Hester revives her gently with smelling salts. He cannot tell her everything, it would be too much, he must focus on the simplest fact.

'Sarah, Joseph is alive.' Hester holds her hand, strokes her hair, while Sarah, face ash-grey stares forward, then shakes her head vehemently.

'It is true, I assure you, Sarah. Soon I'll tell you everything, everything the collier told me. But first, try to accept the fact, for it will help you to recover and find Eve.'

*

Eve brings another silver bracelet and a brooch for Stephen and they set off for Colchester soon after Joseph leaves. Which he does in considerable style in the Wauchope Browne's barouche with its coat of arms and liveried grooms. Boxes of equipment and carefully wrapped blank canvases go with him, several travelling bags of clothes; but anyone looking closely can see the taut skin around his glazed eyes, the tremor in his sweating hands. Eve would cry when she says goodbye to him but knows she must not betray her plan, and the minute he's gone her heart beats with anticipation.

She leaves him a letter.

John Street, 25 August 1814

Dear Joseph,

This letter will surprise you and I'm sorry, for I do not wish to upset you, but I can wait no longer. I must find Mama. Perhaps she is still alive, but even if not (and I know you think she is not) at least I can see the place where she fell into the sea. Someone will be able to tell me something about her end, and, you see, I crave to know.

You have given me a home for twelve years, Joseph, and I thank you for that. Even though I'm not yet of age I am certain I can look after myself. Please do not try to find me and please do not punish Stephen when he returns.

You will surely not mind my taking the sketch of Mama that you made on her last journey. I found it in your studio and as it was like coming across Mama herself I could not resist taking it. Please also forgive my theft of some coins and paper money from a box there. Now that you have your patron, you will have enough money to live on (and no longer have to provide for me!) but I promise to pay back the money when, one day, I have some of my own.

Goodbye, Joseph
Eve Cranch

In signing herself *Cranch* Eve proclaims her allegiance, entirely separate from Joseph Young and from any attempt by him to claim her. And firmly reminds herself of her direction, since for her Cranch will always mean America, and when finally she finds Sarah, that's where they'll go.

Joseph will be hurt by her formality, by the letter's unnaturally stiff tone. She cannot bring herself to mention the terrible drawings that helped propel her away from him. If he checks for the missing sketch and the empty money box he'll probably guess that she has seen them. Is sorry.

Leaving London, the country seems endless, for the little rural existence she's observed on outings, such as the fields of Highgate, of Mortlake or of Sheen, is always quickly supplanted by housing and the City. Now, cottages, hovels, parched August land, tired out and brown, occasional grand gates to an unseen house, all of which would have interested her once, are impediments. She'd reach the sea instantly if she could. And Stephen insists on his stops: despite the lightness of the gig his horse must run no more than twenty-three miles at a time.

*

It is a while before Sarah tries to speak. She is dazed by the information; sits for hours reading Edward's account as given to him by the collier, reliving each awful moment, struggling to adjust her memory without it even occurring to her to speak.

One morning, like a child, she says their names.

'Hester! Edward!' and they hug her as they would a missing daughter.

'Soon, soon, we'll go to London, Sarah,' Hester says.

'When I'm happy that you're well and speaking a little more,' Edward adds. He's concerned they'll go before she's ready, but for Sarah the prospect is a vital spur.

The patience of her two friends is unceasing, but then their own pleasure in her recovery is great. They treat her with special care, encouraging speech in the gentlest way, never forcing it. She and Hester sit together mending stockings and other garments, collecting the clothes they'll need for a stay of an uncertain number of days. Pick lemon balm leaves for a tea.

Edward makes notes for a paper he'll send to the *London Medical & Physical Journal*. He doesn't name Sarah, describes the care he and Hester have given her only in general terms. In detailing his failed experiments and admitting that recovery depended on chance, he doesn't help his profession. But the paper is widely read by intelligent amateurs.

The public celebration at the supposed end of war delays Sarah's journey to London by days. The whole country is afloat with joy, Boney safely ensconced on Elba, sailors and soldiers returning home in ever greater numbers, countless French prisoners of war repatriated or taking themselves elsewhere.

Every town and city puts on its show, processions, balls, bells, flags, street feasts, bands, bonfires, fireworks, fancy costumes from the obvious to the obscure. Even Edward joins Hester and Sarah with Margaret in tow for an hour, to watch the splendour and hilarity in Wakefield as the bells of all the city's churches ring out around them and people cavort to brass and whistles, bang on drums and kettles. In Hawkswith bunting appears, people greet each other in the street, exchange news, when before they'd do little more than grunt.

Hester says to Edward: 'You know, the collier did commit a kind of murder.'

'What do you mean?'

'The attempted drowning of the men caused Sarah to lose her memory and her voice. Not reporting her rescue ensured that both memory and voice were not recovered for years. She lost years of her life. Years withered. She lost her self for years; that's how she put it, wasn't it? She was as if dead all that time. It *was* a kind of murder.'

Hester will take Sarah to London, for Edward cannot leave the practice. Indeed he's so overworked he's begun looking for an apprentice. In the City, though still barely speaking, and nervous of doing so, Sarah will at least try to ask the necessary questions. They have the address for Joseph Young that Henry Sessions found, although a letter already sent to Joseph from Sarah has not brought a reply. The journey will take three days by stage and once arrived they will stay with Mr and Mrs Sessions in their house in Hammersmith village, some distance out of the City. Although his medical training was the same as Edward's, Henry has taken a step up, calls himself Physician, attends well-paying patients and treats one or two in his house for their opium addiction, though he assures Sarah and Hester they won't be disturbed. As students in Edinburgh Henry and Edward had shared cold, cramped rooms. The generosity of old friendship is now well seasoned with curiosity about Sarah's case.

The plan is to find Eve and bring her back to live with her mother and the Bissetts in Hawkswith.

*

Eve and Stephen spend the night at two inns before reaching Colchester and Stephen, with an efficiency that pleases both him and Eve, makes all the arrangements, orders her a suitable room, food she's prepared to eat and enlivens the long evenings of each landlord and assembled, somnolent drinkers. He's discreet about his passenger, but has many tales to tell of life in the City and his erratic, unnamed master. Mysterious anonymity guarantees attentive listeners.

On each arrival, Eve is glad to reach her room after prolonged, shameless stares, the welcome concealment given by her lilac-trimmed straw bonnet merely stimulating curiosity. She aches from the bouncing of the gig on stony roads, and her face and clothes are covered in dust.

As they enter the town, however, she's aware of elegant houses, new buildings and many soldiers among those parading in the high street. They find an inn on the far side, towards the sea. It's altogether less primitive than the previous two, and the landlord is helpful if wary of this young woman, accompanied only by her groom. Irate parents may yet come for her, will pay him well for keeping her from harm.

'Balloon? Yes, I remember that,' he says. '1802, yes. Twelve year now. Particler bad storm, most was indoors keepin' theirselves dry. Somebody come up later from the Naze.'

'The Naze?'

'Walton way, east from here. A few did see that comin' down. Boats set out. Bob Goose that were did pick up the two balloon men.'

'But there were three people in the balloon.'

'Was there now?'

'Yes! There were two men and a woman.' She will tell him nothing more. Not yet. Her *mother*. Oh, she'll tell no one, will keep Mama to herself. Will hold off dread.

'Ah. Now I do think there were mention. Jacob, what d'you reckon? Were a woman in that balloon?'

A man, bent double but not in sleep as Eve had thought, raises his head with difficulty.

'Niver founded.'

'What Jacob don't know's not worth a candle,' the landlord says. 'He do know *everythin*'.'

'Swep' away.'

Eve's eyes cloud with tears, but she wants him to be wrong. 'Were you there yourself, Mr Jacob? Did you see the balloon come down?'

'No.'

The landlord intervenes: 'May I ask, Miss Cranch ...' The young woman is perhaps seventeen, he surmises. Were that her sister, maybe, or a friend?

Eve ignores this. 'Is there anyone living who was there, do you think?'

'We've lost that many. The sea do take 'em, and so do the king. They did press every man jack. Town's full o' widows.'

'People in the nearby houses will have seen what happened,'

says Eve, but the landlord laughs, and a painful wheezing indicates amusement from under Jacob's bent form.

'You'll need be a mermaid for that. All gone. All under the waves. Church went in '98. Last buildin'. The sea been swallowin' Walton in gobs for 'undreds o' years!'

*

Sarah's first attempts at speech are almost farcical. She oscillates between frustration and amusement at the sounds she makes. Having never had a case like this before, Edward feels quite unsure how to help her. Hester is intuitive, offers Sarah unforced opportunities to speak; she asks questions that need simple answers, about what they'll eat, what else to pack for their journey. When they walk in the garden Hester names flowers, fruit and vegetables, and Sarah repeats the words.

Peter glances over from digging up parsnips and carrots, hearing two voices as they pass.

'Peter is am – amazed!' Sarah says quietly.

'Oh, he'll get used to it soon enough. When he hears you talking all the time!' In a loud voice she adds: 'Just look at the nasturtiums!'

'Nas-tur-tiums. They grow and grow!' says Sarah, inadvertently expressing Peter's own thoughts. He growls, longing to grub up the gaudy flowers, for they're nothing but weeds to his mind.

'How I wish I could come with you both,' Edward says to them as they are about to leave, pushing his fingers through grey tufts. He means it all the more because Hester is pregnant, and though she's in good health, he'd rather be with her to make sure of it. No one else knows yet, though Hester agrees that Edward should write and inform Henry.

Hester tells Edward that she always wanted to *have* children, though not to *get* them. In that utterly loveless marriage to Snead, what physical contact there was had repelled her by its aggression and by the awful begging God for forgiveness afterwards, though there were never any prayers after he'd punished her for misdeeds.

'And I was relieved not to have a child whom he'd want to lock in the coal cellar on the slightest occasion. I once called at the school and heard him harangue the pupils as I stood waiting to enter. Each child's nature is corrupt, he told them, and their evil disposition needs constant correction. Imagine how much worse that would have been with any child of his own.'

Now she bears the child of a man she loves. The journey by mail coach will be tiring, the search for Eve and continuing care of Sarah stressful, but she will act wisely and is optimistic that in a week, perhaps two, they'll return with Eve to Hawkswith.

'We'll write to you when we can, dearest Edward.'

'Short notes,' Sarah says.

'Yes, please tell me what you find. Hester will look after you, Sarah. She's a strong woman, and you are such good companions.'

Edward, about to employ a young lad as apprentice, will have to tolerate Margaret's dull, stodgy cooking. And he'll miss the two women. Now, however, there's the shining prospect in six months' time of delivering his own child.

Sarah is excited beyond her still limited verbal expression. As before, what she feels is conveyed bodily and in her face. She sits in the coach straight-backed, leaning slightly forward, her hands pressed together, alternately gazing out of the window and looking intently at her fellow passengers. She searches faces wherever they stop, and when they spend the night in an inn, as they must, for the change of horses.

Twelve years have grown into a grey enormity of time, a block she cannot cut through. Yet behind it are memories that surge up, sometimes refreshing, more often staggering her with their force.

Among them Eve, the baby who brought profound joy and constant misery because of Tom's death, the child so like him that she must mourn and celebrate in the same moment.

She feels the baby's small, vigorous body, the clutch of her fingers, the sucking bird-mouth at her breasts, sees again the deep, unknowing eyes. And the growing child, held on her hip or stumbling to keep up; the poise of the speaking, reading girl, bright with questioning intelligence, for whom she held such ambitions.

She reaches back to pull the child into the present, into the future.

In their shared room at a large coaching inn north of London she looks at herself in the glass:

'I have aged.'

'That's true, though we all have, of course. Your face is thinner and you have a few grey hairs, Sarah.'

'Eve will not recognise me.'

'I think that is unlikely. On the other hand *she* will have changed.'

'She was nearly six.'

'A girl. And now she's almost a woman.'

'They said she looked like me.'

'She probably still does.'

'But darker, like Tom. Shall I recognise *her*?'

They travel for three days, spend two nights in slightly unsavoury beds. Eating amid crowds of travellers, their clothes are drenched in heavy smells of tobacco and broiled meat. Two apparently shy women, no longer young, sitting side by side in a dark corner of a long, low-ceilinged room; talking quietly to each other, aware that people stare, puzzling out their story. Such places are closer to Sarah's experience than Hester's, and for moments Sarah almost senses a call to the kitchen to supervise the meals.

'The coffee house.'

'Was it rather like this, Sarah?'

'Yes. Dark. I wanted to leave the darkness.'

'I can understand.'

'Become a bookseller like Tom. With Eve.'

'Perhaps you will.'

'S. Cranch & Daughter. In Philadelphia.'

'Oh, Sarah, surely you don't need to go to America!'

The coach completes its journey at Charing Cross and Henry's groom meets them with a smart two-horse curricle to take them out of the City.

They bowl along Piccadilly, past Green Park and Kensington Gardens, until houses fall away and they reach Hammersmith village and the river. Sarah has never seen the river this far away from the city. There's little traffic on it, for another decade will pass before work begins on a new London Bridge, and till then no ships get through the old one. A few small sailing boats pass, men row odd bundles, fishermen pull in nets or stand by their rods, apparently transfixed, but it's recognisably that same river, broad, grand, slow, that flowed through her childhood, and above which she sailed under the great, green-and-yellow orb on that fatal day so many years ago.

The Sessions' house, set back up a short drive from the river, is large for a young physician, but Henry is increasingly successful, and in any case his wife Laetitia brought money to the marriage.

The Sessions welcome them warmly. Henry is sprightly, unworn. He picks his patients among the rich, is driven to their houses when called. Unused energy causes him to joke and quip a little too often. Laetitia is polite, considerate, yet much concerned with her timid little dog, Fanny, and apparently sleepy, perhaps as a gentle defence against her husband's liveliness. Both are more curious about their guests than they show.

'You should do nothing for a few days, Hester and Sarah. On Wednesday I shall take the day off from my toils,' Henry announces. 'I want a turn in my new curricle. Phibbs gets all the best spins. It's not fair! I'll take you up to town myself and deliver you to Mr Young's establishment. Till then, rest, take life easy. I expect you're aware that Edward has asked me to force you to take things slowly!'

*

Stephen agrees to drive Eve to the sea, hoping that having found nothing she'll agree to come back to London with him, despite her original plan, for he's not looking forward to facing Joseph without her. The man's strange enough as it is.

In the non-existent village of Walton an enormous brick tower stands back from the sea, once a beacon, more recently a lookout against Boney's ships, though no one's seriously expected invasion for years. The lookouts, friendly, curious, pleased by the unusual diversion, assure Eve they were not themselves present twelve years ago, but willingly take her and Stephen to the log-room and pull out the volume for 1802, leafing through to 28 June.

5h.00m: Wind severe W NW, high precipitation. 59 04. 6h.28m: Gas balloon losing height, approaching from W. 6h.38m: Balloon downed, aprox 300 yards out. Newcastle collier passing, direction N. Visibility very poor due to oncoming darkness and low cloud. Believe three fishing smacks in vicinity. Balloonist and male passenger reported rescued by Jolly Betty, owner Robert Goose.

'But there was another person in the balloon!'

The officers show Eve and Stephen out onto the crenellated roof.

'If the young lady would imagine standing here in a day darkening to dusk, telescope useless in the rain, a gale doing his best to blow you off, how much would you see?'

Eve, her hands on the sun-warmed brick wall, the day dry and still, has little difficulty imagining. Stares out to sea, longing, willing a balloon to surface, Mama holding on to a rope, smiling and calling to her. Stephen exchanges a look with the officers. They help her down the endless spiral, her feet urging her to slip.

'Stephen, please let's go to the water's edge.'

He leads her across feeble, sea-eaten cliff to the sand, where she stands for long minutes. Beneath this grey, unmoving water, so unlike Joseph's painted Mediterranean, is an entire village. She recalls Barker's Panorama, in which the reflection of the grand buildings of St Petersburg looked like a city beneath the river. This is real: out there are houses, barns, inns, a whole church lying silent.

But why silent? Perhaps they're alive down there, walking along the streets, calling their wares, driving their gigs, dogs barking, church bells tolling. Couldn't Mama ...?

Stephen pulls her back.

And she banishes the absurd fantasy. Instead, of a sudden, remembers the moment the sun appeared as Nelson's body was brought on land, the unanimous sigh of amazement. But the sun has gone now, the sea is flat, its line unbroken and she weeps, her life seeming to drain out of her.

*

At first, the thought of waiting four days before the meeting with Joseph is too much, for there will be yet more time after that before they find Eve, if they do. Sarah must know now, wants to urge Henry to change his mind, but the next day is Sunday, the household rises late and it is clearly not a day for action. Henry and Laetitia offer to take Hester and Sarah to church with them, an offer they both politely decline.

Everything in the Sessions' house is pleasing and comfortable:

impressive Turkish carpets, walls fashionably papered or painted precisely; a bathroom and water-closet attached to Hester and Sarah's room. Argand lamps light the principal rooms, with their elegant furniture and framed Italian landscapes, and meals are served on pretty Coalport porcelain.

Even the two paying patients, kept out of the way most of the time, are neat and well mannered, only slightly ravaged by their addiction. Once they begin to relax, Hester and Sarah admit that they are, indeed, exhausted from the journey, from the anticipation of it beforehand, and now from anxiety about the next stage.

Sarah is torn between longing and dread. Joseph has not replied to the brief letter she sent him from Hawkswith, and in a newly arrived note Edward confirms that there's still no reply.

Despite the confirmation of Joseph's address and indirect information that he's alive, he might be dead by now, and then they'd never discover anything about Eve. Worse than that is the dreadful possibility that Eve herself is dead, a fear that grips Sarah in the black hours after midnight, so that she almost wants to search no further. If Eve is dead then she herself no longer has reason to live.

Guessing at Sarah's thoughts, Hester tries often to distract her dear friend during the day, but Sarah's fears run on. The Eve she remembers is a baby in her arms, soothed by song; a small child tottering, holding her hand, walking with her, clinging to her skirts; a girl leaning a hot head against her shoulder as they talk and read together. Affectionate, eager yet still childish at nearly six. That Eve will be a woman now, resentful or remote, *changed*, disconcerts her utterly. What if she is unkind? What if she doesn't want to meet her mother?

Hester writes to her husband:

Hammersmith, 3 September 1814

Dearest Edward,

Here is my second promised note. I am well, in answer to the question I can hear you asking. I am aware that Henry is keeping the discreetest eye on me; he does so without asking me anything at all. I can see him almost invisibly inspect Sarah, too. He and Laetitia are so considerate. Sarah and I have everything we need, even things it hadn't occurred to us to want. We are both obeying your orders, which are conveyed merely as friendly suggestions by Henry.

Rest is certainly what Sarah needs, and yet she finds it hard, for her mind is full of fears about which I can do little. I, too, feel some dread on her behalf.

Henry is to drive us to Joseph Young's house on Wednesday. He says he wants to drive his new curricle, but I feel sure he wouldn't be doing it had it not been for our need to call on Joseph. I'll write to you again after that.

I hope you are getting some sleep, dear Edward, but that when you nod off over your book you are waking yourself up in time before the fire goes out! How is the new apprentice? Has Margaret accepted his presence in the house?

Meanwhile, Sarah sends her love to you. As do I, my dearest, dearest Edward.

Hester

*

Eve has never been so unhappy. Yet what did she imagine? That her mother would be sitting in the parlour of a pleasant house by the sea, expecting her? Reading a book of poems perhaps.

'Ah, Eve,' she'd say, 'I've been waiting here for twelve years. What's kept you?'

How ludicrous to have allowed herself such childish hope! Her bitterness is all the greater for having no one else to blame. There is nothing she can do. She can no longer resist the horrible Jacob's statement, must allow that what everyone except Nursey has said all these years is true. Mama drowned.

She will not speak, nor eat, weeps incessantly; a childhood of grief never properly articulated overpowers her. Eventually, when Stephen suggests they begin the return journey to London early next morning, she nods stiffly and bursts into tears again.

To avoid people, she sits in the garden behind the inn. Cold despite the warm afternoon, she draws a shawl around her shoulders, shrinks into it when aware of someone's approach.

A uniformed man. 'Mademoiselle?'

She looks up, but not at him, at a nearby tree weary from a summer's heat.

'Captain Louis Leclerc, French Navy. May I sit here?'

She looks down at her hands, nods.

'Please do not be afraid. I have been a prisoner in your country for eight years, but now that the war is almost over the English wish us to leave. I shall go soon.'

She inclines her head in minimal politeness.

'You are Mlle Cranch?' He makes it sound nasal, odd.

'Yes.'

'Please do not be offended. I could not help but overhear your conversation with the landlord of the inn, about the balloon. Most probably the balloonist was a Frenchman. But you are concerned about someone else?'

'Do you know something about the accident?' A few seconds of hope.

'Alas, no. But I see that you are very sad. I see that you are alone. I felt it at my heart.'

She wishes he'd go away, for she can dwell only on her misery. Almost *wants* to return to John Street, despite her grand plan not to, where she can run up to her room, lock the door, cover herself in her bedclothes and never get up again.

'I am going home tomorrow,' she says. How dismal!

'You return to London?'

'Yes.' No! She will stay in one of the inns on the way and refuse to leave.

'May I accompany you?'

'Stephen will take me.'

'Ah, that is a pity. I, too, am going to London. From there I shall take a ship to America.'

'Oh.'

'I cannot return to France, even though if I do not I shall be accused of desertion.'

He sees that she is listening. 'France is not the same country I left when I was twenty-two. It is not the same country for which I fought. I believed in the Revolution. At least for a time. But now France has stepped backwards: we have an *emperor*! America is the only place to live.'

She begins to emerge. 'My mother and father went to America. They were radicals,' she says, proudly.

'You are American?'

'My father died in Philadelphia, before I was born. My mother ...'

'Ah. Then I understand.'

There is pity, kindness in his narrow, intense face: perhaps he really does understand. His black hair shows flecks of grey; to her he is old, though not as old as Mr Pyke. Spare-framed, gentle, he's as different from Joseph as possible.

'You speak English very well,' she says.

'My ship was captured in '06 and I have given French lessons for English. It has been pleasant to live in England. Officers have a certain freedom, you see. We may travel one mile from our billet, we keep our own money. We are paid one shilling and sixpence a day for food and rent. I have met many people.'

She says: 'I've wanted to go to America all my life! I'm sure my parents had friends there.' What little she's learned of their life in Philadelphia, told her by Pyke, lives in her mind as if it were her own memory.

Leclerc is pleased. Too many of the English do not want to hear about revolution or democracy; think America, whose war with England ceased only last month, a benighted land.

'In America the people have succeeded where those in France have failed. Only in that country do they practise liberty, equality and fraternity.'

Eve watches the earnest flow of his feelings, the expressive movements of his mouth, hears ideas which in shadowy form she'd first encountered when she'd learned the word 'radical' and, more recently, of course, reading Tom Paine with Mr Pyke.

As Leclerc holds forth, encouraged by the spark in Eve's eyes, a wonderful possibility wells in her. Mama fled to America with Tom. Might she not do the same with this man? Impetuosity floods her like good health after illness. At last! To America!

Would it be the same as Sarah and Tom? Not quite: Sarah fled a miserable marriage. *Marriage!* Oh! If Captain Leclerc would *marry* her, she would be safe from Joseph!

He stops speaking, looks at her quizzically, for she has been smiling while he spoke. 'Yes,' she says, having heard little of what he said. 'I think my mother and father went to America for those reasons.'

How can she make this new plan work? Audacity, determination, the old egotism of her untamed childhood all merge into compulsion.

'Will you help me get to America?' she asks. 'Can I sail on the same ship with you?'

'First the ship must sail to Halifax, for all American ports are blockaded still by the British.'

'Halifax?'

'It is in Canada. North of America. You understand, your country has been at war with America since 1812.'

'Oh. I didn't believe it.'

He sees her face falling. Would cheer her with smiles of hope.

'Don't worry. A peace has been declared. Once I am there I shall travel down to New York or Philadelphia.'

She *will* get her way. 'Can I sail on the ship to this place Halifax with you?'

'It sails in four days. Do you have money for a ticket?'

'Oh, yes!'

'Most surely you have relatives with whom you live in London? I must speak to them first.'

'Oh, I live with a painter, Joseph Young, a friend of my mother. He's quite famous. He's a sort of guardian. But I'm twenty, you know.' It is a small lie, but necessary, she thinks.

'I shall ask permission of your guardian to accompany you.'

'Oh no, I'm sure you needn't do that. Joseph is far too busy to bother with letters. Besides, I'm sure he won't mind.'

'I shall write to him at least. It would not be seemly for me to accompany a young woman all the way to America.'

'You could pretend to be my brother.'

'Certainly not!'

'We could get married.'

He looks at her with amazement. How can she have moved from being so sad that she could barely speak to this proposition of marriage? It is bizarre!

Three days ago, no longer a prisoner of war, he was planning to desert his country, abandon his old parents, siblings, begin life in the New World, where he would find work and in time a wife. And now a wife offers herself! She is charming, spirited. He senses her

240

strong will. But she is young, impetuous, an orphan, her emotions unbalanced, and he knows almost nothing about her.

His eight years in England have been restricted. Apparently welcome in many homes, valued for his graceful manners, his willingness to teach French, give dancing lessons, there's been flirtation from several women but little more. Always he is watched, an exotic insect under a microscope, fascinating but potentially dangerous.

Now he's like a starving man offered a dish of delicious-smelling food made from unknown ingredients. How can he possibly resist?

A compromise is reached. Captain Leclerc will accompany Eve as her *protector* on the merchant ship to Halifax. After which he will ensure she reaches Philadelphia.

'I am a man of honour,' he tells her. 'As your protector, I shall shield you from harm on the journey. And I shall inform your guardian, Mr Young.' His intentions are good, and, he believes, durable.

Stephen is paid well and given a letter to hand to Joseph. Eve fails to tell Leclerc that Stephen's journey will take him three days: a reply from Joseph, even if he were at home, could not arrive before the ship's departure. Nor does she say that Joseph will certainly not be back from the country when Stephen does arrive with the letter. Won't return for weeks. She and the captain will be well on their way to America by the time Joseph realises what's happened.

She regrets Ann and Gilbert cannot see her sail. Cannot see her achieve the ambition they'd sought to delay but understood so well.

They remain at the inn until the day before the boat is due to sail, when they'll take the post-chaise. They talk together, eat together, walk in the nearby lanes. Leclerc, aware that they are not unobserved, determined to carry out his plan of travel, is cautious, immaculate.

But Eve is alight with hope, her face shines, she is an excited child, a new-grown woman, her nerves touched with possibility, alert to each of Louis Leclerc's movements, to every one of his words, every nuance.

*

Sarah and Hester rise early on Wednesday. A housemaid brings them hot water in the room they share and offers to help them dress, which they refuse. They smile at each other: being helped to dress is not something either has ever experienced.

At breakfast Hester eats two hot rolls and coffee, Sarah, taut with anticipation, manages a few mouthfuls only. Her mind, so newly filled with memory, with images, voices, sensations long submerged, is whelmed by uncertainty. Joseph was so volatile, a great child of a man. She recalls the terrible moment in the balloon after the world shone like a wonder before and below them and he, having sketched her face, proposed marriage to her, entirely confident of success. When she had to deny him, crush him. When he seemed to diminish, his spirit shrink. Surely he'll not bear to see her after that, even if it was twelve years ago? Most likely he'll know nothing of Eve. The fear sickens her.

It's a day of shortening autumn warmth. Henry is lively, too talkative. Sarah, comforted by the presence of Hester next to her in the curricle, nevertheless feels herself alone, for it is only she who may persuade Joseph to tell her what she needs to know, only she who may recognise her changed daughter.

As they move from the unfamiliar outskirts to the city itself, and buildings increase in size and self-importance, her fears burgeon, yet mingle with a sense of familiarity, even of belonging. She clasps her hands together, finds her nails digging into her palms.

The women are silent, what is there to say? Henry chatters on.

At last they pass Green Park, move slowly in the traffic along Piccadilly, Haymarket and into the Strand, where Henry turns down John Street to number 6. There's a long wait before the door opens, but as soon as it does he drives away, promising to return in an hour.

At the door is a slight, ginger-haired man with a pock-marked face. Not old, yet too old to have benefitted from inoculation, Hester can't help noting.

'Mr Young come 'ome last night, unexpected like. Row wiv 'is patron, Wauchope Browne. 'E's very unwell. Very. Too ill for visitors. Sorry, but vere it is. It were better you come beck anuvver day and … *Oh!* Oh my Lord! Oh, I can't believe my eyes! I *can't!* You's Mrs

Battle, Eve's ... *Oh!* Come *in*, ladies. Oh my Lord! 'E'll never believe it's you. Never.'

Stephen shows them in to a musty, airless room, and there, sprawling in a chair, asleep, is Joseph, so much older than Sarah remembers, grey-skinned, bottles and papers at his feet, among them her own letter.

Stephen shakes his master awake, and for a while Joseph stares at Hester and Sarah, apparently seeing nothing.

'Joseph,' Sarah says.

'Oh!' He struggles out of the chair, stands unsteadily. 'Sarah. Oh God, Sarah! It is you. *Is* it you? It can't be. It's not you. You've changed. You're thinner. No, it *is* you! Oh good Lord. Your letter! I took it for a fake. How *can* it be you? Back from the dead. You've come to haunt me. I know it. I deserve it! I do, I do. Oh God!'

His hands press either side of his head, his eyes stare with both horror and joy, not unlike the face of Insanity in *Young's Guide to the Fine Arts*.

Stephen takes control. 'Mr Young, Joseph, sir, it *be* Miss Battle. And 'er friend. Miss Battle'll want to know about Miss Eve, Mr Young.'

'Yes. Do you know where Eve lives, Joseph?' Sarah's voice is frail in its newness, in fear there'll be no answer. 'Please can you tell me?'

'*Where* she lives! Hah! She lives here with me of course! Been living here all these years with me. I took her in after the disaster. With the nurse. But *she*'s dead, and now Eve has gone. *Gone!* She has *left* me.'

'Gone? Where?'

'Would that I knew. No, would that I *didn't* know.'

Hester intervenes. 'Mr Young. Please tell us what you mean. Sarah has been ill for years, you must understand. Now that she is well she must find her daughter and we have come to London for that purpose.'

'You're too late! Eve has run away from me. Wrote me a letter. *Took my money!* Think of that: took my money! I have the letter somewhere.' He rummages in his pockets, removing paint-blotted rags, coins, pieces of food. 'Where is it? She wants to find where you *died*, Sarah! Where the balloon came down!'

'Then she's gone to the coast? Has she, Joseph?'

He's emptied all his pockets, found nothing. 'Oh, *I don't know.* Where did you take her, Stephen?'

'You want ve *uvver* letter, Joseph, sir. From ve hofficer.'

'Yes, oh yes. I have received a letter.' He's on his knees, scrabbling among papers. 'A Frenchman, an officer, informs me he is her protector. A *Frenchman* of all things! Why not an Englishman? Even a Russian would be preferable. Ah, here it is. He's taking her to America via Halifax because of the British blockade.'

'To *America*? Her *protector*? What do you mean? What have you let her do, Joseph?'

'I haven't let her do anything. I wasn't here. I've been away.'

Still on his knees, he thrusts Louis Leclerc's letter at them and Hester, seeing Sarah begin to reel with terror, says: 'This is dated four days ago.'

'Four days ago! We are too late!' Sarah staggers slightly, too shocked to cry.

Hester continues: 'He writes that they will travel to London and take a merchant ship from Wapping to Halifax. That he will ensure Eve reaches Philadelphia where she will find friends of her parents who once lived there.'

Hope leaps in Hester. 'It was written from an inn in Essex. Perhaps the ship has not yet departed. We might still intercept them!'

Joseph struggles to his feet. 'Harness up the gig, Stephen. Take them. The new dock. *Go now!*'

Hester supports Sarah, they follow Stephen, then wait endless minutes for him to appear with the gig. Henry will find they've gone when he returns.

Out of their sight Joseph covers his face with his hands, rocks back and forth.

'Oh, Sarah. Suddenly you are here! Oh God! My life might begin again, but you're *going away. Going away again.* I have lost you and Eve. I've lost everything!'

*

The merchantman *Olympus*, with superior furnished accommodation for a handful of passengers and a cow on board for milk, is due to sail to Halifax, under the command of Captain George Croker, on Wednesday, 7 September 1814. Scanning the passenger list, Sarah and Hester find the names Captain Louis Leclerc and Miss Eve Cranch. Sarah's heart falters at the sight.

'Weighs anchor at high tide, 12.58, miss,' they're told. In an hour.

On the dockside the last barrels, boxes, sacks are swinging on board, sailors stand ready to unhitch, shouts from ship to shore have a last-minute urgency.

Hester embraces Sarah.

'Will you not come with me, Hester?'

'It's better that you talk to Eve alone. If you need me, you can wave down from the deck or send a sailor with a message. There's still time. I'll wait here, Sarah.'

Eve and Louis are among a number of passengers at the rail watching the sailors, the porters and lightermen, the screeching gulls. Louis, deprived of sea and ships for so many years, stands straight, almost to attention, as though listening to the music of his past and his future played by a naval band. Eve, intoxicated with a story that shapes her future from the pattern of her parents' past, their flight, hers, would hold on to this man's arm, his hand, if only he'd let her. They do not touch.

The sun breaks through. River light glimmers; sea-light will outshine it once the ship leaves England. Just below, on the quay, two women hug each other, talk briefly then split apart. They are without luggage. One, a woman of middle age with features that unexpectedly attract the girl, approaches the ship.

Eve sees her mother ascend the gangway towards her.

Author's note

An entry for 28 June in the 1802 *Annual Register* begins:

An elegant afternoon breakfaſt was given At Ranelagh by the directors of the Pic Nic Society, of which about 2000 perſons of the firſt diſtinction partook. About five o'clock, Mr Garnerin, the celebrated aëronaut, accompanied by Capt. Sowden, of the navy, aſcended in his balloon. Its aſcent was, in the firſt inſtance, very gradual, in order that all poſſible gratification might be afforded to the crowd of ſpectators.

Almost four pages are given to the account of the journey, provided by the scrupulous Captain Sowden, who was no doubt used to the detailed reporting of naval encounters. All the main events of this journey are present in the opening chapter of *Sea Change*: the direction in which the balloon travelled, the changes of temperature, the extraordinary experiences of sight and sound, the violent squall, the need for the travellers to suspend themselves from the balloon's hoop to 'ſave ourſelves from being daſhed to pieces', the balloon dragging along the ground, the unhelpful people from the farmhouse, the sudden ascension, the loss of the valve rope.

Of course the difference is that I have inserted my own characters into the balloon with M Garnerin and given the journey another ending. Garnerin and Sowden eventually landed on the ground, but only after much violence and the ripping of the balloon in a tree. They were *fo exhaufted with our numerous exertions, that we had hardly ftrength to follow the balloon, which fell again about 200 paces further, when we completely maftered it, by throwing ourfelves upon it, and by that means preffing out the remainder of the gas.*

Balloon flights had been taking place since 1783 when the word 'balloon' was introduced into the language, though people also liked to refer to 'aerostats' and 'aerostatic globes'. Although spectacular, balloon travel was obviously dangerous and there were many fatal or near-fatal landings both on land and at sea and particularly at night or during storms.

André-Jacques Garnerin, Official Aeronaut of France, seems to have been especially intrepid. In reality he believed women perfectly capable of balloon travel: he caused a scandal in Paris in 1798 when he took the young and beautiful Citoyenne Henri with him and in London in 1802 his wife accompanied him on some journeys. It was in London that he demonstrated his new, frameless parachute, jumping from a balloon and landing in a field near St Pancras.

In 1786 Thomas Baldwin produced a 400-page book of drawings and a minute-by-minute account of a balloon journey he'd made the year before. The book, *Airopaidia: Containing the Narrative of a Balloon Excursion from Chester, the eighth of September, 1785* can be read on archive.org. Irresistibly fascinating!

One other source of importance to me for this novel was a report in *The Times* in 2015, of a Royal Navy sailor who was unable to speak for eight years after seeing two of his colleagues drown. The story had a happy ending, as does *Sea Change*.

Acknowledgements

———

I owe thanks to several people in the production of this book. Firstly, thank you to my agent, Véronique Baxter, who has had faith in my writing from the start and encouraged me greatly with her enthusiasm. Thank you to both editors at Serpent's Tail, Hannah Westland and Leonora Craig Cohen. Before she went off to give birth to her daughter, Hannah successfully steered the first draft of the novel off hidden rocks. An excellent combination of precision and appreciation has made Leonora's editing hugely stimulating and the final draft owes much to our pleasing emailed dialogue. Serpent's Tail itself – Valentina Zanca, Flora Willis, Anna-Marie Fitzgerald, Niamh Murray, Penny Daniel et al. – which, even under furlough, has seemed like a collection of kindly daughters.

In the early stages I was helped enormously by my dear friend Catherine Humphreys whose expertise, experience and wisdom over much coffee and through countless emails were invaluable with decisions about Sarah's condition and treatment. Thank you, too, to Dr Nicholas Howell who was generous with his time and knowledge, crucial in his support of my presentation of both Sarah and Edward. Thanks to Sarah Harding, a fine painter, and, though she won't be aware of it, I was much inspired by the mother/daughter theme in Polly Clark's wonderful book *Tiger*. Thank you, Polly!

A big thank you to my sons, sister, brother, family and the many friends whose kind enquiries and great patience in the face of over-long answers have kept me going. My very dear friend of decades, MaryRose Romer, whose own brilliant writing is yet unsung, has been there throughout. Future writing will not be the same without her.

Above all, to my husband Nicholas, thou day in night, thank you, always.